DON'T POKE
THE BEAR

DON'T POKE THE BEAR

ROBIN D'AMATO

a novel

atmosphere press

PROLOGUE

JIM, 1987

A strange copper liquid dripped slowly onto Manhattan's East-28th-Street subway platform, rhythmically breaking the late-night silence of the mostly deserted station. Jim wouldn't normally think this was unusual, except that there hadn't been rain or snow in over a week. Then what was leaking? Something toxic, no doubt. He hurried over to the other side of the station.

It was never encouraging when there were no signs of a train in either direction. He leaned over the platform edge so far that he had to hold onto one of the iron beams to keep from tumbling onto the track-bed. Nothing. In the absence of train activity, huge rats were running all over the tracks, expertly avoiding the third rail. Jim pulled himself back from the ledge and lit a cigarette. He sucked long and hard on his freshly lit smoke and blew rings into the frigid air.

Since his best friend, Ephram, had chosen to stay home and catch up on some schoolwork, Jim had gone to their usual Saturday-night watering hole by himself. It was an old-school Irish bar in Murray Hill, the kind that opens around noon but is perpetual night inside. No one in this bar ever asked him, or anybody else, for ID, but it did help that Jim looked a lot older than his chronological age of 17. Could have been his prematurely receding hairline or his stocky build. It might also have been the three-packs-a-day.

Jim had had a few beers with a pair of retired cops, and the three became immersed in a heated political discussion about Watergate, Jim having just seen the hearings on the History Channel, the cops having seen them the first time around. When one of them asked Jim if he had voted for Richard Nixon, he didn't have the heart to tell them he wouldn't have been born yet. Although passing for older did amuse him, he left soon afterwards.

Not much was moving in the station, and Jim could still hear the rhythmic dripping and its echoes. Mayor Koch had announced that week that crime rates were down, but, as a native New Yorker, Jim knew that empty streets or stations were treacherous. His leather bomber jacket made him look tough and unapproachable though, should some untoward soul join him there.

Someone emerged from the far end of the platform and walked purposefully toward him.

"Shit," Jim muttered and quickly put out his cigarette.

The officer already had his book out and was writing a ticket.

"You know there's no smoking in the subways, including on the platforms?"

"Yes sir. Sorry sir."

"Can I see some ID?"

"I don't have any," he said. He had left his Stuyvesant High School ID at home. He motioned at his pockets but made no attempt to go into them. Then, hoping this worked as an explanation, he said, "I don't drive."

The officer frowned and continued writing.

"Name?"

"Jim Smith."

The officer glared at him.

"What, you think I'm stupid? Don't give me that 'Jim Smith' shit."

Jim fought the urge to chuckle.

"That really is my name: Jim Smith." Not his fault his mother had chosen the most common name in the United States for her only son. At least it wasn't "John Doe."

The cop grabbed him by the collar, lifted him off the ground, and slammed him into the tiled wall.

"What — is — your — name?"

He thought of telling him his name was Yitzhak, which was his Jewish name, and Stein, which was his mother's last name, but since he didn't want to poke the bear, he said the next thing that came to mind.

"Harold Callahan." With any luck, this guy wasn't an Eastwood fan.

The officer wrote the ticket to Harold Callahan.

The train arrived much later, depositing Jim in Forest Hills, Queens, well after two o'clock. The Continental Avenue strip mall was populated by a healthy assortment of shady characters, but the neon and fluorescent lighting from the storefronts made lurking in the shadows rather difficult. Instead, people lingered in doorways, hid in phone booths, and peered around corners from side streets. Jim hurried by all but unnoticed.

He crossed under the archway of Station Square into the wonderland that was Forest Hills Gardens. Tudor homes surrounded by an abundance of flowering plants and trees in perfectly manicured lots, it was an über-exurb, a gated community without the gates. There was a long period in its history when blacks and Jews were prohibited — okay, some say they were merely discouraged — from owning property there. Now, just over a decade after people had protested the policy, there were Jewish families everywhere. Even so, Jim felt more kinship with the lurkers on Continental Avenue.

His family's house was dark and locked; his mother and sister must have been asleep. After a frantic search in his pockets, Jim realized he didn't have his keys. He rang the bell, but that was futile because no one upstairs would hear it. The extra key wasn't under the mat, wasn't in the planter on the porch, wasn't on top of the door ledge, and the closest pay phone was back on the other side of Station Square. Jim shivered and blew on his hands. And where the hell did he leave his gloves? He squatted down and felt around the ground for something to throw at the bedroom windows. Grass and dirt, nothing that would make a good projectile. Defeated, he headed back to Continental Avenue to the phone.

His mother's line was busy. Since his father's death, she tended to leave the phone off the hook when she was alone in the house. It made her feel secure somehow. This meant his sister was with her boyfriend in Astoria. Jim hung up and dialed Ephram.

"Hey. You still awake?"

"Yeah. Still working on this paper. Where are you?" Ephram sounded like he had had way too much coffee.

"Continental. I can't find my keys, and Mom's phone is off the hook."

"Where's Julie?"

"Probably with her dopey boyfriend."

"Well come on over. Don't ring the bell, though; everyone's asleep. Call from the station."

They both knew that the minute Jim arrived would be the end of Ephram's attempts to further his education for the night. The two polished off the cocaine Jim had tucked away in his jacket and stayed up past dawn discussing politics and feeling smart.

A few weeks later, two beat cops found Jim doing the lurch-and-stumble down 3rd Avenue near the Murray Hill bar. Jim had no idea where he was, how he got there, or why he was without clothes. No one answered when the cops called his home, so he told them to call Ephram, who brought him something to wear and got him back to Forest Hills. Jim never did find his clothes, his wallet, or his shoes, and never *remembered how he happened to lose those things in the first place.*

A short time after that, his mother signed him into rehab.

SEPTEMBER 1994

Jim was sitting on the metal table without his shirt on, and he was shivering. The room was white and spotless, as was the lab coat the man with the instruments was wearing.

"Ready?" the man asked.

Jim knew better than to go to a piercer near his mother's house. He also knew better than to go to a piercer near his girlfriend Allie's apartment. His friend Laynie, whose idea this was, always went to the place in Allie's building, but Jim asked her for another option, which is where he was sitting now.

"Uh... uh..." Not ready at all, it turned out.

The piercer grabbed hold of Jim's nipple, stretched it out, and picked up a pair of scissors.

"What the —"

The piercer laughed.

"Relax. I'm kidding."

The piercer applied something freezing to Jim's nipple, supposedly so he "wouldn't feel anything." This didn't work out as planned.

"YIIIIIIIIIIIIIIIIII!!!!!!!" People in apartments down the block could hear Jim bellowing.

"And we're done."

The piercer put in a small ring.

Jim chose that moment to have second thoughts about the piercing. Allie would hate it. His Jewish mother could never know about it. The only person who would be happy for him would be Laynie; she liked people who were pierced all over, like she was. Maybe he should have revisited his motivations before he had this done. But Jim never questioned his motivations.

The bell tower of the Ukrainian church on East 6th Street was chiming ten. Even though it was a weekday, this Manhattan neighborhood was barely awake. Stores here wouldn't open until the afternoon, and it would be hours before restaurants saw many patrons.

The Java Café was on the second floor of a residential building on St. Marks Place, making walk-in traffic rather rare. Jim, who was the manager, was sitting at the table nearest the cash register, uncontrollably yawning. Although there was a stack of college textbooks beside him, Jim was reading the New York Post. It was the fastest read of the four New York papers, and its apparently deliberate lack of journalistic integrity was always good for a few laughs. He'd move on to the Daily News next, and then settle in for some serious reading with the New York Times and the Wall Street Journal. Maybe later he would open one of his textbooks.

Halfway through the Daily News and his third cigarette, his first customer arrived: one of St. Marks Place's resident homeless men. He was wearing tree branches on his head and torso, duct-taped in place.

Jim went behind the counter and got silverware, napkins, and a glass of water.

"Hello, sir. The usual?"

The man nodded and stood by the table nearest the door. Jim set the table and said, "Have a seat."

Jim filled a cup with coffee, added half-and-half and six spoons of sugar, and brought it over to the table.

"Here you go, sir. Your sandwich is coming up."

The sandwich was the same every day, too: ham and

butter on darkly toasted white bread. Had to be practically burnt or he wouldn't eat it. When Jim placed it on the table, the man nodded at him.

The café door jingled open. Jim hoped it might be another customer, but it was Allie. Short and lean, she had over-dyed black hair that stood up like a hairbrush. Jim had to lean down to kiss her hello, which he loved, not being so tall himself. She was over a decade his senior, but her smaller stance and youthful features made people think Jim was older. He grabbed her, looked into her eyes, and said, full of innuendo, "Latte?"

"Can I get decaf? I've been working all night. I gotta crash soon."

"Hasn't your job heard of labor laws?

"Labor laws? Uh... no," she said. "I freelance. Labor laws don't apply to me."

"I'm pretty sure they do."

"Yeah? Tell my employers that."

"Still, it's gotta be better than working in a café with no customers."

Allie tilted her head towards the tree-branched man and said, "Don't be silly. You have customers."

"Yeah. I have a feeling this place won't be around very much longer. My boss has not been very happy."

Allie saw the Post headline and read it aloud: "'Albany's Plan to Bilk the Rich.' I see Page 1 is still their Op Ed page."

"Appeals to their mostly working-class readership."

"How do you figure?"

"It's America's carrot-on-a-stick, the idea that anyone, at any time, can become rich. And you wouldn't want *your* millions taxed away."

Allie shook her head. "Did you see this thing Giuliani is doing? Something about 'Quality of Life' issues? What, is he going to hire more street cleaners?"

"More police, fewer homeless, no squeegee guys."

"Fewer homeless? Where are they going to go? New Jersey?"

Jim set her coffee on the table and sat across from her.

"You know," he said, "you're one of the few people who orders decaf here... who gets decaf."

She raised her eyebrows at him and smiled behind her latte.

"So, I wonder," he said sotto voce, indicating Tree Man, "if you're going to wear dirty socks, shouldn't they at least match?"

"That's what you're wondering? Not, 'Why the tree branches?'"

"That's easy: camouflage."

That got a laugh.

"Actually," Allie said, "if he really wants to be camouflaged in the City, he should wear black."

Tree Man stood up and began rummaging through his pockets. Bits of change and buttons and lint poured onto the table.

"That's okay, man. That's okay." Jim headed over to him.

The man nodded and shuffled out.

Jim picked out the change from the table and cleared away everything else. When he sat back down with Allie, she said, "What's your take?"

"61 cents."

"See? What are you worried about? Business is booming."

He smirked at her and drew from his cigarette. "So, my sister... she's such a disaster. She told her stupid husband he doesn't have to work if he doesn't want to. He can just sit at home and get fatter and stupider."

"How would they live?"

"She's a nurse. I guess she thinks she can support them both."

"Doesn't she have a house? Aren't there, like, payments and stuff?"

"My mother owns it. Like she owns my apartment. Except, I pay rent. Julie just lives there."

"Ohhhhhh."

"Yeah."

The door opened again with another visitor. Jim saw Allie frown and roll her eyes. Laynie had entered the café.

"I'll be right back," he said. Allie took this opportunity to put out his neglected cigarette.

"Hey, Jimmy!" Then she mumbled the rest; she could barely talk.

"Laynie? You just back from the dentist?"

She stuck her tongue out. Jim wondered how it even fit in her mouth, it was so swollen. Her tongue was skewered by a small silver stud, hard to see beneath all the swelling.

"Ouch," he said.

She said something that Jim interpreted to mean, "It'll be fine by tomorrow," and she stuck her tongue out again so he could admire it further.

"Was this the only place on your body left to pierce?"

"Jus' bou'." Then she mumbled something that sounded like, "Ooush geh wn."

"I should get one? Ha. Allie hates what I already have. I don't dare add more. Besides, you said it wouldn't hurt."

She laughed. "I lied."

"Yes. You did." Jim looked back toward Allie, who was pretending to read the Daily News. "Well, I guess you don't want coffee. Can I get you some water or something?"

"Nah. I'ff gah tmee chas."

Okay. What was that now?

"What? Oh! You're meeting Chaz. Got it."

Jim sat back down with Allie, and she said, "You gotta be kidding me," and when he laughed, she said, "Seriously. That girl is ridiculous."

By Saturday, the café was shuttered. Jim and his boss, Arun, moved all the chairs and tables into the truck. Soon they were down to the appliances. Arun had hired two huge men with belts to do the heavy lifting, which left Jim to do the heavy cleaning. Behind the refrigeration and the sinks and cabinets was black, inky soot. Arun paid Jim quite generously for the day, more than double; the guy was a mensch.

A gloved and masked Jim with his mop set down his bucket filled with industrial cleaner. His boom box and CDs were on the floor against the wall, and, as the Pet Shop Boys began to sing at full volume, he dove into his task. Allie was sick of this CD, but it was Jim's favorite. He bellowed along at the top of his lungs, occasionally breaking into a dance with the mop.

As the CD came to an end, Jim decided to grab a smoke. The cleaner was so toxic he didn't dare light a cigarette inside, even with the windows open. He put down the mop, took off his gloves and mask, and when he turned toward the door, he saw a smirking Chaz and Laynie standing in the doorway.

"Holy fuck, you wanna give me a heart attack?"

"Watcha doin', Jim?" Laynie's tongue was once again working properly.

"Cleaning up."

"Can we hang a bit?"

Jim looked around the completely empty café space.

"Uh, yeah, okay. Sit near the windows; the cleaner fumes will kill you."

"We'll watch you dance," Laynie said, and Jim did a little rumba.

They sat on one of the window ledges, and Jim went out to smoke.

Someone somewhere was blasting the oldies station (WCBS), and Aretha Franklin began serenading the St. Marks Place people parade with "Chain of Fools." Jim watched a cluster of giggling coeds wearing NYU sweatshirts stroll by, and he nodded hello from his perch on the top stair. He was sharing the stoop with three stoned headbangers, who surely would have hidden the joint they were smoking if they had noticed the pair of cops crossing over from the other side of the street. A few doors down at the old Electric Circus building, a stream of recovering alcoholics poured out of their AA meeting. One of the participants walked by with a white rat perched on his shoulder as a silver Ferrari that looked a lot like a spaceship pulled up to the stoplight. This street was rarely boring. Jim was going to miss working here, not just because it was down the block from Allie.

He went back inside to find Chaz and Laynie hunched over a mirror.

"Is that coke?" Jim sounded angrier than he had intended.

They looked up. Something weird was going on with their eyes, like they weren't focusing or were focusing on something far away. "No, man. It's dope."

"Oh..." He could just hear what Allie would have to say about that.

"Wanna try it?"

"Uh... no thanks, man. I'm working."

"Next time, then. You'll dig it."

That's what made him worried.

In a dimly lit room, in a Tudor-style house in Forest Hills Gardens, three figures were gathered around a huge dining table, immersed in an action-packed, nail-biting, fight-to-the-death game of gin. The oldest, a heavy-set woman in her late 60s, was contemplating her next move, while the younger, male version of her and his friend waited impatiently.

"You know, it doesn't matter how long you stare at the cards. They aren't going to change," Ephram said.

Jim's mother looked at him through her fish-eye-lens glasses.

"Don't think you can rush me into making a mistake, now," she said in her deep, husky voice. She took a long drag on her menthol cigarette and changed the order of cards in her hand again.

"Seriously. It's a card game, not surgery," Jim said.

His mother, a retired doctor, raised her eyebrows and glared at him. She took a last puff from her cigarette, ground it out in the ashtray, put down her cards, and said, "Gin."

"What — You — Hey!"

His mother's laugh was hearty and congested.

Jim shook his head, then looked at the clock.

"We should get going."

"Ask Allie if she'd like to have lunch with us next week. I'd like to meet this girl before you two start having children."

His mother's sarcasm aside, Jim knew children were not in Allie's plans. He kept that to himself. "I'll ask her. Her schedule keeps changing. Maybe she can make it this time."

The traffic crawled along Queens Boulevard until it stopped altogether. Jim opened his window. He couldn't see much up ahead. Car horns were starting to blow, and some of the drivers were yelling. The longer the wait, the louder this would get. Jim closed the window.

"So..." Jim said. He hesitated. Did he want to discuss this with Ephram? "Laynie and Chaz stopped by the cafe yesterday afternoon."

"Laynie and...?" Ephram said. "Oh, those guys. They get something else pierced?"

"Nah. What's left? Maybe Laynie's uvula. Anyway, I was helping Arun clean out the cafe, and they came by."

"And...?"

"I stepped out for a second, and when I came back, they were snorting H."

Ephram grimaced and rolled his eyes. "Jim, those lowlifes are not your friends."

Jim tried not to get mad. He inched the car forward and stopped.

"Did you try it?" Ephram said.

"No, I didn't try it."

"But you're thinking about it."

Jim's silence answered the ques'

"Seriously, Jim..."

"I didn't try it. You know, I' addict or something. I'm just thinking o̤ ᵕ see."

"See what? How fucked up you can get?"

Jim wasn't going to acknowledge it out loud, but Ephram did have a point.

"What did Allie say about this?"

"Haven't told her. I'm not sure I'm even going to try it. Just thinking about it."

"Well, it's stupid that you're even thinking about it."

Jim tried to think of a good comeback. This was not the kind of subject he and Ephram were used to debating. Usually they stuck to something safe, like religion or politics.

"It's not like it's coke or something. I'm not going back to doing that."

Ephram threw him a side-glance. Okay, that was lame.

"Besides, Chaz said you can't get addicted when you snort it."

"The hell you can't." Ephram became very interested in something outside of his window. When the silence between them got too weird, Jim turned on the radio.

By the time Jim dropped Ephram off at his apartment in Chelsea, it was after 10 o'clock. Allie would be wondering where he was, but he had one more stop to make; he was out of cigarettes. He double-parked in front of a tiny store on Avenue A that sold candy, cigarettes, and ice cream. He'd leave the car idling. He'd only be a minute.

ment was three flights up, and while a person on
d would have trouble seeing into Allie's window, a
standing in a window across the street would have a
iew of the bedroom if Allie's lights were on. Jim pulled
chain of her overhead light to turn it off.

They flopped onto the bed. Jim began to chew on her neck,
which she loved, and after he had the area covered, he started
to plant small kisses down her arm.

"Wait. Wait. That tickles."

"Should I go back to chewing?" He kissed her some more.

"Yeah. Really. You gotta stop that." She pushed him away
from her arm.

"Well, okay."

But when he moved, he was suddenly in pain.

"Oh my god. Ow ow ow ow ow!"

"What? What?"

"Ow! Don't move your arm. Your watch is attached to my
nipple ring."

Allie burst out laughing.

"It's not funny."

"Oh, yes, it is."

She held up her wrist so he could detach himself.

"Stop laughing. If I didn't know better, I'd think you did
that on purpose."

Once freed, Allie took off her watch and put it on her
nightstand.

"The health hazards of piercings," she said.

She was still laughing when he grabbed her and said,
"C'mere, you."

He knew he shouldn't feel unnerved — they'd been
together almost two years now — but he couldn't help
wondering if she ever compared him to other, older men. In
fact, their first time, he envisioned her laughing at him. She
didn't. Tonight, he forced those insecure thoughts out of his
mind and tried not to be tentative. Fondle her breasts, kiss her

all over, get her worked up. Allie always made it seem easy.

As Allie fell asleep next to him, Jim thought about wrapping his arm around her, but she'd likely wake up and punch him. She wasn't a sleep cuddler. It was some time before she'd even let him stay over; he shouldn't push it.

He was in a dead sleep when Allie shook him awake.

"Jim. Hey. I'm heading out."

He opened his eyes and saw her bending over him.

"C'mon. You gotta move the car."

He squinted to see her more clearly.

Oh, no.

He fought the urge to laugh. "Uh... think you better wear a scarf today."

"Why? It's not that cold."

"No. Go look in the mirror."

He waited. Then he heard the shriek.

"Jim! My neck is totally bruised! I look like I've been strangled!"

Now he could laugh freely.

"It's not funny," she said.

"Oh, yes, it is."

PART ONE

OLD: *Let the Boogie Woogie Roll* (Ahmet Ertegun and Jerry Wexler)

— recorded by Clyde McPhatter and the Drifters, released 1960

CHAPTER 1

ALLIE, 1986

The borough of Manhattan was Icelandic cold, and although Allie was standing on the curb shivering, her eyes kept closing. There is a point where one's body just takes sleep, even if its owner is too stupid to lie down. The bars closed an hour ago, and there was no one on the street, but because Allie was so exhausted, walking the ten yards to the bustling Third Avenue to hail a cab was out of the question.

Despite her hypnagogic stupor, she spotted a taxicab across the Avenue with its "available" light on. Allie shot her hand into the air and the cab headed towards her. When it got closer, she was pleased to see it was a Checker cab, one of those fabulous rolling relics with spacious back seats. Allie opened the oversized back door, pushed her black duffel bag and her shopping bag full of wrapped presents to the far side of the cab, and climbed in.

"Good morning," the driver said and looked her over in the mirror. "Or are we still on 'Good evening'?"

"Kind of both," she said. "LaGuardia, please."

The driver nodded and turned on his meter. "You got it. Terminal?"

"Delta. Domestic."

"And am I driving crazy or normal?"

Allie smiled. The guy was a veteran New Yorker. He looked

21

and sounded like he should be taking bets at the OTB or standing in the middle of Times Square hawking the latest edition of the Daily News. In any case, he would know where LaGuardia was.

"Normal. My flight's at 6:30."

She was asleep in the back seat before her eyes were completely shut.

A procession of little winged Macintosh computers floated by, each one with the black and white "Hello" greeting on its screen. They seemed friendly, but they had her surrounded, and Allie wasn't falling for it. She didn't have to be back at work until after New Year's, and they knew it.

Her head bounced gently against the window, and she woke to see that her taxi had turned in to the terminal.

At this hour, there was no guy standing on the curb offering to help with her bags, and no attendant at the Information Desk. The Delta counter was manned, but there was no line there or at any other counter that she could see.

Allie handed the Delta guy her ticket and New York State ID, and in return, she got the fisheye.

"Everything okay?" she said.

"Allegra Squerciati..."

He looked her up and down and not so subtly shook his head. Maybe he was confused because her purple spiked hair didn't match her ID photo. Maybe he didn't like her studded leather jacket or her "Je Ne Regret Rien" t-shirt. He was a 40-something blue-collar soul in an airline uniform, and it seemed he wasn't too keen on the whole rock-'n-roll-chic phenomenon. To be fair, Allie's young-adult life didn't take her north of 14th Street very often. Her world was even smaller than she assumed his was.

To Delta Guy's dismay, Allie's ID appeared to be real, and with no bags to check, Allie soon had her boarding pass in hand and was negotiating the terminal's linoleum maze to get to her gate.

And this is where all the people were: Allie's gate. She found a free spot in the far corner, put her carry-on bag on the floor beside her and her shopping bag under the seat. From out of the carry-on, she extracted a pair of sunglasses, which she put on her head, and a recent issue of Spy Magazine, *which she opened to the cover article, "The Spy 100: The Worst People, Places and Things of 1986." Drawing the oversized sunglasses down from her forehead, she closed her eyes and pretended to be reading.*

"Excuse me?"

She flipped up her shades. A pleasant-voiced, older man was addressing her. He was beige, everything from his down jacket to his khaki trousers to his Nubuck boots.

"Would you mind watching my bag?" he said.

"Not at all," Allie said, then added with a grin. "What's it gonna do?"

A question mark appeared over the man's head.

"Nothing," he said. "I thought maybe you could look after it a minute, so no one takes it."

She bit her lips. "Sure," she said. "No problem."

Oh, boy.

She looked around. Chubby, blushing, cheery faces, pastel-colored, freshly pressed, casual clothes, clean, unmussed hair, everyone perky and easygoing and engaged in lively conversation.

Tourists. Probably all came in to see The Radio City Music Hall Christmas Spectacular.

Okay, there was nothing really wrong with the Radio City Christmas Show, other than the constant, cloying television commercials, and nothing wrong with tourists either, as long as they were the kind who knew how to walk on a sidewalk without getting in everybody's way. There might not even be anything wrong with being awake this early, unless a person had just worked the late shift, as Allie had.

Since she was not going to be able to sleep amid the gaiety of these merry, chirping travelers, when the bag's owner returned, she gave up her seat and wandered over to the overpriced breakfast place to drink a large cup of coffee, sulk, and curse her parents for moving to Ohio.

Allie had requested, and was granted, a window seat. With the help of a much taller stranger, she got her bags loaded into an overhead compartment, and nestled into her seat.

"Good morning!"

An older woman and her pre-teen daughter were taking the seats next to her. Allie forced a smile. It wasn't this woman's fault that Allie had had only two hours of sleep or that she was, as a rule, suspicious of people who exuded too much happiness. The woman pulled a book out of her bag, and for a moment Allie thought this might be a conversation-free flight.

"Okay, where were we?" the woman asked her daughter.

Her daughter reached over and opened the book to a happy pink bookmark.

"This was the last one we read."

"Okay. Next: 'Two ropes walk into a bar. They sit down, and the bartender says...'"

Allie turned her attention to the safety of the window.

It had been a few years since Allie had been on a plane, the last time having been a post-college-graduation trip to Jamaica with some friends. A Rastafarian who called himself Charlie had turned them onto the most exquisite weed and later took Allie on a tour of the local record stores. Allie scored a couple dozen locally produced reggae 45s, and her friends came home with three pounds of locally grown ganja, carefully hidden in a hollowed-out, wooden, Rastafarian mask. After the weed was smoked, Allie took ownership of the mask and hung it in her kitchen, hoping it would annoy her roommate.

If she was remembering correctly now, planes leaving La Guardia flew the length of Manhattan, and if one were on the correct side of the plane...

Yes.

Allie pressed her face against the glass, always exhilarated by a view of her City's skyline.

Except for one intrusion, when her seat neighbor took her life into her hands to wake Allie and tell her breakfast was being served, Allie did manage to sleep through the flight, actual deep REM sleep. This made her reluctant to leave when the plane landed. Her sticky eyes watched the other passengers advancing to the exit, and it occurred to her that, in her black leather jacket, black jeans and black t-shirt, she was the only person on the plane who was wearing anything remotely dark in color, and certainly the only person sporting purple spiked hair.

Were people staring at her?

She deplaned and headed into the main area of the airport. Unlike the institutional decor and confusing corridors, staircases, and escalators that made up LaGuardia, she found herself in a vibrant, friendly mall. She was about to enter a Dunkin' Donuts to get another coffee, when a mild panic came over her: She had forgotten to change her New York money.

Reality hit her seconds later, and she laughed.

How did that go? Something about not being in Kansas anymore?

The bubbly girl behind the counter at the Dunkin' Donuts had no problem accepting Allie's New York money in exchange for a large coffee.

OCTOBER 1994

Jim was a snoring mound of flesh beside her, but that wasn't why Allie wasn't sleeping. It might have been the coffee she had had at work, although it seemed to have worn off hours ago, allowing her to sleep comfortably until her cat, Tuna, jumped on her head. Now, Tuna and Jim were asleep, and Allie was wide awake.

She carefully removed herself from under the cat, crawled over Jim, and went to sit in the window. She put both her feet on the sill and hugged her knees. The streets were quiet, unusual for her block. From her perch, she could see across the street to the punk clothing store, Trash and Vaudeville, and to what used to be a long-standing bathhouse. These days it was a karaoke bar. Allie didn't think that establishment was going to last long; no one ever seemed to go in it.

Her friend Rihanna had invited Jim and her to dinner in Chinatown this coming Saturday. When Allie told Jim, he was less than enthusiastic.

"Let me think about it."

"My friends will be nice. I'll put the fear of God in them."

"I'm sure you will. Let me tell you Friday, okay? I'll call you if I'm coming."

Not committing was customary for Jim, but in this case, she knew it was because of her friends. They were a lot older than he was, and he found them intimidating. They all met at her birthday dinner last May, and Jim was so anxious, he chattered on and on about anything he could think of. Her friends began talking behind his back, and one of them murmured, "Keep talking fast so you don't have to listen to anyone else." Jim wasn't supposed to hear it, but he did.

She was now contemplating, for the umpteenth time since they got together, their age difference. Jim had a way about him that camouflaged his 24 years. People used to mistake him for his dad, and everyone said Jim looked ten years older than Allie, instead of the other way around. But there were those times when his youth leapt out of hiding, and then Allie felt like an old woman, or worse, his mother.

"What's wrong?"

Jim was up. Tuna was following him into the room, yawning.

"Can't sleep. I'm having a caffeine flashback."

He reached his hand out

"C'mon. I'll make you tired."

Allie smiled and jumped down from the sill. If she wasn't going to be sleeping, what better way to spend the time?

In the center of the apartment, right off the kitchen, there was a closet. This was considered somewhat of a luxury by Manhattan standards. Towering and cavernous, it stored all of Allie's clothing, and as she stood in front of its deep, imposing maw, she realized there were probably things buried in there that she hadn't seen since the 80s. Someday she'd go through it. Tonight, she just needed something to wear.

Allie hadn't heard from Jim, so it was clear she was going to this dinner thing by herself. Which was fine, except for the part where she didn't really know for sure she shouldn't be waiting for him. Jim did have a penchant for surprises. Could he say, "I'll call you if I'm going to come," and then not call and show up anyway? Yes, he could.

She decided not to call him, though. He didn't even have an answering machine (hello, it's 1994 already, get with the program). Truth was, she was a little tired of having to track him down all the time. Jim wanted to surprise her? Let him pick up the phone and tell her his plans. That would be a major surprise.

She spotted a shirt she liked, and as she climbed her stepladder to reach for it, the phone rang. She grabbed her shirt and got down to answer the phone.

"Hi."

"Hi, Allie, it's Rihanna."

Okay, so not Jim.

"The restaurant wants us to come earlier because there's so many of us. Is 7:30 okay with you?"

That gave her an hour. "Sure. See you then."

Crap. Now, did she call Jim to tell him the time changed, or not? Seriously, he wasn't coming.

She got dressed, put on make-up, then stalled for as long as she could. Finally, she put on her leather jacket, grabbed her keys, and headed out.

It requires a certain amount of indefatigability to navigate an adventure to Chinatown, especially on a Saturday night, when all seven million inhabitants of Manhattan Island, with every one of their bridge and tunnel friends, converge at the intersection of Canal Street and Broadway, with and without their vehicles, to look for restaurants. Allie exited the subway, and as usual, the traffic on Canal was at a standstill. She walked past the vendors selling their knock-off handbags, the loitering delinquent youths, and the genuine neighborhood residents, to join the succession of hungry people heading to Mott Street.

The best part about Chinatown was going to those little hole-under-the-street places, where the food was cheap and tasty, the hours were early to extremely late, and the ambiance bordered on abuse. Allie was not going to one of those places. If your party was more than four people, there would be no room for you there.

No, they were meeting at the Royal Imperial Hunan Dragon, upstairs on the corner of Mott and Pell Streets. A huge, red, seething, dragon's-head sculpture loomed over the sidewalk, its body painted on the building, covering most of the wall. A swarm of beautiful Chinese lanterns hung in the upstairs windows and lined the outdoor staircase leading to the entrance. It occurred to Allie that she had never been to an upscale restaurant in Chinatown, not once in her 35 years as a resident of the planet and of New York City.

The menu had so many pages it was broken into chapters, and as the discussion turned to what everyone would or would not eat, Allie started to feel anxious and guilty. Maybe she should have called Jim. Was he sitting on her stoop right now, waiting to surprise her? Or buzzing her apartment, wondering why she hadn't waited for him? By not calling him, did she stand him up?

"Excuse me, everyone. I gotta make a call."

The phone booth was an enormous Chinese lantern, a large version of the ones hanging in the windows. Two dragons were guarding it. Allie took a seat inside and dialed.

Ringing.

Be home, Jim.

Still ringing.

If he had a stupid answering machine, she could leave a message. At least he would know she had called.

Ring, ring, ring.

That was already a dozen rings.

She hung up and sighed. Maybe he was off having fun somewhere else. Not, as she imagined, sitting on her stoop, waiting for her.

And somewhere in the distance, a phone was ringing.

Ringing, ringing.

Was that really a phone, or was it coming from the neighbor's stereo? Allie thought about pounding on the wall, but then, that would require her to wake up.

Actually, that really was the phone, not part of her dream. Her real phone.

Allie struggled to get up. She tried lifting an arm, then a foot. Sleep was pressing down on her limbs, but she had to answer that phone; it could be Jim. With much effort, she shook herself awake.

Still ringing.

Allie nudged Tuna off her legs and got up to get the phone. "Hi."

A pause. Then, a low, gravelly voice said, "Hello, is this Allie?"

Okay, why on earth would Harvey Fierstein be calling her?

"This is Jim's mother."

Really? Holy crap. "Mrs., uh, I mean, Dr. Stein. Hello."

"Jim was going to call me when he was leaving. Is he still there?"

Allie caught her breath. "Still here? He never was here. I didn't see him last night."

"That's odd." Allie could hear Jim's mother take a draw off a cigarette. "He borrowed money from me yesterday so he could go to dinner with you."

"He did? He never told me he was coming."

"Well, I guess he wanted to surprise you."

"Yeah. I hate that."

Jim's mother grunted a laugh, punctuated with some coughing. "So, you didn't see him last night?"

"No, but I ended up leaving earlier than I had expected, so I guess I missed him."

"Well, we had plans today. Maybe he's on his way."

"That's probably it."

Damn it. She did stand him up.

Allie sighed and dialed Jim. No answer. He must have already left to go see his mother. Or maybe he had been out with his friends and crashed at one of their places.

This was her first Sunday off in a while, and although she had a strong urge to go back to sleep, she decided she might as well start her day. Tomorrow she'd be back at work, but today there were coffee shops to go to, urban decay to photograph, and a large, odd assortment of people to watch. She couldn't remember the last time she had a day to herself. The novelty was refreshing. She'd talk to Jim later.

It was now nine twenty-nine in Astor Place.

It had been nine twenty-nine in Astor Place for years and would continue to be nine twenty-nine for at least a dozen more. The clock on the Carl Fischer Building had stopped working sometime in the 80s, and although it had been painted and restored, it continued to be lifeless.

Allie knew this but couldn't help looking up at it for information every time she passed. Right. Of course. Nine twenty-nine.

Everywhere else in the City, it was closer to three o'clock in the afternoon, and, anyway, Allie really had no reason to be looking at the clock. Late or early never mattered this time of year. When Goldfish Graphics was in the middle of its busy season, everyone worked around the clock, and shifts were approximate. A freelancer's dream, for the money; a nightmare, for the lack of sleep and sanity.

The usual ragtag group of musicians was set up in front of the uptown subway stairwell. They were playing something that resembled swing, although with the tuba, washtub bass and child's piano, it wasn't obvious exactly what they were going for. When Allie was a kid, she used to think how magical it was that the City streets were dotted with musicians and other street artists, there just to entertain her. When she got older, this perception changed, and she realized the more practical implications of people playing music on the street.

Allie gave them a quarter as she passed by.

Allie was too agitated to go down into the subway, and since Goldfish wasn't that far away, she decided to walk. Jim still hadn't called. She assumed he was mad at her for not waiting for him on Saturday. She had ruined his surprise. They'd been together almost two years, and he was always trying to surprise her; she should have anticipated it.

"Allie! Good. You're here."

Allie could smell Sal's cologne and cocaine sweat from the other end of the corridor. He entered the production area and stood beside her desk with his coat half on, his face involuntarily twitching.

"There's a stack of photos on your chair. They're due in the morning."

Yes. She could see them. "No problem," Allie said.

He went back into the corridor, put his other arm in its sleeve, and then came back.

"If you could get those done, that would be great. Really great. We need them in the morning." Perspiration was building up on his forehead and around his neck.

Allie strained a smile. "Okay, Sal."

He tried to put on his gloves, but when that failed, he put them in his pocket. "Get on it right away. They're due in the morning."

"Got it."

He fumbled with the buttons of his coat.

"I'm heading out."

Thus, the coat.

One more, quick circle around himself, and he was gone.

"Allie, get to work. Those photos are due in the morning." Rihanna had waited until Sal was gone to enter the area.

"God, he's really tweaked today," Allie said.

Rihanna put a finger on one side of her nose and pretended to snort.

"Yeah. He wreaks of it. The heavy cologne isn't fooling anybody." Allie moved the stack of folders off her chair and sat down. "Have you heard anything about our checks?"

Rihanna shook her head. "Nothing. I didn't get mine, either."

"Really? But you're the Production Manager. Aren't you staff?"

"Doesn't matter; the client hasn't paid the bill."

"Great," Allie said. "I'm sure my landlord will be very

understanding. He actually likes getting the rent late."

"One good thing about my living with Dylan; no rent to pay."

Allie was going to say "Yeah, the only thing," but for once she held her tongue.

Models in pantsuits. Models in sun dresses. These photos obviously couldn't be placed in the catalogs if the models had no feet, could they? Allie wasn't opposed to a little Franken-steining, but every photo? The problem with mind-numbingly dull work is that it does just the opposite. Allie's unsettled mind was taking a long walk, first wandering past some CDs she wanted to buy at Tower Records, a safe place for it to go. Then it turned left and headed to the Laundrobot where she had a bag of laundry to rescue. There, it did an abrupt U-turn, skipped past the Kiev where some cheese blintzes were calling out to her, and landed right back at Saturday's Chinatown dinner, with Allie wondering how mad Jim was and when he would call.

She decided to get some coffee. Walking across the studio might help her get her mind back to work. After pouring a cup, Allie sat down in an empty office and picked up the phone.

"Ephram. It's Allie."

"Hey. What's doing? Uh, no, I haven't spoken to Jim."

"What? How did you —"

"Dr. Stein called me. He was supposed to see her yester-day."

"Yes, she called me too. Wait, he never showed?" Jim rarely disappointed his mother. The fallout wouldn't be worth it.

"I know why he hasn't called me," Ephram said. "I pissed him off."

"You did? How?"

He hesitated. "Not important. It'll blow over. But it's weird he hasn't called you either."

"I saw him Wednesday. We sort of had plans on Saturday,

but nothing concrete. I may have inadvertently stood him up."

"Inadvertently, huh?" Ephram said. "You know, he probably went drinking with Chris and Mike. You know how they get. They may still be hungover someplace, trying to figure out what day it is."

"Right. And then he'll have to deal with his mom, and I'm sure he isn't looking forward to doing that."

"Yeah. I wouldn't worry about him."

Allie put down the phone. If Jim stood up his mother because he was out drinking, it might take some time for him to resurface. She would hear from him soon.

She picked up her coffee and shut out the light before she left the room.

Allie finished the photos around midnight, a lot earlier than she had been leaving lately, early enough to walk home. Wrapped in a personal, protective envelope of darkness, her path illuminated by silvery streetlights, Allie walked unnoticed through this movie set, taxis barreling by, people conversing and laughing, stores closed and bars open. She took a deep breath of the cold, clean, night air. Walking in her City at night always managed to quiet her most unsettling thoughts.

Allie was feeling tall.

There was no reason for this phenomenon. She wasn't wearing high heels or standing next to anyone shorter than she was. In fact, she wasn't standing at all, but was lying on her bed in her apartment, flipping through a new issue of the kinder, gentler — and less funny — resurrection of *Spy Magazine*. It was something about the way she was stretched out there — one knee slightly bent, her jeans hugging her thighs and then slightly flaring out below her knees, ending just shy of the base of her Nike'd feet — that was giving her an idea of what it might be like to be tall. Not altitudinous, but certainly more elongated than usual. She hadn't achieved the state of calm she had been looking for but had instead achieved the pretense of height. This illusion vanished when she clambered off the bed to answer the phone.

A telemarketer. She groaned and hung up.

Allie's hopes of achieving placidity were dashed. Forget relaxing; what she needed was a diversion.

Maybe she'd make a mixtape.

She surveyed her crates of albums and CDs. Allie liked to make tapes that had a theme, even if the theme was only apparent to her. She had made plenty of tapes: happy tapes, sad tapes, party mixes, tapes from every decade, but she had no particular reason to be making this tape. Calling it a "Something Else to Focus On" tape seemed stupid.

Old, new, borrowed, blue. She hadn't created one of this genre in a while, as it tended to be rather labor-intensive. "Old" was easy, of course. "Borrowed" was any cover, which was only tricky because Allie tended to prefer originals. "Blue" could be a lot of things, actual blues or R 'n B, or anything sad, or anything with blue in the title or, in a pinch, in the band name. But "new." That was a short, transient list.

She stopped a moment and had the thought she had been trying to avoid:

Where was Jim? It was now over a week.

She took a deep breath and let it out slowly. Jim disappearing for a day or two was one thing, but this was more than a little worrisome.

She forced herself to concentrate. She scanned her collection for CDs that had come out in the past year or so. Nirvana? Luscious Jackson? Hmm, yes, and yes. Beck? Maybe something off *Mellow Gold*. Bonnie Raitt? Too mainstream. Insane Clown Posse? Too disturbing. Green Day? Too... something.

Just as she admitted to herself that her heart wasn't entirely in this project, the phone rang.

"Allie?" That now familiar growl with the Darth Vader breathing technique could only be one person. "Still no word, and I've been calling everyone." Then the pitch of Dr. Stein's voice sunk somehow lower. "This is strange now."

Allie sat at her kitchen table. She was getting a nagging feeling.

"You know, Dr. Stein, at this point I don't know whether we should be mad or worried."

The nagging feeling turned into a voice, an internal voice, and it sounded a lot like Jim's voice, whispering urgently in her ear, "Not mad. Please don't be mad." It was not quite real enough to make her think she was having a psychotic episode, but it did make her uneasy.

"Allie, Dear, do you have keys to his apartment?"

"I can't find them. I think I might have left them there."

"That's okay. I do." The tobacco-damaged voice on the other end of the phone perked up a bit. "This is what we will do. I have to come into the City tomorrow for an early appointment. I will go to the apartment and see if he's there. Either way, you and I will get some lunch. It's time we finally meet."

Allie hung up the phone. She sat staring at it for a minute, and when it told her nothing and didn't ring again, she picked it back up and dialed.

"Hi, Ephram."

"Hi, Allie. I'm guessing Jim still hasn't called."

"No. Listen, you know those two losers he thinks are his friends?"

"Mike and Chris?"

"Ha. No. The two lowlifes that have been hanging around my building."

"Oh. Yeah. He does find them fascinating. All they do is get high and get pierced."

"Well, you don't think... I mean, he hasn't touched the stuff for nine years."

"He hasn't done coke. They weren't offering him coke."

Allie paused, confused. "Wait. What did they offer him?"

Ephram hesitated. "They were... snorting dope the other day in the café. It got him curious. When I told him he was being stupid, he got mad at me."

"He got mad because you said snorting dope was stupid?"

"He said he just wanted to try it once. Maybe that's what he did. And you can bet he'd be unwilling to materialize if that's what he's been doing."

Allie put down the phone. Armed with this new insight, she grabbed a coat and headed out.

The piercing shop, Fleshtopia, was on the second floor of her building, and Scott, the head piercer, was sitting on the stoop, smoking a cigarette. His face and much of his body were covered in tattoos and piercings. His earlobes were stretched to fit two palm-sized disks, and his dreadlocks were almost as long as he was tall. Allie would have found him kind of handsome if he didn't have all that ridiculous body ornamentation.

There was plenty of downtime at the shop, and Scott spent most of it sitting in that exact spot on the top of the stairs. It made him a great source of neighborhood gossip, the East Village equivalent of those Italian matriarchs who hung out of windows in Little Italy.

"Hey..."

He looked up. "What's going on, Allie?" He shifted over so she could sit.

"Listen, you know that couple who've been hanging around here lately? You pierced the woman's tongue, like, a month ago."

"That doesn't exactly narrow it down."

Right. "The guy's got a Prince Albert. His girlfriend has something, uh, similar, and they have a chain that links them together. They've been practically living on this stoop."

"Oh. Yeah. Chaz and Laynie."

"Have you seen them?"

"Not since last weekend. Why?"

"Jim seems to be missing. Thought he might be with them."

Scott's usual expression of boredom and distain turned to concern.

"You guys have a fight?"

"Not exactly," Allie said. "But he's been hanging with those two lately, and we're kind of running out of people to ask."

Scott took a long drag that finished off his cigarette and flicked the butt to the street, barely missing a passerby.

"Don't worry," he said. "He'll turn up."

"Yeah," she said, not convinced. "He eventually does."

They fell silent and stared at the sidewalk traffic. Allie would have liked nothing better than to stay on the stoop and people watch, but she was too unnerved. Allie said goodbye to Scott and bounded down the stairs.

Okay. She was worried.

"Damn it, Jim, where the hell are you?" she said aloud. This elicited a startled look from a group of passersby. *Not New Yorkers*, Allie thought. She walked all 20 blocks to Jim's apartment building. When she got there, she stood across the street and stared at the entrance of his building.

Now what?

If she buzzed the apartment and there was no answer, that would be it; there wasn't anything else she could do without keys. Maybe he would come home while she was standing there.

After some time, she noticed she was cold. She climbed the stoop and rang the bell. She didn't really expect an answer.

Not a sound from the street outside. No giggling revelers staggering home from the bars, no speeding taxis trying to make the light, no fire trucks, not even the distant rush of traffic from the FDR drive. Quiet, cool, early morning blackness, the calm before the cacophony.

A streetlight shone on Tuna's attentive face. If anything was awake out there, she would know about it. Allie watched Tuna on the lookout, and it kept her mesmerized for a full minute. Not being able to sleep was torturous, but the silence was so unusual Allie was temporarily absorbed.

Allie waited for the sun to rise before she got up and got dressed. Then she paced around her apartment, making herself miserable with her own thoughts. Jim's mom wouldn't be calling for some time. She couldn't keep walking back and forth, talking to herself, until the phone rang.

Or, in truth, she could.

She went to the closet and got out her black denim jacket. Her Pentax camera was hanging on a hook inside as well, and she grabbed that, too. She closed her apartment door behind her, locked the bolt and the two Fichet locks, and headed east.

For three blocks, East 8th Street was called St. Marks Place, starting at 3rd Avenue, where Allie's apartment was, and ending at Tompkins Square Park. Allie loved Tompkins' beautiful landscaping, its cobblestone paths, and century-old trees. She crossed over to the basketball courts on the Avenue B side, across from the notorious Christadora apartment complex. The first luxury condo building in the neighborhood, it had been renovated for that purpose in 1986. At the time, Allie and her neighbors had thought it ridiculous that someone would invest in that decrepit, monstrous building on Avenue B, an area populated by crack and heroin addicts, low-rent prostitutes, and various other conmen and conwomen. Then a few years later, the City discovered it had some money and decided it could no longer tolerate chemically altered people having their run of things on the Lower East Side. So one day, the park's old band shell was taken down, the cardboard refrigerator boxes that housed a community of homeless people disappeared, and Tompkins Square was closed for renovation. When it reopened, developers were buying up property in the area, and upper-upper-class folks began wanting apartments there. A renovated Christadora was no longer that laughable.

Allie sat on a bench with her back to the high-end building and put a roll of film in her camera. The only other person in sight was shooting hoops at the far end of the court. Her plan was to spend some time, just her and her camera. She needed a few moments devoid of disquieting thoughts. If she could figure out how to do it, she would spend the time having no thoughts at all.

When she got home, she found her answering machine flashing with a message. Dr. Stein's raspy voice was full of distress.

"I found Jim in the apartment. He has been murdered."

Allie froze. Stunned and paralyzed, she was not ready to allow this reality in just yet. It took a few moments, but then she picked up the phone and made various S.O.S calls to her friends. She called back Dr. Stein last.

"Allie, there's blood everywhere. I'll call you back after the police are finished."

It wasn't long before someone was buzzing Allie's apartment. She looked outside, dropped the keys down to her friend Natia, and slumped back over her kitchen table.

Natia knocked softly and eased into the apartment. "Heard anything else?"

Allie mumbled a "No," and lifted her head. "You know, I can just see Jim pissing somebody off enough to get himself killed."

Jim had asked her not to be mad, but Allie found anger to be the most accessible emotion at the moment.

When Dr. Stein called back, it turned out it was not the result of foul play, but, more likely, a drug overdose. She had found Jim on the couch, shirt off, blood all over his chest and all over the cushions. She hadn't seen the small glassine packet with remnants of white powder on the table beside him. It wouldn't take much effort to confirm what it was. Experienced with cocaine and not with heroin, Jim did not know how much was too much. Whatever it was must have hit him fast, the cops told her, because there were no signs he even tried to reach for the phone.

While Natia sat across from Allie at the kitchen table, the phone kept ringing, as if time had not stopped and the world was still turning. There was a wrong number, the Harris Poll, several of Allie's friends returning her calls, and a telemarketer. Then came a call from Sal, wondering why she wasn't coming in to work.

"Rihanna said you needed the day off. Can't you come in for part of your shift?"

"I don't think... I can't..." She was trying not to say, "My boyfriend is dead."

She paused to think this through. "I can't do anything today. I've just gotten some very bad news."

How stupid that sounded. For a moment she contemplated asking if tomorrow would suffice, but instead of giving in to pressure, she came to her senses.

"I'll be in Monday."

"Monday! You know we have a very tight schedule. You still have a computer at home, don't you? What if we send a messenger over with some work?"

"I'm sorry."

Natia took the phone out of her hand.

"That's it. You're not answering the phone anymore today."

Ephram called Allie later that evening. Their conversation artfully skirted around the issue of guilt, even though all Allie could think about was how Jim must have come to her apartment, found she wasn't there, and hooked up with those two deadbeats with the heroin. And Ephram, well, his last conversation with Jim was three weeks ago.

Ephram, however, was not choosing guilt this evening.

"Allie, you know Jim. When the rest of us sees a rabid dog, we say 'Oh my God! A rabid dog! Run away!' Jim says, 'Look! A rabid dog! Cool! Let me check that out!'"

This made her laugh for the first time in many hours.

Friday would find Natia, Rihanna, and Allie in a car heading to a funeral being held in a synagogue somewhere near Jim's mother's house in Queens. Jim's friend Chris had picked them all up — as Jim would've said, he was a real mensch — and he was now cursing and swerving in and out of the Friday morning traffic, with Natia and Rihanna cringing quietly in the back seat. Allie, sitting shotgun, was staring blankly out of the window.

Her mother had tried to console her the night before, saying something like, "God will forgive Jim, and he will eventually have a place in heaven."

Allie had nothing to say to that, because, as far as she was concerned, Jim had nothing to be forgiven for, except stupidity, and everyone was guilty of that at one time or another. When Allie did not react, her mother tried something like, "You know, there's a reason for everything that happens. God has a plan."

Allie did not believe there was a plan. She felt that people who believed that everything happened for a reason were just denying the accidental nature of life, hanging on to the illusion that people had some control over what happened to them, or worse, that there was a mysterious force watching out to make sure they didn't fall down a manhole or something.

And then there was that afterlife thing. Why would everyone be so sad if dead didn't mean dead, really dead, like gone, dead? But for two days, she had had the feeling that Jim was following her around, and as Chris turned his dad's black Ford Escort into the parking lot, Allie could feel Jim holding her.

Allie scanned the vista of sad faces across the parking lot and tried to guess which ones were related to Jim. The male guests were wearing yarmulkes, and many of the women were wearing small, round pieces of lace on their heads. Allie found she was suddenly as nervous as she was bereaved. She was an outsider clumsily invading someone else's solemn ceremony.

She spotted Ephram and headed over. He leaned down to the plump little woman standing beside him and said something, and when the woman turned to face Allie, she revealed her teary eyes. Dr. Stein was maybe half a foot shorter than Allie, and a lot older than a woman would normally be having a 24-year-old son. She was wearing one of those little circles of lace, attached to her hair with a few bobby pins.

"Allie. We finally meet."

Allie was not much of a hugger, but she hugged Dr. Stein.

Everyone entered the synagogue and was led into what looked like an office, except for the rows of folding chairs and the podium. Allie and her friends joined Ephram at the back of the room, and when Allie faced the front, she saw the casket. Ephram put his hand on her shoulder; she must have reacted out loud.

After the funeral, everyone assembled at Dr. Stein's house, where there was quite a feast. Natia offered to make Allie a sandwich, but Jim's sister, Julie, approached and took Allie aside.

"Allie! Oh, Allie! Oh, God! This is so terrible!" She was crying.

Allie had not yet resorted to crying. A bizarre guttural howl had come out of her when she heard Dr. Stein's message, but since then she was immersed in a murky fog. And now a woman she did not know was sobbing at her.

"I was so awful to Jim when we were growing up. I was terrible. Now he's gone. Did he tell you I was an awful sister?"

What was Allie going to say, "Yes"? She put on her best I'm-sorry-for-your-loss face and shook her head.

"Do you think he forgave me? Did he ever say anything about me?" Julie was staring at Allie with a hopeful, guilty look.

My sister is such a disaster. That's what Allie remembered. That and something about Julie locking Jim in a clothes trunk when he was four.

"Sure, he talked about you all the time."

Julie was interrupted by her mother before she could ask anything else, and Allie was relieved, but not for long. Dr. Stein led her into a bedroom and closed the door.

She sat on the bed, literally looking down at Allie, who had been shown to a chair much closer to the floor. This was the first time Allie had gotten a good look at her. Like Jim, her face was round, with high cheekbones, a straight, long, thin nose, and eyes that crinkled. It used to give Jim kind of an elfish look. It did not do the same for his mother.

Dr. Stein lit a cigarette, drew on it hard, and savored the exhale. Allie would have liked nothing better than to jump out of her skin, but her body stubbornly refused to go.

"When I found Jim," Dr. Stein said finally, "he wasn't wearing a shirt."

Jim's mother motioned toward the general vicinity of her breast. "He had a... a..."

Oh, crap. Jim's stupid nipple ring.

"Piercing." Allie finished the sentence for her. Dr. Stein nodded.

"Do you know anything about this?"

I was having sex with your son. Of course, I knew about this.

Great. Did Dr. Stein think this was her idea? Allie was not amused by the irony.

"That was his decision, not mine. I really hated that thing."

Wow. Allie wouldn't have believed that explanation herself. Although there was still a distinct look of suspicion and disapproval on her face, Dr. Stein nodded slowly. Allie let out what she hoped was an imperceptible sigh of relief.

And she could feel Jim laughing.

The next morning, Allie entered Tompkins Square, this time without her Pentax. She tried to walk on the cobblestones that encircled the fenced-in lawn of the park, until she realized how uneven they were and had to switch to the paved sidewalk. The old and gnarly trees in the park formed a canopy, and even without leaves, there was no unobstructed view of the sky. It gave the impression that, as long as the adjacent bench was unoccupied, a person could be alone with her thoughts.

Allie found a spot in front of an old willow that was growing out of the pavement. It leaned away from her, its bark split open with a gaping wound. The band shell used to sit across the way, but now that area was a wide, empty walkway leading to an exit. Allie looked around. She had this part of the park all to herself.

She had dreamt about Jim the night before. Rather, he had walked into another dream she was having, and dragged her out of it. And she did exactly what any book you'll ever read on this subject tells you not to do: If someone who has died visits you in a dream, you are not supposed to say "Oh my god! I thought you were dead!"

Jim kept avoiding her questions, and then they had a laugh together over nothing, and then he had to leave. That was it. And all she had to say to him was "I thought you were dead. Oh my God. You're not dead? You are, aren't you?"

Several months earlier, they had talked about the inevitability of their separating one day. Jim wanted to go to grad school, most likely not in the City. He eventually wanted to get married and have a pack of children, not something Allie had any interest in doing. Allie was reluctant to ever share her living quarters again after her experiences with her last roommate, and kids had never been part of her life plan.

"You don't want a family now, do you?" she had asked him.

"No, no, not until I finish school. I figure not until I'm at least thirty."

"Well, then, we're fine for now."

And they would part friends, they both agreed.

Allie knew she wasn't deeply in love, but actually, she didn't miss it. She was proud of her emotional independence. Her oldest brother, Nico, used to complain about his "clingy" girlfriends, and Allie had made the decision early on to avoid being one. But whether in love, deeply or not, she felt a lot like that willow, with a huge chunk of her now torn off.

She wasn't feeling him around her anymore. The dream was it. He came to visit one last time, said something funny to her that only her subconscious got to hear, then a goodbye, and now she was alone, sitting on a cold park bench, staring at a tree.

When a life ends early, there's a story left yearning for a punchline with none forthcoming. God has a reason for everything? She didn't think so.

She headed back to her apartment.

CHAPTER 2

RIHANNA MEETS DYLAN, 1986

Rihanna set the bicycle down on its back wheel so she could lock the apartment door, then maneuvered it down the stairs to the street. The first time she tried this, she became trapped by the bike, its front wheel having been wedged in the banisters between the second and third floors, where she stayed until a neighbor came home and rescued her. It took weeks to get the bicycle grease out of her sun-bleached curls, and she never did get it out of her jeans.

Rihanna was staying with her friends Maya and Lindsey in their moderately sized studio in Chelsea. The three women had been living on top of each other since Rihanna moved to the City a few months ago, and Rihanna knew that, if she didn't move out soon, they would no longer be friends. Therefore, mornings she would leave with her bike and head to those battered piers on the Hudson to sit by the water. By the time she returned to the apartment, her friends would have left for work, and she could concentrate on finding a job and a more permanent living arrangement.

Today she wanted to venture out of Chelsea, be brave, and try another neighborhood. Rihanna put on her wrap-around shades, as much to prevent pieces of City air from flying into her eyes as to block the sun and climbed onto her bike. She headed down 7th Avenue with the flow of traffic, passing an array of restaurants, newsstands, bars, mom-and-pop store-fronts, various apartment buildings and row houses. At 14th Street, the street grid collapsed, and the cross streets became a mad jumble. Eventually the entire diorama transformed into cement office buildings and warehouses. She turned west towards the river. A bit further south, there was a pier and some boats, and she decided to stop.

A vendor had parked his cart in the middle of this nothingness. She bought a coffee and a donut, then walked her bike to the end of the pier, secured it to one of the cement posts that lined the edge, and sat down, legs dangling.

The Hudson River was looking clean and green, no longer the steady flow of raw sewage, dead bodies, and detritus it had been for the past several decades. There was word that these days certain residents of this planet could be surviving in the Hudson's lightly salted water, and that some of them might even be fish. Rihanna had never seen the Hudson when it was a cesspit. To her it was a fresh, clear waterway, a happy place, a place of reflection and meditation.

A seagull landed on a neighboring pier. A flock of smaller birds circled and took off to the north. Motorboats dotted the river on the Jersey side, ready to take a tour around Manhattan, and a clock chiming seven in the distance told Rihanna there was nowhere she had to be for a while. With the wind blowing a briny mist into her face, she closed her eyes.

She jumped. Something was sniffing at her donut.

"Dizzy! Stop that! Leave her alone!"

Rihanna turned around. The dog's owner was coming up behind her.

"Okay, now, sit." The big floppy puppy obeyed. "Sorry. There's never anyone out here at this hour, so I let her run without the leash."

His jeans were ripped and full of holes, and his white tee shirt was worn thin, but his clothes were clean, and there were definitely muscles there.

"Dylan Gillespie," he said.

She smiled. "Rihanna Strauss."

He nodded at her bicycle. "Where'd you ride here from?"

"Chelsea."

"You come down West Street?"

"Seventh most of the way, then I turned right onto West Houston."

She pronounced it "Hew-ston." Dylan chuckled.

"You're new to the city," he said.

"Just moved here. What gave me away?"

"It's pronounced 'How-ston,' here. Not 'Hew-ston.'"

"Wow. How would I know that?"

"You wouldn't. Someone has to tell you."

"Well, it's spelled like 'house,' not 'hue.' Maybe the rest of the world's got it wrong."

"Are you sure you just moved here? Because you think like a New Yorker."

Dizzy started whimpering.

"Okay, Dizzy, stop that."

Dylan produced some dog treats from his jeans pocket to divert Dizzy's attention from Rihanna and her donut. He didn't have any such treats for himself, however.

"Do you live near this pier?" Rihanna said.

"I live on this pier."

He pointed toward an old ferryboat that was moored to the pier.

"She was in bad shape when I got her, but we've been renovating her. It'll be a long time before she's seaworthy. Hell, right now she's hardly dock-worthy".

"That's where you live? On that boat?"

"You wanna see her?"

"Heck, yeah."

Dylan gave Rihanna a hand to help her up, and they walked over to the partially painted ferry.

The boat was a floating antique, desperate for repair. Most

of the windows in the main deck were blown out. Rihanna could see two men on the upper deck hammering and sawing. The side of the ferry that was facing the dock had a large gash in it, with several of the outer sideboards worn or torn away.

"I've put a lot of money into her," he said. "I'm lucky; my guys Casey and John there are working in exchange for their rooms."

Rihanna raised her eyebrows. "Rooms. You mean, on the boat?"

Their eyes met for a second, but Dylan deflected.

"Well, yeah." Interesting; he was suddenly stammering. "Someone has to be on board at all times in case a pipe bursts or something."

"So, you're all living on this boat."

He beamed. "Wanna see the inside?"

There was a small wooden footbridge connecting the pier to the boat. Dylan took Rihanna's hand and helped her aboard. It was shadowy and musty inside the enclosed main deck, and waves were knocking the boat around. Rihanna grabbed onto Dylan to keep from being thrown off her feet. He put his hand on the ceiling for support.

"Yeah, it takes some getting used to," he said. "C'mon, have a look inside."

They went down a narrow, uneven ladder that led to a hallway and several small rooms. Dylan showed her the one he had made into an office. All over the walls were sketches and photos of the ferryboat in her prime.

"I found all this reference material. We're going to have to do some hunting to find parts that will keep her looking authentic."

Dylan hung back in the doorway as Rihanna walked from wall to wall. At each photo she stopped to study the caption, at each sketch she traced a diagram with her finger.

"This is really impressive." Rihanna could feel Dylan watching her every move. She turned her head and looked him

in the eye.

She smiled.

In a few months, she would be living there, too.

NOVEMBER 1994

"Wow. The boat has changed a lot since I was last here."

Allie no longer wanted to talk about Jim. She had been compulsively chattering about him, and surely her friends were as sick of the topic as she was. These days she preferred conversations on just about any other topic: Frisbees. Horseflies. Ductwork. Lemons. Cattle prods.

"You haven't been here in ages," Rihanna said. "Dylan and the guys have done a lot of work. Let me show you around."

First stop was downstairs in the office, which had been recently paneled and painted. There was a huge, new desk and matching file cabinets. Further down the hall were several bedrooms, one where Dylan and Rihanna slept, then others for the crew.

Rihanna and Allie went back upstairs to the main deck, where Rihanna had her paints and easel set up. Allie went over to the windows to look out onto the Hudson River. She let her eyes look as far as they could go, spotting a tiny motorboat further uptown. Having no real view from her apartment windows, this was a treat.

Next on the tour was the top deck, which hadn't been safe the last time Allie visited, but was now finished. It was smaller than the other levels of the boat, and, with a 360° view, made a great perch.

"Why do I want to say, 'Ahoy there, Mateys'?"

"Because you watch too many old movies."

The women ended their tour in the galley. They were

drinking beer and talking about nothing — really nothing: avocados — when Dylan returned home.

"Hello..." He kissed Rihanna and nodded to Allie.

Dylan made Allie uncomfortable. She knew from Rihanna that he was a cheating whore-slut (Allie's word). He had since promised to stop sleeping around, but Allie didn't trust him. It was all she could do to keep her mouth shut.

"Uh... I probably should go," Allie said.

"You have the evening off," Rihanna said. "Want to stay for dinner?"

"No, thanks. I haven't been home much lately, and I'm working Sunday. I think I just want to go catch up on my life." Allie realized that sounded stupid, but she wanted to get out of there. "Good to see you, Dylan. Rihanna, I'll see you Monday."

"Yes. You will."

"You guys have that party tomorrow night, right?"

"Yes," Dylan said. "We'll be spending tomorrow setting up."

"Ok. Well, hope it goes well. Have a good night."

Allie knew her exit was abrupt, but she couldn't stand to be in the same room with him. The man was uncivilized. Rihanna had put up with him these last eight years because she loved him, but Allie didn't have that problem. Being a little rude still wasn't as bad as calling him a whore-slut to his face.

Dizzy was barking.

Not a friendly bark. Not an angry bark. It was a worried bark, tentative, punctuated by the occasional whimper. Dylan, Rihanna, and their crew were busy getting the boat ready for some corporate bigwig's retirement party that evening. Rihanna put down her paintbrush.

"What's up girl? What's the matter?"

Dizzy was pawing at the door of a storage room. She barked again.

"What do you want in there?"

She opened the door, screamed, and slammed the door shut again.

Dylan was on the upper level clearing off piles of tree branches that a storm had deposited there the night before. He called down the stairs.

"Everything all right down there?"

"Dylan, we have rats again. Really big ones."

He climbed down the stairs to investigate. Rihanna had her body against the storage room door, keeping it closed.

"Hmmm," he said. He was taking this lightly.

"Dylan, they're enormous!"

"Did you get a good look at them?" he said. "What did you see? Were they racing around, climbing on things? Did they scurry away when they saw you?"

"Well... no."

"They're big because they're fat. And lazy. They can't move very fast, even if they wanted to. Which they don't."

Obese rats. Maybe not as scary, but still disgusting.

John and Casey went into the storage room and came out pushing the fat indignant rats with brooms. They swept them overboard, and the round furry boulders hit the water and were floating and bobbing pathetically in the river's current.

"Casey, John, find the hole where they got in and fix it," Dylan said. "And see if there's any rat poison left. Just keep Dizzy out of there."

He grinned at Rihanna. "Can't have chubby rodents lolling around when our rich clients get here."

When the first party guests arrived, Rihanna was still hanging lights, and Dylan wasn't quite dressed. By midnight, the clients and their friends were loud, drunk, and happy. Club music was thumping loudly, and the boat was rocking from energetic, if not proficient, dancing. Rihanna had stopped her hosting duties about an hour earlier and was starting to relax. Beer in one hand, shoes in the other, a velvet wrap around her shoulders, she walked across the footbridge to the pier, sat on the wooden rail, and watched the party carrying on in its full-tilt glory.

Casey's girlfriend, Jeanie, spotted her and began to tiptoe across the footbridge. She was wearing a form-fitting black sequin dress, about a pound of sparkling costume jewelry, and a long, white, faux-fur stole. One of her spike heels sunk between the planks, and she cursed. She stumbled over to Rihanna and sat beside her.

"Where's Casey?" Rihanna said.

Jeanie took a long drink from her beer and let out a little gasp for air.

"Upper deck. He started this shots competition with some pompous guy in a tux."

"I just sat down for the first time tonight. I haven't seen Dylan for a while."

"You know, I haven't either."

"He's probably downstairs, trying to get a poker game going."

There were happy shouts, then the sounds of chanting, then counting, and then a very large splash. In a moment, something was swimming toward them. Casey grabbed one of the moorings and climbed out of the water.

"Of course, it was you," Jeanie said. She took off her stole and put it around him.

Casey was smiling through his chattering teeth. "Lost the drinking contest," he said. "That old fart can put it away, wasn't even feeling it."

"You idiot." Rihanna knew she shouldn't be amused, but she was. "You're going to die of hypothermia."

She stood up and brushed the wood splinters off her dress.

"Well, I know when I need to get in out of the cold," she said. "I'm going to go find Dylan. Get Casey inside before he freezes solid on the pier. That'll be hard to explain in the morning."

Rihanna negotiated the footbridge back onto the boat and then searched the crush of dancing bodies on the main deck. She climbed the ladder to the upper deck, but Dylan wasn't there either. She went back down to the main deck, then down one more flight. And there she found Dylan, in their bedroom, in their bed, with two inebriated, practically teenage women.

He bolted upright. "Rihanna."

Thing was, he had been behaving himself. Suddenly Rihanna wasn't getting enough air.

"Get out of here," one of the girls said. "This is a private party."

Dylan glowered. "Girls, time to go."

"But Dylan," the other one said. "We're not finished with you yet."

He guided her out of the bed. "Yes, you are. Go."

The girls were pouting, but they gathered their clothes and left the room.

"Honey, I'm so sorry," Dylan said. "You know they mean nothing."

Rihanna hurried back up the ladder, wiping her eyes dry as she climbed. She could just hear what Allie was going to say about this. She'd probably call him something worse than a whore-slut.

Jeanie and a dripping, fur-clad Casey were dirty dancing on the main deck.

"I'm keeping him warm!" Jeanie called to her over his shoulder. "Hey, did you find Dylan?"

"Yeah. Downstairs."

"Was he playing poker?"

Poke her, she thought bitterly. Yeah, there was a joke there.

"No. He'll be up in a minute."

Now fully dressed and abashed, Dylan climbed to the

upper deck. Rihanna was sandwiched between two young men in tuxes. Dylan motioned to them to go away, and when Rihanna tried to follow them, he grabbed her arm.

"Really. I'm so sorry," he said.

"Got it. You're so sorry. I can't hear it now, Dylan. I don't want to hear anything from you right now."

"Can't I talk to you?"

"No, you can't."

Rihanna was finding Dylan's oozing emotions of shame and remorse oddly seductive, but she was not going to give into it. He could sit, stand, kneel, beg, roll over, or play dead, anything he wanted, as long as he kept his mouth shut.

"You can sit beside me if you want, but you can't say anything," she said. "And you have to let go of my arm."

Rihanna drank, laughed, and danced until the last guests left. And Dylan sat by her, stood by her, and waited on the sidelines, silently, for the rest of the night.

At dawn, Jeanie made a pot of coffee, and Dylan and the crew started cleaning up. Rihanna changed into a big fluffy sweater, a pair of jeans, and boots, threw on her grand-mother's fur coat, and went out to sit on the edge of the pier, coffee in hand, Dizzy by her side.

This was not the first time she was out there after a party, a drunk and disorderly Dylan having gone off with one chippy or another. But it had been several months; this behavior was supposed to be in the past. Yet, here she was again, sitting on the end of the pier just before sunrise, watching the still-dark Hudson River waving and splashing as if nothing could ever be wrong.

He wasn't even that good in bed.

Okay, that was cruel. Accurate, but cruel. Too much alcohol turned Dylan into a compulsive predator, and it did nothing for his technique, which was quick and choppy and short-lived. He had a taste for young women when he was in that condition, and they usually didn't know any better or were too drunk themselves to care.

Dizzy nuzzled her, and Rihanna put her arm around her. She felt someone sit down on her other side. After a long silence, Dylan cleared his throat.

"Nope," she said. "Not yet. You can't talk to me, not yet."

"Okay, then. When?"

"Tomorrow."

"It is tomorrow. The sun is coming up."

"By disco rules, it's not tomorrow until we've gone to sleep for the night."

"Since when do we go by 'disco rules'?"

"We run a party boat. We always go by disco rules."

"Okay. But I have to tell you something."

Rihanna stared out over the Hudson. He wouldn't get her that easily.

"It's important. It's about the client."

Against her better judgment, she shrugged and nodded yes.

"Turns out, the corporate dude who put the down-payment on this shindig doesn't have any more money. Says he'll probably pay me the balance in the next couple months."

"But wait, that's $10,000! You mean you're out $10,000?"

"For the moment. I'd like to think positively."

Rihanna glared at him with a huge, stupid grin, then looked back out over the river. She let out a hearty laugh.

"Serves me right?"

"Absolutely."

Rihanna entered the office Monday morning clutching the two large coffees she had bought from the food cart in front of the building. Her curls were pulled back unceremoniously with a hair-tie, and her clothes were somewhat mismatched and disheveled. Lucky for her, Goldfish Graphics had no dress code.

"Rough night?" Allie greeted her.

Rihanna turned around to face her. Allie's eyes were half closed. Even her hair was having trouble standing up.

"Allie. Were you here all night?"

"Yeah. How was the party?"

"It didn't really end for us until Sunday. It takes me about a week to recover from these things."

"How was Dylan?" Allie said.

"Not so great."

"Again? But I thought..."

Rihanna sighed. "I know."

"You need to toss that guy overboard."

"Wouldn't help; he can swim."

"You're going to forgive him, aren't you?"

Rihanna looked at her sadly, and Allie grimaced. She handed Rihanna two different-sized disks and some paper-work and said, "Anyway, the latest files are on the optical. The ones we didn't get to are still on the Jaz drive."

Allie hesitated. Rihanna knew the question without her asking it.

"No news yet on our checks, Allie."

"Should we be looking for other work?"

"Well, this client has just placed a new order, so we're going to be really busy. And they have to pay us before we'd start on anything new."

"So, we'll get paid eventually."

"Right. Probably soon. They want these new catalogs right away."

"Gotta sell women those pantsuits."

"Right."

"Okay." Allie put her jacket on. "I've been living on my credit cards, but if we'll be paid soon, I'll be alright. I'm not keen on trying to find work just before the holidays. Besides, I've been saying 'no' to everybody. Employers like freelancers who always say 'yes.'"

"Availability trumps ability."

"Exactly."

Rihanna was feeling a lot like Allie looked. This was going to be a long day.

Most days, a bike ride to or from work would take Rihanna about a half hour, but lately she was running out of steam halfway home. Today she rode just a few blocks before she had to stop and rest at the mini-park on 8th Avenue, something called Jackson Square, although it was triangle-shaped. It seemed that any tuft of grass growing out of the sidewalks in New York City might get designated a "park" if it proved advantageous for some local official. Probably a real-estate broker thing: "two-bedroom luxury apartment, overlooking the 'park.'"

Her bicycle was propped up against an adjacent bench, and while she sat and waited to reclaim her energy, she considered heading to the subway. No, riding would be faster and more direct, and she wouldn't have to hoist the bicycle down and up the subway stairs. Carrying her bike on any day was hard for Rihanna, not just lately. She was an average height but had a tiny frame. Her feet were so small she had to buy children's shoes, and her hands couldn't reach around her bike comfortably. Meanwhile, no matter how much drinking or smoking or gallivanting Dylan did, it never seemed to affect him. Rihanna was athletic and health-conscious, yet she was aching all over and feeling like she couldn't stand up much less pedal the rest of the way home.

She considered maybe seeing a doctor. She was one of the few people in her office who was on staff, which meant she had insurance. But maybe not. She was taking a week off for Thanksgiving, so that should help. She had been working exceedingly long hours, plus she had been helping prepare for that latest party. Add to that Dylan himself, whose mere existence these days was raising her blood pressure. A doctor wouldn't be able to fix any of that.

Her life was wearing her out.

On the other side of the park, a blanket-covered homeless person was picking through garbage. Rihanna thought at first that he or she was looking for food, but then she realized there was a much more practical mission: cans and bottles with a nickel deposit. Male or female, black or white, old or young, it was impossible to tell. This person was wrapped in so many layers of clothes and blankets there was hardly any skin exposed, and what was visible was leathery and covered in grime. This was once somebody's child. How does this happen?

The human pile of clothes made it to the exit and was now moving snaillike up the avenue. Rihanna decided this was as good a time as any to continue home. Maybe if she didn't think about it, she wouldn't notice how run-down she was. She walked her bike out of the park, climbed on, and rode across to West Street.

The proximity of the river was causing a temperature drop of several degrees, and the headlights from the oncoming cars on the West Side Highway were aimed directly into her eyes. Through the glare, the boat came into view, a floating sanctuary rocking peacefully beside its pier.

Rihanna paused by the river's edge and leaned against the railing. A plastic coffee lid was floating in the water below. And yuck, was that a condom? She quickly changed her sightlines back to the boat. Dylan appeared in the window, setting the table for dinner. Then he disappeared back into the galley. She was thinking about that first day, when he showed her the boat, how proud he was of that floating wreck. It took some time, but now it was a beauty. Rihanna had spent the last eight years floating on the river with Dylan. Unlike other relationships in her past, she felt safe with him; he took care of her. Despite his drunken dalliances, life had been good, hadn't it?

She waited a long while before she walked her bike onto the pier. Dylan spotted her as she started across the footbridge. He hurried to the door. She let him take her bike to put it up on the wall rack. Then he followed her to the dining area, where she pretended to be intrigued by a picture of a seagull that was this month's calendar art. She heard him pull out her chair and pour two glasses of wine. He waited. She lingered as long as she dared and finally sat down.

As she reached for her glass, Dylan put his face in front of hers, forcing eye contact. Even without words, it was the longest conversation they had had since the party. Then he smiled, and she couldn't help but smile back. Dammit, she couldn't stay mad at him.

Penn Station was ugly. Uglier than LaGuardia Airport, even uglier than Port Authority. It was a cramped station with inadequate fluorescent lighting and old linoleum, filled with fatigued, unhappy, hurried people. Rihanna was sitting on the cold floor, her back against a wall, her bags and coat in a pile beside her. There were no benches free to wait on, and nothing to eat but fare from unkempt fast-food restaurants or stale trail mix from the newsstands. She had rushed there without breakfast, lugging her bags under the weight of her grandmother's gigantic fur coat, only to find the train to Syracuse would be delayed. There was plenty of time to go out to 7th Avenue and find something decent to eat but going outside would require her to stand up. The train, if it ever arrived, would have a café car, so she would get something there. Since they said it would be over an hour, Rihanna took out her sketchpad and tried to create something, if not beautiful, at least interesting, out of her current surroundings.

Sometime later, it started to snow hard, and, many more hours than the trip should have taken, Rihanna was off the train and heading to the parking lot to wait for her ride. The noisy detrained passengers around her were complaining about the time delay, the difficulty walking, and, it seemed, anything else they could think of that needed to be complained about.

Finally, her mother's car pulled into the lot. Wait, she sent Tom?

The olive station wagon pulled up in front of her and the side window opened.

"Hop in."

Rihanna glared at him. Her mother's beau was clueless, as always.

"Oh wait. Sorry."

He put the car in park and got out to open the back of the wagon and take her bags.

"Where's mom?" Rihanna said.

"Your mother is home. Cooking."

"Cooking?"

"Yes. She's taken up cooking. She's decided this is something she should know how to do."

"She's decided that now? Where was she 25 years ago?"

He laughed. "Teaching biology, I guess." Tom closed the top part of the tailgate, and they got in the car.

Traffic was barely crawling along the icy, snow-encrusted roads. Tom and Rihanna were trapped together inside the car, settled into their usual uncomfortable silence, but without Rihanna's mother there to act as a buffer. Rihanna turned on the radio and found a rock station: Guns 'n Roses singing "Sweet Child O' Mine." Tom caught her eye and gave her a nod. She turned it up.

The house had a large kitchen, complete with a butcher-block island and racks of hanging pots and pans and various other kitcheny things, but for years it had been just for show. At least, Rihanna and her older sister, Jill, never benefited from anything her mother might have created there. But now, here was their mother, wearing an apron, inundated by serving plates and carving knives. There were two open cookbooks, pots on the stove, and whirling exhaust fans. When the sisters were growing up, this kitchen's shelves and countertops held strange aquatic creatures preserved in jars of formaldehyde. If someone wanted food, she would have to look elsewhere. Jill learned to cook in high school, which was great, because then the family would get to eat something other than frozen pizza.

"Mom, what are you doing?"

"Cooking the sides for Thanksgiving dinner tomorrow. We're going to have turkey," her mother said, with some pride in her voice. She saw Rihanna's face and said, "What?"

"You're going to cook a turkey."

"Why not?"

"Do you know what you're doing?"

Her mother was indignant. "I've been practicing, you know. Tom can tell you."

Tom and Rihanna shared a smirk.

"Okay," Rihanna said. "But who's gonna call the paramedics if we all get ill?"

Tom smiled at Rihanna. "Your mother's been cooking for months. They know where the house is."

Okay, so Tom wasn't so bad, not really. They had been getting along better these last few years. Someday she might stop feeling awkward around him. Maybe in another decade.

"I can't believe Mother is cooking." Jill's tone was appropriately incredulous.

"I was as shocked as you are."

Jill and her husband, Mitch, had rented a car for their trip. The minute they arrived that morning, Jill wanted to go shopping. As Rihanna was kind of desperate to get out of the house, the sisters headed over to the mall, leaving Mitch to socialize with their mother and Tom. Mitch was a good sport.

"Are you sure it isn't going to be one of her lab creatures? It's not squid or something, is it?"

"No, it's a turkey, a whole, giant turkey. We could have, like, 20 people over for dinner."

"I guess we'll be eating leftover turkey this weekend."

"And next week."

"And beyond!"

There was still snow on the ground, though much of it had melted off the roadways. Rihanna could see kids throwing snowballs at each other in their front lawns. While Rihanna liked looking at snow, she was never one to roll around in it.

"I'm glad some stores are open today," Jill said. "Hanging around that house would make me insane. Have you thought at all what you're getting people for Christmas?"

"Well, Christmas isn't even our holiday. I never go too crazy."

"What are you getting Tom? He's always so hard."

"That's because he's not interested in anything," Rihanna said. "I thought I'd buy him socks."

"Damn. That's what I was going to do."

"Well, a person can never have too many socks."

Jill laughed. "Poor Tom. We treat him like crap."

"Well, he kind of deserves it. He is still married to some mysterious woman he never talks about."

"True. He spends all his time with Mom, though. He can't be that married."

She turned the car into the mall's parking lot. "How's Dylan? Too bad he couldn't come up this year."

Rihanna was going to delve into the whole should-she-still-be-with-Dylan issue but didn't have the energy. "Yeah, he couldn't leave the boat. Casey's off to meet Jeanie's family, and John's in Florida."

"I like Dylan," Jill said. "He's very charming."

Rihanna smiled weakly. "Yes. Yes, he is."

"Hmmm, that sounds convincing."

Jill parked, turned off the engine, and, without looking at her sister, said, "Seriously. Everything okay with you two?"

Rihanna held her breath and exhaled slowly. "Well..."

"Rihanna..."

"No, no, not like Robert. It's just... he's still sleeping around."

"Oh. That."

"Yeah. That," Rihanna said.

"But he's not..."

"No, not at all."

Jill became quiet, which was very un-Jill-like. She looked at Rihanna.

"Well, you've been with him a while. I guess you know what you're doing."

"Hardly."

"You look like hell, you know."

"Why, thank you."

"No, not like that. I mean, dark circles under your eyes, your skin is kind of greenish. Seriously, are you okay?"

Rihanna sighed. She could never get anything past her older sister. It was incredibly annoying.

"Honestly, I don't know. I have a doctor's appointment when I get back." Not really, but she might make one. Her sister was looking at her as if that were not enough information, so she added, "I've just been really tired."

"Well, you work crazy hours. Maybe it's exhaustion."

Rihanna laughed. "Well, I don't need a doctor to tell me that I'm exhausted."

"No, I imagine you don't." Jill opened her door. "C'mon. Let's go buy some socks."

CHAPTER 3

NATIA MEETS DANNY, 1988

On the top of the sheet of notebook paper, Natia wrote the name "Adam." She bit her lip, twirled her long, dark brown hair, and scribbled an image in the bottom corner of the paper that started out looking like a bird, or maybe a horse, but then became covered in anxious, random pen strokes until it became a blue, inky cloud.

She looked around her apartment, a one-bedroom in the West Village that featured a skylight, a terrace, and a reasonable rent. When Adam lived there, the bedroom served as the practice room for Adam's band, Funky Pancake, and he and Natia shared the main room. This is where she was now sitting, on a beat-up convertible sofa rescued from her first apartment. Adam never added much to the furnishing of the place, didn't even bring his own linens.

That should have been a clue.

When Adam left to live with that model Ariel, Natia quickly found a roommate, her current tenant, Rich. She wrote down "Rich." Okay, and his girlfriend, what's-her-face. Was it Isabel? Yeah, something like that. She wrote down "Isabel."

She chewed on the end of her pen.

Well, Allie, of course. She wrote "Allie."

And Adam's friends from the band, Anton, Danny, and Marcos.

Okay. The list was getting a little longer. She added a few names of people she knew from college, not that she had been to any of her classes lately, and one or two people from her job. And she would tell everyone to invite people. Except Adam, because he might bring that stupid Ariel and that would defeat the purpose of the party.

Ariel wasn't treating Adam well these days, and Adam had been calling Natia to get sympathy. Ariel never took him out with her, as if she didn't want to be seen with him in public. It would be, *"This wouldn't interest you, Adam; you're not in the business,"* or some other condescending nonsense. Adam assumed it was because he was black and figured that blonde, pasty Ariel didn't want her fancy friends to see him with her. He was tired of being put down, so he turned to Natia, someone who never made him feel anything but important, certainly more important than he would truly ever be on this planet.

While nothing had been said — yet — about his moving back in, or even about rekindling whatever it was they had had, Natia decided to jump on this possible opportunity. And so, the party.

Natia bought an Italian whipped-cream cake from Rocco's on Bleecker Street, and Allie supplied an eclectic selection of music in the form of home-recorded cassette tapes. Rich and his girlfriend, Dawn (as it turned out, not "Isabel"), spent the afternoon moving furniture out of the way and hooking up his stereo in the main room.

The party consisted of a few dozen twenty-somethings, fueled by good music on a good stereo system, kegs of beer, and equal amounts of lust and cocaine. It went on into the wee hours of the morning. And while Adam never showed, the rest of Funky Pancake did. Anton, the band's front man, had just trimmed his circle beard and was looking like a beatnik in his beret and thin, black sweater. Marcos was their guitar player, much shorter than the other members of the band. His Latino roots might have seemed like an odd choice, but he could play *just about anything and had the funk rhythms down. The bass player, Danny, was a bit shy. He was all but hiding behind the other band members, but Natia noticed him, and when she approached him to introduce herself, his kind, round face burst into a goofy grin. He stayed all night and never left.*

An affordable, good-sized apartment in the charming and desirable West Village was not something that was easy to hang on to, especially if one didn't have a stabilized lease and had a landlord who was less than sympathetic — less than scrupulous, even. The landlord began turning off the heat in the winter and turning on the heat in the summer. He would turn off the lights in the stairwell, and then turn off the hot water. There were outright threats and other intimidations, but when it was finally time for the lease to be renewed and the rent was quadrupled, Natia had to admit defeat. She had had a good run — almost three years in the neighborhood — but now she, and therefore Danny and Rich, would have to find housing elsewhere.

Elsewhere for Danny and Natia turned out to be the then uncharming, undesirable Clinton Street. Remarkably, a dozen years later, the street would be chic and trendy and the rents unaffordable, but in 1988, despite a considerable clean-up effort that had started a couple of years back, it was still a questionable place to be living.

Danny and Natia moved into an efficiency apartment in a building that would clearly topple over if there weren't two buildings leaning against it on either side. The gloomy, stuffy, decrepit, rat-infested firetrap they moved into was much smaller than what they were used to, and the rent was almost double. Natia was going to have to get a full-time job and stop pretending she was going to college. Somehow, she would explain this to her parents, although, perhaps, not in great detail.

Danny hung a sheet from the ceiling down the center of the room. On one side he set up his home recording studio, and he and Natia would live on the other. Any normal couple living in such tight quarters would surely kill each other.

Danny and Natia, however, were no ordinary couple.

═══════════════════

DECEMBER 1994

In the years that Danny Benton and Natia Stojanovich had been living together on Clinton Street, the neighborhood didn't change much. Many of the buildings on the block were still boarded over and covered in graffiti, and the sidewalks were scattered with people who were clearly inebriated or otherwise stoned or involved in or planning on being involved in something illegal. And every day Natia had to walk through a chorus of catcalls to get to and from the building.

There were two storefronts on the first floor of their building. One side had curtains covering the front window. Natia assumed there were people living there. The other, though dark and uninviting, looked like it might be a store. Sometimes Natia would see someone being buzzed in, but the tinted display window hid whatever was going on inside. The stoop to the building entrance that rose between the two stores was uneven and crumbling, the front door lock only worked every so often, and the metal, indoor flight to their apartment was steep, perilous, and poorly lit.

Natia hoped to find a better living arrangement before her parents learned how she and Danny were living, but years went by, and they were still on Clinton Street. Her family lived in Georgia, so it wasn't as if they would ever just stop by.

They arrived on a weekday afternoon.

Natia was at work, and, with no warning, Danny found himself on the other side of the door from Mr. and Mrs. Stojanovich.

Danny wasn't prepared for company. The tiny apartment badly needed cleaning and decluttering, and Danny, who was in the middle of a recording project, had not bothered to get dressed that morning. He had said "hello" through the door to find out who was there, so he couldn't now pretend he wasn't home. The best he could do was say, "Nat's not here."

"That's all right. We want to meet you."

Mrs. Stojanovich's tone was all business, and Danny did not feel encouraged. He hurried around the room, gathering up things, attempting to make neater piles.

"We've been driving for hours. Please let us in."

"I'm sorry," he said with a nervous laugh. "I'm not dressed."

It was three in the afternoon. There was an ominous, judgmental silence seeping through the door.

"Ok," Mrs. Stojanovich said finally. "We will wait for you to get dressed."

Danny began to talk to himself. "This is not good. This is really not good."

He picked up the phone to call Natia, and in a hushed voice said, "Come home. Now. Your parents are here."

With no one there to rescue him, he had no choice. He found some reasonably clean clothes, covered the dishes in the sink with a dishtowel, closed the curtain to the recording studio, and opened the door.

Danny saw the scene reflected on Mrs. Stojanovich's horrified face. Not only was the small, filthy, cluttered apartment in a neighborhood that clearly wasn't safe even in broad daylight, the man her daughter had taken up with was home doing nothing in the middle of the afternoon, while her daughter was out supporting him. To make the scenario even more unpleasant, his skin tone was several shades darker than he figured she deemed acceptable.

Mrs. Stojanovich crept into the apartment, followed by Mr. Stojanovich, who gave Danny an apologetic nod of greeting as he entered. While Danny cringed in the doorway, Natia's parents slowly inspected every inch of the place.

Natia arrived just as her parents were on their way out. Her mother strode by her without the slightest eye contact. Her dad's greeting, although warm, was solemn and silent.

Natia ran up the stairs. "What happened?"

"They were here! They were all over the apartment! Your mother gave me the evil eye!"

"She did?"

"Well, not literally."

"She didn't speak to me when I saw her downstairs. She didn't even look at me. I'm in big trouble."

"What's she gonna do?"

Natia knew how easy it was to get on her mother's bad side. Being related to her made no difference. Her mother had stopped speaking to her own father when she was in her twenties, which ended that relationship forever.

"I don't know. Never speak to me again?"

Christmas season in New York, the happy hustle and bustle of the City. Delighted shoppers stroll along the streets with their purchases, sharing a laugh and a hot cocoa. Children sing songs, horses and their carriages merrily trot by, and snowflakes gently fall on this snow globe of happiness.

Beneath this charming, fantasy view of the City, Natia and Allie were waiting on a local subway platform with about a hundred of their fellow New Yorkers. There were signs this crowd of wannabe straphangers, despite their best efforts, were getting a little unglued: checking watches, huffing and sighing, staring down the tracks in hopes of seeing a tiny light in the tunnel, cursing under their breaths when it turned out to be an express train. Not one of these things was making their train arrive any faster.

"Your parents just appeared on your doorstep? They drove all the way from Atlanta?"

"Savannah. Yeah. My mother insisted, so my dad drove her up here."

"And now she's not talking to you."

"Right."

"And the holidays are coming up."

"Right. And I'm not invited."

"In my family, you have to be in jail or something to not come home for Christmas. Have you talked to your dad?"

Natia shook her head. "It's not allowed."

"Just because she's not talking to you, doesn't mean he can't."

"Yeah, it does. When she gets like this, there's no reasoning with her."

The conversation paused while yet another express train thundered by.

"Okay, so, excuse this stupid question," Allie said, "but does your mother disapprove of Danny because he's black?"

Sadly, not such a stupid question. "Not just because. I think it's less that he's black and more that he's not Serbian," Natia said. "And I think she'd find him less objectionable if he had a job she could understand. You know, like a lawyer, or a bank manager, or something. Definitely not a recording engineer who works out of his apartment. Our apart —"

A train was approaching on the local track. As it reached the platform, it blasted its horn, and sped on through the station without stopping. The crowd shouted in protest.

When it was quieter, Natia continued. "Also, my mother blames Danny for my dropping out of school, even though I was well on my way of my own accord."

"Yeah, you sure were," Allie said. "I could call her and tell her that, if you like."

"Ha. No, thank you."

Allie's eyes zeroed in on something behind Natia, who

turned around and saw the crowd dividing. An escapee from Bellevue was taking a late afternoon stroll on the subway platform, waving his arms, and howling at an invisible moon. He was wearing a paper-thin t-shirt with what looked like a teddy bear on its front, hard to make out through the several layers of grime. He was also wearing loose, flimsy, boxer shorts, which left nothing to the imagination. A shoe was on his left foot without a sock, and a sock was on his right foot without a shoe.

"That guy must have been waiting here a really long time," Natia said.

"It's kind of amazing that more people in the City don't just lose their shit and start screaming and thrashing around."

Natia was feeling like that a lot these days, like she wanted to start screaming and thrashing around, but it had nothing to do with trains.

Eventually, the train came, as they eventually do, and soon every square inch of subway-car floorspace was occupied.

"What are all these people doing here, anyway?" Allie said.

"Shopping. You know, three weeks until Christmas."

"Oh. Right. That."

Right. That. Natia was starting to cry, and she looked away from Allie.

"Is this thing for Danny a Christmas present?"

The train was so loud it took Natia a second to realize Allie had spoken. "What? Oh, no, it's for the studio. We've looked in other stores, but they were out of stock."

The train spit them out at 59th Street. Music Planet was a short walk away, and for a moment, Allie and Natia were part of the happy, holiday, street scene. Inside the store, swarms of shoppers were exploring the packed aisles of impressive-looking equipment. Price tags whispered "retail price: $xxxx.xx" and screamed, "OUR PRICE: $XXXX.XX."

"Wow, this isn't much better than the subway," Allie said. "Do we take a number or something?"

Natia reached into her bag and took out the scrap of paper where she had written down the model information. A man sporting a Music Planet badge was heading toward them.

"Excuse me," Natia called out. When he looked at her, she started to say, "We —" and he said, "In a minute," and was gone.

Natia tried the next one who came by, and the next, and the next. Finally, she looked around. "Let's see if we can find this ourselves."

Stacked to the ceiling against the back wall were black and silver boxes with pretty, red, green, and blue lights. Natia read aloud from her piece of paper.

"Okay, we're looking for a Demeter VTCL-2a stereo tube compressor/limiter."

The women stared up at the flickering boxes and tried to determine what such a thing might look like.

"You don't have a picture there, do you?"

"No, no picture," Natia said, and then, for no reason, really, added, "Danny said it'll cost around $2000."

"You're kidding. Can't we get him a smaller Delimiter whatever that was?"

The women read the labels on each shelf but did not see what they were looking for. There should at least have been a floor model.

"Sure could use some help here," Allie said.

A large man pushed by, causing Allie to stagger.

"Hey! Son of a bitch."

And then a tall, bored, metal head with faded tats covering his skinny arms appeared out of nowhere.

"You ladies need help?"

Natia presented the slip of paper. "I'm looking for this."

He read it and handed it back to her. "Yeah, we're out of stock. Try back after the holidays."

And he was gone.

"Damn it. What am I going to tell Danny?" That came out

with more distress in her voice than Natia had intended. "I mean, he needs this thing to compete with other studios."

"Well," Allie said, "if they're out of stock everywhere, no one else can buy it either."

Natia hadn't considered this.

"Maybe you'll have your Christmas bonus by the time they're back in stock, and you won't have to use your credit."

"Hah. Christmas bonus? I'm freelance."

"You are? But you work in an office. You're like a secretary or an assistant or something."

"Doesn't matter. I'm a permatemp."

Allie waited patiently for Natia to give her the next cue.

Natia sighed. "Let's just go."

They pushed through the revolving doors and were greeted with a gush of frigid air. Despite the cold, going back down into the subway did not seem like their best option.

"Feel like walking some?" Allie said.

"I guess we won't freeze to death if we keep moving."

If one were to observe a Manhattan street-corner for an extended period, one would conclude that pedestrians in the City have little or no fear of cars, busses, or taxis. The bolder ones dart into the street against oncoming traffic, getting across with seconds to spare. What seasoned New Yorkers are most concerned about, and what keeps their eyes aimed at the ground as they walk, are broken sidewalks, detached steel gratings, bent and abused metal basement doors, steaming manhole covers, vermin, and refuse. Once they get to a curb — and everyone, every single person who spends a lot of time walking around New York City, at one time or another, does this — they look up to see if they have the walk light, and, no matter what color it is, without looking left or right, they step off the curb.

They assume there's one car width between the curb and the lane of traffic, one car width they can stand in to wait for the light to change.

Deep underground, approximately 80 feet, to be more precise, Natia was sitting on a packed F train. The man standing over her in the suit was reading his vertically folded New York Times and dangling his briefcase back and forth in front of her nose. Beside her was a bony rock chick unabashedly playing air drums. The sound coming from her Walkman was so loud Natia could hear the hardcore punk streaming out of the headphones, and she was not enjoying the concert.

Natia surfaced at the 51st Street subway station, and, with her eyes glued to the ground, pushed through a swarm of "excuse me," "pardon me," "sorry," and "so sorry," often said with such irritation it didn't qualify as politeness. She got to the corner, saw that the walk light was red, and stepped off the curb.

"Jesus, look out!"

There was an ear-splitting horn blast. Someone grabbed her coat and yanked her back to the sidewalk. A bus, veering towards the curb to collect passengers, missed her by inches. It was so close, in fact, that at first Natia wasn't sure it had missed her.

"Are you okay?"

Heart racing, strangers staring at her... She felt like a complete idiot.

"Yeah, I'm fine."

The light changed, and the people around her started to cross. The man who had pulled her to the sidewalk gave her one last concerned look before hurrying across the street with the others. She couldn't get her feet to move. The light changed three more cycles before she dared cross.

As she entered the office, one of the secretaries greeted her with, "Griffin is looking for you."

"Good morning to you, too," Natia said under her breath. On her desk, stacks of hand-written notes and letters were waiting to be typed, piles of folders were waiting to be filed, and several of the phone lines were ringing. Except for almost getting hit by a bus, not one thing about this day was going to be interesting.

She hung up her coat, turned around, and Mr. Griffin was standing in front of her.

There were other secretarial assistants, but Vice President Ralph Griffin always wanted Natia. She was the one he could count on to plow through and finish just about any mindless task, usually without taking personal breaks.

"You're late," he said. It was kind of refreshing the way no one in this office bothered with the formality of common pleasantries.

Natia wasn't late. She was, in fact, early, but 15 minutes later than she usually came in. Any other day, she would be apologizing. She was not in the mood for this today; as clichéd as it was, the near-death experience was giving her a modified perspective this morning. Instead, she stared blankly at him.

"I need this typed up right away," he said. "It's for a noon meeting."

Natia looked over the pages and tried to put Mr. Griffin's insufferably dull words into some kind of order that made logical sense, which was more than he had done. Just as she started typing, the phone rang again. Natia was preparing to put the call on hold or forward it elsewhere when she heard a familiar voice.

"Nati?"

Natia stopped typing. "Daddy?"

"Is this a bad time?"

She couldn't tell her father that, indeed, it was. She put the phone on her shoulder, moved the notes closer to the computer so she could see them better, and resumed typing.

"I have, like, a minute," she said.

"Okay." She heard him take a deep breath. "Nati, I think you should come home for Christmas."

A rush of adrenaline, a glimmer of hope. She couldn't believe what she was hearing.

"But what about mom?"

"Well, she would be happy to see you, if you do what she wants you to do. And I think you should do what she wants you to do."

Hopes dashed, glee turned to gloom.

"You mean, leave Danny."

"You wouldn't have to leave right away." There was a pause, as if her father were waiting for her to say, "Sure. Okay, Daddy." "If your mother knew you had plans to leave, she would welcome you."

Mr. Griffin stuck his head out of his office and glared at her.

Her father continued. "Come home for Christmas, Nati. This is tearing us apart."

Nothing like a little emotional blackmail for Christmas.

"Don't you think this is tearing me apart? You're asking me to choose between my family and the man I love."

Mr. Griffin came out of his office, stood in front of Natia, and pointed to his watch.

"Daddy, I have to go."

Mr. Griffin frowned and stormed back to his office.

"You'll think about this?"

"I have to go."

She put down the phone and resumed typing. Mr. Griffin charged out of his office.

"I told you I need those notes by noon," he roared. Natia silently noted that the clock on her desk was reading 8:55. "Whatever personal business you need to conduct, it can be done on your lunch break or after hours!"

"Yes, sir." Natia couldn't remember the last time she had taken an actual lunch break.

"I'll be in my office."

The door didn't quite slam behind him, but it made Natia flinch. The door reopened, and Mr. Griffin was coming over to her again.

"And another thing. No personal calls! And while you're doing work for me, the other girls should be picking up the phones. Those notes are important, damn it!"

Natia was in no position to tell the other "girls" to do anything, seeing as she was so very low on the food chain. This time the door did slam behind him. When it opened again, so did a door down the hall.

"And another thing —"

"Ralph, why are you yelling?" Mona Moore, the CEO's administrative assistant, had come out of her office. "Can't you see she's trying to work?"

Ralph puffed up indignantly as she approached. Mona caught Natia's eye and threw her a conspiratorial smile. She walked up to Ralph, forehead inches from his chin.

"How can she get anything done with you yelling at her like that?"

Mr. Griffin stepped back and said, "Stay out of this."

"Seriously, you made your point. Let it go, and let her work."

He glared at her and said something like, "Hrmph."

"Ah, Ralph. You know I'm right."

He backed up some more, then retreated to his office.

Mona picked up the box of tissues on the adjacent desk and offered it to Natia.

"You okay, Kid? You're getting tears all over Ralph's notes."

Natia took one and said, "I will be. Thanks."

She used the tissue on her eyes, then took another one to mop up the saliva Mr. Griffin had sprayed all over her desk.

"Griffin is a bully. Don't let him get to you."

He's not what's getting to me.

"That's easy for you to say; he's afraid of you."

Mona barked a laugh. "Well, he oughtta be."

All the notes and all the letters were typed up in time, all the folders were filed, and all the phones were answered, just like every other day, and at 6:30, Natia called Danny.

"I'm leaving. Do we need anything?"

Danny laughed. "Are you kidding? We need everything."

They hadn't been to the market in weeks.

"Right. Let me see what I have."

She was sure she had at least twenty dollars in her wallet, but it was a ten and a couple of ones.

"How would you feel about hot dogs?"

"Fine, fine."

"You're not tired of them?"

Danny laughed. "I didn't say that. But it's food, right? I'm not tired of food."

"Maybe I can get some rolls as well."

Natia managed to get to the subway without getting run over by a large vehicle and took the long escalator ride deep into the ground to catch the F train. Her subway car was full of people holding shopping bags adorned with Christmas trees, cartoon Santas and snowflakes.

Sure. Rub it in.

She climbed out of the subway at 1st Avenue and started the eight-block walk to her apartment.

A dialogue of unproductive thoughts ran through her head:

What am I doing to my parents?

Am I being selfish?

She crossed Allen Street, passed the Turkish joint on the corner, passed Katz's Deli...

What am I still doing in New York, anyway? I'm not doing

what I set out to do.

... passed the Mercury Lounge and that other club on the corner that used to be a bank, stepped off the curb at Essex Street, and waited for the light to change.

Should I just go home for Christmas? Maybe I should tell them I left Danny.

No, they'd know. Mom would know. She always knows.

Should I have stayed in school?

Should I have stayed in Georgia?

By the time she reached Clinton Street, tears were frozen on her cheeks. She climbed up to her apartment, fumbled around for her keys, and decided to knock instead. Her neighbors were blasting a Latin-music radio station, so she had to knock a few times before Danny heard her. The door opened. Danny frowned and greeted her with:

"You didn't get the hotdogs?"

A simple enough question. Natia gaped dumbly.

He smiled. "You forgot."

"I... uh... yeah."

He laughed. "I can't believe you forgot. We talked about it just before you left."

His smile faded fast when he saw the look on her face.

"Don't worry about it. It's cool," he said and sat down to put on his shoes. "I'll just run across the street to the bodega."

Natia burst into tears.

"Oh my God." Danny was on his feet again. "What's going on? Are you all right?"

Natia was sobbing. "I'm fine."

"Do you want a beer? Wait, we don't have any beer. Do you want a cookie? Wait, we don't have any cookies. Can I get you some soda? Wait, we don't have any soda."

Natia's sobs started to mix with laughter. Danny put his arms around her.

"Give me a gun, I'm going to shoot myself," she said.

"No, you're not. Besides, even if we had a gun, we wouldn't

have any bullets." He held her until the sobs were mostly gone and sat back down to put on his shoes.

Natia watched him a minute. "Don't go out," she said.

"Don't go out?"

She shook her head. He studied her. "Yeah, okay. I'll make mac and cheese. Wait, we don't have any mac. Or cheese."

Danny and Natia spent the rest of their evening snuggled together in front of the television, eating cold, dry cereal. No milk. They didn't have any milk.

It was the Friday before Christmas, and their next-door neighbors were having a party. Loud Latin music had started playing early that morning, and the festivities were bursting into the hallway. Occasionally someone would teeter into Natia and Danny's open door and offer them a beer or a flauta, which they would gratefully accept.

Frosty air was blowing in through Natia and Danny's open window, but it didn't matter. Even with their door open to create cross ventilation, the apartment was a steam room, its radiator's unrelenting heat blasting into the tiny space. Danny, in shorts and a t-shirt, was making newspaper chains to decorate a small potted pine tree Natia had appropriated from one of the Christmas displays at her office. Natia herself was home from work with a bad cold. Propped up on the bed (an old futon), a cup of tea on the nightstand (a milk crate with a board on top), a notepad and pen in her lap, she was making a grocery list of things they could buy with the $23.40 they had to live on until next week.

The phone rang.

"Hey, are you guys going to be around?"

Natia laughed. "Allie, where are we going to go?"

"Stay there. I'm coming over."

"You're not working?"

"In a while. I'm going home tomorrow morning, and I got you guys something I wanna bring over."

About twenty minutes later, Natia opened the door to see Allie holding an Allie-sized box wrapped in silver Christmas paper with an oversized white bow.

"What the heck is that?"

Allie struggled to lower the box to the floor. "You have to open it now."

Natia was about to rip open the wrapping paper, but Danny stopped what he was doing and hurried over.

"Save the paper! I can use it for the tree."

Danny carefully undid the tape on the silver paper with a boxcutter and then cut open the packing tape that was holding the box closed. Inside, there was a whole frozen chicken, several white and sweet potatoes, fresh broccoli, a can of crescent rolls, butter, stuffing mix, cranberry sauce, salad fixings, and a bottle of wine.

"How did you know?" Natia said.

"What do you get people who have nothing?"

"Wow. Thank you."

Allie shrugged. "Feed the world."

Now it felt like Christmas.

CHAPTER 4

ALLIE AND HER ROOMMATE, 1983

"Does your life play like a movie, or a series of snapshots?"

Allie hadn't seen this letter in years. It was sent to her when she was still in college, and Allie had since lost track of its writer. The letter had fallen to the bottom of a box of various other items: ticket stubs, rubber bands, Salada-tea-bag tags (with the tagline on the back), marbles, a couple of jacks, a few menus. When she read this question the first time, posed to her buried within the contents of an otherwise innocuous stream of consciousness, she wasn't sure why her friend was asking it. Perhaps it was because they both shared a passion for photography, and her friend was just waxing poetic. Obviously, there was only one answer: a movie, of course.

But here it was, four short years later, and Allie was experiencing an unhealthy form of introspection, the kind that kept her looking backwards instead of forwards, a THC-style slowdown of thought processes that was making every action subject to scrutiny. Her brain was full of knots. In a feeble attempt to create some semblance of sanity, she had sat down at her kitchen table to sort through some papers, and she happened upon this old letter. Rereading this question, she had to answer: Snapshots. Definitely snapshots.

She heard keys in the lock of the apartment door. Allie's whole body clenched.

"Hi."

"Yeah. Hi."

Her roommate went into her room and shut the door. In a minute the sound of Dan Fogelberg was in the air.

On days when Allie was in a better mood, she might respond to this act of aggression by putting the Buzzcocks on the stereo and cranking the volume. But Allie was tired. Not sleepy tired, but cabin fever, road-to-nowhere, bored-with-everything tired. She had spent that last year trying to fight her roommate's hostility without turning into a bitch herself. Allie had had the misconception that talking things out, trying to be understanding, would result in the two parties coming together with renewed closeness. At least, that's the way it worked in the Squerciati family. This approach turned out to be ineffective in this situation.

Allie sorted through her mental snapshots (the clock, the cat, the dresser, her clothes, her shoes), and climbed into the shower. At least Dan Fogelberg wouldn't follow her in there. The water was a little cool, and she carefully nudged the hot water up just a bit. Cold water blasted on her, and she jumped back.

"Son of a...!"

It took several tries to get it to a reasonable temperature, but eventually the water was warm and soothing. As the rushing water drowned out Dan Fogelberg from her earshot, she wondered what she should do next. Fighting her roommate had become an all-encompassing task, and as much as she kept trying to be the "good guy" in this mess, it turned out that whatever she did didn't matter at all.

She started weeping.

She stayed there long after her skin had started to pucker. When she finally emerged from the shower, Dan Fogelberg was still singing.

She got dressed. The snapshots continued.

(Shirt. Jeans. Socks. Shoes.)

She went to the closet.

(Coat, cat....)

"Where the hell are my keys? Ah..."

Under the cat.

(Keys. Door. Stairs. Street.)

She would go sit in the St. Marks Bar and Grill, have a beer, and talk to herself. It was a Tuesday night, and when she got to the bar, it was just about empty. Her plan to sit and talk to herself was pretty much a go.

(Barstool. Bottles. Bartender.)

Allie wanted beer in a bottle, something she could easily carry around. There was something new, Budweiser Light, which was being advertised everywhere lately, and so she decided to try one. She brought it with her to the jukebox and started flipping through the pages of singles.

She fumbled through her pockets for a quarter, and when she was thinking maybe she'd put in a whole dollar and get five songs, she felt someone standing beside her.

"Hi Allie. What are we playing?"

A familiar voice.

"Steve! How's it going? You here with Laura?"

"No, she's at the restaurant. They changed her nights again."

(New snapshots: Steve's beer. Steve's nose. Steve's chin.)

He reached into his pockets and took out a handful of change. They poured a couple of dollars' worth of quarters into the machine, made their selections and went to sit on the ledge of one of the bar's oversized windows.

(Car. Parking meter. Punk kids with Mohawks. Aging hippie in poncho. Cute dog.)

"What's up, Allie? What are you doing here alone on a Tuesday night?"

She stopped staring out of the window. "Going a little crazy," she said, making an effort to look him in the eye, or at least, in the chin. "Bitchface was torturing me with that slit-

your-wrists music of hers, so I had to get out of there."

"Hmm, the spiteful bitch drove you out of your own house with Gordon Lightfoot?"

"Fogelberg."

"You can't get her out of there, huh? I'm guessing she's on the lease."

Allie smirked at him as a reply. Nothing like stating the obvious.

"You just need to fight back harder."

"Yeah? How?" Allie began to peel the label off her beer. "The woman emptied the garbage onto my bed the other day."

Steve took a long swig of his inky draft beer, and it occurred to Allie that she wasn't really enjoying her Budweiser Light.

"That may be, but you know she's just trying to get you out of there. You've got to get your power back," he said.

Allie sighed. She had the top corner of the label off. A little pile of paper flakes was forming on her leg.

"Thing is, I don't know how to fight her without becoming as petty and bitchy as she is. I don't want to become someone I'm not."

"Really? You're just going to let her drive you out? You've got some kind of martyr complex?"

"I'm a martyr because I don't want to fight dirty?"

Head turned away. (Juke box. Bartender. Bottles. Bar floor. Bar exit.)

"Allie?"

Head coming back. (Floor. Bar. Steve's knees. Budweiser bottle.)

"You know, she'll always out-bitch me," she said. "That's a losing battle, any way you look at it."

Steve sheepishly drank from his beer and contemplated his next thought. He reached into his pocket and handed Allie a metal straw and a glass vial.

"Oh, man, you got coke? You've been holding out on me?"

Steve produced a pocket mirror and a matchbook cover.

Allie made a tiny line and snorted it. Her adrenal gland sprang to life, and the snapshots faded away. No doubt, they'd be back tomorrow. She handed the vial back to Steve, who smiled.

"As I recall, you're a pretty cheap date," he said.

"I'm a social snorter. Besides, the one time I tried to keep up with you and Laura, I thought my heart was going to explode."

The line he created for himself was about the size of a cigarette. It disappeared in an instant.

"So, do you want to know what I think?" he said.

"Besides the fact that I'm pathetic?"

"Yes, besides that." He took a large gulp of beer. "You're a rat in a cage."

Allie managed a laugh. "How do you mean?"

"Experiments with rats and depression. A rat sits in his cage, and researchers give him an electric shock. He moves to a different part of the cage. After a while, he gets shocked again, so he moves again."

"That sounds like my living situation. Go on."

"The researchers speed up the rate of shocks, so that the amount of time the rat gets with no shock keeps getting shorter and shorter. Eventually, the shocks happen so frequently that whenever the rat moves to a new place, he is instantly shocked."

"Nice."

"And do you know what the rat does?"

Allie shook her head.

"He stops moving."

"Huh," she said. "She stops moving, you mean."

Unusual for people with a coke buzz to have a moment of silence, but there it was.

Steve made a few small lines on the mirror and handed it to Allie before he spoke again.

"Maybe you can't out-bitch her," he said, "but maybe you can out-crazy her. Right now, she thinks she's got you. And she does."

They sat in the window drinking beer and snorting coke until well after the bar had closed and the after-hours crowd had filtered in. At sunrise, they headed over to the Kiev Diner. Pushing past the tables that crowded the entrance of the long skinny restaurant, they took a booth in the back corner. A haggard Ukrainian waitress dropped two giant menus on their table.

"Coffee?" she said. They nodded.

"Ugh," Allie said. "I'm full of cocaine and that wimpy excuse for beer. What the hell do they put in that stuff, anyway?"

"Dog piss," Steve said to Allie's delight. He picked up a menu. "Are we really going to eat now?"

"I dunno... I think it's a federal crime to be out all night without coming to the Kiev, even if we just stare at our food."

"True, true. How about blintzes?"

They shared an order, finished half of it, and had the rest wrapped to go.

The sidewalks on 2nd Avenue were filled with indigent people who were trying to make a buck peddling household possessions, not necessarily their own. Their wares were displayed on blankets and tablecloths, an outlaw flea market the locals had taken to calling "Little Calcutta." They would be there all night, many of them sleeping, others tweaked and shouting their hustle out to Allie and Steve as they walked by.

"I think I saw someone selling my cowboy boots," Steve said.

Steve walked Allie to St. Marks, where they parted, he continuing up 2nd Avenue, Allie turning west to 3rd. She gave the blintzes to the homeless man who slept under the stoop of the old Electric Circus building, and then proceeded home.

Allie took a moment outside her door to pray that Bitchface

was still in her room, but when she opened the door, she was right there, in the kitchen, concocting some incredibly smelly breakfast of eggs and hummus and garlic and bean sprouts and anchovies and God-knows-what-else. When she saw Allie, she scowled and shook her head.

"What?" Allie said.

"Your cat's been crying for hours," she said.

"Did you try giving her some food?"

"She's your cat. Not my problem you were out all night."

Her roommate was such a braying ass.

"If her crying bothered you that much, you could have just fed her. But no, you'd rather bitch at me about it."

Allie opened a can of food and put it in the cat's dish. She petted the cat and cooed, "Poor baby," and was about to retreat to her room, but stopped. She opened another can and put it on a plate.

"What are you doing? You just gave her food. And that's not a cat plate."

"Not for her."

Allie stuck a fork in the center of the food.

"Oh, yuck! You're not going to eat that! That's disgusting!" Her roommate was looking at her in horror. Now, that was a snapshot.

Who knew she would be such an easy target? Steve was a genius.

Allie took the plate into her room and closed the door. She set the food on the floor in the corner for the cat to find later. Then she turned on her stereo, put the Buzzcocks on the turntable, and turned up the volume.

She wouldn't be sleeping any time soon, anyway.

DECEMBER 1994

Poughkeepsie was not, nor would it ever be, Brooklyn. On the other hand, it also was not Cincinnati, and it was a lot less Cincinnati than it was not Brooklyn. Although Cincinnati did have its own miniature Brooklyn Bridge (a.k.a. The Roebling Suspension Bridge, which was pretty great), Poughkeepsie had its own miniature Grand Central Station, and more importantly, from what Allie could tell from the handful of people she ran into getting off the train, it seemed to be populated with a generous amount of facetious people. This was something Allie found to be decidedly lacking on visits to her parents when they were exiled to that flat, land-locked state of Ohio.

Allie stepped off the train and looked around for her brother Nico's car. It would be something expensive and right off the assembly line. She knew it would be black — his cars were always black — but that didn't narrow it down. Then she spotted it: a shiny, sleek Jaguar, a stand-out among the family sedans that filled the parking lot.

Allie opened the back door and put her bags on the seat.

"Hey, can you throw your stuff in the trunk? I just had the car detailed."

Surely, he was joking.

"C'mon," he said. "I want to get back to the house. Mom made crab sauce, and I'm starving."

Allie glared at him, but took her bags out of the backseat, threw them into the trunk, and got into the front passenger seat.

"Nico. You had this car detailed?"

"I use this car to drive clients around. It has to look new."

"It is new. If it were any newer, it would be a concept car."

Nico forced a smile but let out an exasperated sigh.

Allie let it drop. These days, although their exchanges would start out with good humor, they often wouldn't end that way. For one thing, she and Nico couldn't talk about work anymore. Allie would tease Nico about being an agent for "the

Dark Side," and in turn Nico would make fun of Allie for working on a "toy" computer. This IBM vs. Macintosh banter would devolve into a debate on the evils of corporate culture versus the naiveté of the artist, and the brother and sister would stop speaking for a while.

"How's the new house?" Allie figured that would be a neutral enough topic.

"Nice. Enormous. I think our parents think the four of us still live with them."

"Or that we all might move home if the place is big enough."

"Well, Dad can afford it, and it makes Mom happy. Don't forget, he made a lot of money when he sold the brownstone in Brooklyn."

"Meanwhile, while everyone else in the world retires to someplace warm, Dad retires to Poughkeepsie."

"Mom doesn't like Florida. Something about hurricanes."

"There aren't hurricanes in Poughkeepsie?"

"I think it's more about being closer to *la familia*."

"Right. Then they should have moved back to Brooklyn."

Allie was sorry she said it the minute it left her lips. It had been Nico who convinced them about Poughkeepsie. He was doing well there. A former salesman at IBM, he had been promoted to an executive position of some kind several years earlier. When he first started working for them, he made a huge effort to drop his Brooklyn accent and had changed his work name to Nick Shine — said it would make him more "marketable," whatever that meant.

"Carol back at the house?" Allie realized as she said this that there was a lot of disdain in her voice, even though she was trying to be nice. Nico's wife wasn't her favorite person.

"Yeah, trying to help Mom in the kitchen."

"And Mom's letting her?"

"Ha. I said 'trying.' Allen drove up yesterday. Gianni, Trish, and the kids should be there by now, too."

"Are they staying over? How big is this house?"

"No. They're just coming for dinner. They're staying in a hotel."

The traffic slowed just enough for Nico to make his left turn. If Allie had been in that intersection with her brother Allen in his old beater, they would have been sitting in there a lot longer. They turned onto a stretch of road where building after building displayed signs that read "IBM," and Allie no longer felt like talking.

The Squerciati house was in an older neighborhood, one with hundred-year-old trees, stone walls and even an occasional barn or two, long since converted into garages or storage sheds, but still quite definitely barns. The family's house was at the top of a hill, barely visible behind a mammoth weeping willow that had command of the front yard. Allie recognized Allen's 1982 Honda Civic parked on the street.

"What is it with Allen and that car? He's gonna be buried in it," she said, knowing Nico would laugh.

Her parents' car was in the driveway, no doubt so Nico could store his Jaguar in the garage. He let her out before he pulled in. The front door was immense, and it confused her. Had her parents bought a mansion? Where was the doorbell? She tried the handle and heard footsteps hurrying toward the door.

"Wait a minute! Wait a minute!" her father called from inside.

There was some fumbling of locks on the other side of the door before it opened.

"Hey, Dad."

They hugged. Behind him, her Irish-twin brother, Allen, was waiting.

"Hey, Al."

"Hey, Al!"

He bent down to hug her. "Where's Nico?"

"Parking the Jag'." Allie put as much sarcastic inflection as possible into this simple statement. "And getting my bags."

Three small, screaming children entered the room, followed by Gianni. The children ran up to Allie, practically knocking her over trying to hug her.

Gianni was laughing. "Allie! Good to see you!"

The children released her and went running and screaming out of the room.

"Where's Trish?"

"In the kitchen with Carol and mom. I don't think mom wants the company, but she hasn't thrown them out yet."

Allie looked around. There was an enormous Christmas tree in the corner of the room.

"What's with the sequoia?" she said.

"Well, we have such high ceilings," her father said, "I thought we could get a taller tree. Your mother doesn't really care for it, though."

"That's because she's the one who's been decorating it," Allen said, and turned to Allie. "C'mon, I'll give you the grand tour of *La Pensione Squerciati*."

The house had two floors, plus a finished attic, and a finished basement that served as a playroom for the kids when they visited. First stop was the kitchen, where they were immediately shooed away by Allie's mother. A large staircase bifurcated the living room, and another smaller one ran up the back end of the house. Allie counted four bedrooms, five if you count the attic, and three baths.

The various Squerciatis gathered in the dining room, a room that could encompass Allie's entire apartment. Her father, poised over the seafood salad with a giant serving spoon, was engrossed in a conversation with Nico about Jaguars. Gianni's kids were fighting about where they would sit, and Allen waited patiently as their parents sorted it out. Allie ducked into the kitchen. Her mother greeted her with a platter of crabs.

"Go." Her mother turned her around and pushed her.

"Take that to the table."

Allie wasn't sure, but she thought her mother might be shrinking. She had always been tiny — slight and less than 5 feet tall — but decades of smoking and sun worshipping, not to mention catering to her husband, her four children, and various relatives, seemed to be finally catching up with her.

Allie took one step, and her mother said, "Wait," and Allie did an about-face.

The dish was hot and heavy, and Allie was having trouble balancing it. Carol took pity on her and took the plate into the dining room.

"Are you going to stay awhile this time?"

"I'm working the 27th."

"The 27th! You can't stay a few more days? All of your brothers are here."

"I'm a freelancer. I work when there's work."

"But who works the week of Christmas?"

"Freelancers."

Allie's father called from the dining room, "Rose! Allegra! C'mon!" and the conversation was over for now.

Around the table, food was passed, plates were filled, and the banter became relaxed and punctuated with laughter. Eating was something this family could always agree on.

Allie woke from a strange dream to find she had no idea where she was. Oh yeah. The new house. She was sleeping in the attic. Everything was black and silent, like death, only quieter. When it became obvious sleep was not coming back, she peeled back the covers and fished around for her slippers. She wrapped one of the blankets around her shoulders and shuffled over to where she thought the door was.

"Ouch."

Okay, that was a chair.

Several bruises later, she found a doorknob and turned it. There were hints of sunlight on the attic stairs.

She had an urge to sneak downstairs, as if she was five years old this Christmas morning instead of 35. She groped around for her clothes, pulled on her jeans and sweater, and headed down. When she got to the base of the Gone-With-the-Wind staircase, she could see it was getting light outside. An early bird was already chirping.

Her Dr. Martens were where she had left them, by the front door, but she wondered what happened to her leather jacket, because she didn't see it in the hall closet. She grabbed something that must have belonged to one of the men — way too big for her — and contemplated her escape.

Front door? Back door? Side door from the porch room? What would they not hear from upstairs?

Porch room seemed easiest, and it did not appear to be self-locking. Was there an alarm system? That would really suck if she set something off slipping out to take a walk. Give everybody apoplexy at six a.m. Real smooth, Allie.

There was no keypad by the front door, no stickers or sign alerting intruders that a security system was in place, and she didn't remember anyone setting an alarm before everyone went to sleep last night. She took a chance and opened the side door.

Nothing started shrieking. She was in the clear.

The neighborhood was Christmas-card perfect: old, shingled houses with shutters and smoking chimneys. She would have to pay attention so she could retrace her steps. If she got lost, she'd have to call the house from a payphone somewhere. Assuming there were payphones somewhere. Then again, why would there be, in this rural postcard?

She would go in a straight line. The house number was 142.

House number was 142. 142. 142.

Two years ago, Jim had come with her to the house in

Ohio. There was a lot of eye rolling between her brothers and her parents. Okay, so he was younger. A lot younger. And he talked a lot, because they made him nervous. And he was short. Really short, especially compared to her pituitary-freak brothers. She tried to explain to Jim that the onslaught of sarcastic ribbing was the Squerciati way. It meant they liked you. Really.

Then last Christmas, Jim wasn't answering his phone. Ephram said he thought Jim had taken a trip somewhere; didn't he tell her? Allie spent the last two weeks of the year wondering why she hadn't heard from him. By the end of the second week, she was, much to her surprise, distraught. She decided she was never letting a guy do that to her again. She would never get so attached. In fact, she shouldn't have let someone have that power over her in the first place. She certainly would never spend another Christmas or New Year's pining over some guy. Turned out, he had taken an impromptu road trip with his mother to their house on Lake Erie. No phones.

"Didn't you get my letter?" he said when he got back.

She eventually got it, at the end of January, long after he had come back. But the damage was done. She felt differently. Less attached. And it took nearly two months for her to let her guard down again.

Now there was this Christmas. Was mourning the same thing as pining?

It started to snow, and now that she had walked a while, she was feeling sleepy again.

Yawn... 142. 142. 142.

Back to the house, she crept in through the side door, hung up the jacket she was wearing, and climbed up the back staircase to the attic. As she bundled up under the covers, she heard others in the house stirring.

She drifted back to sleep. Her family wouldn't be expecting her to get up for a while, anyway.

Snow had fallen on the City, enough to mute a boisterous Manhattan. So much less car noise, people noise, bus noise. It would be a temporary reprieve. The City wanted to keep moving; its stubborn inhabitants needed to get to work, to school, or to the park to throw snow at each other.

A melancholy Allie was walking down 1st Avenue on her way home from a friend's New Year's Day party. She was finding it hard to get excited about much of anything lately, but today she had risen to the occasion. Now that she was on her own time, she was indulging her sadness. A flash of guilt, a common occurrence these last couple months: What if she had called Jim that day? What if she had been home when he came by? What if she had insisted that he come to dinner? She shuddered; it was such a sensitive subject, and a person could drive herself crazy with the what-ifs.

What was strange, even suspicious, was the disappearance of Chaz and Laynie. No one had seen them since Jim's death. Did he get high alone, or had they been with him? Did they know he was in trouble and left him there to die? Were they also dead? These are the kinds of things the universe might never divulge.

As she approached 10th Street, she found she was becoming distracted by the sound of music and cheering emanating from Tompkins Square. A little closer, she could see several dozen people jumping around and could just about make out the strains of rockabilly. Curious, she headed into the park.

The band was a disheveled quartet draped in layers of hooded sweatshirts and beat-up leather jackets. The lead singer/guitarist was stunning. He had sleek black hair, piercing eyes, and an athletic build, but Allie had to wonder: Why do taller guitarists always play their instruments down at their knees? The Harpo-like, curly-haired rhythm-guitarist seemed put upon every time he had to come in on the vocals, the bass player's stance was awkward but efficient enough, and the drummer was hidden under a pile of heavy fabric behind a drum set. Allie was not a rockabilly fan per se, but she liked this band's take on it. Theirs was not that clean-cut-boy-next-door-let's-stand-here-with-pompadours kind of stuff, but more an edgy, dirty, pre-Elvis r 'n b.

After a couple songs, Allie realized this band was playing many flavors of rock: rockabilly, rock 'n roll, country rock, heavy metal, even power ballads. The lyrics were clever, what she could hear of them, and the front guy had a versatile voice, ranging from hiccuppy Buddy Holly to screechy Nazareth vocals to straight-on crooning.

The band paused a moment so their lead could put down his black Les Paul and switch to a misty green Fender, and then the band dove into a very melodic, pyrotechnic song with indescribable guitar work.

Allie felt something click off in her head: Who the hell was this guy?

She thought she heard the large drunk next to her calling out song titles, so she turned to him and said, "Excuse me. Do you know the name of this band?"

"Pest and the Caterwaulers."

Allie smiled and thanked him. Of course, they would have some crazy name like "Pest and the Caterwaulers."

It was her first moment of real pleasure since October.

PART TWO

NEW: *City Song (NY State of the World)*
(Jill Cunniff / Gabrielle Glaser /
Curtis L Mayfield)

— recorded by Luscious Jackson, released 1994

CHAPTER 5

IZAAK ("PEST"),1987

A newly formed band, the Sizzling Hounds, were imbibing in a Ukrainian dive bar on 6th Street, a place that had an unpronounceable name, something with strange and backwards letters and lots of extraneous consonants. It was so crowded the patrons' voices were drowning out the pathetic little juke box that was playing in the corner. Around the pool table were the band's lead vocalist, Roy, with guitarist, Izaak, keyboardist, Stan, bass player, Matt, and drummer, Tony, and looking on were Roy's girlfriend, Jeanne, and Matt's girlfriend, Ellen. These big-haired women, in tight jeans and tighter blouses, were pouting.

"You should let us play," Jeanne said.

"Hell no, not you," Roy said. "You're a shark. You'll just embarrass us."

"If she can play, let's let her play," Izaak said. "Maybe she can show us something."

"Sawicki, don't cause trouble," Roy said to him. Jeanne smiled at Roy, her large brown eyes open wide.

"Okay. Come on."

Jeanne turned to Ellen, who shook her head. Jeanne grabbed a cue. She proved to be more than competent, and in fact, she was much more competent than the guys were.

"Damn," Izaak said, as Jeanne sunk another ball. "You are

embarrassing us. Where did you learn to play?"

"She grew up with a pool table in her house. Her father was a pro or something."

"So, you're a ringer."

"He warned you."

"And you have the biggest eyes I've ever seen," Izaak said. Roy glared at him. Jeanne smiled.

"Are you flirting with me, Izaak?"

"Just stating a fact." He began to sing, "'She's got great big eyes and great big thighs.' Know that song?"

She laughed. "No! What the hell is that?"

"'She's got great big eyes and great big thighs,'" he sang again. "It was sung by a dude named Archibald in 1950."

"Well, it's not very flattering."

"Sure, it is."

"Izaak. Don't be a pest." Ellen found Izaak insufferable.

"A pest?" Izaak laughed. As he went back to humming the song, Jeanne playfully hit him.

"What? It's a great song."

"We should cover it," Stan said.

"We are not going to cover that song!" Roy was amused but adamant.

Jeanne sunk another ball while everyone was distracted.

"God, she's killing us," Roy said. "Good thing we didn't bet."

"Yeah, I'd be waiting a long time to get any money from you guys."

This hit a nerve, and everyone stared at her. No one spoke for a moment.

"Sorry," she said.

"It's okay," Izaak said. "It's true. You're just stating a fact."

The game continued with little conversation after that.

JANUARY 1995

Pest looked in the mirror, which was never a happy moment, especially first thing upon waking. His left eyelid was drooping more than usual, and, on further inspection, it seemed the rest of his face was starting to sag as well. If this was what he looked like in his thirties, what would happen to his face as he got older? He imagined it hanging down to the sink, then dripping down to the floor, then bouncing back up to normal. He took one last look, then turned on the water.

He lathered up his face with the bar of Castile soap he bought at the bodega and started shaving. He wished he were one of those guys who didn't look so bad if they skipped shaving occasionally, but Pest's facial hair grew back fast, causing a rather dark five o'clock shadow. He left his thick, black, random-length hair alone, except to grab his scissors to hack off about an inch from his bangs.

He headed to the kitchen. There was enough coffee left in the bag to make a few cups, so he put on a pot of water to boil, then checked to see if there was anything edible in his refrigerator. Great. There was still some pizza he had rescued from rehearsal the other night.

He had gotten, what, three hours of sleep? The gig with the Sizzling Hounds had gone late the night before, and the club made everyone wait forever to get paid. They played pool and drank beer to pass the time, but when the money finally materialized, the club stiffed them 25 bucks each. Pest threw a fit, broke several chairs and got his sorry ass banned from the club. The rest of the band were welcome to come back, if they wanted to; they'd just have to have their keyboardist take all the leads. Pest was pretty sure they wouldn't bother, though. Unless Pest pushed them, those guys were happy just to sit around and watch television. The music part of this band seemed secondary. Yet, they always kicked ass when there was a gig. He didn't know how they did it.

His knew his van wouldn't start in this cold weather, so he'd take the train to rehearsal, this time with the

Caterwaulers. Thirty minutes and three cups of black Cafe Bustelo later, Pest was boarding the F train at Essex Street, switching to the A train at West 4th Street. He took a corner seat so there would be room for his guitar and amp, but just as he sat down, a source of annoyance boarded the train: a person who needed everyone's attention. Most days it would be someone begging for money or food, or someone might sing or play an instrument to get a donation to his cause. Or maybe it would be a person selling candy or Street News. Today it was someone with a burning desire to save souls.

"Good morning, and angels be praised! Angels be praised!" The man, clad in a monk's robe, held up a large, tattered book and said, "People! Have you read your Bible today?"

Pest would not ordinarily pay attention to someone ranting on the train, it was so commonplace, but the pontificator was on Pest's end of the subway car, and, possessed as he was with a generous vocal capacity, he was hard to ignore. The monk's robe was weird enough, but on closer inspection Pest noticed that the Good Book he was carrying was a dictionary. Saving souls was one thing; sharing the crazy was another.

"People! I said, 'Have you read your Bible?'"

The man had chosen a hard audience, these early-morning straphangers. The riders responded by trying their best to feign deafness or sleep. A few gave themselves away when an uncontrolled grimace flashed across their faces. Others shared an eye-roll and a smirk with a near-by stranger.

"Jesus and the Angels want to warn everyone about Hell."

Heads down, people adjusting coats, eyes checking out the subway map or glancing at a watch under a coat sleeve. It was at this point that Pest noticed the man was not wearing shoes.

"Jesus Himself wants you to know that physical torment awaits all sinners!"

Some cringing, some fidgeting. Pest thought he heard

someone groan. He raised his hand as if asking permission to speak.

"I'm already in torment. Do I get credit after I'm dead?"

Little smiles formed on the faces of the passengers. The man spun around. Clearly Pest was someone who needed to be saved.

"Physical torment awaits you if you die without knowing Jesus Christ as your personal Lord and Savior." He stood in front of Pest. "Do you accept Jesus as your personal Lord and Savior?"

Pest raised his hand again. "I'm Jewish."

As if bitten, the man's attention snapped back to the other riders.

"The unbelieving, the liars, the murderers, shall be thrown into the lake which burneth with fire and brimstone!"

Again, Pest's hand went up.

"What exactly is brimstone?"

Agitated and no longer able to pretend otherwise, the evangelist was now full-on shouting.

"He shall cast them into the furnace of fire! There shall be wailing and gnashing of teeth!"

Pest raised his hand again, but the man was too insistent for Pest to interrupt.

"And the fire will not be quenched! The fire will not be quenched! The fire will not be quenched! Say it with me, people."

He was waving his arms up and down trying to get his captive audience to chant with him, but these MTA benchwarmers were not cooperating.

Pest got up and began dancing a little jig.

"The fire will not be quenched! The fire will not be —"

Some of the riders were chortling. The evangelist pirouetted around to see his heckler dancing and mocking him.

"He is the Devil!" he shrieked, pointing at Pest. "HE — IS — THE — DEVIL!"

Pest stopped his dance and raised his hand again.

"If I'm the Devil, why am I on the A train? Wouldn't I take a limo?"

In God's merciful wisdom, the train chose that moment to pull into the next station, and the doors opened. The evangelist stormed off the train, no doubt hoping for better results in the next car. Several of the sleepy, irritated New Yorkers applauded.

"Sawicki! C'mon! Orders are piling up!!"

Pest did not like being yelled at, especially first thing in the morning. How was he supposed to cook faster? Things cook as fast as they cook.

"C'mon! *Ruszać się szybciej!*" (Move faster!)

Pest got this job because he knew some Polish. This ultimately proved to be a problem, as his boss now liked to shout at him in Polish, whether Pest understood what was being said or not.

"*W porządku!*" Pest answered, hoping that it meant "Okay!"

Not his fault the other cook called in sick. At least Pest wasn't the guy making pierogis; that was time consuming. He got into a rhythm, though, and soon pancakes and eggs were flying off the grill. He had done his boss a favor coming in today, and anyway, Pest could use the extra cash. This was supposed to be only a half shift, but he had the feeling they wouldn't want him to leave at noon. He would have to. He was going on the road.

"Sawicki!"

"*Tak?*"

"Can you stay after noon o'clock?"

"*Nie.*"

"I'll double your money."

"Can't. Sorry."

He'd never see the "double his money" thing, anyway. He'd fallen for that before. At "noon o'clock," he took off his apron, the boss paid him, and he headed for his apartment.

Guitars?

He had one strapped to his back. The other two were on the floor in front of him.

Check.

Amps. He'd have to come back upstairs for those.

But... check.

Extra strings, tuner, picks.

Yeah, in the Fender case. Check, check, check.

Changes of clothes in the messenger bag hanging across his chest. Check.

Wallet in his pocket, keys in his hand. Check and check.

He picked up the guitars and headed to the door. The phone rang.

"Fuck."

He stared at it. He willed it to stop ringing. 10 rings, 15 rings.

Oh, c'mon.

He knew better, but he put down his keys and the guitars and answered it. "Yeah?"

"Izaak."

He sighed irritably. "What's up, Ma?"

"What took you so long to pick up the phone?"

"I'm trying to get out the door."

"Don't snap at me."

"Sorry. I'm in a hurry. What's going on?"

"Are you coming by this weekend? I want to clear out those closets, and they're full of you and your brother's things."

"Ma. I told you. I'm going on the road. I won't be back until Tuesday. I'll come by when I get back."

"You're going on the road? No, you didn't tell me."

Yes, he did. He chose not to argue, though, because he needed to get off the phone.

It was his mother's turn to utter an irritated sigh. "Well, then I'll just use my own judgment on what to put into storage and what to throw out."

"Why does this have to be done this weekend? I told you, I'll help you when I get back."

"Because I want to do it now."

Pest resisted the urge to start yelling.

"Ma, really, I gotta go. I'm going to be late picking up the guys. Can you please just hold off until I get back? Don't throw anything out."

He all but hung up on her. His mother would have kept him on for another hour if he let her, but now he was fighting his need to obsess about what may or may not be in the closets she wanted to empty.

He looked at the clock, which changed his attention elsewhere.

"Fuck."

He picked up the guitars again and looked around for his keys. Where the hell did he put them?

The phone rang again.

"Fuck. Fuck. Fuck." He really needed to get an answering machine.

Answer it? Ignore it? Get the hell out of there? What if it were important? And where were those fucking keys? He just had them in his hand.

10 rings...

"AHHHHHHHHHHHHHHHHHH."

He picked up the phone.

"What?"

"Dad?"

And the exasperated train screeched to a halt.

"Kolby. Everything okay, Bud?"

"I just wanted to say hi. When are you coming over?"

Pest wanted his kids to feel they could call him at any time. Just not... well, he shouldn't have answered the phone.

"Next week. Okay? Right now, I'm on my way out to pick up the band. I'll call you as soon as I get back."

His son didn't respond.

"Maybe I can sneak a call to you guys from the road. Okay?"

"Okay." He sounded disappointed. It was killing him.

"You sure everything is okay?"

Then he spotted his keys, left precariously on the arm of the sofa.

"Sure, Dad."

"Mom's okay? Hanna's okay?"

"Yeah."

"Okay. Well, I gotta go now. Hug your sister for me and I'll see you guys real soon. I love you."

"Me too. Bye, Dad."

"Bye now."

He picked up the guitars again, got to the door, and the phone rang again. He pushed the door open, locked it shut, and headed down the stairs.

He could hear the super, his friend Erwin, singing from the front sidewalk.

"*Don't know why/*
They don't serve no apple pie/
Starvation."

Erwin's voice was very deep, practically *basso profundo*. There were many nights when Pest and Erwin would sit out in front of the building, sharing a couple six-packs, and sing doo-wop songs until the neighbors started throwing things. Erwin was old enough to have been in one of those Harlem street groups back in the day, and he knew some obscure tunes. Many found their way onto Pest's master play list over the years.

"Hi, Erwin."

Erwin was collecting the building's garbage to put out on the curb but stopped when he saw Pest. "Hey, Izaak, my man, how's it hanging?"

"Going on the road. Gotta pick up the guys."

Erwin stepped aside so Pest could get by. Halfway down the block, Pest called out, "You should come sing with us sometime, Erwin."

Erwin snorted a laugh.

"Okay, Izaak," he said. "Okay."

The Caterwaulers' drummer lived on East 3rd Street, which would be the first stop. Carl was supposed to be waiting on the corner. Pest turned north onto Avenue A, but when East 3rd Street came into view, there was no Carl.

"Fuck. Damn it. Fuck."

This meant he would have to park and buzz Carl's apartment. More time wasted. Never mind. Pest knew it was his fault. When you're late, you're wrong. Fortunately, he saw a place to park just up ahead, and was about to pass East 3rd, when he saw Carl coming out of the pizza place on the corner. He slammed on his breaks. Car horns honked behind him. Carl jogged across the street towards the van.

"Sorry!" Carl said to the irritated drivers. "We're really sorry. Sorry. Sorry!"

He climbed into the front seat and Pest started the van before the door closed.

Those two slices of Sicilian he was carrying smelled great.

"Just don't get sauce on my seats," Pest greeted him. Carl pulled out a wad of napkins from his jacket pocket and tossed them onto his lap. He turned his baseball cap around, feeling it would be easier to eat.

"Damon on 12th?" Pest said.

"13th."

"Oh. Right."

Damon, the bass player, was leaning against a building, his black jeans ripped at the knees and his black button-down shirt partially open. Beside him was a leather-clad blonde chick wearing red shiny boots with spike heels.

Damn.

Damon spotted the van. As he reached for his things, the blonde grabbed him and gave him a memorable goodbye kiss that almost knocked him over. Pest liked his women more curvaceous, but her leather jeans were tight, and she did have a great ass. Good for Damon.

Pest stopped the van in front of them and rolled down the window.

"Hey!" he yelled. "He's only going to be gone a couple days. Save some saliva for when he gets back!"

The blonde didn't let go of him all that easily, but Damon finally jimmied her off and got into the van.

"She new?" Pest asked.

"Yeah. About a week."

"Nice."

They picked up Trevor, the rhythm guitarist, on East 18th Street, and then Pest continued north. He figured he'd take the FDR Drive, pick it up at 23rd Street. Maybe they could make up the time if there wasn't much traffic.

"Hey Pest." Damon was trying to make himself comfortable on the fold-up chair Pest had supplied for him, but it was sliding all over the metal floor of the van. "You remember to bring that amp?"

The amps. Still in his apartment.

"Fuck." Pest pounded the steering wheel. "Fuck, fuck, God damn it. Fuck!"

"You forgot."

"Christ. Yes. Both amps."

"I have mine," Trevor offered.

Pest steered the van into a U-turn, which threw Damon

and Trevor from their chairs and into the side door. Horns were blasting all around them.

"Pest," Damon said from the floor of the van, "Maybe we can borrow something at the club."

"But if we can't, we're screwed."

There wasn't much southbound traffic on Avenue A, so Pest gunned it. Carl braced himself against the dashboard, the remainder of his pizza now flat against his t-shirt.

At his building, Pest was in full panic mode.

"You guys go. Take the keys. I gotta stay with the van."

Damon hesitated.

"Just go. Go!"

"What apartment? Which key?"

"Fuckin' damnit. This is the front door, this is the top lock, this is the bottom. 5B. And fuck it, hurry up!"

"Which building?"

Pest pounded on his side window so hard that he cracked it, which made him even crazier.

"Right there! Right there! Are you stupid? We're right in front of it. 163! Go. Go!"

The guys hustled out of the van and ran up the five flights, two stairs at a time...

"Man, he's crazy. Did you see his eyes?"

"Yeah, he's like, possessed or something."

... only to have trouble getting the keys to work. They would have done anything not to have to go back down to the van and report they couldn't get in, but they were taking too long, and they could hear the van's horn. After several attempts, they knew they had to cop to their failure.

"One of you guys go," Damon said. "I'll keep trying."

Carl and Trevor looked at each other.

"Odds or evens?"

Carl lost.

He was halfway down the stairs when Trevor called him back.

"Carl! He's got it! We're in!"

Meanwhile, back at the van, Pest was becoming unhinged. One could argue that Pest was never quite hinged in the first place, and besides, he never was, and most likely never would be, good at waiting.

He pounded the steering wheel several times. What the hell was taking those guys so long? If he had gone himself, he'd have been up and down the stairs by now. Maybe he should have done that, just gone himself. But would he have wanted to leave those guys alone in his van?

"Can't be everywhere at once," he said aloud.

A nanosecond of sanity, then he started thinking again. The clock was ticking, and now they would be leaving over an hour late. Would the club let them play? This was all his fault. Everything, his fault. And where the hell were those guys?

Pest went back to pummeling the horn. Two women who were walking by looked over, and one of them yelled, "Jesus! Take it easy."

Pest leapt out of the van.

"Take it easy?" he said. "Take it easy?"

The women started running down the sidewalk. Pest tore off the side of a cardboard box that was sitting near the garbage and Frisbee'd it towards them. They squealed and dashed to the other side of the street.

Pest turned back and saw his band standing beside the van holding the amps.

Pest lowered his head and said quietly, "Get in."

Sometimes a trip is just cursed.

Once they got onto the FDR, Pest made attempts to sound likeable.

"Sorry guys. I was angry at myself, not at you."

His bandmates hadn't uttered one word since they left Attorney Street. They had placed one of the amps in the passenger seat and had climbed into the back and settled onto the floor. Pest looked at them in the rear-view mirror. They were not smiling.

"I just needed to let off some steam."

They remained expressionless.

"It's how I've survived all these years," Pest said. "If people think you're crazy, they won't fuck with you. Not that you guys were fucking with me. I mean, that's how I deal with things, it gets results."

Still not smiling, but Carl nodded.

Pest sighed. Well, he had the whole trip to win these guys back over. Fuck 'em, this is who he was, right? No, they didn't deserve his wrath, and he did take it out on them.

"Anyway, sorry to take it out on you. I just really hate being late."

Those were the last words spoken in the van until they got to Massachusetts.

Attorney Street was unusually quiet for a weekday, and it was almost noon when Pest rolled off his futon to start his day. The first thing he wanted to do was add to his journal.

"January 23, 1995."

Pest twiddled his pen and pondered how best to deface this pristine page.

"Weekend trip went okay but had to cajole the guys to stay in the band. I just can't spend time finding other players right now. I think they'll be okay."

The journal, started when he was in middle school, was bulging out of its three-ring binder.

"Met a girl named Chelsea. Or maybe it was Veronica? Anyway, she was wearing a very short, very low-cut dress, and I went home with her. The guys slept in the van. I didn't get her number, but hell, she's in Brookline. When would I ever get back there again?"

He had things to do today, so he cut his entry short, put

the binder back in his clothes trunk full of memorabilia, and got ready. His rehearsal was on Stanton Street, so it was walking distance. Pest put his guitar on his back and grabbed an amp. He was singing to himself, trying to figure out the lyrics to his new song. He was thinking so hard he almost crashed into Erwin washing the floor in the vestibule.

"Hey, Izaak... Izaak."

Pest heard him on the second try.

"You hear? The old man is selling the building."

Now he had his attention. "What? Shit. You're kidding."

"Nope. Hope you got a lease."

Ropes of nerves circled Pest's head and began to crush his temples.

"Fuck. I don't."

"How come you don't got no lease?"

"Never needed one."

Erwin stared at him a moment, then continued mopping the floor.

All Pest could say was, "Fuck. I don't believe this."

Pest struggled to hold it together. Didn't need to freak out in front of Erwin. And there wasn't anything available to punch that wouldn't cream his hand.

"How much time do I got?"

Erwin shook his head. "There's no telling."

With great effort, Pest kept his external composure. He said goodbye to Erwin, walked to his van, and got in.

His brain, meanwhile, was doing this:

Holy fuck what am I going to do I can't find an apartment I don't have any cash everybody wants to fuck with me I can't win but where will I go I could sleep in the van I could stay at my mother's no I can't live that way where am I going to put all my stuff holy fuck Holy FUCK. HOLY FUCK.

He sat there several minutes before realizing he didn't need his van; he would be walking. This crisis needed to be put on hold right now. He got out of the van and headed to Stanton Street.

Pest waited to have his full-blown tantrum about his apartment when he had the time to have one, and in the privacy of his soon-to-be-vacated home. He called the landlord. The building was already sold, and the landlord was kindly giving him about a month to find a place. Pest called everyone he knew but got nowhere. Then, out of desperation, he decided on his next plan: fliers. And who better to take on this mission but his kids who would be visiting this coming weekend?

He opened a beer and sat down to create something to Xerox.

A motley trio was making their way down East Houston Street. The tallest one was wearing a tattered leather jacket, over a hoodie, over a long-sleeved t-shirt. His jeans just touched the top of his faded, holey, high tops. Walking on his left was a seven-year-old boy in Yankees gear. Holding his right hand was a small moppet in a pink jacket. She was trying to perfect her Tarzan swing. Occasionally, her feet would touch the ground.

"C'mon, Hanna, walk."

She walked a few steps, and then grabbed her father's wrist again and swung happily. This was annoying her older brother more than her father.

"Quit it!" Kolby said. Hanna giggled.

Pest stopped walking and extricated the child from his arm. "Sorry, but you have to stop swinging on me before you pull my arm out of its socket. And, also, you're making Kolby crazy."

"I'm not crazy."

"Okay, annoyed, then. Look, we're almost done. Let's see if we can walk normally for the next few blocks."

Pest contorted his body into a hunchback and, dragging

one leg as if it were dead, lurched a few steps down the sidewalk. The kids laughed. He continued a few more feet, then stood up and grinned. They ran toward him.

They moved on and stopped in front of the next lamppost and attached a flier:

"Wanted: Room to Rent

"Rock musician with inconsistent salary history getting tossed from his long-standing hovel. Don't smoke, don't do drugs, just play music. I promise: Rent will come before food. Call number below."

This was possibly a futile enterprise, but at least he was taking charge. When they reached the corner at Ludlow Street, Kolby said, "Dad, look."

A red vinyl wallet was lying by the curb. Pest picked it up. "Can we keep it?"

He opened the wallet. There was $35 in it. Would really help with food this month.

"No, we can't. If you lost your wallet, wouldn't you like to get it back intact?"

Kolby and Hanna thought about this and nodded.

"C'mon. Let's call..." He looked through the wallet for ID, "... Lisa Milner, and tell her we have her wallet."

Back on Attorney Street, Pest and his kids were singing together:

"*How can I miss you if you won't go away/Keep telling you day after day...*"

Before they could finish the song, the buzzer went off. Pest pressed the door button and stepped out into the hall.

"Up here. It's five flights."

When Lisa got to the fourth floor she called up, "Izaak?"

"One more, and you got it."

Lisa was heroin pale and wire hanger thin. Her hazel eyes

bulged out from their dark sockets. As she got closer, Pest could see she was holding a flier, pulled right off from where Pest had taped it.

Pest handed her the wallet. "I see you have my flier."

She flipped through her billfold, and, satisfied everything was there, she said, "Really? You're looking for a place?"

"Yeah. I'm getting kicked out of here in a month. You know somewhere?"

"Yeah. My apartment. My roommate's moving out."

Pest wanted to weep with relief. "Shit. No kidding. Where is it?"

"Christopher and Hudson."

He'd be leaving the neighborhood. Lisa surveyed what she could see of the apartment and said, "The kids come with you?"

"No. They live in Jersey with their mom."

Lisa nodded. "The room's tiny. Not like here."

Pest had a large apartment. It killed him to leave it.

"You see that van out front?" he said.

She looked out of the window.

"Yeah."

"The room larger than that?"

"Kind of," she said and laughed. "It's taller, anyway."

"I'll have to get storage somewhere, but it could work."

CHAPTER 6

NATIA, 1979

Natia had the windows open so the wind could blow through her hair, and the AC was on because, even at night, it was over 90°. The car she was driving was a sweet-16 birthday present from her parents, a new Pontiac Phoenix. She reached over to crank up the volume on the radio; the station was playing Rod Stewart's "Tonight's the Night."

How appropriate.

Except for the heat, Georgia nights were gorgeous in the summer. The plants and trees were lush, and the air was filled with smells of greenery and tar from freshly paved roads.

A perfect night to see Connor.

Connor's family had a farm, a real bona fide farm, with chickens and cows and horses. Natia pulled up onto the lawn where other vehicles were parked and went to the front door.

"Just a minute, Dear, I'll get him," Connor's mom took two steps away from the door and hollered, "Connor! Your friend is here." And then back to the sweet voice she used when she answered the door, "He'll be down in a minute. Would you like to come in and wait?"

Before Natia had to answer that, Connor bounded down the stairs. He kissed his mother.

"Bye, Mom."

"What're y'all seeing again?"

"'Raiders of the Lost Arc'," Connor said. "It's at that theater in the center of town."

"Okay, well you have fun now."

No way they wouldn't.

Connor and Natia waited for the inside front door to close, then they raced to the barn.

"Okay, we gotta be kinda quiet, okay?" Connor said. "They might hear us from the house."

They started kissing and grabbing at each other's clothes. This was going to happen.

This was going to happen!

Connor led her over to a pile of hay. They were settling down onto it, and Natia giggled and said, "Now, here's a cliché."

"A what?"

He didn't have to be smart. He was adorable.

Natia tried to get comfortable on the hay, which was itchy and smelled nasty, but when Connor began kissing her, the hay was no longer a problem. The lights from the house went off, leaving them with just the glow of the moon. Connor ran his hands up and down her back under her shirt, and Natia took it off, then realized he was looking for the back of her bra to unhook it. She was finding the simple act of starting to undress thrilling. She unhooked her bra and then reached down to unzip Connor's shorts. Remarkably, Connor stopped and sat up.

"You're sure you want to do this." It was a statement, not a question.

What Connor did not know, and would never know, was that he had been a topic of serious discussion among Natia and her friends. The consensus in this group was: Lose your virginity. Lose it soon. Lose it now. The fact that Natia was currently in no condition to think straight was also a contributing factor to what she said next:

"God, yes."

He went back to kissing her. As more clothes were tossed aside, he stuck his finger in her, a move that always made her wild. He used his other hand to fondle her breasts, but finally stopped everything to put on the condom that he had in his wallet. Natia was annoyed; he was taking too long. He started to kiss her again and reinserted his finger. He continued kissing her, slower this time, and pushed his finger in deeper. Natia arched and groaned. What was he waiting for, anyway?

Then she felt pain and almost told him to stop. No, it would get better. Okay, maybe not. While Connor had been careful, practically tentative, at first, now he was getting a little rough. Still, she didn't want him to stop. Strange, these simultaneous feelings of discomfort and elation.

Then Connor got a blank look on his face, as if he had suddenly become dumber. They were finished, and there was no fanfare. Connor rolled off her. It wasn't what Natia had expected. She wasn't sure what she had expected. But somehow, although not physically, emotionally she was satisfied.

After several minutes of breathing hard, Connor said, "So, what do you want to do now?"

FEBRUARY 1995

The wind outside sounded like a train whistle. Not a subway train, because they don't have whistles, they have irritating, low, blasting horns, but a proper, rural train. The cold gusts of wind demanded to be let in, and the tenement windows were rattling loudly in their flimsy frames, no match for the power of nature. Inside the radiator clicked and sighed, as if it was about to say something, but all it did was start to blow a lot of hot air.

Natia woke with the feeling that she was in her parent's house in Georgia. Didn't look quite right, and seconds later the apartment on Clinton Street came into view, eerily lit by a swaying streetlamp. The plastic shower curtains Danny had tacked up over the windows were ballooning into the room, and Natia could see snow accumulating.

Danny was sleeping soundly, unaware of the tempest going on just a few feet away. Natia was enervated, and though her brain registered the snow starting to collect in the window covering, she rolled over, unconcerned, and fell back asleep.

In the morning, there were several inches of snow on the inside of the window frame.

Her winter coat was one of the nicest articles of clothing she owned, a Christmas present from her parents the year she moved to New York. It was a beautiful, gray wool, with a black satin lining, and it was a bit oversized so she could pile on several layers underneath. By the time she was ready to walk out the door, she looked like Charlie Brown, bundled up in so many clothes she could barely move. She made it to the bottom of the inside stairs and found a group of people in overcoats speaking Spanish in excited tones. Natia excused herself and squeezed past. Then she understood the problem: Something had been dripping on the doorframe, and now the exit was iced shut.

This was not a time to panic, except that everyone in the corridor was doing just that. One man went into his first-floor apartment and came back with a crowbar, but the only place to get leverage was the doorknob, and it just flew off with the door still closed. He and another man began to argue in Spanish — at least, Natia assumed from their tone they were arguing — and when the guy started waving the crowbar in a threatening manner, she realized something had to be done.

"*Un momento,*" she said. Everyone was so stunned that she had spoken, and in Spanish, they fell silent and looked at her.

She pointed up the stairs. "*Mi esposo...*" she said, and did an up-and-down motion with her hands, hoping they might understand her. At the very least they had stopped trying to kill each other. She ran up the stairs.

"Danny!"

She shook him. He batted her away.

"Danny, I need you."

He opened his eyes and groaned.

"I'm sorry," she said.

"What's up?"

"Door's iced shut downstairs. No one can leave the building."

He blinked a few times and rubbed his eyes. Then he laughed. "Really?"

"Yeah."

He climbed off the mattress.

"Okay" he said. "Get your hair dryer."

"But the cord won't be long enough."

Danny pulled on some sweats and ducked behind the curtain to his studio. He came out holding a large, orange, industrial, extension cord.

"Let's go. Where's the dryer?"

It would take some time, but the door was beginning to thaw. Through the door's window Danny saw that there was a homeless man sitting on the top of the stoop, propped against the door.

"Hey. Anyone know this guy?"

Since no one in the corridor spoke English, no one responded, and Danny continued thawing the door. This was going to be a long operation, and people started to go back to their apartments to wait. Natia went upstairs to call her office. She wouldn't be going anywhere any time soon.

When Danny finally got the door open, the homeless man fell into the corridor with a sickening thud. He was ice blue, face frozen in a permanent stare.

The next day the City was having yet another snowstorm, its third in as many days, and it was slowing the subways and shutting off electricity in the outer boroughs. It was worse out there, of course, since the subways and electrical wires were mostly above ground, but the storms were starting to take their toll all over Manhattan as well, with people taking to travelling on skis down yet unplowed streets and avenues.

Natia had offered to go into the office, but as fewer and fewer people were able to get there, the office management reluctantly decided to close. Instead Natia would be spending her day at home working on a special project. She had a package of construction paper, some white glue, and some glitter, and was happily seated on the edge of the futon, using one of the milk crates as a table.

The phone rang. Natia considered not answering it, but when the machine picked up and she heard Allie's voice, she went to the phone.

"Nat. Your mother just called me."

She caught her breath. "Really?"

"Checking up on you. Well, me, but really, you. The storm, you know. We're all going to freeze to death here in Manhattan. I got a hysterical call from my mother earlier this morning."

"Did you talk to her? My mother, I mean. I know you talked to your mother."

"Yeah, I listened to her, anyway. She gave me an earful about how you are throwing your life away, how you need to go back to school, get a degree..."

"Did she mention Danny?"

"Do you really want to know?"

"Yeah, I can guess, anyway, so you might as well tell me."

"She kept referring to him as 'that man.' As in, 'she's throwing her life away on that man.'"

Natia sighed, and Allie continued. "I wanted to say, 'His name is Danny, not "that man,"' but that would have ended the conversation right there. And forever."

"Right."

"I got the feeling she was hoping I would talk you into dropping everything and moving back to Georgia or something."

"That's exactly what she's hoping."

"Really. Should I not talk to her?"

Natia considered this. "Well, you don't have to if you don't want to."

"No, it's okay. Isn't some connection better than nothing?"

"Yeah. It is."

"Who knows? Maybe I can convince her to surrender."

"Ha!"

"Okay, maybe not."

Natia hung up and went back to her project.

"Everything okay?" Danny called out.

There was half a moment where Natia considered relaying the conversation to him.

"Yeah, everything's fine," she said. "That was just Allie seeing how we're faring in the storm."

"Nice."

Her mother was a prickly issue. No sense in getting Danny upset, too.

Danny emerged from behind the studio's curtain and stood over Natia and her project.

"Whatcha doing?"

"Making a birthday card for Dad."

"Oh. You gonna send it to his office?"

Natia had cut out a picture of a jumbo jet from a magazine and now turned it over to put glue on it.

"I can't. I mean, I can, but my dad wouldn't be comfortable with that. He can't get over being behind the Iron Curtain; he keeps thinking people are going to read through his mail. I guess once you experience that it never goes out of your head."

Natia pasted the picture on the front of her homemade card.

"Not a rocket?" Danny said. "I thought your dad's a rocket scientist."

"He's an aeronautical engineer. He doesn't work on rockets; he works on aircraft."

Danny watched as she drew the words "Happy Birthday" on with glue, and then sprinkled them with glitter.

"What about your mom?"

Natia shook off the excess glitter and waved at the card to make it dry faster. Then she carefully wrote with a marker, in script, "Love, Nati."

"It's not for her," she said.

Danny shook his head. "Okay..."

"I gotta try, right?"

Danny shrugged. "You might as well." He stood and watched her, then said, "Can I help?"

"Can you make me an envelope?"

He knelt beside her and reached for a sheet of construction paper. "No problem."

How great was he?

Danny had placed his second ad in the Village Voice, and it was starting to pay off. On Saturday he was seeing the third of his clients he had booked this way, and there would be more next week.

Natia was just about dressed when musicians invaded the apartment. The band greeted her with barely noticeable head nods and grunts. They abandoned their partially consumed coffees and bagels beside the kitchen sink and found places to sit on whatever free surface they could find.

The song they would be recording was a hard-rock tune

with an abrasive guitar riff and an unfortunate drum solo. Danny had suggested recording the tracks individually, due to lack-of-space considerations, but his clients insisted the song be recorded as a group. At least they had agreed to have the drummer record his tracks separately the day before. Natia was happy she had been at work during that session.

The first nine or so takes were sort of interesting, but then Natia retired to the other side of the curtain to do, well, anything else. She could watch TV, but she couldn't hear it, so she decided to read her book. John Grisham's sentences, however, weren't loud enough to compete with the sounds coming from the other side of the curtain.

(shouting) *"THE GIRL!"*

(pound pound pound)

(shouting) *"THE GIRL!"*

(pound pound pound)

"Not easy to let her GOOOOOOOOO."

Maybe she would go for a walk. No, it was late for this neighborhood, and besides, it was cold. Maybe she could go into the hallway and read her book. She could sit on the stairs.

"THE GIRL!"

(pound pound pound)

"THE GIRL!"

(pound pound pound)

Maybe earplugs. But they didn't have any earplugs. And now came the abrasive guitar lick.

"TWANG! Twang twang twang twang TWANG!"

She grabbed her book and exiled herself to the hallway.

After many more takes of that stupid eight-word song, the guys still weren't happy with the recording. Natia decided to take a walk. She got out her coat and grabbed her keys. The street life began creeping toward her as soon as she got down to the sidewalk. She might as well have been wearing a bell around her neck.

There were kissing sounds, then whistling. Then it was:

"Yo, mamacita, can I ask you a question?"

"Chica, where you goin'?"

"All right, mommy. Come 'ere."

She headed north to the safety of civilization that was Houston Street. She felt like Ichabod Crane trying to cross the bridge; anyone who was up to no good instinctively stopped short of this main road. Cars and cabs and City busses sped by in both directions. There was too much light and activity for foul play.

She walked a few blocks west, but when the wind picked up, she decided this walk was going to be a short one; she wasn't wearing her usual number of layers. She turned around and headed back to the apartment. Destroying her eardrums seemed far better than walking in the February air.

She broke into a jog on the last block and practically ran up the iron staircase. She slipped inside the door, but before she could go up one more flight to her apartment, she found she was being held back.

"Your money. Now."

All she had taken with her were her keys, not her wallet. The man was behind her, clutching the top of her arm so tightly it was going numb. There was a glint of something metal dangerously close to her face.

"I have nothing on me," she said.

"I'm not playing. Give me whatever you got." From the way he was breathing on her hair, Natia could tell he wasn't much taller than she was.

"I have nothing. See?" She turned her pockets inside out.

Something sharp was pressed against her neck.

"Here. Take my coat." She began peeling her coat off. "Take it. That's all I have. Take it."

This guy was robbing people in the wrong neighborhood. If he wanted something of value, he should have tried Greenwich Village, near the university. One of Natia's first-floor neighbors opened his door a crack, and although no one came out, it was enough to startle her attacker. He grabbed the coat from her and escaped out the door, down the stairs, and somehow vanished when he reached the street.

"What about this one?"

Danny was holding up his grey trench coat. Natia shook her head.

"Are you sure? It's got a lining."

"Too much like the secret police in the old country."

"Okay, but freezing is like the old country, too."

Natia sighed. "I can't believe he took my coat."

Danny picked out something else. "What about this?"

It was a red silk sports jacket.

"God, no. Just give me the trench coat."

She put it on. She looked like a four-year-old playing dress-up.

Danny laughed. "Yeah, you look ridiculous, but you won't freeze."

There can be a huge amount of significance in a simple gesture. A hug, for example, a wink, a middle finger, a single rose.

Natia arrived home from work to find a piece of mail, a fat, legal envelope, postmarked from Georgia. The address was typed on an Avery label, but there was no return address.

She sat on the futon and held the envelope in front of her. Her dad must have sent her something, maybe a letter he gave to his secretary to mail. Not his style to use office resources for personal matters, but current events were creating an extreme case.

Just holding this letter was a source of great comfort. She

ran her thumbnail under the seal and pulled out the tri-folded sheet of paper. It was holding something lumpy.

This was not from her father's office.

It was her Daddy's birthday card, torn to bits.

CHAPTER 7

RIHANNA, 1972

The screen door slammed behind Rihanna, then bounced a few times for good measure before clicking shut. Her mother and sister were having it out again, the same stupid argument about their mother's gentleman friend, Tom. Honestly, sometimes it seemed her sister just wanted to pick a fight. Rihanna didn't like Tom any better than Jill did, but she had learned to keep it to herself and just ignore him.

Rihanna got on her bike and drove across their leaf-covered lawn to their leaf-covered gravel driveway, and then onto the paved road, where she zoomed down the hill. She could still hear them screaming at each other, their voices lingering in her ears until she got to the very bottom. It was the only flat patch of land for miles, this place where these five roads came together. If she continued straight ahead, the steep hill continued down. It was tempting, but the problem with choosing all down hills is that, of course, you have all up hills on the way back. She could take a hard left and loop around Madison Pond, but that would bring her back home too soon. So, it was either turn right, towards the school and then the park, or the soft left, past the cemetery and the dairy farm, a route with the potential to get very lost.

Soft left it was.

Rihanna had that Todd Rundgren song running through

her head. She had just about all the lyrics down, just a few words that she had to hum through. If she let her mind go where it wanted, she would be singing the line, "There was not another soul in sight/Only you, only you," over and over, but here in the middle of upstate New York's nowhere, she made herself start the song from the beginning and sing it through. It lasted until she reached the cemetery. There had been those months, just after her father died, when she would come every day to sit on the grass beside his plot and talk to him, but eventually the shock of losing him subsided. Most days now she would acknowledge him with a "Hi, Dad," and ride on.

Past the dairy farm there was another intersection. Turn left, and she would be winding her way home. She turned right, then left onto a road that was less familiar, and then right onto something even less. She was in deeper woods now, so unexplored it was comforting.

"'There was not another soul in sight, only you, only you.'" What was it about that line?

She wondered if she'd still be riding her bike once she got her driver's license. Would she feel as free in a car, considering the responsibility attached to it? She stopped by the side of the road and parked her bike. There was a short wooden fence, its purpose seemingly to keep cars from going off the road into the ditch. Rihanna doubted it could really prevent that, and anyway, seeing as this stretch of road was relatively straight, a person would have to be drunk or asleep at the wheel to miscalculate that badly.

She sat on the fence and took a joint and some matches from her back pocket. She had rolled this one herself, and when she lit it, it started to fall apart. No matter. She inhaled as deeply as she could and immediately began coughing and coughing, and soon was worried that maybe she wouldn't be able to stop. Okay, so it was home grown and green and budless, but it was a nice high if one smoked enough of it.

She studied the multiple varieties of foliage around her and began composing her next painting. She wouldn't need to come back here to paint this, set up an easel and all that. She was developing what her art teacher called an impressionistic style. Rihanna liked to say it would be the idea of trees, not actual trees. Her sister said that "impressionistic" meant "not very good," but Rihanna chose to believe her sister was trying to be funny.

There was no time, because she had no watch, but in the last few minutes there had been some cars driving past her, signaling the end of the workday. Instead of turning around to head back, though, she went on ahead until she found a left turn, and then another left turn, and then she was on a familiar road that she knew would lead her home.

The screen door bounced closed behind her, and Rihanna, red-eyed and reeking of pot, went into the kitchen. She tried not to look at the jars of ocean creatures in formaldehyde that were lined up on the counter. At least the bulk of the collection was kept in her mother's lab at the university, or the whole kitchen would look like some mad scientist's lair.

Her mother called out from the other room, "You have a nice ride?"

"Yeah, Mom." It was times like this Rihanna was happy her free-spirited mom didn't pay that much attention to... well, most things.

"Pizza all right tonight?"

"That sounds great. Can we get it soon? I'm starving."

"Tom is coming over for dinner. We'll order it when he gets here."

Rihanna grabbed a box of crackers from the cupboard, which were probably Jill's, and carried it down the hallway to her bedroom. The door to her sister's room was closed and the radio was blasting Casey Kasem's top 40. Number 16? Todd Rundgren's "I Saw the Light."

Rihanna stood by the door and listened until the song was over.

MARCH 1995

The wind picked up for a moment, and Rihanna grabbed her hat so it wouldn't blow off; trying to work on a painting on the upper deck had its difficulties. She pulled her oversized scarf tighter around herself and leaned over to choose a color. Cadmium Blue was her favorite, as could be seen by the half-spent tube left in her paint box amid the other, fuller ones. She mixed it with a little white, black, and green. The resulting color was still much more vibrant than the actual Hudson River, but she'd add streaks of grays and blacks to tone it down. She put her fingerless gloves back on and began painting.

The corporate dude who had stiffed Dylan for the party last November had finally come by and paid cash, brought over a sack full of money just like you'd see in the movies. Dylan was down on the main deck counting it. Rihanna doubted they'd ever see the guy again, even if the amount wasn't right, but she supposed it did make sense to know how much was there. This past winter had been particularly slow for parties, plus Rihanna was still waiting on money owed her from Goldfish. Their survival for the next couple months might well depend on what was in that bag.

Dylan climbed up to the deck and stood behind her.

"No boats? Or is that smudge supposed to be a boat?"

Dylan always wanted boats.

"That smudge is part of the water."

"How about ducks?

"Ducks? On the Hudson?"

"Why not? There are ducks on the Hudson. Aren't there? Okay, seagulls, then."

Rihanna stopped painting and looked up at him. He was

flashing that sexy smile of his. She sighed. "Okay, seagulls. But in the air, not on the water."

"They're not really going to be seagulls, anyway," he said, "just the idea of seagulls."

"Exactly."

Dylan watched over her shoulder a minute before he spoke again.

"Anyway, it's all there. All $10,000."

"Really?"

He nodded.

"Oh, Dylan. Thank God."

"You said it. Hey, would it bother you if I came over here and did some work on the railing?"

"Not at all."

"Are you sure? 'Cause I can do something somewhere else."

"No, come keep me company."

As he turned to get his tools, Rihanna said, "Dylan, bring the boom box."

The sun had set, and the Hudson River was glimmering with reflections from New Jersey and Manhattan. There was a faint sound of aircraft overhead, joined by the distinct, closer sound of a helicopter. A huge party boat invaded the scene, its music loud, its passengers inebriated and rowdy.

Rihanna was watching from the galley window. She had let her mind drift off for a moment, but then went back to making dinner. She had a knife in her hand; it made sense that she paid attention.

Dylan called out from the other room. "Holy fuck! Damn it, I don't believe it."

"Dylan? Everything okay?"

"No."

She stopped chopping peppers and wiped off her hands, but Dylan appeared in the doorway before she could go to him.

"Oh God," she said. "What?"

He handed her two hundred-dollar bills.

"I thought you said it was all there."

"It is. Sort of."

"Sort of, how?"

"Look at those bills. Notice anything?"

Her stomach knotted up. "Well, they're hundreds."

"Yes. Anything else?"

The faces were Benjamin Franklin, not Alfred E. Neuman or other such silliness. She rubbed them to see if any ink came off, put them side by side to see if she could see any difference, flipped them over, nothing. She looked questioningly at Dylan.

"They have the same serial number," he said.

She felt her jaw drop.

"The whole bag, all of them, the same serial number."

"Oh my God." She was in tears. "What are we going to do?"

Dylan shook his head and shrugged. "We're going to live on it."

She wasn't sure if she could cross this line. Passing bad money? She could just hear her mother going on and on about this. It certainly wasn't ethical. Or legal. And it wasn't like she didn't know about it. Why didn't Dylan just let her be ignorant?

On the other hand, what were they going to live on?

It was a nice justification.

No amount of staring at the stack of hundreds Dylan had left her was going to turn it into real money. Go to jail, go directly to jail.

She took one of the hundreds, put it in her purse, and then

went to put the rest of the stack somewhere safe before she headed out.

When the elevator doors opened on her office floor, she was greeted with commotion: Two of the proofreaders were fighting, actually throwing punches that contacted chins and noses. Jason was a lot younger than Gerry, but Gerry was bigger and taller. The other proofreaders and computer operators were feebly trying to make them stop.

"Hey, guys? Guys!" Rihanna said. "What's going on?"

The two men backed off from each other and mumbled something that sounded like "Uh, nothing," and then, from twenty-something Jason, "It's all good."

"Sure doesn't look good."

"Sorry, Rihanna." Gerry was a Korean-War vet, with the kind of limp that had everyone assuming he had a fake leg. He was usually the least flappable of the employees. "We've been here all night. We're overtired."

The latest catalogs were wrapping, everyone was working ridiculous hours, and people were still waiting on checks. Not surprising everyone was on edge.

"Jason, how about you take a walk to Taylor's and get everybody some coffee?" She handed him the hundred-dollar bill. "See if they'll break this. Get some brownies and some of those giant macaroons. Get enough for everybody."

If her religion believed in hell, she'd be going there. Better start making amends now.

She soon had seventy-seven dollars and 22 cents in real currency in her wallet, and a large cappuccino and a macaroon on her desk. She would just forget about all that fighting and the going-to-hell stuff. Speaking of hell, there was a note that Sal wanted to talk to her. He would have to wait, though. She wasn't going to talk to him on an empty stomach.

"Rihanna."

So much for Sal waiting for her. She suppressed a groan.

"Good morning, Sal. What's up?"

He closed the door behind him and sat down. He stared at Rihanna a long time before he said anything.

"It seems that some people who used to work for us have been applying for unemployment."

Rihanna feigned horror. "No."

Sal frowned. "But that's not the problem. The problem is the IRS has contacted us about our freelancers' payroll taxes."

"But we don't take out... oh."

"Right, so here's what we're going to do: Starting with the new catalogs, we're going to charge everyone for the use of their desks."

This was why Rihanna didn't like talking to Sal before... well, ever, but certainly not before she finished her coffee.

"What?"

"I know what you're thinking but hear me out. Obviously, the freelancers won't go for it if we *actually* charge them for their desks. So, what we do is, we bill them $100 for the use of their desks every month, which they pay up front by check, and then we give it right back to them in cash. This way, we can say we are renting them the desk space, even though we're not, and then we aren't required to take out payroll taxes."

"Or pay FICA."

"Right. A perfect solution, right?"

Wrong, but she had almost $80 of ill-gotten funds in her bag. Who was she to judge?

CHAPTER 8

ALLIE AND A FRIEND, NYU DORM ROOM, 1977

Dialogue:

Friend: "I was just in Second Coming Records, and I saw John Lennon."

Allie: "Lennon was in Second Coming? You're kidding."

Friend: "Nope, it was him. He was looking through the Beatles' bootlegs."

Allie: "No way. Did you talk to him?"

Friend: "Yeah, I asked him for his autograph."

Allie: "No! His autograph? You did not ask John Lennon for his autograph. That is so... well ... What did he say?"

Friend: "He said, 'Sorry, I don't do that anymore.'"

Allie: "Damn. You should have asked him what he thinks of the Talking Heads or something."

Friend: "I know. I panicked. I wasn't thinking. I mean, it was Lennon."

STILL MARCH 1995

Third Avenue was a continuous stream of north- and south-bound traffic that was barely stopping when the traffic light told it to do so. A City bus on Cooper Square was trying to turn north onto the Avenue, but the equally non-stop pedestrian traffic was making this a difficult maneuver.

Customers hurried in and out of the magazine store on the corner to secure their gum and lotto tickets and girlie mags. Next door was a one-story building that housed a club called the Great Divide. On its roof was a large dinosaur that was peering down at Allie as she approached the bus stop that was in front of the club. The bus finally turned its corner and collected the group of riders that now included Allie and whisked them up the avenue.

Allie had a song going through her head, a song that had been following her around since she heard it in Tompkins Square back in January. She used to have a pretty good idea of how it went, but by now the memory of it had faded. She kept trying to hum it, but couldn't remember exactly how the melody went, and yet, there it was, haunting her, forcing her to try to sing it.

It followed her to her office building, up the elevator, and all the way to the 4th Floor.

Goldfish was dead quiet. The new catalogs the client had promised had been trickling in all week, but the bulk of the work had not yet arrived. Management had been hiring more freelancers in anticipation of soon needing to, as Sal kept saying, "hit the ground running" (an innocuous expression, but a favorite of Sal's and, therefore, irritating to Allie), but right now everyone was restless and bored. The chances that anyone would have to hit the ground, running or otherwise, seemed slim.

Allie sat down at her desk, still trying to hum that song, and when Rihanna asked her, "Allie, what song is that?" she had to say, "I wish I knew."

"Explain."

"It's a song I heard in the park. I can't remember exactly how it goes. It's making me crazy."

"Whose song is it?"

"A band called Pest and the Caterwaulers."

Mark, one of the other freelancers, spoke up. "Oh. Yeah. That guy Pest. He's a maniac, but a great musician. He can play anything. Plays guitar for the Sizzling Hounds sometimes."

"The Sizzling Hounds?"

"They're like a country band. But where did I see something about the Caterwaulers?" Mark said. "I think they're playing the Great Divide this week."

Mark rummaged in his knapsack and handed her a Village Voice, open to the ad.

"That's tomorrow night," Allie said.

"I guess you'll be calling in sick, then," Rihanna said.

Allie smiled and coughed.

The Great Divide was a smoky dive catering to NYU students, punk aficionados, and weathered rock kinda-beens. The interior walls were lined with photographs featuring various bands that had graced the stage in the past. Some were recognizable; others were so obscure Allie figured the members must be related to the owners of the club.

The Caterwaulers were already on the platform stage when Allie and Natia walked in. Pest, wearing a Metallica t-shirt, was drinking something from a thermos. His eyes were dark and wild, his jaw pronounced, his nose distinct, and his build lean and muscular, as if he had been chopping wood all his life. The Caterwaulers' drummer was quietly practicing drum rolls. He had dark skin but hazel eyes, a striking contrast Allie could see now that he wasn't hidden under winterwear. At the edge of the platform stage sat the rhythm guitarist, sucking down a beer and looking bored, while the bass player tuned up.

Hard rock was being piped in from the house sound system, and Pest started playing along to it. Soon, though, he was all business, plugging in cords and tuning the three guitars he had brought with him. When he finally took the mic, he tapped it impatiently and looked out across the crowded room, in the direction, Allie assumed, of the sound guy.

"Hey, can you turn off the house music?"

"One two... one two... can you turn up the monitors? Yeah, still more. One, two..."

This went on for a while. A voice behind Natia and Allie said, "Jesus, that guy spends more time doing the sound check than he does playing. I just want to say to him, 'Pest, just plug it in and play it!'"

Allie thought Pest's obsessive behavior was kind of charming.

Pest continued. "Okay and turn down the treble a little."

The guy behind them groaned.

At last, the monitors were right, the treble was right, everything was right, and Pest said into the mic, "Hello. We're Pest and the Caterwaulers."

A nod to the band, and they started with a cover of a fifties rock 'n roll song called "Great Big Eyes." Allie knew it from somewhere. Early fifties? Mid-fifties? Allie thought the song was great, but the audience reaction was only polite. The band blasted out another song, this one at breakneck speed. Pest was setting himself on fire playing guitar, brandishing a maniacal sneer as he played, but most of the crowd was responding as if... well, as if it was a Tuesday night.

Dissatisfied, Pest approached the mic.

"What do you usually listen to?"

Silence from the crowd. He put down his guitar and bent down to pick up the thermos. Steam wafted in front of his face as he poured, and Allie noticed a tea-bag tag hanging from the rim.

"What are you all, 23? 24?"

"Add like 10 to that for us," Natia said. Allie winced.

"You know, you can listen to something other than MTV," Pest was saying.

He continued with his complaints: music industry this, young audience that, landlords, Giuliani, anything he could think of that was pissing him off that night, which was a lot. Allie was becoming concerned that everyone would leave, but at last Pest put down his tea and reached for a guitar. Four beats into a heavy-metal song, he backed into the microphone and knocked it off the platform into the audience. The bass player stepped down to retrieve it and got it set back up in front of Pest just in time for him to sing into it.

The audience applauded.

People started dancing. Natia and Allie soon joined them, unable to resist now that others had started. As the audience continued to wake from their work-day stupor, the band switched to a rockabilly song. Pest became more playful with his guitar riffs, throwing in a line of the Popeye song, then something that sounded a lot like Aqualung, then Pop Goes the Weasel, and then a classic big-band riff.

Allie leaned over to Natia and said, "One O'clock Jump."

"What?"

"The last thing he threw in there. It was 'One O'clock Jump.'"

The band soaked in the now exuberant audience's reaction. They started their last song, a power ballad.

"That's it!" Allie said. "The song that's been haunting me. That's it. That's the one."

Natia listened a moment.

"Wow. That's almost a love song. Sort of."

Allie listened, too, now that she could hear the lyrics properly.

"Sort of. More of a stalker song, really." Allie sighed. "Okay, I just died and went to heaven."

"I don't think they let you into heaven unless you believe in it."

"You're probably right. One of those 'Catch-22' things."

Pest put down his guitar and grabbed the mic.

"Thank you. We're Pest and the Caterwaulers. Come up and say hello. Don't be shy."

"Come on," Natia said, "We gotta go talk to him."

Allie balked. "No. We don't."

"He said, 'Don't be shy.' You heard him."

"So?"

"You should talk to him. Tell him you noticed that he threw 'One O'clock Jump' into the middle of that rockabilly song."

"Everybody knows 'One O'clock Jump.' I'm not the only one who noticed that," Allie said. "Really, the guy makes me nervous."

Natia rolled her eyes. "Why? He's not going to be anything but polite to his fans."

"I know, but he has those Charlie Manson eyes. You go."

"Oh, I see. I should be the one who talks to the mass murderer." Natia put down her drink. "I'm sure no one else here tonight knew that was 'One O'clock Jump.'" And she went off to talk to Pest.

Pest was obscured by a mob of fans, but Natia maneuvered herself into a position where she could get his attention.

When his eye caught hers, she said, "Hi, Pest. Great show."

"Well, thank you. And you are?"

"Natia." He kissed her hand, and she said, "There's someone I want you to meet."

Pest looked around, puzzled.

"She's shy."

He laughed.

"Come with me."

Allie was standing by the bar when it occurred to her that perhaps Natia could not be trusted. Maybe she should make a run for it. This thought came too late. She turned just in time to see Natia leading Pest toward her.

"Pest this is Allie. Allie, Pest."

Natia was smiling triumphantly.

Allie smiled back, but said through her teeth, "You are so very dead."

They were being pressed together by the crowd, and Pest leaned over to talk into her ear. He was warm and intense, and Allie felt her knees buckling. Pest was a flurry of words, which Allie could just about hear over the noise in the crowded bar, and then he said something about the next gig, and would she and Natia be coming?

"We didn't hear about that gig. When is it?"

"Next week, Friday, at the Rodeo Bar. Hey, give me your number. Then I can tell you when our gigs are."

Natia pulled out a scrap of paper, wrote Allie's number on it and handed it to him.

"Why don't you give her yours as well?"

The next band began their set, now making it impossible to hear any further conversation. Pest handed Allie his number, smiled, and in a few minutes, they were out on the street.

"I cannot believe you did that."

"What? He's really nice. Wasn't he nice?"

"Right. How does that go? 'That Ted Bundy. Wasn't he nice?'"

But Allie did have to admit it hadn't gone so badly.

"Besides, he asked for your number."

"That was for gigs."

Natia sighed. "He asked for your number. He didn't ask for mine, now, did he? If you weren't so extremely neurotic, you would have picked up on that."

"But I'm not —"

Was Allie going to say she wasn't interested? They both knew that would be a big fat lie.

Allie got home and flipped through her stockpile of LPs to see if she had the original version of "Great Big Eyes." She found it, on a collection of early 50s rock songs she had picked up when Tower Records was switching over to CDs and practically giving away their vinyl. The album was still in the shrink-wrap. She put it on her automatic turntable and eventually fell asleep to it.

One thing the East Village had in abundance was stores that sold trendy, slutty clothes. Saturday found Allie on the hunt for a new dress. She had just received a check from Goldfish; she could spend some money, right?

She started her search across the street at Trash and Vaudeville, and then she headed over to Broadway to see what they might have there. Not satisfied, she returned to her neighborhood and entered a store on 9th Street that looked interesting.

She froze. There was music playing. Wasn't that one of Pest's songs?

Couldn't have been. Probably it was something from that Pulp Fiction soundtrack everyone was playing to death lately. Great, now she was having audio hallucinations.

But several beats later it was obvious that was it indeed Pest singing, and it was something live, something she heard the other night.

"Can I help you?"

The man behind the counter was probably wondering why this short woman with black spiked hair was standing motionless in the doorway.

"Where did you get this music?" she said.

"It's a band called Pest and the Caterwaulers."

"I know it's the Caterwaulers. Where did you get this?"

The guy took a moment to size her up.

"Do you know Pest?"

"Not really. I mean, I met him once."

He nodded. "I tape local concerts and sell them for $10 a piece. I have lots of stuff."

"Does that mean you're selling this tape?" This was too good to be true.

"This is my only copy right now. If you give me your number, I'll let you know when I have copies to sell."

Although sensing this was a bad idea, she wrote down her name and phone number...

... and immediately regretted it. Something wasn't right.

When she got to her apartment, suddenly it all became very clear.

"God, am I stupid."

The guy was selling Pest's music without permission. And by giving the guy her number, Allie was complicit.

"Damn it. Damn it. Stupid!" She hit herself on the forehead a few times. "Damn it. So stupid."

Fine. It was fine. She would see Pest next week at his gig, and she would tell him. It was going to be fine.

She hit her forehead a few more times.

"Damn it."

Wait a minute. She had Pest's number.

Allie searched through her pockets until she found the little scrap of paper with his number on it. She called and got a machine, but that was okay. She briefly explained the problem, left her number, just in case, and as she hung up, she felt her karma shifting back toward neutral.

The window in Allie's bedroom faced the street, and, in perfect Feng Shui style, her bed was placed so she could see the door. Allie was lying on her bed, sometimes staring at her ceiling, sometimes at the photos and posters on her walls. The framed, black-and-white photos she had taken over the years made her wonder when she'd have time again to take out her camera.

Meanwhile, across the room, a poster of Ella Fitzgerald was looking down at her, amused.

Allie had missed Pest's phone call. He had said something about being in D.C., that he'd be back tonight, and he would call again after he dropped off the guys. She had brought the phone in from the kitchen and dragged it up on top of her bed. And now she was waiting for it to ring.

"Stop being such a girl, Allie," she said aloud. And Ella laughed.

She turned on the television and flipped through the stations. *Law and Order* was on; she could always watch that. Except she couldn't watch that. She couldn't concentrate. She nervously flipped through the stations again. What was this? *Bay Watch*? That stupid show was still on the air?

And with that, the phone rang. She muted the TV.

"Allie? Hi. It's Pest."

"Hi."

"I got your message about that guy. Do you know who he was?"

"Never saw him before. He said his name was, like, Andy or something. He has a band."

Pest chuckled. "Everybody has a band."

"Well, he works in a store over here called Little Angel."

"Shit, I'd like to get a copy of that tape."

Wouldn't we all.

"Well, I'm sure he'd sell it to you."

He didn't seem to have picked up on her tone. "No, I'll just send my manager over there to talk to him. I'm sure he'll give me one."

"Pest, do you really want that guy selling tapes of your concert like those street vendors who sell knock-off designer bags?"

"Well, no."

"It's not like he asked you if he could tape the show and you said, 'Yes, go ahead, and please, sell copies of it.' Right?"

There was a pause while Pest considered this logic.

"Okay. I gotta find this guy," he said.

"That sounds very ominous."

"Ha. Yeah. Hopefully this Andy guy will think so too."

There was a moment of silence. Allie tried to think of something smart to say, but Pest spoke first.

"So, hey, what are you doing now?"

Allie's heart jumped. "Nothing. I'm watching television."

"Wanna meet me somewhere? Somewhere near you."

"Sure."

A recording of a phone operator broke in asking for another 15¢.

"Wait a minute, I gotta sort through this shrapnel and feed the phone."

There was a clatter in the line as the coins dropped, and Pest was back.

"Where are you?" he asked.

"St. Marks and 3rd."

"Give me 15 minutes and meet me at Veselka."

Veselka was a Ukrainian coffee shop that had been on the corner of 9th Street and 2nd Avenue for decades. It was always busy, serving some of the best blintzes and pierogis in the neighborhood (although not quite as good as the Kiev down the block) for very little money, and, like most coffee shops in New York, a place one could get breakfast any hour they were open. Very cramped and a bit damp, it had a strange, sour smell and even stranger clientele.

The sidewalks on the block between St. Marks and 9th Street shimmered in the streetlights. Someone once told Allie that sidewalks shone like that in New York because crushed glass was mixed into the cement to make the sidewalks glisten. Maybe to impress tourists? She thought it was a Mayor Koch thing, but that part she didn't remember.

Pest was already standing in front of Veselka when she got there. He smiled and opened the door for her. The fluorescent lights were way too bright, unnerving, really, and Allie almost wished she had her sunglasses. In front of them was a man sharing a table with a tuba case. Four Goth kids were at another table, their empty plates pushed aside to make room for the pile of change they were counting to pay the tab. Two young women were having a loud argument about their apartment, and in the corner an older man who looked like Socrates was reading a large book, his pierogis getting cold on a plate in front of him.

Allie and Pest sat at the counter and ordered coffee.

"So that guy taped my show the other night. How did it sound?"

"It sounded great. He must have been using really good equipment."

"Can we walk over to the store later so you can show me where it is?"

"Of course." He was staring at her as if expecting her to say something else, so she said, "How was D.C.?"

Pest enthusiastically related the altercations with irritable Jersey drivers, how he threatened some of the more aggressive ones and blew by the slower offenders. The serious drinking and resulting flakiness of the substitute drummer particularly annoyed Pest, who explained he was not only notoriously obsessive compulsive about his music and his gigs, but he rarely drank when he was working. In Pest World, you never start your set 30 minutes late if the club is ready for you to start, and in most parts of anyone's world, if you want to get anywhere, you certainly don't start late because your drummer is temporarily unavailable due to his having to throw up in the parking lot.

"Do you want to show me the store?"

Out onto the refuge of the street, Pest took her hand. They ran into a couple of Pest's friends, and Allie stood there patiently while they talked. Pest would turn to her and smile periodically, and at one point introduced her to his friends, although she completely forgot their names the minute he said them, as she knew they did hers.

After Pest and Allie walked over to the store, where there was truly not much to see, Pest walked her to her building, and they stopped in front of her stoop.

Although not as tall as her brothers, he was much taller than she was. He had almond-shaped, dark brown, almost black, eyes that sunk deep into his face. They were not at all, it turned out, like Charlie Manson's. Allie took a step toward him, which he took as an invitation — and rightly so — to reach for her waist. She shuddered and offered him her lips.

She thought she detected a slight hesitation, but then he leaned down and kissed her. The proximity, the placement of his hands, Allie was suddenly feverish. When they took a moment to breathe, Pest pressed against her, and dramatically panted.

"Can we go inside?" he said.

Her turn to hesitate. "Uh... Yes."

He took her hand, and she led him up the stairs. Outside of her apartment door, she stopped and turned to him.

"You're not an axe murderer or anything, are you?"

Pest shook his head.

"A girl's gotta ask." She unlocked the door. "Don't trip over the cat."

She led him through the unlit kitchen into her room, where she flicked on the lights.

"Wow! Look at all the records!"

Pest began studying Allie's music collection. The albums were alphabetical by artist, so he was seeing Adam and the Ants, Aerosmith, Artie Shaw, the Bad Brains, all respectable, but then Allie started to think about it.

Please don't notice the Jim Croce. Please don't notice the Jim Croce.

Pest turned to her. "Quite an eclectic collection you've got here."

He gently pressed against her. Their lips not quite touching, he slipped his hand underneath her sweater. She gasped, and they were kissing again.

Was she going to let this happen tonight?

She put her hand on his chest and pushed gently. She could be an adult if she tried.

"Just fooling around tonight, okay?"

"Got it."

They were necking like two teenagers in the back of a movie theater, feeling under each other's clothes, but with nothing coming off. Allie had the early shift the next day, and she soon had to send him home. He shot her a grin as he left. She closed the door and leaned against it.

She could have some fun with this rock-'n-roll guy.

Tuna was carefully watching the goings-on outside Allie's bedroom window. There were scores of people carrying on in the street, it being the first day in a while that was over freezing. People were giddy and howling, intoxicated by something, not necessarily alcohol. Tuna flicked her ears. Between the street noise and Blondie's *Parallel Lines* blasting from Allie's stereo, a cat could hardly get any peace.

Allie was assuming she would be having sex tonight. She took a shower, sprayed on some Calyx, and put a change of clothes in her bag, even though she probably shouldn't stay over since she was working in the morning again. Condoms? Would Pest have some? She threw those in the bag, too.

Pest's roommate, a skeletal woman whose skin was an unappetizing shade of pumice, greeted Allie at the door. It looked to Allie like she might be a vampire, not in the Goth, fashiony way, but in the this-person-really-needs-a-blood-transfusion kind of way. The woman had pins in her mouth and was wrapping some plain, off-white fabric around a dress form that was seated at the kitchen table. She pointed Allie in the direction of Pest's room.

The room was tiny. Taller than it was wide, there was a lot of space to be gained by turning the whole thing on its side. To the left of the doorway, there was a ceiling-high stack of milk crates filled with books, records, and clothes, and against the wall there were several guitars. A short bookcase was set up in the middle of the room, which functioned as a room divider, with a twin-sized mattress stationed behind it. A record was spinning on a turntable that was on the divider, its arm bumping gently against the record label. Way to wear down your stylus, Pest.

"Hey. Have a seat. I'm almost finished practicing."

Allie sat on a free milk crate. Pest was sitting on a folding chair playing classical music on a full-sized acoustic guitar. A quick lean over the music told Allie he was playing Bach. This was not smooth, delicate, playing. This was the meatpacking version of Bach, raw, hard, and brutal. Heavy-metal Bach.

"I know this isn't very good," said Pest, reading Allie's mind, or more likely, the expression on her face. "I think it's important to play something I'm not very good at. Something that's unfamiliar that I have to really work at." He laughed. "I have such a huge ego I need to knock it down a bit sometimes."

Allie studied his face, his hands, his arms, his neck. His nose was slightly bent, like maybe it had been broken a few times. One of his shoulders looked a lot lower than the other one, but Allie thought maybe that was just the way he was sitting. His fingers were thick with callouses that were fighting the nylon strings, and when he hit a particularly difficult passage he grimaced as if he were in pain. He struggled through another page and stopped.

"You have a great face," he said.

It took Allie a moment to realize he was talking to her.

Pest leaned over to kiss her. They looked each other in the eyes for half a moment, then they started kissing like they were running out of time, gripping each other so hard there was a possibility something might break. Allie yanked at Pest's shirt until he helped her remove it, and as he continued to kiss her, she struggled out of her jeans. Their fumbling intensity carried them over to the tiny mattress, where they landed with a thud, neither of them noticing the room divider tilting and swaying as they knocked against it, the album still spinning on the turntable above them. Allie put her hands behind Pest and pulled him towards her, but now he was taking his time with her. What started as a powerful storm gradually changed into a windy, autumn shower.

Unlike any guy Allie had ever known, Pest did not fall dead asleep afterwards. He was a talker. She got the whole rundown of his wild days with his first band, how much he'd calmed down after he got married, and how, long-time Loisaida that he was, he happened to be living in the West Village.

"They sold my building out from under me. Then I found Lisa's wallet on the street, and when she came to retrieve it, she said she had a room."

"That's really the only way to find an apartment in Manhattan if you don't have a lot of cash: by accident."

"Is that how you found yours?"

"A friend of a friend was moving out, and we moved in."

"'We'?"

"My crazy roommate. And not crazy in a good way. But that was a while ago. Now it's just me and the cat."

"Do you think I'm crazy in a good way?"

She laughed. "I guess that remains to be seen."

"I'm pretty nuts, but at least I try to keep it entertaining."

Allie was shivering. The one scratchy blanket Pest owned didn't quite cover both of them.

"You know, we kept hitting the radiator, so I know you have one, but does it ever turn on?"

"Usually like five in the morning for a half hour. Want some tea?"

"Sure."

He pulled on a t-shirt and some sweatpants. Allie wrapped herself in the blanket and, after taking the turntable arm off the record, followed him into the kitchen. The roommate had retired to her room, but the mummified dress form was still seated at the table.

Allie sat next to the mummy and tried unsuccessfully to wrap the blanket tighter around herself. Pest put some water in the kettle and lit one of the burners. "We've got Lipton or chamomile."

"Lipton. Really strong. Human beings should not drink chamomile."

Pest placed two cracked mugs on the table.

"So, what's 'Allie' short for?"

"Allegra."

"Like 'Allegro.'? Does that mean you're fast?"

She answered with a smirk.

"What's 'Pest' short for?"

He grinned. "Izaak."

Pest filled the cups with hot water and sat down beside her.

"You have work tomorrow?" he said.

Allie sighed.

"Unfortunately, early. I'm doing a double shift until they can hire more people. This catalog company I work for just landed a whole lot of work, and the deadlines are crazy."

"My mother used to work for a catalog company."

"Lucky her."

"Actually, when she met my father, she was a jazz singer."

"And that's where the music comes in?"

"That, and my grandfather was a cantor. My mom was raised an orthodox Jew."

"Wait... your mom's an orthodox Jew? But you act like you were raised by wolves."

Pest laughed. Allie did not think it was possible that no one had said that to him before.

Pest's roommate came out from her room.

"Oh, great. Tea."

"Lisa, have you met Allie?"

"Not officially. Hi."

Pest got up to get her a mug and poured her some tea. She sat down and started engaging Pest in a dialogue about the apartment building's other tenants and the possibility of a rent strike. Allie started to feel extremely self-conscious, undressed as she was under the blanket.

Allie took a few more sips of her tea and said, "I'll be right back."

She collected her things from his room and ducked into the bathroom. Except, it was just a water closet, no sink or shower. Allie guessed there must be a tub in the kitchen somewhere, hidden under a board or something, a common tenement feature.

"Damn."

She got dressed.

Allie reentered the kitchen dressed and carrying her coat and bag.

"You going?" Pest looked disappointed.

"Yeah. Sorry. I'll stay next time."

He nodded as if it was okay, but his expression said otherwise. He gave her a bear hug and a kiss before he let her go.

She walked down to the sidewalk. As it sometimes happens in Manhattan, even after midnight, Allie saw a free cab the minute she got to the corner and put her hand up.

PART THREE

BORROWED: *You've Really Got a Hold on Me*
(Smokey Robinson)

—covered by The Beatles, released 1962.
Original by Smokey Robinson and the Miracles.

CHAPTER 9

NATIA, 1980

Natia was in the serenity of her room, surrounded by the beautiful bedroom furniture her parents had presented her for her tenth birthday. Beside her was her princess phone, also a birthday gift, for her fifteenth. Her closets were filled with nice clothes and good shoes, there were several shelves of stuffed animals and two overflowing bookcases. Ironic that all the things that made this room a refuge were supplied by the very people from whom she was presently seeking respite.

Natia considered her next course of action. Yes, she had been filling out the college applications, and yes, she had taken all the math and science prerequisites. So far, all was going according to her mother's plan. Natia had gone on interviews for all the schools her mother had chosen for her, and it was looking like Natia would be getting into a good pre-med program.

Except Natia didn't want to be pre-med or any other kind of med. She wasn't quite sure what she wanted to do, but whatever it was going to be, she wanted it to be her own choice.

It hadn't gone over well when she finally had the courage to explain this to her mother.

"Well, you have to do something." This was a demand rather than a statement of fact. "What are you going to do instead?"

"I don't know."

"You don't know. Well, that isn't acceptable."

"I just want to go to a normal college and figure it out."

"You are above normal; you won't be going to a 'normal' college."

"It's my life! I should be deciding this for myself."

"And you will. You can figure it out while you are in a pre-med program."

"No. I can't!" Natia stormed off to her bedroom and slammed the door, signaling an end of this round of the conversation.

So here she was, in the room, behind the slammed door. She turned on the radio, cranked the volume on high, and lay on her bed. What did she want to do, really? Run away to New York and get in a Broadway show, like the kids from Fame. That would go over like the proverbial lead balloon.

There was this boy, a football hero from her high school, a couple of years her senior, a boy she'd had a mad crush on for a while. And he was going to Georgia State. The school was close enough to drive to, so she could get herself there, and it had a theater program. She would apply there. Her parents needn't know unless she got in. And after a year there, she could transfer to a school in New York.

She was accepted to Georgia State.

"Mom, Dad, I've picked a school." Keeping it positive.

"That's wonderful," her mother said. "Tell us what you've decided."

"I'm going to be a theater major at Georgia State."

Natia prepared for outrage and fury, but when her mother finally spoke, she said, as calm and pleasant as she'd ever seen her, "I'm glad you've made a decision." Then she turned to leave the room. "I'm going to go make dinner now. Is steak all right with everyone?"

It was almost more disturbing than her usual rage. It seemed the way her mother was going to be dealing with this *betrayal was to ignore it.*

Natia needed to visit the school and find suitable housing. Sensing help from her parents was not forthcoming, she took her own car there later that week. She toured the school, found a place to live near campus, and even secured a job at a local coffee shop. Before heading back, she called her dad to check in.

"Just be careful on the road on the way home, Nati."

Natia thought it was cute that her father still worried about her.

"Don't worry, Daddy, I'm always careful."

"I know but be extra careful not to speed or get any other kind of ticket," her father said, and paused before he added, "Your mother has reported the car stolen."

"She what?!"

"Just be careful."

"But it's my car!"

He sighed. "I know. Be careful."

APRIL 1995

The members of Funky Pancake hadn't played together in a while, and Danny was surprised to hear from them. They had landed a gig somewhere in Jersey. This wouldn't be a regular thing — they were filling in for a funk trio that couldn't make it — but it was money, so Danny agreed to join them.

The sidewalks started buckling as soon as Danny, clutching his prized Music Man bass, reached the bottom of the stoop. He took several deep breaths, which made this illusion stop. He was determined not to let a little panicking keep him from walking to the subway. As the streets swirled around him, he headed over to the entrance at East Houston and First.

The West 30s were a strange part of town. There were more vacant lots, brick warehouses, and car repair shops than there were apartment buildings, and the buildings that were residential had a vaguely abandoned look to them. Anton, Adam, and Marcos were on the street in front of Anton's apartment building. Anton's head was under the hood of the van.

Danny stood by them for a moment and then said, "What's going on?"

"Anton's working on the van. Shouldn't be too long," Marcos said.

"What's wrong with it?"

"Dunno. Loose wire or something."

Danny took note of the "Car Repair" sign hanging over the van; they were maybe six feet away from a professional mechanic. He decided against pointing this out.

"Hey, I think I got it." Anton's head appeared from behind the hood. "Try it."

Adam turned the key, and the van came to life. Everyone scrambled in. The part of Jersey they were heading to was farther than Danny had anticipated. They arrived two hours and a rest stop later.

The way back started out smoothly. The van started on only the third try. Having learned no lesson from the trip there, Anton made the mistake of parking the van at a rest stop instead of leaving it idling. It didn't want to start back up. Anton turned the key in the ignition, causing the van to make a sound a vehicle should not be making, like that of a baby squirrel stuck between the floorboards of a house. Danny was convinced they would all be walking home. Just as well. The brakes had been working about as well as the ignition was.

To everyone's relief, the engine finally turned over. Danny and Marcos climbed into the back seat with the gear, Adam got in front with Anton, and the van started moving. Natia would probably be asleep by the time they made it to

Manhattan, but she'd be happy; Danny had a hundred dollars from the gig. Life was good.

A gray stream of smoke floated in front of Danny's eyes.

"Man! Pull over. We got smoke and sparks back here."

Anton tried to steer the van over to the right shoulder, and the vehicle, only stable when driven in a straight line, began to bump and wobble. They felt the shoulder of the road, but Anton couldn't get the van to stop. The smoke was getting thick, and someone had the idea to open the side door. Eventually the van slowed down enough that they felt it was safer to abandon ship than stay on board. Marcos rolled out first, with lots of yelling and cursing. Next it was Adam's turn, then, with great apprehension, Danny. Anton managed to get out just before the rolling van burst into flames, and he probably would have been cursing as well, if he weren't coughing and choking.

All the equipment and instruments were ablaze, which included Danny's $100, safely tucked away in the case of his burning bass.

Poor Danny didn't get home until early morning, and he was bruised and singed. Natia had waited up for him, and then she slept for two hours before getting ready for work.

On her way home the next day, Natia saw something wonderful. She couldn't wait to tell Danny. Maybe it would make him feel better after losing his bass and money in the fire.

"Dear! You'll never guess."

Danny came out from behind his studio's curtain. "What's going on?"

"I think I found you a job."

He was less than excited. "You mean, a client?"

"No. There's a help-wanted sign in that coffee shop on the

corner of Stanton."

"But you know I get crazy talking to people I don't know."

"That's the thing: I've already talked to them. They said they still need people and that you should go in and fill out an application. It's already set."

Yes, but he didn't want to. It would mean talking to strangers.

"Please, dear? You don't have to do it full time, just get something until the studio takes off. Anything."

He looked at her.

"Can you go now? I just talked to the guy and said you'd come in."

"Now?" But he looked at her face and had to say, "Yeah, okay."

Danny put on some nicer clothes and stepped outside. A cold sweat engulfed him, and when he got to the bottom of the stoop, so did the sidewalk. He waited, taking deep breaths. The street came back into view. There weren't many people out. That made it a little easier to begin walking.

All he had to say was, "My wife was in here earlier and told me you might need someone." He repeated that sentence a dozen times before he got to the end of the block. Then, on the corner, though he told his feet to keep going, they halted. The corner had four stop signs and no traffic. He could easily cross. One foot. Take a step. Go, already.

He repeated his sentence to himself a few more times before his feet would move.

The door jingled as he walked in.

"Yes, can I help you?" The waiter was already grabbing a menu.

"Uh, no. I mean, yes. Uh... my wife... she was in here before... and uh... she... my wife... uh... anyway, she said you guys were looking for someone."

The waiter stared at him.

"Like, you know, the sign you have in your window?"

The waiter put down the menu. "We've already hired what we needed."

"But my wife said.... she was just —"

"Already hired."

What the fuck?

Danny almost said, "You mean, you expected someone white," but starting that conversation was unlikely to get him anywhere. He fought the urge to start yelling. This episode did little to quell his overwhelming anxiety. He backed out of the diner and hurried back to the safety of the apartment.

During the silence of the early morning, Natia heard the front door of the building slam. The upstairs neighbor was just returning home from his night shift, which meant it was five a.m. Natia listened to him walking up the stairs, heard his keys turning in his door, and heard his door open and close. She would have to get up in two hours, but she was already painfully awake.

Bills were haunting her.

Rather than just lying there with her eyes affixed to the ceiling, she sat up, turned on the lamp, and grabbed the stack of envelopes on the milk crate beside her. This couldn't be as bad as she thought.

Con Ed had to be paid this month, close to on time. All of it. She put the Con Ed bill to her left, which became the Pay First pile.

The rent notice would have to wait until everything else was figured out. That went to a pile to her right.

The next few were credit card bills. She chose one with a low minimum and put it on the Pay First pile on top of the Con Ed bill. After that was paid, they could get a cash advance from that one and pay the minimums on the other four because they were due later.

She put those bills in a newly formed Pay Second pile.

And that left... oh God.

"Argggh!"

She hadn't meant to scream. The pile of Danny that was sleeping next to her groaned and shifted.

"What?"

"We have no money."

"Oh. That."

"You've got to get a job. Something. Anything."

He squinted at her. "Right now?"

"Yesterday would be better."

"Who's gonna hire me? Besides, I get, like, crazy when I leave the house."

"This is another month where, even if we pay only half our rent, we're still short."

"Can't you get money from the cards?"

"That's after taking money from the cards."

"Well, I can't do a regular job. I get all weird and I feel like I can't breathe." Danny sat up. "Hey, how about the money from the studio?"

"That money has been going back into the studio. There hasn't been enough to make a profit. How about working across the street at the deli one day a week? Just one day."

"They won't hire me."

"Why not? It's a deli. They don't even care if you're legal."

"Yes, but I don't look like them."

"Look like them? Why would that matter? You can't make change for crappy sandwiches because you're not Latino, or whatever they are?"

"It mattered in that coffee shop. And if I work all day, I'll come home too tired to do anything else."

"Like me?"

"Well, yeah. I mean —"

"ARGGGGH."

Danny covered his ears. "Ow. Stop yelling."

"Okay, fine. I'm going to get ready for work. At my stupid job where I work all stupid day and am too stupid tired to do anything else."

Natia flung open the closet door. Danny pulled the covers over his head, and then threw them off again.

"What am I supposed to do about the studio? That's work. I do work. I work all day."

Natia pulled some clothes out from the closet and fished around for a pair of shoes.

Danny climbed off the futon. "And there's still a whole bunch of things I don't know about mixers and audio editing, and then there's all that midi stuff I'm still trying to learn."

Natia reeled around. "Well, think about how hard that's gonna be when we're on the street!"

She ducked into their bathroom and locked the door. The shower at full blast drowned out most of Danny yelling and pounding on the door. She stepped in and let the water pour onto her head.

"It'll be okay, it'll be okay, it'll be okay," she whispered.

CHAPTER 10

THE WOLVES THAT RAISED HIM, PART 1: 1957–1962

It was a slow night in the club. There were a few patrons sprinkled here and there, pressed together in private conversations with their tall exotic drinks. Judith Katz was sure she wasn't going to make much money tonight, but her cousin said he was coming with a couple of his army-medic friends, so she couldn't not sing. Besides, some money, however little, was better than no money. The bartender would keep her happy with as much whiskey as she wanted, anyway, so the evening wouldn't be a total loss. And who knew? Maybe one of Jacob's friends would be interesting.

The pianist had been playing and drinking for hours. Judith headed over to him.

"How ya doing, Evan?"

He turned towards her, holding the piano for support.

"Fine. Fine. You wanna start?"

"In a minute. Here."

She handed him some pills and a fresh beer.

"What's this? Diet pills?"

"I want you to stay awake for my set."

"Why, who's coming? Rockefeller?"

They exchanged scowls, then he swallowed the pills with a

gulp of beer.

Jacob Katz and his party arrived a few minutes later. They looked completely out of place in this west-side dive, with their neat clothes and freshly scrubbed faces peering out of the smoky darkness. To Judith's horror, they sat in front. Judith quickly snorted something the club owner told her would help her "sing better," and went up to the mic. Her pianist raised an eyebrow at her.

"Those squares your friends?"

"Just play," she said.

Judith decided to make the most of it and sang directly to her cousin's table. One of his friends seemed promising. He had black hair and black eyes, big broad shoulders, and a wide knowing smile. He was chain-drinking shots of scotch and puffing on a cigar. His energy was restless and extreme. And when she caught his eye, she didn't want to let go.

Jacob later took Judith aside.

"Listen. Stan can be very charming, but I gotta warn you about him."

"Warn me how? I can take care of myself."

"Yeah? You might think so, but don't fall for him. He's a bad guy."

Like a moth to a flame, a lemming to the sea, a fly to a bug-zapper, the girl could not resist. Not only did she fall for him; she married him.

They got married soon after he left the army. He immediately got a job as an EMD. Derisive, loud, rude, and ill tempered, Dr. Stanley Sawicki did not make the best of husbands for the petite Judith Katz. He was an irascible man with the patience of a boiling teakettle. His army-tank build made him an imposing figure, as did his overbearing personality. He spoke several languages, had a quick, caustic wit and an explosive temper. But with the right combination of stimulants, alcohol, and narcotics, he could also be great fun.

Their first son was conceived sooner than they would have

liked. They did not intend to stop having a good time just because a baby was on the way. It was long before any government agency even considered warnings or guidelines for mothers-to-be, and, anyway, the Sawickis ignored even the slightest common-sense precautions. They drank heavily, chain-smoked tobacco and weed, stayed out all night snorting heroin and speed, and fought violently until the day Izaak Michal Sawicki was born. The baby stayed in an incubator for weeks for detoxification. If only he could have stayed there indefinitely.

The baby changed nothing in the Sawicki household except to add complications to an already thorny relationship. Izaak was barely two when, during one of his parents' frequent fights, Stanley grabbed the baby by his arm and dangled him overhead, cackling, as a frantic Judith tried to reach her son.

"What are you doing?" she screamed. "Put him down!"

The baby was shrieking, and Stanley was laughing. He finally let go, sending Izaak tumbling down toward the floor.

Judith caught him.

Although his father would insist on treating most of the baby's injuries himself — no big deal popping an arm back into a socket — Izaak would visit the hospital often. Being the child of an ER doctor ensured that the visits would be kept surreptitious.

MAY 1995

It was worse than a usual hangover.

As soon as Pest opened his eyes, he knew it was going to be a Soup Day. That's what Pest called days like these. It did not mean he was going to be eating soup or even making soup. It would mean an entire day, or two, or three, where his brain would become soup.

The problem with Soup Days was that they often became Quicksand Days. The latter often were accompanied by an unrehearsed, unruly chorus of brutal thoughts intent on taunting him, or even, threatening him. In comparison, a Soup Day was much easier.

He didn't overdo the drinking that often these days, but last night someone else was buying. He propped himself up and climbed off his thin futon mattress to standing. There wasn't much sense in making coffee on a Soup Day because the caffeine would do exactly nothing. Since Lisa was at work, he decided to take a bath.

He removed the board that was covering the claw-footed tub in the kitchen and turned on the water. It was ice cold, a fact that wasn't registering in his muddled brain. He got into the water and, after a lost moment, soaped up. The water was gradually getting warmer, and it was almost comfortable by the time he finished and got out of the tub.

The phone rang, and Pest dripped across the floor to answer it.

"Yeah?"

A voice on the other end of the line said, "Izaak Sawicki?"

Somewhere in the functioning part of his brain the phrase, "Who wants to know?" floated by, but all his mouth was capable of was, "Yeah."

"This is Ricky Gleason from Lightweight Records. We spoke a couple of weeks ago?" He had an AM-top-40-DJ-I'm-peppy-and-excited-and-you-should-be-too kind of voice.

Ricky Gleason. Ricky Gleason. Why was that name familiar? Oh. Right.

"Yes. Of course."

"We'd like you to come in to discuss your album."

Getting on a label, on most days, would have made Pest delighted. Today the soup was thinking, *God, I can't deal with this, go away*, but sanity reached out of the clam chowder and grabbed Pest's vocal cords.

"Yes, absolutely. When?"

"How's Friday for you?"

"Uh... uh..." Think, Pest. Friday. The day after Thursday. "How about in the afternoon?"

"Like, say, 3 o'clock?"

When Pest hung up, he lumbered over to get his calendar, and with great difficulty wrote "Lightweight 3p" on the page for Friday. On today's page, above the entries "do laundry" and "practice," he wrote "Soup Day."

Since Soup Days usually lasted only one day, Pest was his perfectly abnormal self before Friday rolled around. After he got home from his appointment with Lightweight, Pest picked up the phone to dial Allie. She was already on the line.

"Pest? I didn't even hear it ring," she said.

"It didn't. I was about to dial you, and there you were."

There was a pause, and then Pest said:

"You know, I think we should go on a real date next time, instead of just falling into bed together again."

Pest heard Allie laugh. She said, "Okay. Sure."

"Not that I don't love having sex with you."

"Glad to hear it. Me too."

The next night, Pest arrived at the Film Forum at 7:15 for an 8:10 movie. Allie was supposed to be getting out of work in time for them to see a screening of *Faster, Pussycat, Kill, Kill*. As it got closer to the hour, he began to worry. What if she couldn't leave work? He had already bought the tickets. What if she changed her mind?

Allie got there in time, but hadn't eaten, so they stopped at the theater's concession stand and got her a brownie and a ginger ale. Then they settled into two seats in the third row, and Allie scarfed down the brownie and soda before the movie started. She curled up against him, and he put his arm around her.

The movie was not exactly a romantic flick, and Pest was thrilled that Allie not only agreed to see it but seemed excited about it. They stayed wrapped together throughout the movie, with Allie letting little burps escape from the ginger ale she drank so quickly. Pest gave her a squeeze, and she pressed against him tighter.

The next day had Pest thinking. This thing with Allie might be more than a short fling, and before he saw her again, he had better make this phone call.

"Hey, Allie. I gotta tell you something." Had to just jump in. No other way.

"Okay."

"Here's the thing... I've been to jail."

Silence.

Okay. Here it goes.

"In and out of juvie. Didn't finish high school."

"Okay..." Allie didn't sound too alarmed. He continued.

"Disturbing the peace, disorderly conduct..."

He paused to let her absorb that.

"...driving while intoxicated, resisting arrest, possession..."

He was reciting this information as if it were a shopping list. Better not overly dramatize.

"...assaulting a police officer, armed robbery... ummm, I think that's it."

After a beat, Allie burst out laughing. Was that good or bad?

"Oh my God," she said. "I guess I should be running in the other direction."

His heart sank. "You should?"

"Well, are you still robbing banks?"

"Nah, I cleaned up my act when I got married. Stopped doing drugs, stopped getting into so much trouble. And there weren't any banks, just a store."

"Right. Okay."

Pest waited.

"Well, thanks for telling me," she said finally.

"Are we're okay?"

"Yeah. I'm not scared off. Seems I have a thing for rabid dogs."

He wasn't exactly sure what she meant by that, but he felt relieved just the same.

Night Crawlers was a squalid bar on 2nd Avenue in an area that real-estate agents had been referring to as the East Village for decades, but anyone who had any history in the area still called the Lower East Side. Parts of the neighborhood may have become safer and cleaner, but Night Crawlers had not yet succumbed to the neighborhood's gentrification. Two doors down, a fancy bar had opened, complete with a velvet rope across its entrance to act as a riff-raff deterrent, but in front of Night Crawlers, homeless people found refuge in refrigerator boxes or slept in crude tents. While the words "Night Crawlers" were still legible over the door, the painted wooden sign was old and badly peeling. The rusting metal gates that once protected windows during off hours now served as the outside walls, the windows having been smashed in a decade earlier and never replaced.

Pest was playing a gig there the night they were smashed in. It was entirely possible he had had something to do with the windows' destruction.

Inside, there was a bar on the left, and a small platform directly across that served as a stage. Next to the stage was a jukebox that held a wide-ranging collection of singles, and in the back, there was a battered pool table and two genderless water closets. Drinks were cheap but watered-down, even the soft drinks. All this, for just a $5 cover.

Tonight's event was a reunion of Pest's first band, Those Little Reds, the members who were still alive, anyway. Except for Pest, the survivors had risen from the bar-band scene, and when they discovered they were all going to be in town on the same night, they decided they should converge on Night Crawlers for old times' sake. Even though this was an unadvertised event, the crowd outside of the bar was a lot larger than usual, forcing the homeless folks to move their makeshift homes further away from the entrance.

When Allie arrived, she seemed intimidated by the crowd, and just as she looked like she might turn and run, Pest grabbed her hand and led her inside.

"Hey. They renovated the place," Pest said. "They washed the floor."

Four of the original six band members were there, and there were plenty of other musicians in the audience who had been in the band at one time or another who could take turns filling in for the absent two. The show was crazy with energy and nostalgia, the music unrestrained, the musicians in a mind-meld. And although Pest was super-charged, he found he was fighting back a huge amount of melancholy.

Pest introduced Allie to his friend Jake, co-founder of their old band and Pest's best friend back in the day. Jake barely acknowledged her and proceeded to chew Pest's ear off about his new life in Salinas, California. Not only did he have an album coming out on a major label, but he had also just landed a gig scoring some music for a mainstream film.

This was hard to hear.

"It's great out there, Pest. There's a lot of work. I got a little house that's 15 minutes from the ocean. I got a car and a Harley. There's a pool in my back yard and plenty of fresh air and girls in bikinis."

"Fresh girls in bikinis? Wow."

"Ha, yeah. But really, man, you should come out."

"Well, you're right, I gotta do something," he said and

hugged Allie a little tighter to tell her he hadn't forgotten about her. "It's getting harder and harder to get decent gigs here. There was a time when a band could play two, three nights a week. Now we're lucky if it's two a month, and then we're often sharing the night with four other bands."

"Exactly. You're not going anywhere staying here. New York's dead, man."

This was all a nice fantasy, but Pest knew it couldn't happen. He raised his head as if to think, then looked back at Jake with a pained look on his face.

"Can't do it. My kids are here."

"What? They won't visit you?"

"It's not the same thing. They're still little. I'm already missing a lot of their growing up by not living with them. My son has turned into a Yankees fan, for fuck's sake. If we lived on different coasts, I'd miss everything. I'd be lucky if I saw them at Christmas."

Jake turned around to the bar to put his empty beer down and order another. "No, you're right, man," he said. He took a swig from the new beer and threw a tip on the bar. "That would be tough. But listen, any time you want to come check it out, you're always welcome."

Pest didn't have much to say on the walk back to his place. Not only were the musicians who were there tonight his caliber, but they also were guys he'd known for years, guys that he could simply glance at, and they knew what to do. They had all moved on, and he was still where he was seven years ago. Ten years ago. Twelve years ago. True, the Caterwaulers were finally on a label, albeit an indie one, but these guys were now fairly well-known country stars, and a couple of them had been Pest's students.

Allie walked silently beside him. Nice that they didn't need to be talking all the time. Her hair had a great smell to it, some kind of flower or plant or something, and he was tempted to put his hand up her short skirt. But that could wait until they got inside.

When they got to his place, Pest took out a tape Jake had given him and put it in the stereo. "Listen to this."

Allie's face was full of recognition.

"That's... that's your stalker song."

That made him smile. "That's what you call it? Yeah, It's on Jake's new album."

"That's a good thing, right?"

He shrugged. "I guess."

Jake had given the song a southern-rock feel, very different from Pest's power ballad version. Pest let it play and waited for her reaction.

"I like your version better," she said.

"I know you feel you have to say that but thank you."

"No, really. He flattened out the melody, so there's no bounce or urgency to it. And the middle eight doesn't build like your version does. It's just not as good."

Despite his grumpy mood, this made Pest smile. He kissed her, and she pressed her body against his. The time for melancholy was over.

Allie snuggled against him afterwards, and they lay in silence. Pest would have gotten up to turn off the lamp, but he was too cozy, oddly content after the tricks his mind had been playing on him all night.

Then he said, "Listen."

Allie's face scrunched up quizzically.

"It's so quiet in this part of town you can hear a train whistling in New Jersey."

And by her expression, it seemed that she did hear it: a lone train whistle, barely audible unless a person knew to tune into it.

Allie whispered, "So, tomorrow morning, I'll probably be gone before you get up." He held her tighter and said, "Okay," but it wasn't, really.

CHAPTER 11

ALLIE, 1981–1991

Allie's first job out of college was as a proofreader for a large corporate law firm in lower Manhattan. Benefits included: four weeks' vacation, twelve sick days, three personal days, paid holidays, medical insurance, dental insurance, optical insurance, and life insurance. There were two bonuses a year, comprised of an extra two-weeks' pay each, one at the end of the fiscal year in September and one at Christmas. Overtime was given for working more than a seven-hour day, with dinner money supplied as cash in a generous amount. All of this for an entry-level position.

"How can this be?" Allie asked the personnel coordinator who had been explaining the benefits.

"Honestly? The company wants to keep unions out, so we offer our support staff comparable benefits."

As the 80s continued, the federal government began reducing tax incentives for employee benefits, and, with less powerful unions as a result of the August '81 air-traffic controllers' strike, the law firm began scaling back. Vacation time was cut in half, the optical and dental benefits were dropped, and fewer sick days were allotted. Rather than offering overtime pay at time-and-a-half, the company began hiring from temporary agencies, which also led to replacing staff less often, and instead hiring agency temps to fill shifts, not by day or week, but for months at a time.

Partly due to the aforementioned changes, and partly due to a new gadget called the Macintosh computer, Allie left the law firm and began life as a freelance desk-top publisher. By the end of the 80s, New York's workforce, in general, and the publishing business, in particular, became flooded with free-lancers, temporary employees, and independent contractors. The once powerful International Typographical Union refused to acknowledge desk-top operators as kindred workers, and many felt this contributed to its eventual demise as the need for traditional typographers vanished into the long night. Why hire a typesetting company to set your book at $60 a word, when you can hire your own people and pay them $15 an hour?

A lot of New Yorkers who had been busy getting high and having sex with inappropriate people in the last decade began embracing a new compulsion: workaholism. Paid by the hour with no benefits, work security, or overtime pay, they would work marathon hours, pumping out books and magazines and advertising and packaging, honing their skills on as much software as they could get their hands on to maximize their marketability in an increasingly crowded workforce.

They were all under the delusion that freelancing afforded them more free time and independence. In a city like New York, where rents were extortionate and nightlife was so relentlessly fascinating, who could resist the promise of "flexible" hours?

Many employers all but swore off the notion of hiring staff. Pay a freelancer a little more per hour than they would pay a staffer, offer her abundant work, and she's yours for the duration. Three months, six months, 10-hour days, 16-hour days, 60-hour weeks, 90-hour weeks, the "permatemp" was born, bringing about the death of company loyalty, pensions, health insurance, payroll taxes, overtime, and job security, and bringing in a generation of nervous workaholics trying to keep their virtual jobs.

Allie often theorized that many people only do the right

thing if an authority figure, either with threats or bribery, orders them to do so. And it is people, after all, who run corporations.

"This is why God invented religion," she liked to say. "It's the adult equivalent of 'You're in trouble. I'm telling Mom!'"

In this free-for-all of computer-operator subjugation, an unlikely hero arose. It wasn't God or the Long Arm of the Law, but a much more fearsome enforcer: the IRS. As permatemps began to realize their jobs weren't all that permanent, they started filing for unemployment benefits. They worked six months at the place; they earned it, right? During the battle to get their unemployment, they also discovered they were getting socked for a mess of taxes their employers would normally pay. What the heck was this FICA, anyway? Freelancers began reporting their former employers to the taxman. After a few friendly phone calls from everybody's pals at the IRS, things started to change.

By the early-nineties, although permatemps were still a mainstay of the work force, many of them were now getting income taxes withheld, half of their social security taxes (a.k.a. FICA) paid, and in some cases, even time-and-a-half for each hour worked over forty hours in a week. Just like Robert Owens intended.

Paid holidays, sick days, vacations, health insurance, and job security, however, were still the privilege of the lucky few.

JUNE 1995

The 7 train was packed with happy, albeit realistic, Mets fans. Allie was taking a rare afternoon off to go to the game and was currently hanging on a bar above her head that she could just about reach. The train got more and more crowded until it got to Shea Stadium, where practically everyone got out. Ephram and his friends Mike and Chris were waiting for Allie at Gate C.

Allie looked at her ticket. "We're in the Bob Uecker seats?"

"We're lucky we have seats at all," Ephram said.

"Last year at this time, we could have gotten field seats," Chris said.

"Hell, we could've sat in the dugout," Mike said. "No one was coming to the games by this time last year."

Not quite all the way to the top, it turned out, but there was no one sitting in the one row of seats that was above them.

"Wow, I forget how high up this section is." Allie was feeling a bit of altitude sickness and quickly sat down. "There's a seagull sitting in the next row."

"That's what he gets for buying his tickets at the last minute."

By the top of the fourth inning, the Padres were leading 2-0, with one out and the bases loaded

Allie sighed. "God, I get to one stupid Mets game this year, and they're losing."

"Well, then this is your fault," Ephram said.

"I think it's time for another beer run," Chris said. "Maybe the Mets will stop sucking if we're not watching them."

Allie didn't want to go down and up those stairs any more than she had to, so she opted to stay where she was, and Ephram volunteered to stay with her. As Chris and Mike retreated under the bleachers, the Mets pitcher threw his second strike in a row.

"Hey, that worked," Allie said. "Maybe Mike and Chris should watch the rest of the game from the men's room."

The Mets pitcher threw a third strike, and everyone was on their feet and making as much noise as they could.

The pitch to the next batter was a ball, and the crowd groaned and sat down. Then a single voice bellowed:

"MILICKI, YOU PUTZ! TRY GETTING THE BALL OVER

THE PLATE! OV — ER — THE — PLATE!"

Ephram turned to Allie. "Hey, do you know anyone who might want my apartment?"

"What? Why?"

"I'm looking for a job. In Japan."

Allie raised her eyebrows, and Ephram chuckled.

"Nothing's doin' in the job market here, but I do have a few leads in Japan from when I spent a semester there. I'm thinking, if I get a job there, I'd sublet at first, like a year, and if the job goes well, I'll turn over the lease."

"Well, that..." She was going to say "sucks" but instead said, "is great for you. And my friend Natia might want your apartment if it comes to that."

"Yeah? Good. I'll let you know."

There was a pop fly, and the Mets were finally up again.

"So, what about you?" Ephram said. "How's it going with what's-his-name?"

"Izaak. It's going well." Allie sighed. "I just work too much."

"So, stop working so much."

Allie considered this. "Problem with being a freelancer. The more you say yes, the more you get hired. And competition for jobs is fierce these days. The market is flooded with people like me, although maybe not as experienced. When the deadlines are tight, like they are now, we're expected to stay until everything gets done. Jim would complain about my schedule, too, although this has been much worse."

Something about the way Ephram was looking at her made her feel like confessing.

"I have to admit, I still feel guilty for not calling Jim that weekend. If I had known he was coming, I wouldn't have left without him."

Ephram smiled a you-poor-pathetic-thing smile. "Or you would have known for sure he wasn't coming."

Allie frowned. "How do you mean?"

"Allie, it's never occurred to you that maybe Jim told his mother he was coming to see you, but that he had plans to meet Laynie and Chaz all along?"

The look on Allie's face told him that no, in fact, that had never occurred to her.

"Think about it: He left Queens at like, three or something. It doesn't take four hours to take the train to Manhattan from Forest Hills. Jim might have been gone even before you met up with your friends."

As Allie processed that new thought, the crowd was on their feet again. Ephram stood up to check the board.

"It's 2-1," he said.

The cheering and shrieking and high-pitched whistling going on around Allie did not stop her from having a clear picture in her mind: her dialing Jim from the restaurant, the phone ringing in his apartment, and Jim on his couch, already dead.

Damn.

Another 15-hour day. Allie was so cross-eyed she could no longer see her computer screen. This wasn't worth it. The money they promised her in overtime wouldn't happen unless they finished this project on time, but what was the point if she turned into Adele H in the process?

Allie didn't even try to walk home. She arrived at the L-train station and hurried down the subway stairs. Two a.m. was not a great time to be on the trains, but there were more people than Allie expected. The crowd was a goop mélange of hipsters heading to Williamsburg, Russian immigrants heading to Greenpoint, St. Vincent Hospital staff, still in scrubs, heading to outer Brooklyn and Far Rockaway, and various other tired workers on their way home. Allie, still color-correcting in her head, was scanning the crowd's rainbow assortment of skin tones, her subconscious taking notes and storing the information away to be acted upon some other time. Occasional, accidental, eye contact would necessitate Allie's gaze to dart away. Everyone stared in the subway, but it was bad etiquette to get caught.

Allie got home and flung herself across her bed. As she lay there, Tuna jumped up and purred in her face.

"You poor neglected cat. You'd probably like some food."

She sat up and went into the kitchen, with Tuna following at her heels. As Tuna gulped down her food, Allie opened her refrigerator. Nothing to eat, just two rolls of toilet paper.

"Jeez." These long hours were changing both her body and brain chemistry. She grabbed the two rolls and put them in the bathroom.

The phone rang. She waited a moment but picked up.

"Hey, I was wondering if you could come by." Pest sounded rattled.

The last thing she wanted to do was go out again.

"I'm sorry. I'm fried," she said.

There was silence on the line.

"Pest?"

"I could really use the company."

There was something in his voice that told her she had better go.

"Okay. But I just got home. I'm going to need at least an hour."

"That's okay. I'll see you when you get here."

She hung up. "Damn it."

Allie took a shower and quickly gathered up clothes for the next day. Then she went outside and hailed a cab. Pest's bizarre roommate was already asleep when she got there, and Allie followed Pest to his room.

"Thank you for coming over." He shook his bangs out of his face. His beautiful eyes were dilated so much they looked like black marbles.

"I'm fucked up, Allie."

"How many have you had?" she said, indicating the bottle of beer in his hand.

"This one was all I had in the house. This and a couple of tomatoes. But that's not what's fucked up."

"What's going on?"

He looked away from her as he spoke.

"Just been having a very dark day. Reliving some stuff."

"Okay..."

"Nothing's working. Thinking I should quit everything and start over. Maybe go somewhere."

"Like California?"

He looked at her and smiled slightly. "I was thinking Mars."

"That far."

"Yeah. Or farther."

Pest put his arms around her. She could feel him sigh deeply, and she held him tighter. Calmer now, Pest gave her his first detailed account of his damaged childhood. His father was abusive to his mother, and in turn, she would abuse Pest. This was almost more than Allie's unworldly brain could take. The worst she had ever experienced from her family were simple disagreements. No one dribbled anyone down the hallway like a basketball or smacked someone over and over like Punch and Judy. She couldn't imagine a world like that.

In the early morning light, they made love, and though Pest fell asleep fast, Allie was wide awake. There was a moment where she thought she felt the quivering soul of that abused toddler, and she found herself thinking, *I will never hurt you, no matter what.*

Once she saw his soul, there was no turning back.

One of the better places to hear music in the City was the Rodeo Bar, half restaurant on one side and half music venue on the other. The actual bar was built into the shell of a bus, a vehicle retired long before the establishment came into existence. Overlapping stickers of various bands covered its white metallic skeleton, and past the bus, near the tables and the platform stage, were framed, and some signed, rockabilly posters hanging on the walls. Top this off with a head and torso of a buffalo, breaking through the wall at stage left.

Pest was well into his set when Allie arrived with a few members of the Goldfish crew. He spotted her and beamed.

The patrons were unresponsive that evening, so, guitar in hand, Pest walked out into the audience. He climbed up on one of the tables, balanced himself by putting his hand on the ceiling for a moment, and then continued playing and singing. People stared blankly at him and applauded politely at the end of the song but seemed more intent on drinking than on listening to music

"How about pretending you're out to hear some music tonight and have a good time?"

No response.

"What did you think you were gonna hear tonight? Cover versions of 'Sweet Caroline' and 'Brown Eyed Girl'?"

Some people turned their backs to him.

Pest walked from tabletop to tabletop, bending down to glare at each patron. Still getting little attention, he stood up straight and yelled out, "What's the matter? You afraid of me?"

A voice called back, "Hell, yes."

During the break, Pest came over to Allie's table, took Allie's hand and led her outside.

"I'm so glad you're here. Hey, can I follow you home later?"

"Please."

Pest grinned and hugged her. He had taken to hugging her tightly these days, not letting go for some time. When Pest eventually released his grip, they sat on the bench outside the entrance.

"This crowd is making me nuts. I could cut off my penis and put it in somebody's drink and they wouldn't react."

"Well, please don't. I still plan on using that."

They stayed outside until Pest was called back inside for the second set.

"Ok, it's time to serenade the tone deaf. If anyone shouts out 'Free Bird,' I'm gonna have to hurt 'em."

Middle of the night, Allie was sleeping soundly. Pest had left some time earlier, not wanting to leave his van full of equipment on the street all night. Tuna was curled up by Allie's elbow.

And Allie had a dream.

Jim was climbing into bed with her. When were they together last? Eight, nine months? But what about Pest? What would she tell him? No, wait. What was she going to tell Jim?

She awoke, shook off the dream, and sat all the way up. Tuna lifted her sleepy head and said, "Mrrr?" in protest.

"Hey!" Allie said, addressing the ceiling. "You left me. I didn't just go off with someone else. YOU left ME. Got it? That was your dumbass mistake, not mine!"

She was glaring at the ceiling, almost expecting it to talk back.

"Deal with it!"

She stared at the ceiling for a moment more and lay back down. Tuna curled up again and nuzzled against her.

"Deal with it," she said to herself now and went back to sleep.

The offices were empty, the corridors were dark, and the air was hot and muggy. The clock above the reception desk was about to close in on three a.m. And there, in one corner of the floor, were the inhabitants of the late shift. Floor fans placed strategically around the production area were making it just about bearable.

A group of intelligent but socially desperate misfits with little or no life direction, otherwise known as the proofreaders, were hunched over color proofs on a large table, looking for misspelled words and errant italic periods. The text was small and plentiful and was starting to look more like indefinable squiggles than readable letters. There was a lot of silent protest, with weary bodies wondering why their owners didn't just stop and go to sleep.

The computer operators weren't doing much better. Allie and Mark, their faces inches from their screens, were unsuccessfully fighting sleep. Rihanna walked in with a large pile of folders. People looked up at her and groaned.

"Sorry guys," she said. She put the folders on the "To Do" pile, then sat down at an empty desk near one of the fans to do some paperwork.

To stay awake, Allie began to hum a Marvin Gaye song. No one in the office was shy anymore about bursting into song, or rage, or tears, or, less frequently, laughter, and usually these random outbursts would go uncommented on. This was especially true the later the shift went.

As Allie continued the song, she started to include lyrics:
"'*There's something wrong with me loving you...*'."
Rihanna giggled.
"What?" Allie said.
"That's not how it goes."
Allie was genuinely confused. "It's not?"
This made Rihanna laugh harder.
"No. It's, 'There's *nothing* wrong with me loving you.'"
"It *is*?"
Allie looked to Mark.
"It *is*?"
He nodded.

"I think that says something about the guys you date," Rihanna said. "Okay, I added it up. I worked 118 hours this week."

"Damn. Really?"

"How about you? You've been here more than I have."

Allie took out her time sheet and did some calculating. This wasn't possible.

"124," she said. "How many hours are there in a week, anyway?"

"This is ridiculous. We're not saving lives, we're not creating great art, we're not training for the Olympics."

"If we were training for the Olympics, we'd be getting a decent amount of sleep."

The phone rang. Rihanna looked at the clock and smiled at Allie as she reached for the phone.

"Can't be Pest," Allie said. "He's got a late gig in Jersey."

"Hi, Pest. Yeah, hang on a sec." Rihanna handed her the phone.

"Hey, what's going on?"

Allie heard a deep breath, then: "My band fell apart at the gig. This was a new place for us, and we blew it. *I* blew it."

"Well, wait a minute. How is this your fault?"

"OF COURSE, IT'S MY FAULT. IT'S MY BAND!"

Allie held the phone away from her ear.

"Of course. Sorry. Tell me about it."

Allie could hear an exasperated sigh on the other end of the phone.

"Ken and Luke couldn't agree on a beat, not once. They're rock musicians, for fuck's sake. And Trevor, shit, he's useless unless he has strong players behind him."

Ken and Luke?

"And you didn't kill them?"

A breathy laugh came from Pest's end of the phone. Allie loved his breathy laugh.

"No, but that's still a possibility. Thing is, I totally lost my temper, and I fired them. Now I need to find two new guys before I go on the road next month."

"Well, hopefully you'll find people who aren't rhythm deaf."

Pest laughed again, a signal this crisis was winding down. Then Allie thought she could hear someone talking to Pest.

"Okay, I gotta go," he said. "How are you doing?"

"The same. Stressed times ten."

"Well, I'm seeing you tomorrow. I'll de-stress you then."

"Mmm, can't wait."

Allie put down the phone. Rihanna was studying her.

"Everything okay?"

"Pest is having a hard night," Allie said.

"So you have to drop everything and fix It for him?" Mark said. Allie bristled.

"No. And there are certain things one person can't fix."

How did that go? Something about how the other half lives? Allie was standing in front of the largest apartment building she'd ever seen. It was maybe thirty stories high, and it was wide, maybe three buildings wide, and there was a crescent-shaped driveway that curved around a fountain. Allie felt compelled to check for a moat with alligators, but after amusing herself with this thought, she figured she better get on with it.

Pest was waiting for her.

She couldn't believe he grew up in this place. The doormen had red and black uniforms, and she had to be announced to get in. She felt stupid in a tee shirt and jeans. Maybe she should be wearing a dress or something.

Pest met her at the elevator, dressed in his usual rock attire, and reality returned.

"Thanks for coming up here. Lisa's got her boyfriend over,

and I figured four's a crowd."

A tight hug and a butt squeeze, and they went inside.

It was a mansion.

Okay, not really, but it was huge by Manhattan standards. There was an oversized living room with real furniture, a dining area, and a sizeable kitchen. And that was just what Allie could see from the foyer.

"Wow. This place is enormous."

"Yeah. Three bedrooms, rent controlled. There's a terrace, too."

Allie couldn't believe it.

"My mother is on the other side in her bedroom watching television, so we'll have some privacy. We'll be over here in my dad's old library."

Library?

Allie woke early the next morning. The library was even smaller than the room Pest had on Christopher Street. The twin mattress they had slept on took up all the walking space. The rest of the room was filled with floor-to-ceiling book-shelves. Allie collected her clothes and went to take a shower.

It was a real shower in a real bathroom, clean and tiled, with guest towels and water pressure, hot water that was hot, and cold water that was cold. After she got dressed, figuring Pest was still asleep, and, with no sign of Pest's mom, she ventured out through the kitchen into the main room.

Against the far wall, there was a large gold couch and a gold matching lounge chair next to it. The wall-to-wall carpeting was gold as well. To Allie's right was a blonde-wood upright piano.

There were photos on it: Pest's wedding picture in a frame, several snapshots of Pest's son and daughter, a studio shot of an earlier configuration of Pest's band that Allie recognized from the Voice review of his CD, and one photo that made her stop. It was an 8 x 10, black-and-white headshot of a hand-some, light-haired man. He looked a lot like Pest, without the sunken eyes and crooked nose. She noticed another photo of this same man, this time with a woman, maybe his wife, because there were also three little boys posed with them.

His brother?

"Damn," she said aloud.

She stared at this photo and couldn't help but wonder: Seeing a face that would likely have been Pest's had his not been broken for him a couple dozen times, what would Pest's life have been like had he been given half a chance?

CHAPTER 12

RIHANNA AND ROBERT, 1980–1984

Rihanna's mother and sister didn't approve. Rihanna was too young, just out of college, and Robert was in his thirties and a bit battle worn: leathery skin, pronounced scar on his forehead, track marks. Without discussing it with her family, though, Rihanna married Robert at Town Hall.

Robert told Rihanna she could quit her job at the local newspaper because he was making enough at the car dealership to support them both. Then he turned his extra bedroom into a studio so Rihanna could spend her days painting. Rihanna had hit the jackpot.

However, as time went on, Robert's personality started to change.

Rihanna was looking for her sunglasses one morning, trying to be quiet so she wouldn't wake Robert. He had turned off the alarm when it rang. These days he would wake up irritable, so Rihanna let him sleep if he wanted to. She spent a few more moments searching, but finally chose to take her bike ride without her shades.

"Where are you going?"

Rihanna jumped.

"Oh. Hi. I thought you were asleep."

"You didn't answer my question."

He seemed angry, but Rihanna couldn't see why he would be.

"Just for a ride. I'll be right back."

He stretched, spent a few seconds scratching his back, and looked at the clock.

"Damn it! Why didn't you wake me? I'm going to be late."

"You turned off the alarm. I thought you wanted to sleep."

He slammed the door to the bathroom before she finished her sentence. This crankiness was new, and Rihanna hoped it would pass soon. Maybe it was work stress. Rihanna had tried to ask him about it, but he snapped at her and told her nothing was wrong. It could be time for him to find another job, but in his present state, she was reluctant to suggest it.

Robert came home and immediately passed out on the couch, so there would be no talking then either. Was he keeping something from her?

The phone rang. Robert groaned, but the sound did not fully wake him.

"Oh, hi Evan," Rihanna said. "Robert's asleep. Can I take a message?"

"Well, I wanted to talk to him about what's been going on at work. Is he all right? He seems moody lately."

"He is moody, but he won't talk to me. Everything okay?"

"Probably. He's been nodding off at work. Is he sleeping okay?"

"Well, he crashes on the couch when he gets home."

"Okay. Well, maybe he's not sleeping at night. Anyway, I'll talk to you soon, Rihanna. Tell him I called. Thanks."

When Robert was awake, he began snapping at the slightest transgression: a dish in the sink, bed not made, can't find the TV remote. She waited for him to settle down.

"Hey. Are you alright? Evan called. He says you've been nodding off at work."

"It's nothing. I'll work it out. Everything's fine."

Rihanna almost said, "If everything's fine, what is there to work out?" but hearing his agitated tone made her think twice.

Everything was not fine, however. Robert lost his job. After that he moped around the house, mostly sleeping in a morose lump on the couch.

"Robert? C'mon. Talk to me. It's been over a week."

He grunted and waved his hand at her dismissively.

"Were there layoffs? I don't get it; you were their senior manager."

More grunting, then a mumble of, "I got fired."

"Fired!"

He looked at her. "Yes. Fired. Okay? I've been falling asleep at my desk. I've had really bad insomnia. Finally, they just fired me."

"That doesn't seem right. They should've been more understanding."

He sat up in a rage and shouted, "Well they weren't! Okay?"

He was scaring her. She backed out of the room, ran upstairs to her studio, and locked the door.

"Damn it, Rihanna, come back here. I'm sorry."

Behind the door, she was panicking. Neither one of them was working now, and Robert seemed too despondent to start looking for another job. And the anger was unnerving. Something wasn't right.

While Robert went back to his position on the couch, Rihanna dialed Evan.

"Evan, Robert won't talk to me. What happened at work? Why did he get fired?"

Evan paused. "Listen, Rihanna." Another pause. He was stalling. "He's been getting stoned at work. We found his works in the restroom."

"What? But he's sober."

"I thought you should know. Looks like he's using again."

Robert had gotten off the couch and was now knocking on the door.

"Hey! Who are you talking to?"

Rihanna quickly put down the phone. "I was talking to Evan."

"Damn it, Rihanna, open this door."

She hesitated.

"Open the door!"

She unlocked the door and let him in.

"What did he say?"

Rihanna thought better of answering him, but he came closer and shouted, "What did he say?"

"He said you're using again."

He glared at her, and then he laughed bitterly. "You believed him?"

"Because you've been so moody lately! And you won't talk to me! And then you got fired. Something's wrong, Robert!"

He stared at her a long time, and she wondered if maybe she shouldn't have provoked him. But then he smirked.

"Everything's just fine," he said and left the room.

"Everything is not fine!" she yelled down the stairs after him.

She waited a while, then went downstairs to make dinner. Robert said he wasn't hungry, but Rihanna made burgers and hoped it would entice him to eat.

He appeared in the kitchen doorway, and Rihanna braced herself.

"Look. I'm sorry," he said.

"I'm just worried about you."

"I know. I appreciate that. I've been a louse. I'm sorry."

He held her from behind while she was cooking and nuzzled her neck.

"Hungry now?"

"Sure. I'll take a burger."

However, the bad days kept coming. Robert no longer was hiding the fact that he was using, choosing to get high right there on the couch. Rihanna had only Evan to talk to, since she surely was not going to discuss this with her mother or sister. Evan didn't have much advice to offer, though. Robert's dealer would come over, and they would get high together, often *snorting coke in addition to shooting H.*

When Robert was high, he was either euphoric or a sleepy kitten. When he was coming down, he was angry and uncontrollable.

"Robert. I'm leaving."

"Oh? Where are you going?"

"I mean, I'm leaving you."

He laughed. "No, you're not."

"I can't take this anymore. And the bills are piling up, and you're unpredictable, and —"

"You're not going anywhere. And even if you do, I will find you."

"Find me?"

"And bring you back."

"If you can get off the couch!"

He took a swing at her, but she ducked. She ran upstairs and locked the door to her studio, with Robert chasing her.

"You're not going anywhere."

Rihanna was now hiding in her studio, although with Robert just outside the door, she was also trapped there. He settled onto the floor, lit a cigarette, and stayed until it got dark. He was right; she wasn't going anywhere.

The next morning Rihanna thought she'd at least take a ride, but she couldn't find her bicycle. It was usually right in the foyer. Where was it?"

"Looking for something?"

Robert was calm and smiling.

"My bike. I wanted to take a ride."

"You won't be doing that anymore."

Rihanna studied his face. He didn't look evil. Where was this all coming from? In any case, she knew she was in trouble.

JULY 1995

It was one of those City nights where the air temperature refused to go below 85°. Rihanna, Natia, and Allie were leaning on the rail on the upper deck of the ferry, trying to catch what little breeze there was. The rest of Casey's birthday party was going on below. There was a DJ playing 60s music and a couple dozen inebriated people in period clothes attempting to dance on the main deck.

"Where's Danny tonight?" Rihanna asked. She pushed the toe of her most recent shoe acquisition — a pair of crazy, glittering platforms from the vintage store — between the rails.

"He's got a client," Natia said. "Besides, I don't see Danny in a tie-dyed shirt."

"Meanwhile, we're dressed like the B-52s," Allie said. She had been growing out her hair and tonight was donning a *That-Girl* style flip.

They heard the intro of the Rolling Stones' "Get Off My Cloud," and Allie stood up from the rail.

"Ladies, we must go dance."

They went down to the main deck. Rihanna spotted Dylan, standing by the makeshift bar. He was wearing cut-offs and a Hawaiian shirt, not exactly 60s era, but somehow it worked. He caught her eye and smiled. Rihanna slowly took off her shoes, trying not to break his gaze. He raised his can of cola to her in a salute. He had promised not to get drunk tonight. Looked like he was keeping his word.

Now the dance floor was getting crowded. She lost sight of Dylan for a few moments, and when she found him again, she saw a woman sashay up to him. Rihanna froze mid shimmy. What was this, now? When the DJ started to play *My Girl*, she heard the woman ask Dylan if he wanted to dance. Dylan nodded "yes." He handed the woman his soda and joined Rihanna on the dance floor.

The boat had a lot of large fans, but no air conditioning, and although the guests were trying to dance to the great music, they started to feel like they were in a sauna. Casey took off his t-shirt and, without fanfare, jumped into the Hudson.

Allie was appalled. "Is he crazy?"

"No. Just hot," Dylan said.

"I can remember when they used to drag your ass to the hospital if you fell in that water."

"Not anymore. We swim all the time. In fact..."

Dylan took off his Hawaiian shirt and dove in. Considering how sweaty people were and how much they were drinking, jumping in seemed like a logical plan. They started to follow Dylan and Casey's lead.

"Wanna go in?" Rihanna said. "I could lend you guys shorts and t-shirts."

They changed out of their 60s outfits and, although Allie was still hesitant, the three of them jumped in. Rihanna sank under the surface, came up, and shook the water out of her face. The entire party was treading water around her, the music still playing on the now empty ferry. Rihanna started swimming. She didn't go farther than the end of the pier; she never quite trusted the river's current beyond that. When she reached the end, she flipped over and did the backstroke back to her friends, who were still getting used to soaking in something other than sweat.

Many of the party guests were singing along with the boat's music. It started with a few people humming along, then grew in force. When the song "Happy Together" started to play, Casey climbed onto the pier and conducted everyone in song, although they were no longer in sync with the Turtles.

As the last song from the ferry's mixtape ended, the drunk, water-logged swimmers began to climb out of the river. Dylan swam over to Rihanna and said, "Coming?"

"In a minute." Shriveled as she was, she was in no hurry to leave the water. Nights like this, with everything going well and everyone, including Rihanna, being happy, had become rare. She needed to bask in the moment.

Goldfish Graphics was busy again. Sal informed the hourly employees and freelancers that, while they could now expect regular paychecks, they would have to wait for any overtime pay until the end of the project. The payment for the free lancers' desks would be due the first day of the month; $100 cash would be distributed at that time. Meanwhile, the studio would now be hiring temps from the MacTemp agency to fill some of the freelance positions. Despite anyone's objections (mostly Allie's), the agency was told to send the first candidate this morning.

And there he was, sitting in Rihanna's office.

Bram Baxter Bennington arrived with his Ken-doll face and, wow, look at that suit. The agency must not have told him about the casual dress code. Rihanna tried not to make assumptions about him — like, he might think this place was beneath him or something, which it probably was — so, after she introduced herself, she led him to Allie.

"Nice to meet you, Bram," Allie said, and then to Rihanna. "Where's he sitting?"

"The desk on the other side of Mark."

"Really? That computer is too old for... Does it even have Photoshop on it?"

"Tech installed it last night."

"Hmmmm. Okay, Bram, you'll have to do your best. And I apologize in advance." And in an aside to Rihanna, she added, "Are we charging him for that desk?"

"No, he's from the temp agency," Rihanna said, then realized Allie was being flippant.

Twenty minutes later Bram was back in Rihanna's office.

"How do you expect me to work like this? That version of Photoshop doesn't even have layers. And there are no fonts, and... you know, never mind. Can you just sign my time-sheet?"

Turned out, this place *was* beneath him. As he stomped over to the elevators, Allie appeared in Rihanna's doorway.

"He's right, you know."

"I think I understood every other word of that. What does he mean, Photoshop doesn't have layers?"

"The newest version lets you layer pictures, so you can overlap and still move things around without affecting what's underneath. Like painting on an acetate overlay instead of right onto the canvas."

"Ah. Got it."

"That machine is too old for the latest version. That's a IIx. It's a beater. Good for word processing and not much else."

Rihanna sighed. "We're supposed to be getting new machines. I guess I better talk to Sal. Again."

"Sorry."

"Me too. Should we call Bram back when the machines get here?"

"Nah. He lasted twenty minutes. Gotta have a stronger stomach than that to work here."

Rihanna was able to leave the office before midnight, but it was likely if she hadn't, she wouldn't have made it home. The exhaustion was brutal tonight.

Dylan took one look at her and said, "Are you alright?"

She didn't feel alright. "Not sure."

"This job is killing you. Go lie down. I'll bring you some dinner."

This wave of fatigue did seem worse than usual. She pulled her shoes off and sat on the bed. Before she had a chance to change out of her clothes, she had slumped over, fast asleep.

Dylan came into the room moments later. Concerned, he checked to make sure she was breathing, and when he determined that she was, he pulled the covers up over her and turned out the light.

PART FOUR

BLUE: *Boogie Blues* (Gene Krupa, Ray Biondi)

— recorded by Gene Krupa and his orchestra,
released 1946

CHAPTER 13

THE WOLVES THAT RAISED HIM, PART 2: 1962

Judith Katz Sawicki went about her morning, cleaning the kitchen, collecting laundry, and pretending she was having a normal day in a normal household. Stanley had left for the hospital, and her three-year-old son, Izaak, was sitting in the living room, playing with a toy train. She had a large bruise on the side of her face from a disagreement she had had with Stanley that morning. She had been nagging him, and she kept at it several minutes past the time when she knew she should have stopped.

She was asking for it.

Putting the house back in order would calm her down, perhaps even make her hands stop shaking. Several glasses had broken when she slammed against the counter, and she had cleaned that up first. It was lucky she hadn't fallen; she was three months pregnant. She poured Ajax powder into the sink and let it sit while she went to the bedrooms to collect laundry. She crossed the living room several times, and each time Izaak called out "Mommy?" and she would say "In a minute, Izaak."

She returned to the laundry bag and was stuffing more clothes into it when Izaak appeared in the doorway.

"Really, Izaak, what do you want? Can't you see Mommy's busy?"

He almost said "Mommy?" again but stopped when he heard her tone and saw the annoyed look on her face.

"Don't stare at me," Judith barked. "It's just a bruise. It'll go away."

Izaak wasn't looking at the bruise. He just wanted to be in the same room as his mother.

Judith barked, "Stop... staring... at... me."

He cowered and hid his face against the wall, but he held his ground.

"Jesus, you're stubborn. Just like your father."

Judith lunged at him as a warning, and Izaak backed away, only to come around the side entrance of the kitchen and pull at her sleeve.

"Mommy?"

Izaak got Judith's backhand across his face. When he screamed, she hit him again. And again.

"Stop screaming!" She smacked him with her other hand, and he screamed louder.

"STOP SCREAMING!" (smack) "STOP IT!" (smack) "STOP IT!" (smack, smack)

Izaak's screams turned into quiet sobs, but the hitting didn't stop. He tried to run away, but she grabbed him with one hand and continued hitting with the other.

"SHUT UP SHUT UP SHUT UP!"

A few pleadings of "Mommy!" and then resigned silence, but when that didn't make it stop, Izaak began to bang his head against the floor.

Now in his own trance, Izaak continued to hammer his forehead onto the freshly polished floor until Judith gently pulled him upright and propped him up against the wall. She left the heaving child there, went into her bedroom and locked herself in until late afternoon when she emerged to start dinner.

AUGUST 1995

Pest's gig went late, but he was finally home. Allie would be working even later. He dialed her work number to see if she could talk.

"Hey. I'm checking on your stress level."

"Thank you. Let's see. I would say high to very high," she said. "I'm supposed to be training these guys to be better, but it's not working. They screw up, and I wind up redoing their work after they leave."

"You know, what you've got there is a shit sandwich."

Allie laughed.

"You thought you were ordering tuna fish, but that's not what ya got."

Allie sighed, and he thought he heard a sniffle.

"So, hey, you know I'll be gone for like a month, more like five weeks."

"Yeah. You're leaving Friday?"

"Right. Anyway, I'm not real big on mushy talk, but I'm going to really fuckin' miss you when I'm gone."

There was a long pause, and Pest was worried he had said something wrong. But then she said, "Well, I'm not big on mushy talk either, but I'm going to really fuckin' miss you, too."

Pest climbed into the back of the van and sat on the metal floor. Maybe he was being paranoid, but he couldn't afford to have anything screw up this tour. Satisfied there was no place to hide contraband there, he lay down and looked under the two front seats with his emergency flashlight. Yuck, what was that? A piece of an old hot dog, or... let's hope that was a hot dog. That's what he got for letting his kids eat in the van. There were a couple of maps and a shoe that must have been left there by the previous owner, since neither he nor his kids wore golf shoes. He tossed the petrified hot dog and the shoe from the van and climbed out.

"Okay, guys. Load her up."

Everything fit, and there was even room for the guys to get comfortable. The current rhythm section of the Cater-waulers crawled into the back of the van and laid out blankets to sleep on. It would be eight hours to the festival in North Carolina, the first stop on this tour.

Pest popped a tape into the stereo and set the volume on low to keep from waking the guys. It was a Charlie Parker tape Allie had made for him from his LP. It was great to have this to play on the road.

The ride was going without a hitch. Sleeping people are less trouble, for sure, and there hadn't been much traffic. At about the halfway point the guys groaned themselves awake and set up the folding chairs Pest had provided so they could sit.

Sniff... sniff...

"Fuck! Are you guys drinking? It's not even noon!"

He tried to turn around to look but swerved and went out of his lane. The resulting angry horns forced him to face front again.

"Holy shit, man, you crazy?" Max, the drummer, was holding onto his chair and possibly praying.

There was no place to pull over. Pest slammed his hands on the steering wheel a few times. In the rearview mirror he could see the bass player, Sean, stuffing something into one of the suitcases. Pest could either let the throbbing vein on the side of his neck burst, or he could get everyone to the gig.

The guys were sitting perfectly upright in their folding chairs. Yelling didn't stop these guys, but almost ramming into a neighboring truck worked quite nicely.

It seemed to Pest that every heavy-metal band that ever existed was at this festival, novices to legends. The Caterwaulers almost didn't make the cut; they were not just a heavy-metal band, after all, and they didn't have a cool name like Death Scorpions or Murder Patrol. He had to convince the festival they had enough songs on their set list to qualify. Pest was more adamant than ever that the Caterwaulers' set be exceptional. Max, Trevor, and Sean had played great at rehearsals in New York. It remained to be seen if they could continue to be great for these shows. When they got to the club, Pest went on ahead to check in, and the guys went to find a place to get some coffee and food.

Sean's version of coffee was 80 proof, and when he stumbled onto the stage for sound check sometime later, it was everything Pest could do to keep from tossing him off the edge. Sean carried his bass over to his mic and teetered in place.

"Max," Pest said. "Get Sean some coffee." Pest put a chair in front of his rubbery bass player.

"Sit the fuck down. You're making me seasick."

Pest was hoping Sean would be a bit more sober by the time they had to play for real, but exceptional was about to be a fleeting dream.

Pest had decided to start their set with something simple. Four chords, easy changes, straight 4/4, a song Pest could have taught his kids to play. Max and Trevor were doing great, but Sean was musically nodding off. Pest turned around and played at him until he was in sync again, but every time Pest faced front to sing, Sean would lag.

The applause was polite.

Pest tried to push past this unfortunate prelude. He hoped maybe no one would notice the lack of a recognizable bass line if he played loud enough, and sometimes Sean was following the beat. Just as Pest was thinking that maybe the set could be salvaged, Sean began playing in the wrong key.

Their 40-minute set lasted 20 minutes.

Backstage was packed with other musicians who were waiting for their cues. The Caterwaulers were off the stage for only a minute when Pest grabbed Sean by the scruff of the neck and plunged him face first into the wall.

"I should fucking kill you," he growled.

All sound in the room stopped. Without turning around, Pest let go of Sean's neck and quickly left.

Pest heard clapping and cheering behind him, and then he heard someone say, "He let you off easy. I'm not sure I would have let you keep your face."

All things considered, everyone survived the tour. There was that moment when Pest threatened to leave Sean by the side of the road, but otherwise most of their sets went well and the festival ended on a high note.

Pest was now standing in the 8th-floor hallway of an upscale building on the Upper East Side, trying to summon up the courage to press the apartment buzzer. It was one thing to be surrounded by people at gigs; there it was all about the music and the show. But he didn't know how to behave in a conventional social scene. And an engagement party – even an informal one on a Thursday night – you don't get much more conventional than that.

He could just imagine the people behind this door. His friend Derrick's fiancé owned the apartment, and inside there was sure to be young urban professionals wearing cashmere sweaters and $100 jeans, probably talking about finances and retirement funds and other things he knew nothing about, and most likely never would. Derrick had moved in about a year ago, and it changed him. He played fewer gigs, changed the way he dressed, cut his hair. Behind that door, all kinds of normalcy.

Pest wished Allie was there with him, instead of working. He hadn't seen her since he went on the road.

He took a breath and pressed the doorbell.

"Pest, you made it!" He couldn't remember this chick's name, even though Derrick had been with her for a couple of years. She was tiny, sporting blunt-cut, chin-length, blonde hair. She hugged him. She smelled like lavender.

"You can put your jacket in my bedroom, first door on the right," she said. "Derrick! Pest's here!"

He didn't like to leave his jacket unattended, but this was a yuppie affair, and no one here would want that raggedy old thing. He put his keys and wallet in his jeans pocket, just in case.

He wondered how long he could hide out in the bedroom before anybody noticed.

"Hi."

A young woman with a beautiful smile had come into the room to put her lipstick back in her handbag.

"Hi," he said.

"I'm Tracy."

Her pink fluffy sweater was a little tight and bless her heart, she was delightfully, delectably top heavy. He tried not to act too drooly.

"I'm Izaak, but people call me Pest."

There was that smile again. "Right, Janet mentioned you. You're Derrick's friend, right? Another musician?"

Janet. That was little blondie's name. "Yes, that's right." Not that Derrick was musicianing much these days.

"Well, what are you doing hiding in the coat room, Izaak? Come out and let's get a drink."

Tracy took his hand and led him to the drinks table, where Pest gallantly opened two beers, one for her and one for him.

"So, what do you do?" Pest knew about three or four

phrases of socializing language. That was one of them.

"I work for a bank. Assistant manager." She tossed her brunette, bowl-cut bangs out of her eyes. "I know, pretty dull."

Pest tried to keep his eyes off her sweater. "You're not dull."

"Ha! Yes, I am. I graduated early from college, took the first job I found out of grad school. I'm always the 'good girl.' Getting kind of tired of being so... *normal.*"

"Sometimes, I wish I were a little more normal."

"Why?"

Pest was surprised to find this hitting a nerve. Tracy saw his face and got that I-just-found-a-baby-rabbit expression girls get.

"Hey," she said, "you're not here with anybody, are you?"

She took a swig of her beer, and the sweater stretched nicely. The urge to touch was overwhelming.

"Uh, no, I'm not."

She put her arm around him. "Good."

He had her phone number. The question was, would he call?

Thing was, Allie really got him, and the chemistry between them was undeniable. But now there could be a chick who didn't know about his temper or his fucked-up past, a Beach-Boy's east-coast girl with a million-dollar smile and mouthwatering curves.

But could he hurt Allie like that? Maybe it was possible to see them both. Allie was working a lot, and she was cool about his going away on tour. Maybe she'd be cool with this.

No chick would be cool with this.

On the other hand, what would be the harm in calling Tracy? Invite her to the upcoming Irving Plaza gig. That was safe. She could come to the gig, and the place would be so crowded neither woman would know about the other. That would give him more time to figure out what he wanted to do.

He dug out her number and dialed.

CHAPTER 14

ALLIE, 1982

Allie wasn't so sure about that phone call, but she had said yes. Of course, she said yes. A ticket to the Pretenders?

"Are you sure you don't want the ticket?" Allie said.

Her friend Catt laughed. "A rock concert? Me?"

"Okay, true," Allie said. "But it's with Joe."

Now there was hesitation. "Joe and I aren't together anymore."

"What? What happened?"

A long, deep sigh.

"It just wasn't working out for me. He's all over the place, and I'm... not."

"All over the place, like..."

"Like not into me enough."

"Well, I'm sure it's not you, He may just not be interested in having a relationship right now."

"That kind of amounts to the same thing, doesn't it?"

The tickets were one level above the floor seats, a few rows back to the right of the stage. Allie hadn't seen this configuration of the band yet, a new line-up since the deaths of their lead guitarist and bassist. Chrissie Hynde was hobbling about the stage with a cast on her leg. It didn't affect the sound of the band.

After the show, Joe suggested they go for a drink. Allie

suggested Danceteria. They went to the third floor, where there was a lounge, sat at the bar, and talked about music. Two drinks in, Joe leaned over and kissed her.

Wow. Nice.

Allie was letting herself get swept up in the alcohol and the smooching, but there was this nagging, annoying thought that kept going through her mind:

What about Catt?

Despite Allie's irksome conscience, she stayed at Danceteria with Joe until they both were having trouble staying on their barstools. They staggered out of the club, into the warm, sticky, night air.

"So..." Joe said.

Allie wanted to kill herself for what she said next. "You know... not tonight. Okay?"

He looked a little surprised, but he smiled. "Sure. Okay."

"You know, next time."

"Cool. Okay."

When she got home, Allie threw herself onto her bed and pounded the mattress in frustration. What was wrong with her? She wanted to call him and tell him to come over and ravish her. Eventually the alcohol and the late hour forced her to sleep.

The phone woke her up around noon.

"Allie?"

"Catt... hi...."

"How'd it go last night?"

"It was fun. We wound up at Danceteria after the show."

There was a pause, then Catt said, approximating cheerfulness, "Did anything, you know, happen?"

This didn't feel any better to admit now than the night before. "He didn't come home with me, if that's what you mean. I told him no."

"Oh. Good." And there was a nervous laugh.

Wait a minute. "Good?"

Catt sighed. "I thought that if you two got together, then I'd finally get over him, you know, because I would have to, because he would be moving on. But then, I realized that that just would freak me out and make me upset, and I still wouldn't be over him."

"No. No, you wouldn't."

"Thanks, Allie."

Okay, so she had made the right call.

SEPTEMBER 1995

Monday morning, about three hours after Allie had come home and gone to sleep, her phone rang. Tuna had been trying to get her attention for over an hour but had given up and was now sleeping in a ball against her torso. Allie rolled over to get up, and the cat was gently tossed aside. Tuna stretched her back up into a high arch and jumped off the bed to follow her.

"Hey Allie. It's Pest. Did I wake you up?"

Allie looked towards the window with half-open eyes. It was pouring rain. There was no reason in the world to be awake yet.

"Yeah, but it's okay." She sat down at the kitchen table and propped herself up on her elbows. "How was the party? Are you home now?"

"Nah. I'm in Jersey at my ex's. And here comes Hanna. Hey there. You dressed yourself? Don't you look nice."

If Allie was remembering right, Hanna was about five.

"Do you want to say hello to Allie?"

Oh God don't put the kid on the phone.

"Say hello to Hanna."

There was a shuffling sound. Allie said, "Hello, Hanna" into the phone. Then there was silence.

What do you say to a five-year-old who isn't speaking?

"Hi Hanna," she tried again. Okay, she sucked with children.

The wind was blowing outside, and the apartment was dark and warm. Allie wished this conversation was happening later. Her eyes closed. She forced them open when she heard Pest's voice again.

"So, look, I have to tell you: I might not be the kind of guy you want."

Nothing will wake a person up faster than the "I'm not good for you" speech.

"What kind of guy is that?"

"I'm not going to be around very much. I'll be on the road a lot, especially now that the CD is out."

"I don't know if you've noticed, Pest, but I'm not exactly looking for a 24/7 kind of thing. No offense, but I'm perfectly happy when you go on the road."

"Well, you deserve more than I can give you."

"Maybe, but I'm not looking for more right now."

"Okay. Well, good. I just wanted to let you know that."

Allie's eyes were closing again, but then Pest spoke.

"But whatever happens, I hope we'll always be friends."

Friends? Crap. He did not just say that.

"Sure."

She was starting to feel alarmed, but then he said, "You're coming to Irving Plaza tomorrow, right?"

"Of course. Wouldn't miss it."

"Great. I'll see you there. I'm using my ex's phone, so I don't want to stay on the line too long."

"Okay. See you tomorrow."

She put down the phone. Tuna jumped onto the table, purring, and butted her head against Allie's cheek. Allie petted her and sighed.

"Okay, if I feed you, will you let me sleep?"

Sleep, Allie knew, was probably not going to happen now, anyway. Friends? This didn't bode well.

This was a big deal, this Irving Plaza gig. A converted ballroom, Irving Plaza had been hosting punk rock and New Wave acts since the late 70s. The Caterwaulers had never played a venue this large, or this well known.

Rihanna and Allie climbed the old ballroom's staircase and maneuvered into a spot where they could see the stage. There were hundreds of people there. Allie didn't know how she was going to find Pest, but then she felt someone tap her shoulder.

"Hey. You made it," Pest said.

He was looking good, clad in his best rock-and-roll finery. Allie threw her arms around his neck and expected his signature bear hug in return, but none was forthcoming.

"Of course, I made it. Wouldn't miss it for the —"

"Hi, Izaak."

A girl, much younger than Allie, sporting bangs, a big smile, and a skimpy, black dress with low cleavage. Pest turned completely around to talk to her, putting his back to Allie. When he was finished talking with her, he started to walk off.

"Pest..."

"Oh. Sorry." He kissed her on the forehead. (The forehead!) "I gotta get up on stage. Can I call you tomorrow? This gig's gonna go late, and then I gotta pack up my gear and stuff and —"

"Of course. Go."

He disappeared into the crowd.

"That was weird right?" Allie said.

"Yes, that was weird," Rihanna said.

"Should I be worried?"

"No." Rihanna was emphatic, but it did nothing to stop Allie's current surge of uneasiness. Rihanna stared at Allie a moment, and said, "Should I go get us drinks?"

"Yeah. Vodka soda. Thanks."

Allie looked around at the ever-growing crowd, then up at the three-storied ceilings and the balconies and was suddenly feeling oh-so insignificant.

"Hey there. Can I buy you a drink?"

A benign fellow in a brown jacket had entered Allie's personal space.

"No thanks. My friend is getting me one."

Pest and his band were taking the stage to loud applause. Allie was studying him for clues, or... something. He had been gone five weeks, and although now only some 20 feet in front of her, it felt like he was 100 miles away.

"Do you know this band?" Brown jacket guy was still there.

"Yes. The Caterwaulers. We're big fans."

The crowd was pushing towards the stage. Allie had to change her position to see more than just Pest's hair.

"I'm Phil, by the way."

"Allie."

Allie hoped he would not be trying to talk to her during Pest's set. The music started, and Phil leaned over and said, "I do music, too."

Dear God.

"Yeah, not professionally, though." He was now shouting in her ear. "But I write my own music and play guitar."

Allie was gazing intently at Pest, hoping Phil would take the hint.

Phil stood closer to Allie. "I write songs all the time. I just finished one this morning."

To Allie's horror, he started to sing in her ear. She took a step away from him, which made him stop.

"Sorry," he said, although in Allie's estimation, he clearly was not. "I guess you want to listen to the band."

"Well, yeah."

"What are you, in love with this guy or something?"

This was a particularly touchy subject at the moment.

"Have you ever even been on a date with him?" Phil said.

"What, a girl can't want to listen to a band just because she likes the music?"

"Well, she can, but I see the way you're looking at him."

"And this is your business how?"

"Bitch," he said and walked away.

"What's his problem?" Rihanna had returned.

"He was hitting on me. And he was being an ass."

"Did you tell him you're seeing Pest?"

Allie took her drink and slurped some of it down. "No. Hell, I don't even know if that's true anymore."

Pest did call Allie the next day, but it would be a full week before he made plans to see her. The Caterwaulers had been getting a lot of out-of-town gigs, but this week Pest was sitting in with a country band who was playing on her block. Did she want to meet him? He would call her that day and tell her the time.

Six o'clock rolled around the day of, and as Allie had not yet received a phone call, she started preparing for the possibility of being stood up. The world was not going to come to an end if she didn't see him, but somehow it was starting to feel that way. Allie was determined to shake off this hysteria. She lit some candles and filled the bathtub with hot water and bubble bath. She dipped into the warm soapy water and started to relax.

As she was stepping out, the phone rang. It was Pest, calling from the bar.

"We're going on about eight. You wanna come down?"

"In a bit. I just got out of the tub."

"Oh." There was a pause. "Are you still coming?"

"Of course. I just need to put some clothes on. I'll see you soon."

She hurried to get dressed.

The band was set up against one of the walls, where Allie remembered there had been booths at one time, back when the sign outside said, "The Center" and people from other parts of town referred it as "that Irish pub on St. Marks." Allie never could figure out back then why a dive filled with Puerto Rican Lesbian bikers, who had dubbed the place "El Centro," was considered Irish. Maybe because the heroin addict who owned the place had the last name McInerney. Also, there were pickled eggs behind the bar.

Allie climbed onto a bar stool and found she was not far from the band. They were a trio, playing mostly recognizable country tunes. Pest smiled broadly when he saw her, and she felt stupid for doubting him.

The drummer was dramatically balding straight through the middle of his tall, oval head. He was sitting above the others on a platform with his drums, and, though Allie wasn't sure, he seemed to be trying to make eye contact with her. She looked away for a moment, and when she looked back, he raised an eyebrow at her. She suppressed her laugh.

During the break, Pest got sodas for Allie and himself, and they sat together at the bar, his hand possessively on her thigh.

An old friend of his approached them.

"Hey, Cliff! How've you been?"

They reminisced about other days and other bands, and Allie was just about completely ignoring their conversation, when Cliff motioned to her and said, "This your wife?"

Pest caught the stunned look on Allie's face and smiled.

"Nah. Diane and I are divorced. This is Allie."

"She's your squeeze, though, right?"

Pest looked into her eyes. "Yeah. She's my squeeze."

"Your kids' mother, though, that was Diane?"

"Yep. Allie and I don't have any kids." He grinned at her. "Not yet."

Kids? Yet? Squeeze? Either Allie was getting the most

colossal mind fuck, or she had become completely paranoid.

Working over 100 hours a week can do that to a person.

In the distance Allie could hear the melodious tones of Sal, screaming at Rihanna. It usually went something like this:

"Why aren't we making the schedule? Aren't these people working? What are they doing all day? We pay them good money, damn it! We don't pay them to sit around!"

It was true that no one at Goldfish these days was working to capacity, no matter how many hours they were working. Allie was beginning to wonder how much longer she could work at this pace and for these hours. It was one thing to work crazy hours for a month or two, but this was the fifth month, with no end in sight.

"I think I may be hallucinating," Mark said.

"Oh?"

"My screen looks like it's wavering."

Allie looked over.

"That's because it is."

"Oh. Thank God."

"Mark, that can't be good."

Smoke started pouring out of the back of the display.

"Unplug it!"

Mark crawled under the desk and pulled the plug.

"I better go catch tech before they go."

Rihanna came into the production area.

"What's burning?" she said.

"Mark," Allie said. "His monitor."

Rihanna sat down.

"Allie, I don't think we're going to make it."

"God, if the client pulls the job, it'll almost be a relief. This is crazy-making."

"Don't say that, even in jest. They still need to finish paying us."

"Sorry," Allie said. "But seriously, if it weren't for all the overtime Goldfish owes me, I'd be out of here."

"I don't blame you. I think we're all in that boat."

Sal was striding down the corridor toward them. Rihanna and Allie normally would have jumped back into work mode, but instead they stayed in place on their chairs. Everyone else went tense and silent.

"Where's Mark?" he demanded.

"Tech," Allie said. "His monitor blew, and he needs a new one."

"And don't you have work to do? What are you doing?"

Allie looked him in the eye. "Discussing work with Rihanna."

"Oh," he muttered to himself. "Well." And he walked away.

"How does that go?" Allie said. "Something about his bark being worse than his bite?"

Rihanna laughed. "You didn't just sit in his office with him barking at you."

Allie had not seen Pest since their date two weeks earlier at The Center, or rather, The Cave, or whatever they were calling it now. She had talked to him, twice, but even so she was distraught. And depressed. Which was crazy, because he had a gig tonight, so she would be seeing him.

Soon.

Was this what it felt like to be codependent? It was ridiculous, her feeling like this. He had warned her he would be getting busy.

Allie almost didn't want to go. While part of her was looking forward to this show, another had an unwarranted feeling of dread.

Her door buzzer went off. She looked out of her window and saw a FedEx guy, holding a huge box. That was for her?

"Be right down!"

He wouldn't take the box up the stairs for her, so after she signed for it, she asked Scott to lend her one of his guys from the piercing shop to carry it up. Allie attacked the enormous package with a box cutter and just inside there was a card:

"Hope you enjoy your new 'toy.' Love, Nico."

She wanted to cry. It was a top-of-the-line Macintosh. She couldn't believe it. Nico knew nothing about Apple computers, so he probably just told the store he wanted the biggest and the best. She was shaking, she was so happy.

She picked up the phone.

"Nico. You got me a computer? That's just so great. Thank you so much!"

"You're welcome. I know you've been wanting to work at home more. Maybe you can start your own business."

"Wow. You really, really made my day. You don't know how much. Thank you."

And with a new attitude, she got prepared to go out.

Clubs in the City often sprang up in desolate areas. Wetlands was no exception. Situated in the non-neighborhood between Tribeca and Chinatown, it was close to the entrance to the Holland Tunnel and a ten-minute walk from the east-side subway. And if a person was wearing high heels, more like a 20-minute walk.

Plenty of time to become a complete nervous wreck.

What am I doing in this stupid outfit walking along a deserted Manhattan street?

It was, in fact, Canal Street, a well-lit, busy Manhattan street. The wind was blowing hard, and Allie shuddered in her fishnets.

I can't believe I'm wearing this stupid dress. Wetlands is a rock club full of bikers and hippies. People wear t-shirts and jeans.

The club came into view. She stopped and stared at the entrance.

"You're stalling," she said aloud. "Yes, I am. I am stalling."

She hesitated a minute more, but the cold weather won, and she crossed over to the club.

The place was packed. It was hard to get much past the entrance. She saw Pest and immediately relaxed, but then he walked right past her. She called out to him, and he turned around.

"Hi," he said, pleasantly. "Thanks for coming."

He shook her hand but walked on.

Thanks for coming?

Pest climbed up onto the stage and started his usual gig prep. Allie walked up to him. Without looking at her directly, he started telling her something mindless about the rehearsal they had had earlier in the day. When he was finished, he said, "Excuse me," and walked off, over to two women sitting in a booth against the wall. One, a blonde with a short blunt haircut. And the other...

... the girl from Irving Plaza.

Pest sat down across from her and held her hands.

Allie walked up to them.

"Pest?" she said.

He got up from the booth and took Allie aside. She tried to hug him, but he shook her off.

"What's the matter?" she said.

"Just don't be so obvious."

Suddenly Allie was feeling ill.

"You can hug me later. But I'm kind of on a date right now."

Allie was not quite sure she had heard him right.

"I'll see you later, okay?"

Allie backed away from him and pushed her way out of the club. She made it to the curb just in time to vomit in the street.

"Little early to be drinking so much!" a cheery passerby called out.

"Oh, shut the hell up," Allie muttered.

As fate would have it, it had been the mind fuck.

CHAPTER 15

NATIA, 1967

Natia was flying.

She was in her backyard on her swing set, not a thing to think about except how high she could go. She was singing a song, her voice high and sweet, and although her voice carried pleasantly to her parents in the kitchen, she felt it was hers to hear alone.

The chain holding her seat was buckling with the elevation, folding Natia's seat back so it seemed she was even higher. She giggled and kept trying to reach above the top of the swing set.

This time when the seat doubled back, it spun around itself, and Natia found herself hanging headfirst with her pinky finger pinched in the chain.

Her screams could be heard throughout the neighborhood.

Because she was no longer pumping her legs, the swing was starting to slow down, not that the shrieking Natia was aware of it. The back door of her house opened, and Natia could see her father's upside-down legs, running toward her to her rescue.

STILL SEPTEMBER 1995

It was a typical Saturday afternoon in Natia's dingy apartment on the Lower East Side. Inside, the studio curtain was open, and funk music was playing on Danny's recording equipment. In the hallway, neighbors were screaming at each other in rapid-fire Spanish, and the voices of out-of-control children rained down from an apartment above.

What wasn't typical was Natia's despondent friend, Allie, sitting on the floor against the wall, hugging her knees.

"Should I make popcorn?" Natia asked.

Allie didn't look up, but Danny gave her an enthusiastic nod.

"Popcorn it is," Natia said. This was something she and Danny had been eating a lot of lately. "I'm sure there's a movie on. Should I look at the schedule?"

Natia flipped through the Daily News until she found the TV page. Saturday afternoon could usually be counted on for movies.

"Hey. *West Side Story* is starting in 15 minutes. Danny's favorite."

Allie looked up from her cloud of gloom and said, "Sounds great."

Natia put the bowl of popcorn and the beers Allie had brought on the milk crate that was serving as their coffee table and sat on the floor across from Allie.

"So, this girl," Natia said. "Do you know who she is?"

"No idea," Allie said, "She's like, twelve, and has stupid rosy cheeks and porcelain skin, and this big, innocent, glow-in-the-dark smile that makes me want to smack her."

"And have you talked to Pest?"

"He called me this morning and broke up with me using that stupid 'I can't give you what you want' line."

"Well, he can't give you what you want," Natia said. "You want him to not be a complete jerk, and he is one."

Allie couldn't help laughing, momentarily interrupting her rant.

"No, it's bullshit. He just wanted a fresh... uh..."

"... face," Natia said.

"Yeah, we'll go with that." Allie thought a moment. "Everything changed when he came back from the tour. It was right in front of my face, and I didn't want to believe it."

Danny and Natia looked at her with sympathy. Allie sighed. "Turn on the TV. Let's not talk about that Jerkface anymore."

"You're gonna get to hear Danny sing along to 'I Feel Pretty,'" Natia said.

"Can't wait."

The Macintosh SE was a workhorse, the most popular of the Apple computers in its day. It had a shell the size and shape of the original Macintosh, with the same 9" monitor, but it had an internal hard drive. This one had belonged to Allie, and it was a suped-up Chevy: an upgraded processor, a whole 16 MB of RAM, and it was running System 6.o8. Allie had installed one of those add-on cooler systems as well, which was probably why this little guy was still cranking after seven years and not being used as a nightlight.

But now it was being retired.

"I feel terrible," Natia said. Danny began to disconnect its life-support. He unplugged the computer from the midi keyboard, from the DAT machine, and, finally, from the surge protector.

"You're gonna use it," he said. "You said you can do word processing and spread sheets and stuff on it."

"You need to get me Excel so I can learn it."

"I'll hunt down a copy for you. I'm sure someone has it."

"Maybe Allie knows someone. I'll give her a call, too."

The computer was moved to Natia's milkcrate nightstand. Danny took its replacement, a Mac IIci, also from Allie, out of its box, and set it on the milkcrate table. This computer's footprint took up most of the area on the board they were using for a tabletop, so Danny put the DAT on another milkcrate, next to the printer.

Their door buzzer went off.

"Are we expecting anybody?" Natia went to answer the door...

...and found her mother standing there. She wasn't smiling, but there was pleasantness. Warmth, even.

"Would you like to join me for lunch?" her mother said, as if it was the most normal thing in the world.

"Let me just grab a coat."

Her mother stood just inside the doorway. After a moment, she turned to Danny and said, "What is it you do, again?"

"Recording engineer."

"My husband is an engineer. That is not what you do."

Natia returned from the closet. Her mother looked her over, saw that she was wearing Danny's trench coat. Whatever she might have been thinking, she chose not to share it.

"Ready?" she said.

No one with a correctly working brain and a decent amount of spending money would have tried to have a civilized meal in Natia's neighborhood. With very few words, mother and daughter walked down the stairs, over to Houston Street, and hailed a cab.

"My hotel is in midtown. I thought we'd eat there. I made a reservation."

The midtown hotel was the Algonquin, and the reservation was at the Round Table Restaurant. Natia's knowledge of this hotel's history was negligible, only that it had one and that the name had some literary significance. They were greeted by a uniformed doorman, and just inside the main entrance, a fluffy, ragdoll cat, relaxing on a swank, cat-sized lounger. The cat looked up at them, expecting attention, and of course, she got it.

It was not until her mother ordered for both of them that Natia found her voice. "So, why are you in New York?"

"I'm here for a legal conference. I'll be here until Monday. I thought you and I could spend some time together."

Persona non grata for almost a year, and then *presto*: Natia had been pardoned.

Natia saw more of the City that weekend than she had in her entire 12 years there. On Saturday, her mother took her to the Met Museum, then Serendipity for some lunch and frozen hot chocolate, and then they went to a Broadway show. On Sunday they went to the Intrepid Museum, down to the World Trade Center, and then on to China Town. They were both acting like tourists, taking pictures, standing in the middle of sidewalks, staring up at the tall buildings, laughing and pointing. This was the best vacation Natia had had — actually, the only vacation she had had — in years.

They had one more lunch together on Monday before her mother would have to leave for the airport. They stopped in the lobby of Liberty Insurance to say their goodbyes.

"So..." Natia said. She was wistful, but happy. "I guess I'll talk to you soon?"

Her mother smiled and took Natia's hands. "Why don't you think about coming home next week, Nati?"

"That... that would be great."

"Good. We'll sit down and make plans for your future."

Wait a minute. "What?"

"You've had a few years in New York, and I'm sure it has been fun, but now it's time to come home."

"I am home. New York is my home."

Her mother pressed Natia's hands tighter. "Nati, take this opportunity to get out of a bad situation."

Natia pulled her hands away.

"Danny is not a situation. And I'm not going to leave him. I love him. He's everything to me. I have never met a kinder, more thoughtful, more wonderful man."

Her mother's face hardened and cracked.

"Well," she said, "then you have made your choice. You have chosen that man over your family. Do not call, do not contact any of us. I know how close you are to your father, but if he should die, I will instruct everyone not to tell you. You will never know, and you will never hear from us again."

And with that, she exited, taking all the air in the lobby with her.

Steam was emanating from a manhole cover, and people on the street deftly avoided it as if it was something toxic and not just heated water. A street vendor was grilling something that might have been chicken, and the candied cashews from other vendors smelled smoky and sweet. Natia was walking down the sidewalk of that very same street, but the only thing she noticed was the dark cloud hovering over her. And any minute, a storm might erupt on her head.

Allie had been hard to get a hold of that morning, but Natia had finally reached her, and she agreed to meet for coffee. When Allie exited the elevator at Goldfish, the two friends looked at each other and, without a word, walked the handful of blocks to the coffee shop, Florent.

Tucked away on the tiny, cobblestone Gansevoort Street, not far from the river, Florent was a hip bistro in what used to be an old-school, metal, New-York-City diner. It had a simple green awning and an understated neon sign in the window, but inside it would see a huge variety of characters all throughout the day and night. The friends pushed through the hanging plastic strips that kept the outside air from getting in and sat at the counter at their usual spot. Rita, the flamboyant transvestite who worked the counter most afternoons, greeted them.

"My word, honeys, you two are looking weary today."

"We're defeated," Allie said. "Two coffees, please."

"You need more than that, love. How about some lunch?"

They shook their heads.

"Lava cake?"

That seemed like the best idea in the world.

"One piece. Two forks."

"Be right back."

Allie turned to Natia. "Don't worry. I'll cover the cake. Goldfish has been paying us regularly now, just not paying our overtime yet. At the end of this madness, I'm going to be seriously flush. I'll be able to pay off the credit cards I was living on."

A half dozen meatpackers entered the restaurant, still wearing their harshly worn work aprons. They took over one of the back tables and, after a signal from Rita, were immediately greeted by a waiter delivering water and menus.

"So, your mom..." Allie started.

"Yeah. The best and the worst weekend ever."

"Do you think — and I might be out of line here — that it was your mother's plan from the get-go? To convince you to come home?"

"Oh, yeah. This was all planned out from the start."

"Amazing. She really played you."

Natia sighed. "Yes. She did."

The lava cake arrived, and for a moment there was nothing to say, the melting chocolate center was just that decadent. Posted on the board with removable letters, under the list of specials, were local upcoming films. Natia saw that The Film Forum was having a Garbo festival, but she knew she wouldn't be getting to see any of it. At the end of the list it said, "Today's Weather: It's getting cold, folks!"

DON'T POKE THE BEAR

The lava cake gone, Allie and Natia sat in a stupor, sipped coffee, and watched Rita talking trash with the meat guys. Neither friend was in any hurry to go on to the next thing.

CHAPTER 16

RIHANNA, 1984

She wasn't thinking about how she got herself into this. All she could think about right now was how she was going to get out of it. Robert was passed out on the couch. She had to finish packing quickly.

She had packed a backpack and a suitcase. Anything else she needed? Anything she couldn't live without?

Her paintings, but they were too big to take. She had the original sketches.

Take the address book and the letters.

She found her address book on the shelf near the phone. Her boxes of old letters were at the top of her closet and... oh yeah, photographs. She'd want those.

Another sweep of the house. Anything she was forgetting? Anything?

Robert, still in a deep nod on the couch, moved slightly and grunted, "Rihanna?"

She ran upstairs and put the rest of the things in her suitcase.

"Rihanna?"

"Oh, God," she said. "Oh God, oh God."

A rope ladder, one of those ones that attaches to the windowsill in case of a fire. Rihanna threw her bags to the ground and hustled down after them. Lifesaver, indeed.

OCTOBER 1995

The doctor's office was in a run-down, pre-war building. There were four folding chairs in the waiting area, and two receptionists' desks side by side near the entrance. Floor to ceiling metal file cabinets lined the walls. This doctor's practice had outgrown its office a long time ago.

Rihanna followed the nurse out of the waiting area and into the tiny exam room. Dr. Walker was a kindly old man, the sort who would have been the subject of a Norman Rockwell painting back in the day — white hair, reading glasses, tall, slightly hunched.

"How can I help you today?"

"Well, I'm tired all of the time."

"Why are you tired?"

This question surprised Rihanna. "Not just tired. Lethargic."

"Lethargic?"

She was starting to feel stupid. "Exhausted. Lethargic. Tired. Whatever it is, I don't have any energy."

"And why do you think that is?"

"I don't know," she said. "I do work a lot of long hours. Overnight shifts, that kind of thing."

He wrote something down, then looked up at her, doing the classic doctor-takes-off-his-glasses-to-get-serious move.

"Well, I don't think there's anything to worry about," he said. Rihanna was wondering if she should mention that this had been going on for months, but then he added, "I do think you need to stop working so much."

No kidding.

"We'll run some tests. You could be anemic. Don't worry. We'll figure it out."

Rihanna sighed. She hardly had the energy to worry.

When Rihanna got home, Dylan greeted her with. "Call your sister."

"What's up?"

"You mother's boyfriend's wife died."

This sentence took Rihanna a moment to understand.

"Holy crap. Where's my mom?"

"I guess she's with Tom making arrangements. Call your sister."

Death has a funny way of uncovering secrets. After years of judgment, and curiosity, not to mention resentment, the sisters finally knew the truth: Tom's wife was schizophrenic and had been in a facility for decades. Tom didn't have the heart to divorce her, and the sisters' mother didn't feel the necessity to force the issue.

"Now there's going to be a wedding," Jill said. "Ready to call Tom 'Daddy'?"

"No."

"I guess we have to like him now."

"I guess so. Who knew he was being honorable?"

Because Rihanna was living down on the pier, it was convenient to have her drop off packages at the FedEx office on Leroy Street whenever the Goldfish staff missed the seven-p.m. pickup, which, these days, was most of the time. Since the client was in New Jersey, Goldfish could use the ten-p.m., Northeast-Corridor deadline. Unfortunately, some days they didn't even make that, but when they could, Rihanna would strap the boxes to her bicycle and run them down to FedEx on her way home.

Production had been falling behind. Sal refused to let the agency temps work overtime, so the regular freelancers, who they would pay later, were working most of the late hours. Rihanna couldn't understand why Goldfish had so little money when they had all this work. The client must still not have been paying on time.

All Rihanna had left to do this evening was wait for the FedEx parcel. The color printer had started to print everything a pale shade of magenta, and Rihanna sent one of the proofreaders to the storage room to find a black toner cartridge. Two of the production freelancers' machines wouldn't stop crashing, and it being after the tech department had gone home, Allie and Mark stopped what they were doing to try to fix them. Rihanna was pretty much resigned to the fact that nothing would be going out tonight, but sending something, anything, was better than nothing. And so, she waited.

At nine forty-two, Rihanna was en route to FedEx. When she got there, there was a large man in a FedEx uniform on the other side of the door who wouldn't let her in.

"It's not ten o'clock yet!" she yelled through the door. Other agitated people were arriving behind her, carrying armfuls of packages.

"We close at quarter to," the man said.

"Since when?"

"Since today."

While the other frustrated couriers began yelling at the man, Rihanna felt a sudden, urgent, back pain, not like anything she had felt before. She walked away from the mayhem, and when she could stand upright, got on her bike, and carefully rode home.

A few weeks later Rihanna was back in Dr. Walker's office. The nurse showed her right into the doctor's main office, not the exam room, and had her sit in the big leather chair that was positioned opposite the doctor's desk. Rihanna was sure there wouldn't be any good news if they had her waiting in the big chair.

Dr. Walker entered the office, and before he sat down, he said, "I'm sorry to tell you this, but it appears you have hepatitis C."

"What? I mean, how? I don't eat shellfish."

Her doctor put on one of those looks people use when they are about to tell a child there is no Santa Claus. For one horrible moment she thought he might pat her on the head.

"It's not that kind of hepatitis," he said. "You can only get this through blood contact."

Blood contact?

"Have you ever had a blood transfusion?"

She shook her head. Had Dylan's philandering caught up with her?

"Okay, I have to ask you this," Dr. Walker said, "Do you... your boyfriend... any friends... use intravenous drugs?"

"No, of course not."

Except... Damn him.

"My ex. But I haven't seen him in years."

The doctor frowned.

"You probably contracted this a while ago. It can take years to show symptoms. Ever share needles with him?"

"No! I didn't... I wasn't —"

"Toothbrush? Nail clipper? Razor?"

"Razor? Really?"

"You should have your current gentleman friend tested, just in case, but chances are..."

"... I got this from my ex."

Next came a blur of words like chronic, biopsy, interferon, platelets, fatigue, nausea — nothing that seemed to be combining to create a coherent sentence. She let her kindly old doctor prattle on with his list of words, but her head was somewhere else. She was picturing having to explain this to

Dylan, having to explain Robert to Dylan. Dylan would want to kill him.

Rihanna loved that about him.

The doctor had stopped talking and was looking at her.

"I'm sorry," she said. "Say that again?"

"I said, I'd like to schedule a biopsy."

"A what? Yeah, okay."

She chose not to think about what that was going to entail. After another list, this one clearer, including no alcohol, less stress, and more sleep, Rihanna made an appointment with the woman at the desk and got out of there.

She would have to tell Dylan, but maybe not right when she got home. She needed a minute. Okay, an hour.

Maybe a day.

At least she knew what was wrong with her now. She got on her bike, rode across to West Street, and shot down to the pier. Dylan would hang up her bike for her when he got home, so she left it propped up by the door. She collapsed on the bed and fell immediately to sleep.

She awoke to voices and loud music. Shouting, laughing, thumping, high-pitched squeals, sounded like it was coming from the top deck. Dare she go investigate?

She contemplated rolling over and pretending it was a dream, maybe go back to sleep and wake up after it was over.

Instead, she got up and headed upstairs.

Dylan, Casey, and John were drinking beers with two young ladies, one sitting in John's lap, and the other leaning on Dylan. Beer cans were scattered all over, and no one noticed Rihanna until she burst into tears. And she couldn't stop. She was sobbing and sobbing, and the next thing she knew Dylan was holding her. She barely noticed when the little fruit pops hurried down the ladder, with a mortified John and Casey following closely behind.

"Rihanna, honey, what's wrong? Those girls were just friends of John's. Nothing was going on."

"You don't understand," she sobbed.

"Yes, I do..."

"No. No. I just found out I have Hep C."

"Hep C?"

"Yes, Dylan," she snapped. "I probably can't give it to you, so relax."

"That's not —" Dylan started and shook off his irritation. Yes, that was unkind and unfair, and not at all the way she had planned on telling him.

"Listen," he said, "are you okay?"

"No, I'm not okay," she said, and was startled by how distraught she sounded. "I'm scared. And I'm exhausted. And I don't know what to do."

He held her tighter and said, "We'll figure it out. Don't worry."

PART FIVE

OLD: *Bitter Bad* (Melanie Safka)

— recorded by Melanie, released 1973

CHAPTER 17

ALLIE, NOVEMBER 1995

Allie was hitting the anger stage of the mourning process. It was time to purge her apartment of anything that had to do with Pest. There were reviews of his CD from the Voice and the New York Press she had been saving, which she now tossed, as well as an interview in an independent music magazine and some old fliers she was saving because they amused her. She stopped short of discarding a t-shirt, some tapes, and the CD. There could be a day she might regret not having those.

After removing his memory as best she could, she decided to find solace in her record collection. There was no question what the theme of this mix tape would be. When she had a pile of vinyl and CDs selected, she started her official Angry Tape.

This project kept her absorbed throughout the evening, and when it was done, she lay on her bed and played the whole thing through from the beginning.

Everyone who has ever been wronged, or severely misunderstood, by anyone, be it by a lover, a boss, a sibling, or a best friend, eventually writes The Letter. The Letter can include all the things that could not be said, should never be said, really should have been said, and, in the composer's modest opinion, now need to be said. Often The Letter never gets put on paper, but instead remains in a constant state of being composed and never finalized, a perpetual repeating tape loop in the author's head that drives the person crazy with words that come to no resolution. It is general wisdom that, while the physical act of writing The Letter can be very therapeutic, actually sending The Letter is likely one of the stupidest things a person can do.

It was late when Allie finished her final draft, and without doing more than pushing her writing materials to the other side of the bed, she turned off the lights to get some much-needed sleep. It wasn't that long ago that thinking about Pest at night would be a nice cozy place to leave her mind. Now it jolted her awake every hour, invaded her dreams, and distracted her every waking moment as well.

The next day, to ensure that there would be no possibility of ever hearing from Pest again, which Allie had convinced herself would be for her own good, she mailed The Letter.

"I've got this friend..."

Conversations that started like this were always suspect.

"Rihanna, are you trying to fix me up?"

"Well, yeah."

Allie thought about this a minute. "Okay. What's the deal?"

"My friend has a friend. He's a nice guy and single and looking for a girlfriend."

Allie was not fond of blind dates. She preferred to get to know a guy in his natural habitat.

"What's the catch?"

"Maya says he's short."

"Jim was short. I can do short. As long as he's not shorter than I am."

"No living adult in these United States is shorter than you are."

"Thank you. Okay, sure. What the hell?"

Her buzzer went off exactly at eight o'clock. Graham was standing at the bottom of the stoop. He had sandy, curly hair, hazel eyes, the physique of a 12-year-old boy and was wearing a sweater that looked like something his mother might have bought him back when he actually was 12. And he was short.

Much-shorter-than-Allie short.

It was a typical Saturday night in the East Village, and St. Marks Place was its usual swarming, raging mess. There were no longer clusters of rogue street vendors on 2nd Avenue — hadn't been since Giuiliani became mayor. Lately there didn't seem to be any homeless people, either. Allie wondered where they all went.

Seventh Street brought her quite a shock: The Kiev Restaurant was shuttered. Graham waited patiently while Allie inspected the for-rent signs on what used to be the front door, and then they moved on.

They were headed to a sushi restaurant on East 4th Street, Allie thinking that a side street might be more immune to crowds. She was right; there was only a short wait to be seated.

The food was good, and Graham was sweet and eager. They talked her days at college and what she majored in, how many siblings she had, and what was her favorite food, things Allie had no interest in.

She couldn't wait to get the check.

They walked back to Allie's building after dinner, and Allie was happy to see that Graham was shy, for he did not try to make physical contact with her on the way back. She did let him give her a quick kiss when they got to her stoop, and then she jogged up her stairs.

Rihanna did not understand Allie's misgivings when they talked the next day.

"So, he's a little short."

"A little short? Rihanna, he's an adult male who is not even my height."

"But he was nice, right?"

"Yeah, but it was like kissing one of my brothers."

"I think you could give the guy a chance."

Allie sighed. "It's not like I'm a teenager and this is my first date. I'm 36. I can tell if a guy will do it for me. And this guy will not do it for me."

"Maybe it's too soon."

Allie considered this. "And it's too soon."

That last night Allie saw Pest, as she was rushing away from Wetlands after getting sick on the sidewalk, she ran into one of Pest's friends, Kurt Whelan. They talked for a moment, and he asked for her number. Furious as she was at Pest, she gave it to him.

Kurt eventually called, and they made a date to meet at a Mexican restaurant on the Upper West Side. Allie ate half of her enchiladas, and drank half of her margarita, while Kurt talked about his new apartment in the City, bands and music, and where his new band, which Allie had never heard of, might be going.

"Do you want to stop by and hear some of my stuff?"

Allie knew this was the musician's equivalent of "Want to see my etchings?" but she agreed and followed him to his place around the corner.

The apartment looked like a storage room. Kurt had to move boxes out of the way for them to enter. Allie took a corner of the sofa, and Kurt went to work looking for his tapes.

There were two guitars in the corner, and a long table standing on end. Allie wasn't sure how it was going to fit when it was standing upright. A table lamp was on the floor beside the freestanding closet Kurt was rummaging through, and it occurred to Allie that there was no kitchen, and maybe even no bathroom.

"You know," Kurt said. "I've known Pest a long time. I've played in several bands with him."

Okay, that was out of the blue.

"He acts crazier than he really is, you know."

Wait... what?

"I think he just likes the attention. Especially from women."

Allie pondered this statement. What kind of friend was this Kurt?

"You know what? I suddenly realized I've got to go."

"But I haven't played you the tapes yet," she heard him call after her.

Still too soon.

Allie met Norman Kessler one night at the Rodeo Bar, where she and some of her friends had gone one night to see a non-Pest band play. He seemed smart and reminded her a little bit of Jim because of his Queens accent. When he asked her out, although she wasn't too sure about it, she accepted.

It would be Good For Her.

He had chosen seven o'clock to meet for dinner, which said to Allie that he would have a plan for later. She had picked the restaurant, one of her favorite Italian places on Avenue A, and they shared some red wine and pasta and tried to have a conversation.

Norman was a furniture salesman. He had a store in Queens on Woodhaven Boulevard and had lived in Astoria his whole life. Allie smiled and nodded and was hoping that they would be going to a movie or something later, which would give them something more interesting to talk about. One thing that both Jim and Pest had in common: neither of them was ever at a loss for words.

"What do you want to do now?" Norman said as they left the restaurant.

He had no plan.

"I dunno. Do you want to catch a movie?"

Norman put his arm around her waist. "I think I'd like to just walk around the Village."

They walked, they didn't talk, and every so often Norman would stop and kiss her. He wasn't a bad kisser, and Allie was trying her best to find some chemistry there.

Furniture salesman? Could she imagine herself hanging around his shop on Woodhaven Boulevard? She pictured a store with cheap paneling, worn linoleum floors, and big glass windows looking out on a wide street full of traffic. A woman with big hair and too much makeup would be answering the phones, and an older woman, maybe his mother, would be in the office, typing up inventory. Maybe he had a couple of guys he'd known all his life from the neighborhood working as salesmen for him, swayback guys with receding hair, wearing polyester. The furniture would be big and gaudy, something from another era, maybe the 50s, furniture you buy because it looks fancy, and you think you are getting a great deal. He would close shop as the sun was going down, and head back to his place in Astoria to eat a burger, drink beer and watch sports.

Nothing triggered depression in Allie faster than boredom, and the more they walked, the more Norman was becoming dead weight. Allie could feel herself falling into a pool of deep despair. She made excuses and ended their date early.

Allie had been telling herself that yearning for Pest was a luxury. If she were living in a war-torn country, she would have a lot of real things to be sad about. If she were starving, if she were oppressed, if friends were dying, if she were dying, if any of these things was happening, it would make sense to be overpoweringly sad, irate, forlorn, lovesick, depressed, anxious, or whatever it was that she was. But now that she was home alone, not having to be a certain way to the world, it occurred to her that she was in fact, at times, any one or all those things.

She went to her stereo, took out the Smashing Pumpkins' *Mellon Collie and the Infinite Sadness,* and popped the two-CD set into the player. She threw herself onto her bed, and soon, she was sobbing. She had skipped over the bargaining stage of grief and jumped over to depression. It didn't feel good.

Back at Goldfish, the usual clamor of voices was gone. The client had pulled the remaining catalogs, and the studio was suddenly down to a minimum number of freelancers. Allie picked up a work folder from the pile of three and noticed there was a white folded piece of paper between folders one and two. She unfolded it to see where it belonged, and gasped.

Mark looked over. "What's the matter?"

She was already on her way down the hall to Sal's office.

"Yes, Allie?"

She placed the paper on his desk. "I'm a chump."

"INVOICE: Aaron Reyes. For computer services. 40 hours at $35/hour. Amount due: $1400."

This was $15 an hour more than Allie was making.

"Where did you get that?"

"It was stuck between the work folders. You've been paying the other freelancers $35 an hour?"

"Well, only Aaron, because that's what he said he'd work for. We needed people."

"I've been waiting for a stupid $2-an-hour raise for two years. Supposedly, you guys couldn't afford it."

"Aaron was only hired for the crunch. He was pretty good, wasn't he?"

"Not the point."

Allie glared into Sal's stupid face and thought about all that time she had put in working for these clowns to the detriment of other things in her life, all the times she worked at home for them when she was sick so they wouldn't miss their deadlines, all that overtime money she'd probably never see, not to mention the years of loyalty, always giving them priority over other potential clients. It occurred to her that, if she had been in a coma these last six months, her life might be in better shape than it was right now.

"I should sue your sorry ass."

Sal shrugged. "Do what you have to do."

"I'm outta here."

She made a dramatic exit out of Sal's office, out to her desk, and began packing up her things.

"What's going on?" Mark asked.

"I just quit," Allie said.

"What? Why?"

"I have to go home before I kill Sal."

As a way of explanation, Allie handed him Aaron's invoice.

A jobless and single Allie entered Tompkins Square Park. It was late afternoon, and there were people all around, but she walked through to her spot in front of the damaged willow tree and took a seat on an empty bench.

A few feet in front of her, some kids were playing tag. They were so free. Theoretically, she was also free now. No job, no boyfriend; can't get much freer than that.

How did that go? "You are free, and that is why you are lost." Allie let out a bitter laugh and acknowledged that reciting a line from Kafka to herself was not exactly the best way to find consolation.

As far as work went, she wasn't too worried. She had a Rolodex full of potential employers and a brand-new state-of-the-art computer, courtesy of Nico. She would be working soon. She would never see that overtime money Goldfish owed her, which meant she couldn't pay off her credit cards, but she would find work.

She twirled her now-long hair and thought about how much Jim liked it short. With Jim, she never once considered he might leave her for someone else. As frustrated as she sometimes got, she always felt secure. She used to feel that way with Pest, too, in the beginning. He used to make her feel like she was the most important person in the world. Until she wasn't anymore.

The kids' parents were corralling them to get ready to go home. Freedom, it seemed, was a temporary thing.

Jake Ledford was on a motorcycle heading down Highway One in Big Sur and missed a curve. Could have been a moonless night. Could have been foggy. Could have been raining. He could have been drinking or driving too fast. Or he could have just looked the wrong way at the wrong moment.

Allie was sitting at her kitchen table with the Village Voice open to the music events section. And there it was, a notice for a memorial concert for Jake. She had only met Jake that one time at Night Crawlers, but she was mournful. Then, in a selfish moment, she couldn't help thinking that, not that long ago, she would be the one comforting Pest.

She picked up the phone. To her great relief, she got Pest's answering machine. She left her condolences in a short, simple message.

CHAPTER 18

NATIA, STILL NOVEMBER 1995

The tiny elevator was stopped on the 16th Floor. Several anxious business types, which in this case included Natia, camouflaged as one of them, were in the lobby, waiting for the little indicator lights of the floor numbers to start moving again. By Natia's estimation, it would take several trips to get everyone up to their floors, and more people kept arriving.

"Hey, Kid."

Mona had joined the group of cranky colleagues in the busy lobby. As usual, she was impeccably dressed: a nice business suit, accented with a remarkable brushed-silver necklace and matching earrings.

"Hi, Mona."

"Listen, stop by my office when you get a chance. I want to run something by you."

"Sure. Assuming we ever get upstairs."

"Now, now. You've got to think positively."

"Mona, I haven't had a positive thought in about six months."

The elevator car finally began to descend. Mona pushed Natia forward and, with some maneuvering, got them into the car first.

"Can't wait down here all day," Mona said. "Crazy, it'll make you."

The doors were closing, and Natia saw Mr. Griffin break through the crowd. Mona waved, and the doors closed in his face.

Natia's phone was ringing when they got upstairs, and she picked up.

"Liberty Insurance."

"Talk to me," Danny said.

"No," she said and hung up. They had had yet another argument this morning about money, and Natia wasn't ready to end it.

Mona raised her eyebrows. "Someone you know?"

"Well, yes." The phone rang again.

Natia picked it up, listened a second before she said hello, and put it down again.

"Everything okay?"

The phone rang again.

"Yes." She picked it up and put it right back down.

The phone rang again.

"Want me to get that?"

"Sure."

Mona picked up the phone. "Liberty Insurance. Hmmm. Funny, they hung up."

Natia laughed.

"Okay, Kid, stop by later when you take a break."

"If I take a break."

"Take one. I'm fifteen feet away from you."

It was late afternoon before Natia got to Mona's office.

"Hey. You made it."

Mona closed the door behind her.

"Listen," she said. "They're going to be forming a Group Life Department. Interested in working over there?"

"Sure. Is Mr. Griffin...?"

"Staying where he is. You'll be doing more than typing, though. Are you any good with numbers?"

A sore point this morning. "Actually, yes."

"Good. I'll see what I can do. Oh, it would be staff. Still interested?"

"Really? Staff? Yes, absolutely." Natia couldn't decide if she was more excited or relieved.

Mona opened the door.

"I'll have Larry call you."

"Oh boy. Oh boy oh boy oh boy." It wasn't a song, but Natia was singing it, anyway. She hurried up the steps to her apartment.

"What's got into you?" Danny said. "By the way, I'm still mad."

"Oh boy. Oh boy. No, you're not, and neither am I."

"I'm not?"

Natia jumped up and down and said, "I might be getting transferred. More money. Benefits."

"You're kidding."

Natia knocked on the wooden chair, then on her head. "This guy Larry's heading a new department and needs an assistant. And it looks like he might want me."

"So, you'll be getting his coffee?"

"Funny. No. I'll be doing like spreadsheets and other insurance stuff. Not sure yet. They'll train me." Natia jumped up and down again. "So, are you still mad?"

Danny smiled.

"Nope. You're right. I'm not."

"Now we just have to survive the next couple of months."

CHAPTER 19

RIHANNA, DECEMBER 1995

When Rihanna woke, she knew something was more wrong than usual. Her whole right, lower back was swollen and achy. There was no way she could bike to work with this amount of pain. Maybe when this enormous batch of catalogs was done, and her job stopped trying to kill her, she could ride again. For now, she'd have to walk over to Canal Street and take the train.

She was almost afraid to go in. No matter how many hours people were working, Goldfish was not making its deadlines. To save time, the client was coming to look over pages the next day, and as of last night, not even half of what was due was ready.

Rihanna had hoped the overnight shift would do some catching up, but when she got to the office, desks had been pushed aside and the computers were unplugged. The printers were against another wall, also unplugged, and detached from the computers. The proofreaders and computer operators were busy trying to move everything back and get it reattached.

"Guys?" Rihanna said.

"They polished the floors," Mark said. "Sal wanted the place to look nice for the client."

"Crap," Rihanna said. "How long have the machines been down?"

y told us to stop working and go home around one
ock."

Rihanna was feeling weak. She sat in the closest available
chair.

"Don't worry," Allie said. "We got the ethernet hub
connected now so we just need to hook everything back up."

The fire alarm went off.

"Is that for real?" Jason said. "These things are never real,
are they?"

"Never," Gerry said. "Besides, it's a cement building."

In a few minutes, axe-wielding firemen were pouring onto
the floor, knocking on every office door, forcing people to
evacuate. The Goldfish staff proceeded down the fire exit, and
Rihanna muttered, "God hates us," and Allie replied, "No. He
doesn't know we exist."

They crossed the street, stared up at their building, at
nothing, because they could see no fire. Rihanna's back was
feeling worse, and she walked over to the bus stop to lean
against the partition.

"You okay?" Allie said.

"Not really. No."

Allie narrowed her eyes. "What's up?"

"Got a bad liver."

"What?!"

"Yeah. Hep C."

"And you've been working all these hours? Are you nuts?"

Rihanna considered this. "Yeah, I guess so."

"Go home. Mark and I can take care of things for you."

"I'm sure you can."

"Really. Go."

Rihanna wanted to protest, but her liver was winning this
round.

"I'll go when they let everyone back in. Okay?"

Allie frowned, but she said, "Okay."

It had been some time since Rihanna had been home in the afternoon. The sunlight and the shadows were making beautiful latticework patterns on the main deck. She took off her coat and hung it over a chair in the galley, with the intent that she'd make some coffee, but then she decided just to go lie down.

It was also unusual to have the whole boat to herself. If Dylan wasn't home, there was almost always John or Casey at work tinkering with something that wasn't working right. She headed down to the lower level.

Dylan was still in bed. Dizzy was asleep at his feet.

"Dylan? Are you feeling all right?"

But he wasn't alone. He was with a woman who Rihanna recognized as one of "John's friends." Dylan lifted his head with a stupid expression on his face, and Rihanna almost laughed if it wasn't for the onslaught of cursing and name-calling she wanted to unleash. Instead, she said,

"John's friend, huh?"

This time, there was nothing Dylan could say.

Repressing her feelings of anger and pain enough to make it to the stairs, she climbed up to the main floor and broke down.

Now all three friends had been defeated.

Though Dylan pleaded with her for another chance, they both knew he had used them all. This wasn't some one-night stand, nothing that could be explained away with the usual excuses. He had been seeing that woman for months. Happy as she was living on the ferry, Rihanna summoned up some courage and made the decision to move out. In the meantime, she started sleeping in one of the extra bedrooms.

She had never hunted for an apartment in New York before. She had found Dylan, who came equipped with living quarters. Having no idea how to go about it, she turned to her friends, who gave her helpful advice:

Finding an apartment in New York City, Step 1: Throw a lot of money at it.

Step 1 was not an option.

Finding an apartment in New York City, Step 2: The Village Voice

Everyone said that the Voice was the place to find apartments, but this week there weren't that many ads, unless, of course, a person wanted a four-bedroom apartment in the Bronx. Rihanna realized she might have to move to another borough, as distasteful as that seemed, but definitely not the Bronx. That was much too far away from, well, anything.

She'd even take a share, but there weren't a lot of those listed either. She wrote down addresses to open houses, one very far up and east in Manhattan, one in Queens, and a couple on the Lower East Side. Then she wrote down some phone numbers to call.

The first number rang and rang with no answer. It was for a share in Chelsea. She'd try it again later. Another one was in Brooklyn, but when she called, she got, "Why are you calling this number? There're no apartments here!" The others were too expensive, or too far away from Manhattan, or both.

She called the number in Chelsea several times more throughout the day, but never got an answer.

Finding an apartment in New York City, Step 3: Open houses

The first open house she went to was in the Upper East Side, quite a walk from the subway. There was a crowd of people there, spilling out into the street. A woman greeted her, handed her a number, and told her she should fill out an application if she decided she was interested. The ad had said the price was $1,500. Rihanna could just about afford that if she didn't eat very often. When they called her number, she was sent upstairs with a dozen other people. They climbed the stairs single file, all four uneven flights.

While the building seemed a little decrepit, the apartment itself wasn't bad: two renovated rooms, decent size, and there was some light coming in one of the windows. There also was a separate tiny kitchen and a full bath. Rihanna decided to fill out the many-paged application.

She filled in her salary. Other income? No, but she had money she had saved from Dylan's boat parties. Assets? None. Last landlord? Dylan. Then she noticed it said the building required first month's rent, plus the last three months' rent, plus a $300 nonrefundable application fee.

Maybe she wouldn't be applying for this one after all.

Finding an apartment in New York City, Step 4: Agent

There was a real estate agent on the Lower East Side named Margaret Heller who had helped Casey's girlfriend, Jeanie, find her apartment several years before. Her office was a small storefront on Avenue B, sandwiched between a bodega and a funeral home. Margaret was a large woman, probably in her mid-60s, tough-skinned and intimidating. Rihanna had told her what she was looking for over the phone, and when she walked in, Margaret handed her a piece of paper with an address on it and a set of keys and sent her on her way.

The apartment was close to Avenue D on Third Street. There didn't seem to be much else on the opposite side of the street, just a partially boarded-up building and an empty lot with a barbed wire fence around it.

The apartment's building was industrial, and the interior was cement bricks with painted metal railings and doors. Rihanna let herself in and climbed to the second floor. The apartment was huge, a two-bedroom with closets and windows and a full kitchen and bath. The gratings over the windows were in disrepair, bent in as if someone had crawled through them, and the door to the apartment didn't close properly, so those things would have to be fixed, but overall, it was an amazing deal for $600 a month.

Rihanna left a deposit and called Allie with her good news.

"Avenue D? Third Street? Are you nuts?" Allie did not share her enthusiasm.

"I know it's pretty far, but the building looks safe."

"Have you seen that neighborhood at night?"

Since the answer was, "Er, no," Rihanna made plans to go with Allie and Natia to check out the neighborhood.

They met up at Natia's place on Clinton Street. That neighborhood was already making Rihanna nervous, and the new apartment was even further east. On Third Street, there were groups of people huddled together, some offering the ladies drugs as they walked by, some just trying to keep warm around burning trash cans. As the women continued walking, they encountered a group of teenagers, who shouted obscenities at them as they passed. Then the teenagers started following them.

Allie whispered, "Just keep going."

A man was sitting on the stoop of Rihanna's new building, but he ignored the women as they climbed the steps. There were no lights in the vestibule, or the inside stairwell, and none of the three women wanted to go any further inside. While they were standing there, two men hurried down the stairs carrying flashlights and a television, followed by an-other man carrying a stereo and speakers. One of them said, "How ya doing?" to Rihanna as he passed. When the women turned to go, they saw that the man on the stoop was cleaning a gun.

On the way back, a knife fight broke out in the middle of the avenue.

"Can you get your deposit back?" Allie said.

The next morning Rihanna rode over to Margaret Heller's. Margaret was engaged in a conversation with a man, similar in age and temperament — basically, a male version of her — who was sitting across the desk from her.

"Mrs. Heller?"

They both turned around.

"I'd like my deposit back."

"What's the problem?"

"I can't live in that apartment. I'd like to outlive my mother."

Margaret stared at her a moment, but then her friend said, "Good for you."

Rihanna gave her the keys and left with her deposit check.

Finding an apartment in New York City, Step 5: Dumb luck.

Allie came into work one morning with a flier she had taken from her local grocery store's wall:

Efficiency apartment, LES, from owner. Contact super at 212-555-0009.

Efficiency? Could be a shoebox. Still, worth a phone call.

The man on the phone answered with, "Yeah?"

"Hi. I'm calling about the apartment?"

"Yeah. It's small. And no, we got nothing bigger. It's all we got. Still interested?"

"I'm interested."

"Okay. You'll come see it. Buzz me, the super. If you want it, you'll pay my fee, and we'll go see the landlord.

She scheduled a time and got the address.

The apartment was bite-sized, but it had windows. Well, one window. The others were painted over. There was a kitchen area in the corner of the main room, separated from the rest of the room by a skinny, tiled counter. Rihanna stood in the center of the main area facing the window and stretched her arms out to either side. She estimated it was maybe 10 feet wide. She turned in the other direction, which was a little longer, maybe 14 feet to the kitchen counter.

Attached to the main room was an alcove, which had a loft

bed. The loft was barely long enough for a conventionally sized mattress. Maybe it was a child's mattress? No, it wasn't that small.

But the bathroom was.

Rihanna took a step up to a slit in the wall that she thought might lead to a water closet — there was no indication there was a bathroom anywhere else in the apartment, so this had to be it. There wasn't a genuine doorway, it really was just a slit with a board over it that was being used as a makeshift door. She took a step inside and almost fell into the shower. She grabbed the closest thing to break her fall, which was a hot water pipe, and she screamed.

There were going to be huge blisters on her palm. But what luck. There was a sink right there. In the shower. An itty-bitty sink about a foot above the shower controls. Rihanna took the half step past the pull-chain toilet down into the shower well and ran cold water from the sink over her hand.

Rihanna wrapped her hand with a wad of wet, cold tissues and went back out into the hallway, where the bored superintendent was smoking a cigarette.

"How much is this place?"

"700 a month. Landlord wants first and last month's rent. Plus, there's my $500 fee. Cash."

Rihanna considered this. The neighborhood was a bit dicey, but this was Ludlow Street, which was a little more civilized than the rest of the area. The famous Katz's Delicatessen was half a block away on Houston, and around the corner was the Mercury Lounge. Pretty safe, even at night. And besides a safe enough neighborhood, there was only one major requirement for an apartment right now — that she could afford it.

"I'll take it."

Part of the railing on the ferry's upper deck was coming loose. Dylan was trying to hammer it back into place, but it wasn't cooperating. What was wrong with it? Was the wood warped? Were the nail holes too big now? Maybe he needed some wood putty. He had some downstairs.

Rihanna was just arriving home when he got down to the last step. They stood awkwardly, trying not to make eye contact.

"Dylan..."

"This isn't good, is it?" he said.

She held up a set of keys. "I found an apartment."

He did that male thing, where they react indirectly by looking up first as if it were the sky's fault. Then they'll either look you in the eye, if they feel defiant, or look at the ground and avoid you all together, admitting defeat. Dylan chose the latter.

"When?"

"Three weeks."

He nodded.

"Okay."

CHAPTER 20

IZAAK, 1974

Since the lock on his bedroom door was broken, Izaak sat on the floor to act as a doorstop. This was his father's day off, but his parents didn't understand the concept of having a quiet Sunday. If he played his guitar loud enough it would almost drown out the sound of them cursing at each other in their bedroom.

The door behind him pushed open and he slid along the floor with it. He stopped playing.

"Izaak."

He looked up. His father was looming over him.

"Come have a drink with me."

Izaak climbed off the floor and followed him out.

There was nothing special about his father's favorite bar that Izaak could see, other than it was close to their Upper East Side apartment building. It was early afternoon, and there were few patrons. The bartender was wiping off the bar just to give himself something to do. Izaak's huge father sat in the middle of the bar, eclipsing the bar stool. Izaak took a seat next to him.

"The usual, Stanley?" the bartender said. He had a hint of an accent, Izaak guessed maybe German.

"Two glasses."

The bartender raised an eyebrow and said, "The kid's eighteen?"

"Yeah, yeah."

Fifteen. Close enough.

The bartender pulled a bottle from the top shelf, poured two double shots, and left the bottle on the bar. Izaak at this point in his life had mostly been drinking beer, not whiskey, but he'd give it a go. His father took hold of one glass with his beefy paw and offered it up to Izaak to clink.

His father gulped half his drink, and then he pulled out two cigars from his shirt pocket. When Izaak shook his head, he pocketed the extra one.

"There's a doctor I know at the hospital," his father said, unwrapping his cigar. "Friend of mine. Has a wife, three daughters. Even the dog has more say in the house than he does. Doesn't like to go home. I told him. 'You're a fool. What are you doing, letting them rule the house? That's why you don't want to be there.' He works the midnight shift. Goes to sleep when they're waking up."

Izaak drank his whiskey carefully. His father lit his cigar. Plumes of grey smoke blew into Izaak's face. He fought the urge to cough.

"Maybe I should have that schedule, eh? Come home when your mother's asleep?" His father chuckled. Izaak smirked and tried to drink faster. His father was already one ahead of him.

"Tell me something, Izaak. You got a girlfriend?"

Izaak, surprised at his father's sudden interest in his life, quickly nodded.

"She pretty?"

Izaak grinned. "Very."

"Well, don't let her boss you around." His father leaned closer to Izaak's face and raised and lowered his caterpillar eyebrows. "You have to be the boss."

Though happy to be out imbibing with his father, Izaak suspected he shouldn't be taking relationship advice from him. His father reached over and squeezed Izaak's cheeks together. "You hear me? You — be — the — boss."

Izaak leaned away from him, and his father laughed.

"Let me tell you something. Women are only good for one thing. Find a woman who likes sex, and you'll have a lot less grief."

This heartwarming dictum was nothing Izaak hadn't heard from his father before. Cigar smoke wafted into his eyes. He rubbed them as they started to tear.

"Yeah, women can be fun, don't get me wrong," his father continued. "But when you get them to have sex with you, they'll want something in return. They'll want your time. They'll want your attention. And babies. They all want babies."

Izaak nodded as if in agreement. He was enjoying this bonding moment, not just because of the whiskey glow. His father looked over at Izaak's empty glass and refilled it.

"Na Zdrowie!" His father downed his drink in two gulps. Izaak followed suit, then tried not to show how much he regretted it. His father chuckled and refilled the glasses.

"That's better. Try to keep up with your old man."

Izaak slurped his drink. It was going down easier. This was Izaak's third. During the fourth, he found he was slipping off his barstool.

"Looks like he's had enough," the bartender said.

"Well look at that. Having a bit of seasickness, are we?"

Izaak leaned away from his father and vomited on the bar stool next to him. Then he started to dry-heave.

"Okay. Okay. Get us some water here, will ya? Thanks."

Izaak was weaving back and forth. The bartender brought a pitcher of water and a glass.

"Here. Drink."

His father held the glass as Izaak drank the water. Isaac felt the water react with the alcohol in his system. He immediately threw it up.

"Yeah. He's a lightweight," his father said, but with concern.

He refilled the glass and held it for Izaak. Again, Izaak threw up.

His father was studying him. "One more."

Izaak obeyed and vomited again.

"Feeling better?"

Izaak thought it was odd, but he was.

"Let's get you home." His father put a wad of cash on the bar. "Thanks, Günter. Sorry for the mess."

Izaak's father helped Izaak off the bar stool. As the bartender came around with a mop and rags to clean up, Izaak's father led his unsteady son out of the bar.

Despite the retching, Izaak liked being his father's drinking buddy. This was the first of many comparable excursions, which, luckily for Günter, had much less vomiting.

STILL DECEMBER 1995

Ridges formed on Pest's heavily calloused fingers, on the tips, and up the side of his left index finger. As he slid his hand up and down the neck of his guitar, he found that he was too distracted to play well. Allie had left a message on his answering machine. He was still angry about that letter she sent him, but the fact was, he also felt terrible about how he handled the break-up. Should have been up front with her. If there had been a way, he would have kept both women. The world just doesn't work like that.

A knock on his door, and Lisa walked in.

"Izaak? I need to talk to you."

Uh oh. "What's up?"

"Well... I'm getting married."

"Really? Mazel tov! That's great." *Oh, wait....*

"Thing is, I'm going to move in with Tim and give up this place."

Pest tried not to panic. "When is this happening?"

"Well, the lease is up next month."

"Can I get your lease?"

Lisa shook her head. "That's the thing. This place is rent-controlled."

Which meant, he would have to be her son to take over the lease. He thought a moment. "Wanna adopt me?"

Lisa laughed, but Pest was less than amused. This left little time to search for a place. It was a rare moment, but Pest was unable to speak.

"Well," Lisa said. "I'll let you get back to practicing."

She closed the door behind her. Pest threw his high tops at the door one by one and put his head in his hands, hoping that, if he held it tight enough, it wouldn't burst open.

He picked up the phone and called Tracy. He could finish practicing over there, and she would get his mind off this problem for a while.

Tracy was sitting across from him on her bed, legs folded under her, elbow on her knee, chin on her hand, that beautiful, oversized smile on her face. She was enthralled, and though it looked like she could sit there forever, Pest wouldn't make her wait too long. He put his guitar away and went over to her. She began slowly removing his shirt.

"I wish my roommate would let you stay over," she said.

"Yeah, but you don't want any problems with her. And these walls are made out of toilet paper."

She laughed and turned on the radio. He lifted his hands so she could get his arms out of his sleeves. When the shirt was off, she unzipped his jeans, pulled them down, and pushed him onto the bed. Then she put her hand between his legs and squeezed ever so gently. He groaned. She smiled and slowly rubbed up and down. As great as that felt, he stopped her and pulled her down onto the bed. He got on top of her, and she whispered, "Let's pretend we're married."

Pest, not your average guy who might panic and run out of the room upon hearing such a thing, usually found this cute and endearing. This evening, however, he stopped abruptly and snapped: "Don't say that."

"What's the matter?"

"I can't deal with that today." He sat back. "I just can't. We can't even joke about that right now. Okay? I'm serious."

Pest saw the scared-puppy look on Tracy's face, but he kept going.

"I'm sorry. I'm getting thrown out of my apartment. I might be homeless soon. I'm just a wreck. Okay?"

"You can live with your mom for a while."

"No, I can't! I grew up there, and there are too many memories. Every inch of the place reminds me of —"

He had been yelling, and Tracy burst into tears. He hung his head.

"God, I'm sorry," he said. "I just really have a lot of stress right now."

Tears were still all over her face, but she put a hand on his cheek. When he finally let his eyes meet hers, she smiled kindly.

"Really sorry," he said.

She kissed him, and all was forgiven.

There was a place near Tracy's apartment, a deserted block with warehouses and empty lots and barbed wire, where Pest liked to park his van. Since Tracy's roommate wouldn't let him stay over, sometimes it was easier to crash in the van than to drive back to Manhattan late at night, when all he wanted to do was sleep.

This might be something he'd have to get used to if he couldn't find a new place.

The sun wasn't quite up when Pest was awoken by a car

alarm. Today this was a good thing. Last night he slept in the front seat of the van, his legs propped up on the steering wheel. He was going to see his kids in Jersey, and he didn't want to oversleep, which he often did if he slept in the back.

He slowly took his stiffened legs off the steering wheel and stretched out. Then he rummaged through his pile of tapes to find something suitable for the trip. Today it would be Domenico Scarlatti. It was piano music, but there were these dissonant chords and syncopations that sounded like rock guitar. Rock and roll from the 18th century. Good stuff.

There was a long wait to the Lincoln Tunnel, but that did not surprise Pest. Sometimes the wait could be hours. He turned up his music and got in line.

Two hours into a one-and-a-half-hour journey, he arrived. He was taking his kids to a Trenton Thunder game, the closest he could get to affording a Yankees game for Kolby.

"So, you know that each team gets three outs an inning, right?" Kolby explained as they were taking their seats. "And the pitcher gets each batter out with three strikes. But if he pitches four balls, the player takes a base."

Yes, Pest needed the very basic information about the game. A lot of what Kolby was talking about was way over his head. What the hell was a bunt? A double play? A balk? And why, if there were nine innings, would games go to 10, or 13, or 15? Kolby would get frustrated with him, but it was good to see his son so excited about something. Pest just wished he were that excited about music. Kolby seemed to have a natural ability for it. He'd hate to see that go to waste. Much of what Kolby knew about baseball came from his stepfather, who used to play in college. Hanna got bored when anyone talked about baseball, but she did enjoy being in the stands with Pest and Kolby, and both kids brought gloves in hopes of catching the elusive foul ball.

Later, when the kids, their mother, and their stepfather were asleep, Pest went out. There was a tiny bar just down the road that had an old juke box and a pool table. Pest entered the bar and found that the bartender was an old friend of his from high school, Karen Foxworth, or 'Foxy' as everyone used to call her. She had a Brett Butler way about her, tall, blond, pretty, and tired.

"Foxy! Hey. It's been a while."

"Izaak. How's it going? Still drinking Heineken?"

He nodded. She opened a bottle and placed it on the bar.

"How come you and I never hooked up back in the day, Izaak?"

"I was too busy getting arrested."

"Yeah, you did seem to spend an inordinate amount of time in juvie."

"I never graduated. Maybe someday I'll get my GED."

"Why? Do you need it?"

"Haven't so far."

The jukebox started to play "Behind Closed Doors," and before either of them mentioned hooking up again, he gave her as big a tip as he could afford. This meant he would be having only one beer. He headed to the pool table.

There was technique to even just getting the cue to hit the ball in the right place, much less aiming the ball towards something. When he first started playing, that's what he concentrated on for the first few months; just hit the ball so it went somewhere. Once it stopped blooping up or not moving at all, he learned to aim the damn thing. He was an accomplished player now, albeit rusty. This was a skill one had to keep up with, but when Pest had free time, he preferred to be practicing his guitar. With everyone asleep in the house, pool would have to do.

There was someone already at the table. Pest approached and watched him. This guy was excellent.

"Wanna play?" the man said.

"Sure."

"You a betting man?"

"Hell, no. Besides, I just gave my last few dollars to the bartender."

The man laughed. "Well, Foxy is worth it."

This guy was showing off, doing shots behind his back, under his leg, backwards over his head.

"You live around here?"

Pest took a shot, which just barely touched the ball, knocking it out of the way of the pocket.

"No. My kids do."

That was all the conversation either of them had room for. The man hit a shot that bounced off the walls of the table several times before knocking the ball into the socket. Pest laughed.

"Okay. This is why I'm not a betting man. Nothing to bet with, and nothing to bet on."

Kolby and Hanna were on the floor in the back of the van. Tracy was in the front passenger seat. Pest and Tracy had had a fight about this earlier.

"Your kids are here? You just saw them! I thought you and I were getting together this weekend! We hardly get enough time together as it is!"

"I hardly get to see my kids as it is!"

One could argue, as Tracy had, that there wasn't anything wrong with her coming along. There wasn't, except that Pest wanted to see Kolby and Hanna alone. This resulted in Tracy lashing out at him, and Pest lashing back, and next there were tears and Pest gave in.

So, Tracy was in the front passenger seat.

Kolby was leaning against the side door, humming. He was in his own world, and it sounded like he was making up the melody as he went along. Hanna had her stuffed rabbit with her and was having a conversation with it.

"Mr. Rabbit, you have big, long ears, don't you? Why do you have big, long ears?" And then she answered herself in the lower, rabbit's voice, "Because I need to hear everything, silly."

Pest drove the van to Greenpoint and parked in his usual spot. He pulled his guitar out of the back of the van and was about to take Hanna's hand when Tracy beat him to it. The kids walked with Tracy, and Pest took up the rear.

When they got to the apartment, Tracy leaned down to Hanna and Kolby and said, "How would you kids like to make some cookies?"

They looked at their father. "Can we?"

Tracy took out the ingredients and kitchen tools necessary for cookie production. The kids climbed onto two kitchen chairs so they could see the top of the table and be closer to the action. Pest sat in a third chair with his guitar and began to play while he watched. Tracy was great with his kids. It was a happy, homey scene. Not Tracy's fault, but it made Pest anxious and irritable. He needed to find an apartment and soon.

Pest arrived at his mother's door, carrying his favorite guitar and a suitcase full of clothes, shoes, and toiletries. He would be sleeping in his father's library. What he had with him was going into his old bedroom, which was now his mother's office. Everything else he owned was in his storage locker downtown.

"Izaak, I'm going out. You'll be okay here?"

"Of course."

The door closed behind her, and Pest was blissfully alone. He looked around.

"Back here," he said aloud and sighed.

He carried his things into her office and took out his guitar. He sat on the floor and began to play.

Pest had spent many hours playing guitar here while his parents raised hell in the other room:

"Judy, I'm warning you!"

"You think I'm scared of you?"

You should be, Pest would think.

They would go into their bedroom, in an attempt not to be heard, but after the muffled voices stopped yelling, the thrashing and hitting and pushing and falling would be impossible to ignore. A moment of silence, then Pest would hear his father leave the apartment, slamming the door behind him.

He shook off this memory and continued playing. He started with something classical, but soon he wanted to pound on the guitar with something raucous and angry. How could he be in his thirties and living back here?

... He could hear his parents yelling in the other room.

His father came into the living room, drinking and yelling, drinking and cursing, drinking and hollering. Pest continued to play his guitar, although the yelling did make it hard to concentrate.

The enormous bear that was his father stomped around the apartment.

Please don't come in here.

"That's it. I'm going."

"Yeah, where you going?" his mother said.

"Mars. What do you care?" Then, he yelled, *"My life is fucking worthless here!"*

"You're packing? Stop it! Stop it!"

After a while the door slammed. Pest stopped playing. It was quiet except for the sounds of his mother sobbing, "Don't go!"

He snapped out of his flashback.

His breathing was fast, his heart racing. He walked out into the living room and started pacing. He forced himself to breathe slower and deeper.

Who could he call?

Not Tracy. He wanted to spare her from this kind of crap. Crazy thing was, the person who would know what to say, who could always calm him down, was Allie.

He took a few more deep breaths and then called Roy.

PART SIX

NEW: *Bullet with Butterfly Wings*
(Billy Corgan)

— recorded by The Smashing Pumpkins,
released 1995

CHAPTER 21

RIHANNA, JANUARY–FEBRUARY 1996

Starting in the afternoon most days, Ludlow Street would start filling up with aimless bohemians. Tall, skinny men and women would be standing beside parking meters, and others would be smoking European cigarettes in front of the trendy Max Fish bar. Musicians with guitars on their backs headed into the music shop that was across the street from Rihanna's building or continued on their way to one of the rehearsal spaces around the corner. Very few people on this street appeared to have day jobs.

Just below Rihanna's apartment was a bar called the Ludlow Street Café, which was weird because it wasn't a café at all, and next door to Max Fish was an actual café called the Pink Pony, an artsy place with walls donned with black and white photos and bookshelves filled with yellowed paperbacks. Katz's was up the block and vintage clothing shops were down the block. All kinds of places for Rihanna to explore as soon as she got some time off. And now that Goldfish was so quiet, that would be happening in a couple of weeks.

Rihanna hadn't had to carry a bike up a staircase for the better part of a decade, and luckily, this new apartment was only on the second floor. She stood at the bottom of the staircase with her bike and prepared to climb.

"Nice bike."

There was a pleasant-looking shaggy-haired guy smiling at her.

"Thanks." Rihanna was pretty sure he wasn't interested in her bike.

"Listen. We're shooting a music video and need extras."

"We?"

"Titan Video, the production company I work for."

"Oh. And?"

"Thought you looked cool." He offered her a card. "If you're interested, show up at that time and address wearing club clothes. And bring the card."

"Okay. And you are?"

"I'm Greg."

"Rihanna."

"Okay, Rihanna. Maybe we'll see you Saturday."

Rihanna's eyes opened a crack, just enough for her to see light, not enough to be awake. Her bed was softly swaying as the river rocked the boat, and she reached out for Dylan. Instead, her hand hit a wall and she shook awake.

Ludlow Street.

She resisted the urge to regret her decision, to let herself miss Dylan, to long for the river. The cons of staying there had been piling up for years, and by the time she finally left, they were far exceeding the pros.

Except it didn't feel that way this morning.

Rihanna climbed down from the loft and headed over to the kitchen area. From her refrigerator, she took some tofu and veggies to make a scramble, something Dylan abhorred.

"No one really likes tofu," he liked to say. "They just pretend to."

On the counter was the card from Titan Video. Should she go to the shoot? Might get her mind off Dylan for a while. She still had some time to figure out what to wear. What the heck?

West 18th Street consisted of commercial warehouses and was usually populated with double-parked trucks, but today there were two white movie trailers blocking traffic. This was a professional shoot, not just some kids from NYU working on a class project, and Rihanna wondered who the star of the video might be. She checked in with a man wearing a baseball cap that had Titan embroidered on it. He asked for the card, had her sign a release and fill out a W4. Looked like she would be getting paid something to do this.

The scene was easy: Sit at a bar and pretend to be socializing. The other extras were younger than she was, but no one seemed to mind. In a few minutes, they were all laughing and drinking (seltzer), and Rihanna felt like she was genuinely out somewhere for the night, even though it was three in the afternoon.

As she was leaving, she heard a voice say, "Have fun, Rihanna?"

It was the cute scruffy guy who brought her there.

"Yes. I'm sorry, I forgot your name."

"Greg."

They stood awkwardly for a moment, and then he said, "Wanna hang out some time?"

Well, he was kind of cute.

"I'm living with someone. Sorry." She didn't know why she said that. She almost regretted it.

Greg sighed. "Too bad. I guess it's true that all the good ones are taken."

It was too late to now say, "Ha! Only kidding," so she let it go. She stared at him a moment, let their eyes connect, but then she broke her gaze and headed out.

This would be Rihanna's last day at work before she took a needed vacation. With Allie and Mark gone, she had been staying late to help the last two freelancers sort out the remaining work, but, with so little left to do in the studio, she finally could take a week off. Sal would just have to take care of things while she was gone.

When she got to Ludlow Street, there were plenty of Friday-night celebrants hanging on stoops and sitting on benches in front of Max Fish and the Pink Pony. Further down the block, people were standing around in front of the Ludlow Street Café listening to the music emanating from its storefront stage. In most neighborhoods in the City, the music would have stopped at ten o'clock, but no one cared about the excess noise here, and the police had better things to do.

Rihanna climbed her stairs and noted how much easier it was to do without her bicycle weighing her down. She got to her floor, pushed in the door to the pitch-black apartment, and suddenly felt panicked. For a moment, she was four years old and afraid of the dark. She switched on the lights in the main room and locked the door behind her. There was a strange noise, and she froze in front of her door, even though logic would have told her it was the refrigerator rattling. She turned on the light in the bedroom alcove and then in the bathroom. She even peered behind the shower curtain before she came back and put the chain on the double-locked entrance to her apartment. She was breathing fast. She leaned on her kitchen counter and waited for this craziness to subside.

No one was there. That was the problem.

It had been a week of sleeping and more sleeping, and Rihanna was feeling better for it. By Saturday, it was time to go out.

Allie arrived at her door just before nine o'clock.

"You ready?" she said.

Rihanna was. Her favorite jeans, a sparkly top. She was going to have some fun, liver be damned.

The truly exciting, never sleeping, glamorous, laugh-a-minute, Greatest City in the World was often not that at all. Yes, there were great events. Yes, there were great shows. Yes, there were once-in-a-lifetime experiences. But if a person lived there long enough, she found that a silly neighborhood bar having an 80s night was sometimes about all the fun a couple of overworked women could handle.

They didn't see anybody in the place when they arrived. Above the bar was a sign that read: "No Dancing."

"Is that a joke?" Allie said.

The bartender shook his head. "Nope. They've been actively enforcing the City's Cabaret Law. Have to have a license to let people dance."

"Isn't that, like, unconstitutional or something?"

"It's been on the books since the 20s. It's what they used to raid Hogs and Heifers the other night."

"Oh," Rihanna said. "I thought that was a drug thing."

"Nope. The law's been mostly ignored since Stonewall, but now it's being enforced again as part of Giuliani's Quality of Life campaign. Up to a $20,000 fine if a place gets caught."

"Well, this is not going to help my quality of life," Allie said. "How are you having an 80s night without dancing?"

"In the back room. But if the cops show up, you gotta stop."

"You'd think the police would have something more important to do — like fighting crime."

The bartender gave Allie his best, dismissive, not-my-problem shrug, and, after Allie and Rihanna ordered something to drink, the women headed back to the hidden dance floor.

The DJ was playing something by the Cure, and Allie smiled and said, "Love this!" and started dancing, drink in hand. Most of the people there hadn't consumed enough alcohol to join her yet, so there was plenty of room to move around. Rihanna found that if she didn't move too vigorously, she felt okay. Too much shimmying, and she would start to get winded. Twist this way, ow, not that way. Easy left, easy right. Moving felt good when it wasn't killing her.

Gradually, the dance floor filled up. Men and women were falling back into those silly 80s dances, hopping and skipping and jerking around as if they were in their twenties.

A tall, bony man approached the dance floor. His long legs started bending and straightening in syncopation to the music. Then he started moving his arms, making strange shapes, and causing people to duck. He plunged into the funky chicken, gyrated his way across the dance floor, and then started strutting backwards. He did a high kick, nearly lost his balance, but recovered in time to pivot around.

Allie and Rihanna grew tired of dodging his gesticulations and went to dance on the other side of the floor. Undaunted, the man kept dancing.

Allie and Rihanna couldn't take their eyes off him.

"He's like dancing hieroglyphics," Rihanna said.

Then, with no warning, the house lights went on and the music was turned down to radio level. Everybody around them sat down in an impromptu game of musical chairs. Rihanna and Allie exchanged baffled looks.

Two uniformed officers broke in. They did a full sweep of the room, occasionally nodding at people if they caught someone's eye. There wasn't much to see, but the officers circled around a few times, and at one point seemed particularly interested in Rihanna's glass of seltzer. They consulted with each other, and since they hadn't detected anyone exhibiting symptoms of the Boogie-Woogie Flu, they left.

The lights stayed on several more minutes, and then everyone was back in the privacy of dim lighting and the unrestricted sounds of 80s club music.

Going out the night before, even though she had been careful, took a toll on Rihanna, and the next day, she awoke with that now-familiar back pain. She pried herself out of her loft bed around noon and stumbled into the main room to make some coffee.

She sat at her counter and picked up the pile of mail from yesterday she had yet to go through. Please send money, pay or else, buy this, buy that, order now — and then an official-looking envelope with no return address.

The coffeemaker was finished, but Rihanna was curious, so she opened the envelope before she poured a cup. After reading it through, she said aloud, "This must be a mistake. Crap. This better be a mistake."

$30,000, plus. That was what she owed so far for the biopsy, doctor's visits, and several other tests.

Did Goldfish stop paying for her insurance? What the heck was she going to do now?

Call Dylan.

She reached for the phone and stopped. What was she doing?

"Nope, nope, nope. Not a good idea," she said. Then she picked up the phone and called Allie.

Sunrise, Monday morning. Rihanna had been tossing around in her loft bed for what seemed like hours. Sleep was not happening. Might as well just get up and get ready for work.

"Rihanna. What are you doing here so early?" Jolie, the receptionist, greeted her. "I thought you were coming in at ten."

Rihanna didn't want to take her exasperation out on Jolie. She took a breath before she spoke.

"Sal in yet?"

Jolie looked around before she answered.

"Sal's gone. He quit."

"What?"

"Apparently, he's been writing checks to himself and logging them in as something else. It was a lot. He quit just before they found out about it."

See? There were reasons to hate this guy.

"They've been looking for him, but it's like he's skipped town or something." Jolie was speaking so softly Rihanna had to lean in to hear her.

"Okay, then who do I talk to about our insurance?"

"Oh... that." Before she could answer, the elevator doors opened. A group of suited men entered Goldfish. Their suits matched, their ties matched, their expressions matched, even their heights matched. They approached Jolie, and one of them said, "We have a 9:00 appointment."

One of the owners came out to greet them, and they were ushered into a conference room.

"Lawyers?"

"Or accountants, maybe," Jolie said, and then whispered, "I heard something about the freelancers starting to sue for back pay."

"Probably all that overtime." She knew Allie was. She was probably the first. "Do you know which ones?"

Jolie shrugged. "I guess all of them."

"Wow. I'm gone a week, and everything goes to hell."

CHAPTER 22

ALLIE, MARCH–APRIL 1996

A trip to the Ludlow Street Café would give a person some idea of what it would be like to be buried alive. Several steps below street level, it was a long skinny storefront with a ceiling so low Allie could reach up and touch it. A tiny stage was set up in the display window next to the entrance. Most nights it was easier to see bands by standing outside and watching from the sidewalk.

Allie, Natia, and Rihanna took seats at the end of the bar nearest the entrance. Their view of the stage was partially blocked, but it was a crowded Friday night, and in any other part of the bar they would see nothing. The band tonight was not exceptional, but it had a good solid country-rock sound. Something about the band's guitarist looked familiar to Allie, but she couldn't quite see him from where she was sitting.

Small world, this world of music. It was Kurt Whelan.

"Oh, Gees," Allie said.

"What's the matter?" Rihanna said.

"That guitarist. I went on a date with him not that long ago."

"I'm guessing from the look on your face that it didn't go well?" Natia said.

"No, it did not."

Rihanna was looking towards the entrance with a look of concern.

Pest had entered the club.

"Great," Allie said.

"He's alone. Did he ever answer your call about Jake?" Natia said.

"I didn't expect him to. It was like calling Weather and leaving a message."

Pest spotted Allie, caught her eye, and turned away.

"This night just gets better and better," Allie said. She hid her head in her hands. The Letter was proving to be an embarrassing mistake.

"What?" Rihanna said.

"Oh, I'm just thinking about something really stupid I did."

When Allie finally looked up, Pest was standing behind her. He looked her over a moment, slid between her and Natia, and leaned on the bar.

"How've you been?" Allie said.

That was all it took to start Pest talking. He lost his apartment, which meant he was living in his mom's place. Meanwhile, it looked like his kids might be moving to Texas, he was having to rehearse a new drummer for the Caterwaulers, and...

Midway through his rant, Kurt Whelan approached them. He was hunching slightly to avoid hitting his head on the ceiling. He took a moment to smirk at Allie and then said, "Pest, you wanna sit in on our next set?"

Pest slid back out of the space he was in but stopped and leaned in towards Allie.

"The Caterwaulers have a gig at Night Crawlers next week. Why don't you come?"

He followed Kurt to the stage. Although nothing had really changed in the last few minutes, Allie found she was smiling.

◇◇◇

She had not come to this decision without careful considera-
tion. Pest's next gig could be emotionally torturous. Did she
really want to risk seeing Pest with his new squeeze? Would it
be Good For Her to see that he'd moved on? Could she just go
and enjoy the music?

The answer to all these questions was: absolutely not.

In front of Night Crawlers, an older black man was
standing alone. He was singing the bass-line vocal of an old
doo-wop song. He had a nice smooth voice, which made Allie
think he may have once been a professional singer or at least
a serious amateur. He turned around, and Allie realized she
had met him before: Erwin, Pest's super from the Lower East
Side. He didn't come to too many gigs, but when he did, he
liked to wait around by the front door until he heard the band
start. He greeted her warmly.

There was never much of a crowd that night. Most
importantly for Allie, no sign of The Girl. During the break,
Pest was getting a cola at the bar, and Allie sidled up to him.

"They have the worst soda here." She was trying to be
nonchalant.

"It's got caffeine. I need something since I don't do speed
anymore. In the winter I bring tea."

Their eyes locked, and Allie felt that familiar intensity. For
a moment neither one of them spoke.

"Listen," Pest said, breaking his gaze. "I got your letter."

Allie winced. "Oh. God."

Pest sipped his soda and let her thrash around in her
discomfort.

"I'm so sorry about that," she said. "I was just so furious."

"Well, you did cross several lines there." He took the
stirring straw out of his soda and threw it on the floor. "But
on the other hand, I didn't handle that situation well."

No kidding.

"Anyway, Tracy and I are done."

Tracy. Nice to have a name to go with the enemy.

"She kept complaining that I wasn't spending enough time with her. Then she started complaining about me seeing my kids, which really set me off. She's a real needy chick." He paused, and seeing Allie's raised eyebrows, laughed. "And I'm a real needy guy. There wasn't enough room for the both of us."

With that, Pest slid off the barstool.

"I better go play before the last three people here leave."

Allie thought she was being dismissed, but he turned to her and said, "Hey. Wanna get together after the show? You gotta come uptown with me, though, 'cause I gotta unpack the van and park it."

Sometimes a person asks herself "What the hell am I doing?" Sometimes she doesn't. Allie was far too drawn in, so happy to have all that painful longing go away, to have any such second thoughts.

After the show, Pest was immersed in a conversation about Great Guitars We Have Known. The guitar geeks surrounding him were fascinated, and every time the conversation appeared to be waning, someone would think of another guitar to talk about.

This could have gone on forever.

Allie put her hand on Pest's arm. "Pest, I need to run over to my apartment. I'll be right back."

"Okay. I gotta get paid, but then I'll go get the van and meet you back here."

It was only a few short blocks, but 2nd Avenue's streetlights weren't doing their job this evening. There were more people than usual skulking around in the unlit pockets the streetlights were missing. Allie became hyperaware of the short skirt she was wearing and the loud clacking sound her heels were making on the sidewalk. A voice, too close for Allie's comfort, said, "Where are you going?"

"Home." She picked up her pace.

"Alone?"

She was just passing the churchyard on 11th Street. She walked faster, and he tried to keep up with her.

"Can I come with you?"

"No, thanks."

9th Street.

"Oh, c'mon."

She turned onto her block, and he stopped following her.

Allie threw a change of clothes into a tote bag, pet and fed Tuna, and went back out. When she returned to 2nd Avenue, the man was there again, this time standing on the other side of the avenue. He spotted her and followed her all the way back to the club. He crossed over to her side when he saw she was stopping at Night Crawlers. Pest and his van weren't there, and the bar was locked. Allie stood against one of the metal gates to wait.

And someone was singing (to the tune of "Good Night Sweetheart"):

"Pest will be back.
He's getting the van. (da da da da dah)
He'll be right back.
He's getting the van. (da da da da dah)"

Erwin had appeared as if out of nowhere and was standing a couple of feet away from her. He glared at the other man, who was now leaning against Night Crawlers' metal gate on the other side of the doorway. Pest pulled up in the van moments later. Allie put her hand on Erwin's arm on her way towards her rescue vehicle, and he smiled at her.

"I gotta tell you something before I see you again."

And things had been going so well.

"I'm back with Tracy. But I don't want to stop seeing you."

This was the conversation going through Allie's head now, causing a monsoon of upsetting emotions as she walked to her latest freelance job.

"But if we keep seeing each other, you'll have to be The Other Woman. You would have to be a secret."

The "Other Woman." Jeez. She fell in love with him first. Tracy should be the "Other."

Screw it. She didn't need him. Why did she let herself trust him again? It was just sex, that's all. Something a woman could get anywhere.

If Allie had been looking ahead instead of down, she would have noticed a marvelously clear, spring afternoon in the Village. There was a breeze blowing Allie's hair away from her face, the sun was warm, and the streets were filled with people enjoying the afternoon.

She stopped to wait for a streetlight to change. She was getting close to the river. Two more blocks and she'd be at work. She was only a little late.

A moment now where the sidewalks emptied, the wind abated, the traffic halted. Her body shuddered with self-awareness. And in the distance, she heard a train whistling in New Jersey.

There it was, that aching need for Pest, right on the surface, unwilling to keep hidden under other emotions.

What did she think would happen, her falling in love with a feral musician? Chances were anyone who got involved with him would have to share. This was a nice justification for what she was about to do, she realized. Though Allie was not the sharing type, it didn't take long for her to come to a decision: Keep quiet and play along.

How did that go? Something about not being able to stand without a spine?

On one side of the Rodeo Bar stage there was Tracy sitting at a table right under Pest's feet. When he looked her way, she wore a blissful, adoring grin. When he looked away, she glared at Allie.

Allie was sitting across the room, a bit further from the stage. Pest had snuck over to give her a quick hug and a kiss on the neck, which was supposed to tide her over until they could be together again. Judging from the looks she was getting from Tracy this moment of affection did not look innocent.

To shake off Tracy's venomous glare, Allie got up to dance, ignoring the "No Dancing" sign hanging above the buffalo. A jovial man in a curious hand-painted t-shirt — a smoking monkey — joined her on the dance floor. Maybe because no one else joined them, the venue didn't stop them. When the show was over, while Pest was getting ready to leave with Tracy, Buck walked Allie to St. Marks Place. They talked on the corner for quite a while before parting company.

Buck was a corn-fed fellow, born and bred in Illinois, with a stocky build, very pale skin, platinum hair, and a mid-western accent. An easy-going guy with a good sense of humor and a million friends, it seemed to Allie he was the most well-balanced person on earth. He was, in effect, the Anti-Pest.

Allie accompanied Buck and a couple of his friends one night to see a show at the Underground on Bleecker Street. The club allowed dancing, so after spending the night jumping around with Buck and his friends, Allie walked home feeling energized and happy.

They went out often, and one night, there was an attempt at commingling: an awkward kiss in front of Allie's stoop that she was pretty sure was suggested by Buck's wingman friends. Allie had been hoping something would save her from this emotional trap she had gotten herself in with Pest. The kiss proved to her that she wasn't ready to give up Pest, and she didn't feel she could tell Buck what was going on. Besides, Buck didn't make her flesh melt and drip off the way Pest did.

To be fair, no one else did, or ever had.

CHAPTER 23

NATIA, MAY 1996

Natia was up early Sunday morning to gather laundry. She added to the bag until it was too big for both her and the bag to fit on the stairs. She got smart and simply tossed the bag and walked down after it. The resulting thump, thump, and crash sounded like a body falling. Her downstairs neighbor opened her door in alarm, but when she saw Natia and the laundry, she smiled and closed her door.

If one were watching Natia struggling with her giant bag of laundry on the street, one might have wondered why she didn't have Danny carry it for her. Stubbornness was a trait she shared with her mother. Thinking about her mother now, it was hard to fathom being disowned. Before her mother's last visit, Natia still had hope, however misguided. Though she often wondered if she really was disowned forever, her mother was adamant; chances were this wasn't going to change.

Danny was just getting up when Natia returned with their clean clothes.

"Why didn't you wake me up? I would have carried that for you."

The phone rang and he picked up.

"It's Allie."

She took the phone.

"Hey Natia. Might you want Ephram's apartment?"

"Ephram? Where's he going?"

"Japan. For a year, maybe indefinitely."

"Isn't Pest looking for a place?"

"He's looking in Greenpoint. Near Tracy."

"Really?"

"Would I make that up? Says he can park his van out there. Anyway, you get first dibs."

"Where's Ephram's apartment?"

"Chelsea."

"Sounds expensive. Do you know what he's paying?"

"No, but it's stabilized."

"I'll check it out. Yeah, give me his number."

Chelsea was like a whole different city. The buildings were large and sturdy, and not one of them was boarded up or in need of boarding up. The avenues were wide and full of taxis and busses, the sidewalks were humming with people in suits and all sorts of other types walking with purpose, and unlike Clinton Street, most of it legal. Natia also suspected that fewer of them were armed.

When she got to the address, she was pleased to find it had a working door buzzer. Even the intercom worked.

"Come on up. 3rd Floor."

It was a good-sized railroad apartment: full kitchen, then two small rooms — perfect for Danny's studio — and then a large bedroom.

"Whatdaya think?"

"I think I love it. How much?"

"I'm paying \$890, but it'll be a legal sublet, so 10% more for you guys."

Less than what they were paying in the tomb.

"That's great. What do we have to do?"

"Stand on your head. Recite the Torah."

Natia laughed. Ephram was cute.

"No, I'll call the landlord and set up a meeting."

This was singularly the most exciting thing to happen to Natia since she became involved with Danny: packing.

"What's this?" Danny's friend Marcos held up an unidentifiable piece of metal that had been in one of the kitchen drawers.

"Toss it," Danny said.

"This box is full. It's all of your socks and underwear." Allie tore off some packing tape and closed the box. "Got a marker?"

Natia found a small box filled with mixed markers and pens. After trying the first few and finding them dry, she tossed the entire thing. Marcos saw this and picked up the marker he had been using.

"Here."

He waited until Allie was ready and then threw it to her.

"Ten-year-old receipts," Natia dropped them in the trash bag. "Trash. Notebooks from school — trash. Folder of takeout menus we never used — trash."

"Old towels and pieces of old sheets?" Marcos asked.

"Trash."

Danny handed her a stack of CDs and floppy disks.

"Old programs and midi sounds I have backed up on DAT."

"Trash?" In the bag they went.

"This is therapeutic," Allie said. "I haven't thought about Jerkface for at least ten minutes."

"Where is he tonight?" Natia said.

"With Tracy, I guess. I just assume if he's not making plans with me, he's either with the band or with her."

"Do you ever get mad at this guy?" Danny said.

"Sure. I get... well, annoyed, anyway, sometimes."

"He means mad, lose your temper mad," Natia said. "There's a difference between not getting mad and not being able to get mad."

"Okay, no, I don't get mad. I can't. I'm complicit in this. If

I don't like it, I can walk."

There was a moment where everyone in the room had the same thought.

"Except, I can't walk. That's the problem." Allie said. "Give me more stuff to go through. He's back in my head."

Natia pulled out a drawer and handed it to her. "You can start filling the suitcase."

"Perfect. Pest, be gone."

CHAPTER 24

PEST, JUNE 1996

It was after midnight on a Saturday night at the Great Divide, and Pest was playing to a packed house. He had had an argument with Tracy earlier in the day about something stupid. She had called five times today, leaving five long messages. They started off sweet but got more and more demanding. She knew it was a gig night, and she knew that meant he didn't like to talk on the phone. Pest lost his patience after her last message and called her and yelled at her. Luckily, all was well by the time he had to head over to the club. He didn't need the aggravation.

The crowd wasn't dancing, but these days it wasn't the fault of the band. As one a.m. approached, a dozen police officers entered the club and made the management turn on the house lights. They walked around pointing flashlights into corners, inspecting soundproofing and the fire exits, and making sure no one was getting high in the johns. At first, people stayed in their places, hoping this interruption would only last a few minutes. But five minutes turned into ten minutes, which turned into half an hour, and by then the audience numbers were dwindling.

At last, the police were on their way out. The house lights were turned off, and the Caterwaulers were back on stage and picking up their instruments. The police were halfway out the door, when Pest walked up to the microphone and snorted like a pig.

Ouch. Almost made it through the night without doing something stupid.

Tracy was hiding her face in her hands as the police led Pest out of the club.

Pest had been working hard and spending very little to save up money for a new place. But then the show was announced, and it was selling out fast, so he let himself spend some of his stash on tickets to the Iridium Jazz Club. It happened that, by the day of the show, he and Tracy had something to celebrate: Not only had Pest found an apartment in Greenpoint, but he had asked Tracy to marry him, and she said yes.

Pest took Tracy's hand and pushed through to the front of the club, right against the edge of the stage. They each ordered a beer, but then there was a long wait. Tracy went back and forth to the bar a couple of times to get more, mostly for herself, since Pest was driving. Finally...

"Ladies and gentlemen, Mr. Les Paul."

Les started with "Darktown Strutters Ball." Pest was concentrating on his guitar and legendary hands as they worked the strings. After a couple of songs, Tracy went back to the bar. Pest stayed glued to the stage. He didn't want to miss a note.

The music was nonstop, one song right into another. Tracy tapped Pest on the shoulder and leaned in to get a kiss. Then she left to go to the ladies' room. When she got back, Pest reached out for her hand, hoping that would make her less fidgety.

By the end of the show, Tracy was sloshed.

"You ignored me the whole night," she said.

"I was listening to the show. And wow, you've had too

much to drink."

"Well, I had to do something, I was so bored."

"Bored! That was Les Paul!"

"I know. But you were ignoring me."

"What are you? Five?"

Tracy burst into tears. Pest helped her out of the club and drove her home. She had to lean on him to get up her stairs, and then when he tried to leave, she started crying again and insisted he stay.

"Please? You said you'd stay over. My roommate is gone for the weekend."

"Listen. You're drunk. Get some sleep. I'll talk to you tomorrow."

Having an apartment in Greenpoint was convenient for this kind of thing. This would be his first night staying in the new place. He was going to wait until he at least had his futon there, but the floor was fine for now. The only things there now were his guitars and an amp; he didn't even have a fan. In a way, he was happy to be spending the night alone. Between Tracy and Allie, it was getting hard to find any time for himself.

He lay out on the floor in his clothes and soon was asleep.

It took a couple of trips, but Pest moved all his things to the new apartment in under six hours. Then, showered and dressed, he left his van in Greenpoint and took the subway into the City. He had to see Allie tonight; it'd been too long. Tracy could wait a day before he called her. They were getting married, for fuck's sake. That should keep her satisfied for a while.

He climbed Allie's stoop, pressed her buzzer, and waited for her to throw down her keys. It would have been easier if she'd just given him a set, but she never offered, and he never asked.

Allie was wearing a t-shirt and terrycloth shorts, and when Pest hugged her, he realized she had nothing on underneath, and he was instantly aroused. They kissed for several minutes, and then he took her hand and led her into her bedroom.

In the middle of the night, Pest awoke and found he was lying next to Allie. He would have to go move the van, but he was too comfortable to budge. She opened her eyes and said, "Hi."

He laughed. And then he said, "I love you."

To which she said, "What?" and quickly added, "I mean, me too."

Pest was starting to feel like he was in a Chinese finger puzzle. Not just his fingers, his whole being, compressed tighter as he tried to pull in any direction.

He was thinking maybe he shouldn't have told Allie that he loved her. It was true, but maybe he shouldn't have said it. Women expect more from you once you tell them that. Juggling Allie and Tracy was getting harder all the time as it was. There was no satisfying either one of them.

The good news was Carl, Trevor, and Damon were back in the Caterwaulers. With some cajoling on Pest's part, they agreed to accompany him to an upcoming gig in Asbury Park.

Asbury Park, New Jersey, was a once popular shore town that was now a quiet, all-but-forgotten site. There was the famed Stone Pony. There was the deserted boardwalk and decrepit casino. And there was Asbury Lanes, a bowling alley that doubled as a music venue. There was no backstage because there was no stage; bands set up on the lanes themselves. The place had a 50s feel, a perfect place to play a rockabilly set. There was wood paneling on the walls and a little counter that sold hot dogs and beer. On the weekends, they gathered a nice crowd.

Pest was in a good mood and therefore managed to hold it all together without yelling at anyone. The audience was full of rockabilly enthusiasts, and they dressed the part: women in vintage dresses and cherry-red lipstick, men in 50s-pattern shirts and tight jeans. And they all could partner dance. Their response to the Caterwaulers was better than the audiences the band had seen lately in Manhattan or Brooklyn.

Then, there she was: a red haired lovely in a tight, low-cut dress. She was wearing real stockings, the kind with the seam running down the back. Her shoes had chunky, sexy heels, and there was a delicate anklet around her right ankle. Her lipstick was shiny and blood red, her eyelashes were fake and long. And she came right up to Pest after the set and said, "Buy me a drink."

As the woman and Pest began to paw at each other, the rest of the Caterwaulers hung back. Not wanting to incur Pest's wrath, the band left them alone until the place was about to close. Then someone had to talk to Pest about getting home.

They did odds or evens. Carl was the odd man out.

"Hey, Pest"

Pest's eyes were glazed over, but he recognized Carl's voice.

"Yeah." He stopped fondling the redhead and turned his attention to Carl.

Carl pointed at his watch. "We gotta go."

"You can stay with me tonight," the redhead whispered in his ear. "I have a house not far from here."

That's exactly what he wanted to do. But what about the band?

"They can stay in my guest room," she said.

They reluctantly agreed. Pest looked like he was in no condition to drive, anyway.

PART SEVEN

BORROWED: *Missing You* (John Waite,
Mark Leonard, Charles Sanford)

— covered by Tina Turner, released 1996.
Original by John Waite.

CHAPTER 25

ALLIE, JULY 1996

It was nine twenty-nine again in Astor Place.

Astor Place was the home of the Alamo, better known as the Astor Place Cube, a large, black sculpture balanced on one vertex. Weather permitting, any number of freshmen college students could be seen spinning the 8-foot cube around and around, just because they could. Spinners tended to be new to the City; once someone spins it, he doesn't need to do it ever again.

Allie was walking home from her current freelance job and passed the spinning Alamo as it was being serenaded by the sounds of the Astor Place band. Today they were playing a discordant Sousa march. They weren't at their usual spot, but she could hear them. The sound followed her to Cooper Square, to 3rd Ave, and across to St. Marks.

She turned around. It really was following her.

A band of disparate players were marching across the Avenue. There was a tuba player, some flag twirlers, a man with a bass drum, trumpeters, a trombone player, people with hula-hoops, maybe 20 people in all, plus a police escort.

Scott and a fellow piercer, Pete, were watching the procession from Allie's stoop.

"What do you think this is?" Allie said.

"They do this," Scott said. "They get a permit and have like a parade."

Allie sat with the guys and watched the procession. The cordless phone from the shop, which Scott had on his lap, started to ring. Whoever it was caused Scott to quickly stand up and take the call inside.

Pete said to Allie, "Girl trouble."

When Scott came back out, he sat down and lit another cigarette. He flicked the ashes towards the curb a few times while mindlessly shaking one of his legs.

"Everything ok?" Allie said.

"Nah. My girlfriend is moving out."

"Oh. Sorry."

"We've been at each other's throats for weeks. She doesn't want to be in a relationship anymore. She wants to see other guys."

"Hmmm. I know something about that."

"Jim?"

"Oh, God no. My current guy. Jim was a one-woman man. With me, anyway."

"That's me. If I'm not in love, bro, I don't have sex."

"Wow, that's very impressive. You being a man and all."

Scott laughed. "Yeah. I know."

Allie had a moment to ponder that one before Scott changed the subject.

"Hey. Did you see they closed Night Crawlers? Cops shut it down the other night."

"For what? Health code violations?"

"Ha, really. You could get hepatitis from just walking into that joint. No, they're telling people it was because of noise complaints, but actually, their door guy got busted for selling drugs to an undercover cop."

"Ooh. Bummer. Are they going to reopen?"

"There's a sign on the door that says they will, but who knows?"

The cross-town bus rolled by, followed by cabs, cars, and a gaggle of roller-bladers. Tuna jumped onto the windowsill where Allie was sitting, but as it was night and there were no birds to hunt, she quickly got bored and left. Allie stretched her legs out as much as she could and wondered how much longer it would be.

Finally, she could see Pest approaching. He was a good way away, but she could recognize his gait. When he was under her window, she dropped down her keys.

Pest smelled of cigarettes, grease, and aftershave, a mixture of the restaurant he just came from and his prep for this date. They started kissing just inside her door. He put his hands behind her, slipped them under her waistband, and pulled her closer to him. Drifting into the bedroom, they stripped down, their clothes falling in a heap on the floor. Pest softly kissed Allie and ran his hands up and down her back. She placed her hands behind him, wrapped one leg around him, and he lifted her up onto the bed.

Allie got on top first, lowering herself onto him. She wasn't that comfortable in this position; she preferred Pest take the lead. As they rocked back and forth, Pest pulled her more fully onto him. She rolled off and onto her back, and he got on top. For a moment they were looking into each other's eyes, but Allie closed hers. She didn't want him to read her thoughts:

Pest, please don't ever leave me.

It was another Saturday night alone. Allie was looking in the mirror, which was not something she was fond of doing these days. She wasn't just looking, she was studying. Her face was flat and uninteresting, a mass of flesh with no definition. Fine lines were forming around her eyes and lips, not visible unless one was staring into a magnifying mirror, but there they were. And there was no glow. Where did Tracy get all that glow?

No amount of makeup would help this face. Allie half-heartedly applied some anyway. She never felt this insecure when Jim was around, but then, she wasn't competing with anyone then.

Allie decided she would walk up 3rd Avenue to see who might be playing at the Rodeo Bar. She was stopped by a strikingly sexy, inebriated man who needed directions to the Beauty Bar. As they talked, it became obvious that the man, who said his name was Bill, did not need directions at all, but was just hitting on her. When he suggested they go up to his place to smoke some pot, she hesitated.

"C'mon. It's Saturday night. Come smoke with me."

"Okay," she said. "Just the pot though. No sex."

He hailed a cab.

Bill was an import from another state. The company he worked for was supplying his apartment, a small two-room space in a luxury high-rise in midtown, furnished with an unbearably soft, white leather, u-shaped couch, and a black lacquer table with some silk flowers on it. Allie relaxed on the couch while Bill went to get his bong. They smoked a little, and when Bill started kissing her, his perfect body and the marijuana were making her change her mind about having sex with him.

"Do you want to go to the other room?" he said.

The bedroom had a black-lacquer chest of drawers and a tall queen-sized bed covered with a white down comforter. Two things that Allie was pretty sure the company did not supply were the compact stereo, set to the Lite Jazz station, and the lava lamp beside it.

Allie lay on the bed, and Bill unbuttoned her blouse. She was about to ask him if he had condoms, when he said, "Let me cum on your breasts."

Allie somehow suppressed her gag reflexes.

"What?! Yuck! No!"

"C'mon."

He might have liked her idea better.

She rolled off the bed and tried to reassemble her clothes. Bill followed her out of the room, pleading with her.

"It'll be good. C'mon, let me do it." He was grabbing at her, trying to reopen her shirt.

Allie pulled away. "It'll be good? For whom?"

She exited the apartment with Bill still clawing at her. At least he didn't follow her into the elevator.

Allie flagged a cab and told the driver to go through Times Square. It would take longer to get downtown that way, but Allie wanted to see the neon lights. (Sometimes New Yorkers can be tourists, too.) Ever since she was a kid, the billboards in the area, many of them 3D, fascinated her. She remembered one of a giant man smoking a cigarette that had actual smoke, and another one that was a huge can of Chock-Full-of-Nuts coffee. For a long time, she thought it was called Time Square, because she used to see so many enormous, working wristwatches on the advertisements there.

Allie started having second thoughts. Maybe she should have stayed with Bill. She could have told him that, instead of doing something she felt was disgusting, they could have had sex after all. But then, she suddenly felt guilty. She realized, to her dismay, that she was feeling loyal to Pest.

She could possibly be the stupidest person in the world.

The water was warm, the candles were lit, and the bubble bath was bubbly. Allie's feet didn't touch the end of the tub, so she was floating, contemplating the patterns on the cracked walls around her. The walls were lumpy, having been plastered over many times, a condition Allie liked to call Lower East Side stucco. New cracks were somehow coming through, anyway.

Her phone rang. She listened for her answering machine, and soon she could hear the voice of a telemarketer. Often, she wondered if anyone would call her if something happened to Pest. Did anyone in his current world know about her? Or would she find out the same way she found out about Jake: a concert for him, advertised in the Voice?

She was starting to feel a great amount of sympathy toward Tracy, and these thoughts disturbed her so much she had taken to submergence. Her counterpart obviously had strong feelings for Pest; her frustrations were likely similar to her own. Allie would often look across the crowd in those East Village dive bars at Tracy and see herself.

Allie tilted her head back to get the warm soapy water on her hair. There was no telling how long she would be staying in this bath — not until the guilt dissolved and swirled down the drain. Having compassion for Tracy was better than hating her, but it also made Allie feel her culpability. Would Tracy be having an easier time with Pest if Allie weren't around? Or was it the triangle dynamic that was keeping the whole thing together?

Allie shivered. The water was cooling off. She reached her leg down and turned the hot water back on with her foot.

CHAPTER 26

RIHANNA, AUGUST–SEPTEMBER 1996

Rihanna and her bike were halfway up the stoop when she managed to get herself stuck. The front wheel had turned and was now wedged into the railing. Moving it in any direction just made it worse.

"Rihanna."

She turned around. She couldn't quite place him at first, but then she realized it was that guy from the video shoot last winter.

"Hey... What's your name again?"

"Greg. Need some help with that bike?"

"No, I got it."

Greg rolled his eyes. "C'mon, let me help you."

Rihanna softened. "Yeah, okay. Thanks."

He disentangled the bike from the railing, and not only did he bring it up for her, she even let him put it in the apartment.

"Hey, wanna get a drink?"

Truth was, Rihanna could use the company.

"Okay. One drink."

They headed over to crazy-crowded Max Fish. Rihanna forced her way in and took a seat in the corner by the window. Greg went to get their drinks. It could be a while before she saw him again.

The French-speaking group sitting beside her was blocking her view of the rest of the bar, so she looked up. The ornate tin ceiling was two stories up, but that didn't help much with Rihanna's current outbreak of claustrophobia. She took a deep breath and slowly exhaled.

Greg's tousled hair appeared above the crowd. He wedged himself between Rihanna and the French tourists, clinked his bottle of beer with her glass of seltzer, and said, "Cozy, huh?"

As they sipped their drinks, Greg said, "I guess the guy you're living with is awfully small."

It took Rihanna a moment, but then she smiled,

"Yes. He lives in a box I keep under the bed."

"I see. He's a cat."

Rihanna laughed.

"Wanna tell me your real story?"

"Well," she said. "First of all, I met you on the street."

"True. True."

"Second, I had just ended an eight-year relationship."

"Wow. Okay. Got it." He gulped his beer and said, "Well, now that I've rescued you and taken you to this swank watering hole, could I please have your number?"

Rihanna shook her head.

"Please? I promise I won't call you more than three or four times a day."

His goofy grin was hard to resist. She got out her old business card, scratched out the office number, and wrote her home number.

Greg dramatically held the card against his heart. "I'll take good care of this."

The bus left Rihanna off on West Houston Street, somewhat further south than she needed to be. Her latest freelance job, via a connection from Allie, was in the West Village. It was a pleasant walk up Hudson Street. She hadn't been this far west since she left Goldfish, or rather, since Goldfish went bankrupt and left her. With this job, except for her medical expenses, she wasn't doing too badly. The $30,000 she owed might as well be a million dollars; she didn't have it.

She turned the corner when she got to Perry Street, and there was Dylan and Dizzy.

When people say the City is a small town, this is what they mean.

"Rihanna!" He let Dizzy break free to run to her.

Dylan tried to kiss her lips, but she gave him her cheek.

"Hi, Dylan. How are you?"

"God, it's good to see you. You look terrific."

He was giving her his Marlboro Man sexy stare. She didn't respond.

"What's going on?" he said.

"Well, my mom's wedding is in a few weeks."

"Yeah? You need a date?"

He was being charming, which had to be stopped.

"Uh, no. Actually, I'm going with my friend Greg."

His smile disappeared.

"Greg, huh?"

Rihanna nodded. He was looking her right in the eyes. Could he tell she was lying?

"He's... a boyfriend?"

She nodded again.

"Well, then. That sucks for me."

This was killing her, but she was determined not to cave.

"Listen," she said after a moment. "I'm sorry, but I'm going to be late."

"Oh. Right. Sure."

"See you, Dylan."

"Right. See you."

She walked away quickly so he wouldn't see her tearing up.

Mrs. Donna Strauss-soon-to-be-Carrington was having a tra-ditional hippie wedding, the ceremony to be held in the bride-to-be's living room. Members of the wedding party would be barefoot and would be walking across a path of rose petals. Rihanna cynically wondered how many roses were being slaughtered to create such a display.

Keeping with the theme, their mother picked Paul Stookey's "Wedding Song" to serenade her as she walked down the aisle.

There were maybe thirty guests, some family, but mostly colleagues from the university where Tom and Donna taught, people Rihanna and Jill hadn't seen since they were teens. Tom looked a bit silly; he was one of those guys who was too tall to look right in a suit. The tie was too short, and the trousers were so long they overwhelmed the jacket. Rihanna and Jill felt their mother should have just let him wear jeans and a dashiki. It would have worked better with the setting.

The sisters, dressed as flower children, practically ran down the aisle, and then their mother entered. She looked weirdly angelic in her cream-lace, A-line dress. Rihanna couldn't remember the last time she saw her mother in any kind of dress, much less one so elegant. At the makeshift altar, bride and groom looked intently into each other's eyes, something the sisters had witnessed a thousand times over the years. It was the reason they could never be truly mean to Tom.

After a surreal weekend with her family, it was good to be back in the City. Rihanna didn't have work until the next day, so she grabbed one of her sketchbooks and headed out.

The stereo at the Pink Pony was playing "A Chicken Ain't Nothin' But A Bird." Rihanna guessed it was Cab Calloway and attributed having this little piece of musical knowledge to knowing Allie. A great-looking Haitian man — he told her he was Haitian — greeted her. He would have shown her to a seat, but the café was empty, so she had her pick. There were two large front windows, one that had a counter with bar stools, the other with a table. Instead of picking either of those spots, she took a seat on a bench against the gold side wall with the Lower East Side stucco. This gave her a better overall view of the place.

Towards the back was a two-storied wooden doorway made up of two sets of concentric arched doors, a large set that filled the doorframe and a much smaller set that was person-sized. Rihanna took a moment to wonder what that was about, when the Haitian man gave her a menu. The music switched to "White Lines," sung by a musician whose name she didn't know. Rihanna ordered a lox omelet and then took out her sketchbook to draw her surroundings. There was a short bar directly in front of her that had on it a tall vase of flowers and a hard-boiled egg tree. She'd start with that. Beyond the bar were shelves holding yellowed hard- and soft-cover books. One shelf contained a large jar filled with wine-bottle corks, another, framed photographs.

Two men carrying video cameras came in and took seats at the table in the window. They were talking about having to shoot someone's show, how many cameras would be needed, and when they mentioned a famous name, Rihanna assumed that meant they were professionals. After they ordered, their conversation briefly switched to great meals they had had, and then they went back to talking about the logistics of videotaping the show.

Rihanna's omelet arrived. It was light and fluffy, and the home fries had a hint of sage. As the music changed to Iggy Pop, she turned the page of the sketchbook and began to draw the doors.

A trio of art students entered the café. They sat on the

other end of the bench from Rihanna under a piece of poetry that was scrawled across the wall. Their shopping bags were from the art store Pearl Paint, and they were chattering excitedly about their new purchases and what classes they were taking.

This café was an artist magnet.

"Hey, is that Rihanna?" someone outside said. Rihanna looked up to see two women hovering around the entrance.

"Maya? Lindsey? What are you doing here?"

There were hugs all around, and Maya said, "Heading down to our gallery. You?"

"I live across the street."

"With Dylan?"

Rihanna shook her head.

"Good for you."

"It's been, like, forever," Rihanna said. "What's this about a gallery?"

Lindsey took out a piece of scrap paper from her bag and wrote on it. "It's tiny, but it's ours. We show local stuff. We're just getting started. You gotta stop by."

"You still painting?" Maya said.

"Kind of. Sort of. Yes."

"Then we need to talk." Lindsey handed her the scrap of paper. "Stop by. Or call. Whatever."

"I will. Definitely."

Maya and Lindsey exited with lots of waving and fanfare. Rihanna noticed that the video guys were trying to get the waiter's attention. When this failed, one of them took a petal from the flower on the table and used it as a sugar spoon. Rihanna smiled.

She didn't need to live on the river. This was her neighborhood now.

CHAPTER 27

NATIA, OCTOBER 1996

Danny and Natia exited the multiplex movie theater on 23rd Street. This was just one of the many improvements provided by this new neighborhood.

"Do you think that story was true?" Natia said.

"I think William Wallace was a real person. The details in the movie seem hard to prove, though."

It was mid-October and already getting cold. They walked a few blocks up Eighth Avenue, then turned onto a tree-lined street. Danny reached for her hand.

A cluster of people were surrounding a tree by the side of the road.

"Is it real?" one of them said.

"Can't tell," said another.

"It hasn't moved. It looks like it might be made of wood," an older woman said.

Danny and Natia got closer and then saw, on the lowest branch of the tree, partially hidden by the orange leaves, a very small owl.

"I think he's real," Natia said. She looked up again, and the owl opened one of his eyes, as if to say, "Why are you all bothering me?"

The birdwatchers went all atwitter. Danny and Natia left them and continued their walk home. They got to a side street that was lined with yellow ginkgo trees, thankfully, male ones. The City in recent years had gotten smart; there were enough things in the City that smelled like vomit and feces without adding to it by planting female ginkgoes.

One tree was stripped of all its foliage; it was all in a golden pile beneath it. Natia kicked through the leaves.

"Wonder what happened to this tree?" Natia said. "Looks like it lost all its leaves at once."

"Maybe the wind?"

"Must have been an awfully strong wind that aimed for just this tree."

They continued down the block, and as they were approaching the last tree, they heard a noise like fluttering wings. All the leaves rained down on them.

"Whoa!" Danny raised his arms over his head and laughed.

"This can't be normal. Do you think these trees are dying?"

"They look okay. Just naked."

Danny and Natia ran playfully through the leaves, throwing handfuls at each other. People passing by looked on with bemused expressions.

Mondays weren't as bad as they used to be. Natia was getting proficient at this Excel stuff, and her boss Larry — well, he wasn't anything like Mr. Griffin.

She looked up from her computer to see people getting up from their desks and hurrying out of the office.

"Hey, c'mon. There's water gushing all over the street. They're evacuating the building."

Natia was hearing sirens, lots of them, and a quick look out of a window showed emergency trucks surrounding the building and water pouring down the streets. She followed the others down the fire stairs to the ground floor, where the water was gushing into the lobby. Firemen in raingear were leading people through the river of drinking water, past the emergency vehicles, past the local news stations' camera crews, to dry sidewalks a few blocks away. Natia had a blanket from the firemen around her before she was aware of how wet she was.

"You okay, Kid?" Mona was dripping wet herself. Her carefully applied make-up and perfect hair were melting down her face.

"Sure. Just wet," Natia said.

A policeman approached the crowd of displaced workers.

"It's a water-main break. There's no sense in hanging around here. You're not getting back into the building today."

Natia hesitated, and Mona said, "C'mon, Kid, you heard the man. We can go home."

The best ones were the molded cardboard type, though, in a pinch, Danny could use the Styrofoam ones as well. Both buffered sound.

"I can nail some of those up, too, you know," Natia said.

"Nope. I got it."

Danny was transforming the two middle rooms into his studio. He was starting by nailing egg cartons to the wall for soundproofing.

"Do we have enough cartons?" Natia said.

"Not really, but it's a start. And the insulation will help, too."

Down the block was a construction site where Danny and Natia had found some leftover insulating material in the dumpster. It was now sitting in a pink scraggly heap on their kitchen floor. Clean, empty egg cartons weren't easy to come by, so Natia and Danny had been eating a lot of omelets. Danny nailed the last carton to the wall, and then took out the ladder. He climbed up, pushed on one of the ceiling tiles, and when it moved, he said, "Yup. We've got a dropped ceiling."

The phone rang and Natia picked up.

"Nat, your mom called me."

"Really?"

"I thought you were dead to her."

"I am. What did she say?"

"She saw the water-main break on the news and recognized your office building. She was worried."

Danny put on work gloves and dragged the insulation to the ladder.

"What did you tell her?"

"I told her you're fine. That you've moved into a new apartment in Chelsea. I had to explain to her where Chelsea was. It seemed to please her."

With a lot of grumbling, Danny started stuffing the insulation into the ceiling.

"She knows Danny's with me?"

"I may have omitted that piece of information."

"Ha. Good work."

She hung up, and Danny said, "What. Me?"

"No, Allie."

He continued with the insulation.

It was Natia's first day back at work since the building lobby was flooded, and her desk and IBM PS/2E were right where she had left them. She had her Excel cheat sheet on her document stand, her lists of client information to her left, and her cup of coffee to her right. Everything was ready to go.

And her phone rang.

"Liberty Mutual, this is Natia Stojanovich."

"Nati?"

Gasp. "Daddy?"

"I called your other number and they told me you weren't

there anymore. Then someone named Mona came on the line and gave me this number. Everything all right?"

"I have a staff job now, Daddy. Salary, benefits."

"That's wonderful."

Larry MacKensie came into the room. When Natia saw him, she said, "I gotta go in a minute, Dad."

Larry said, "Take your time. Just come see me when you're through."

"Never mind. It's okay. How's mom?"

CHAPTER 28

PEST, NOVEMBER 1996

Tracy had been acting crazy lately, whiny and possessive, and it seemed that just about anything would make her snap or burst into tears. To make her feel better, Pest agreed to let her stay in his apartment over the weekend while he was in Boston with the band. She'd been begging Pest to let her decorate and organize the place; eventually she'd be living there, too, after all.

When he returned home, Tracy was not there.

A trunk that he kept personal things in — memorabilia from shows, reviews and newspaper articles, photos, and the like — was open in the middle of the kitchen floor. Some of its contents were piled beside it, and there, open to a seemingly random entry, was Pest's journal. On top of the journal, written on a scrap of towel paper, was a note that read: "Very interesting."

There was no telling how much Tracy had read, but the entry it was open to described the redhead in Asbury Park. He never did get the woman's name.

Pest started trembling. The idea of losing Tracy was overwhelming. He gathered what few wits he had left about him and picked up the phone.

Tracy's line was busy. Several tries and several busy signals later, Pest gave up.

He wrote several versions of The Letter.

Pest finally passed out from exhaustion sometime in the early morning. One couldn't characterize the hour or so he was down as "sleep"; it was anything but restful.

Then there was the opposite of Soup Day.

He opened his eyes and saw that his room was starting to fill with sunlight. Tracy was the first thing on his mind, and with those thoughts came painful anxiety. He stared at the ceiling and tried to slow down his breathing. Eventually he would have to stand up, as he needed to do something with this onslaught of uncontrollable energy. Making coffee was a bad idea, so was writing in his journal. In fact... he went to the journal, the binder that had been with him since high school and threw it in the trash. Then he kicked the garbage can until his foot was throbbing.

The clock in the kitchen said it was six-fifteen.

He stood a moment, tried to breathe calmly again, then threw his body around in a manic fit.

"AHHHHHHHHH!"

A pause, a few deep breaths.

He began pounding on the wall, quick fists, drumming against a deluge of memories and regrets. The neighbors that shared this wall started pounding back. This brought Pest back to reality.

Deep breaths, deep breaths.

It was early, but he didn't care. He called Roy, and when he didn't get an answer, he called Allie.

It took a while, but he had to pull it together. He had a rehearsal with the Sizzling Hounds that afternoon. Talking to

Allie had calmed him down enough to go about his business. He took a shower, then picked up his razor to shave, and got out a new blade.

Closing the medicine cabinet, he looked in the mirror. He looked down at his chest and drew a long red line with the blade.

The phone rang, and he left his momentary trance to run to the phone.

Could it be...?

No. It was Roy, confirming rehearsal.

"Hey, you okay, Man? You sound out of breath."

Pest was anything but okay, which became evident to everyone when he stormed into rehearsal.

"Let's do this," he greeted the band.

The band had been lounging in front of the television. They were in no mood to get up and start moving.

"Chill, Pest. We want to see the end of this."

Pest put down his guitar and amp, but stood, hovering.

"Sit. You're making me nervous," Roy said.

"I can't sit. I'm too messed up. Tracy left me." The four other members of the band reacted by turning off the TV.

"Shit. You're kidding, Man."

Pest shook his head.

"She found out about that other chick, eh?"

"She read my journal."

The bandmates groaned. "Wow. Tough break, dude."

"Anyway, can we just do this? I wanna get home so I can continue hurting myself."

They thought he was kidding.

After a couple days went by with no response from Tracy, Pest went to her apartment building and waited on the stoop. It took a while, then there she was. She marched up the stairs, passed right by, and just before she unlocked the door, she spun around and said, "You are disgusting," and when he tried to respond, she cut him off with, "You will never see me again."

CHAPTER 29

ALLIE, DECEMBER 1996

Despite what Allie might have believed a few months ago, she was finding no gratification in being the proverbial last one standing. She would rather have been chosen; instead, she was feeling a lot like leftover pot roast. Pest meanwhile was inconsolable but was demanding to be consoled.

Allie was in the unenviable position to be the best and worst person for Pest to talk to during this latest crisis. He always said he felt he could tell her anything, which made it impossible now for her to tell him not to. He was calling her early in the morning, late at night, and many times in between, and the later the call, the drunker he was. Allie really didn't want to hear about how wonderful Tracy was, how well she had treated him, how it was his last chance for normalcy—

"Wait a minute. Normalcy? How so?"

"Well, we were engaged."

Allie almost dropped the phone. "When, exactly, were you going to tell me this? After the wedding?"

"Well, I always sort of felt like you and Tracy were both my wives."

"Great. Tracy must really hate my guts."

"Actually, she doesn't know about you."

Allie doubted that. Even without the journal, Tracy wasn't an idiot.

"How could that be?"

"You weren't in the journal. I didn't write about relationships. She read about someone else."

"Someone else? You needed a third woman? You weren't having enough trouble juggling two?"

"I felt trapped."

Allie moaned.

"It was only the one night. It meant nothing."

Missing the point, as usual.

"Well, that's not a cliché, is it? I have an idea: the next time you feel trapped, how about being with fewer women, not more of them?"

To his credit, Pest laughed.

He arrived at Allie's apartment in a particularly agitated state — mad at his bass player, mad at himself, brought the whole piss factory with him.

"Everything is screwed up. It doesn't matter what I do, someone is going to fuck with me. Everybody always fucks with me."

Pest sat at her kitchen table, opened the beer he brought, and continued his tirade. "That's it. I don't have a band anymore. We have a gig in two days, and I have no fucking bass player."

Allie had seen Pest play without a bass player, and she'd seen him play without a drummer. In fact, she'd seen him play without a bass player and without a drummer. She sensed this was not the time to bring that up.

"Can you call him?" she said. "Maybe he'll change his mind."

"No! I can't call him! I fucking fired him! He's not coming back!"

Allie recoiled and took a step back from the raging Pest.

"I have this gig, and it'll sound stupid with no bass. I can get away with that at one of our usual joints, but this is a new place. I've got to have a full band. I won't be able to find anyone who can learn the songs in two days."

When Pest didn't hear a response from Allie, he turned to look at her. "What should I do?"

She spoke carefully. "You yelled at me when I suggested something a minute ago."

"Sorry. I want your opinion."

"I would call him, apologize, and ask him to do the gig."

"You think?"

"Yes. That's what I think. I think he's probably used to you losing your temper, and when you tell him you are sorry and didn't mean to fire him, maybe he will come back. It may not work, but it also just might."

Pest stood up and held her for a while. Then he said, "Want to go into the other room?"

They flopped onto Allie's bed, but as things started to get hot and clothes were starting to come off, he said, "If we don't have sex anymore, can we still be friends?"

So staggering all thoughts flew out of Allie's head.

"The thing is, I cheated on Tracy with you, so it doesn't seem right to keep having sex with you now."

Allie slowly sat up and started grabbing for her clothes.

"You're angry. I can tell when you're angry."

"For a musician, you have some really bad timing."

Allie concentrated on getting dressed so she wouldn't have to look at him.

"It's not that I don't like having sex with you. I'm thinking I shouldn't be with anyone for a while."

"You know?" Allie said. "It's fine."

This was so very much not fine.

Friends. How was that supposed to work?

Allie had to decide what she wanted, besides wishing things were the way they were the first six months, wishing she hadn't been working so much, wishing she had been able to see where the relationship would have gone without interference. They had both been going through their own form of madness; maybe if they had met at another time, things could have been different. But wishing for something impossible was just a waste of time.

She was standing on her stepladder, trying to get something to wear out of her closet, when the phone rang.

"Hey, Allie, could I ask you to do me a favor?"

"Sure, Pest. What's up?"

"I need some fliers for next months' gigs. Nothing fancy. The Xerox machine at the rehearsal studio is trashed."

"Okay."

"No rush. You can bring them to Saturday's gig if you want. If you're coming."

"I plan to."

"Good. Otherwise let me know and I'll come get them."

"Okay. But I should be there."

"Great." He paused. "How are you doing?"

Missing you, you jerk. "I'm good. You?"

"Less crazy, I think."

"Good. You sound less crazy."

It was all relative.

The next day Allie got a call at work from a very agitated, very drunk Pest.

"Did you do that stuff for me?"

"You said there was no rush; I haven't had a chance yet."

"You don't get it! You don't understand how you're tying me up. It was an easy favor, for fuck's sake!"

"Pest, I told you I'd take care of it, and I will. I'll call you later; I can't talk now."

Her work phone rang again.

"The thing is, I can't wait for people to do things for me, or they never get done. I have to be on them all the time."

"Pest. I got it. Now I have to go." Her infinite patience was becoming finite.

The day of the gig, she got to the bar early, and her better judgment told her to leave the fliers and get out of there before the band got there. Pest's manager, Andy, was early as well, so she gave him the fliers, but as they chatted, the band arrived. Pest was doing his best to pretend she wasn't there.

"You're welcome," Allie said under her breath.

Allie said goodbye to Andy and turned to go. To her surprise, Pest stopped her.

"Hey. Can I talk to you a second?"

It started like an apology. He was having a rough time, he was drinking too much, he never should have called her like that at work, he shouldn't have been so impatient.

"But I'm under a lot of stress, and a lot of things are going on right now, not just this thing with Tracy. I have a lot to deal with, and you promised me you'd get that stuff for me, and I wasn't getting it, so I had to push. That's how I get things done. I have to push people, or they won't do what they say they are going to do."

When did she ever not do what she said she was going to do? She was obsessed with him, after all, and trying to compete with Tracy left little room for falling short.

"This is how I am. I'm impatient and I get stressed and I can't be waiting for things. That's just the way I am. I have a temper. Tracy had to deal with it all the time. Okay? So you can deal with it once in a while too."

Tracy. Pest had found Allie's inner bear and stabbed it with a sharp stick. What was this she was now feeling? Oh yes. Rage.

"No, I do not have to deal with it," she snarled. "We are no longer involved. And you really need to have your gall bladder checked, because you sure have an excessive amount of gall."

She hurried out. She wanted to get as far away from him as possible.

How did that go? Something about a fish without a bicycle?

Allie was about to do what would have been impossible just a month ago.

Disengage.

She finally was being honest with herself. What was she still hanging on to? Didn't matter that she still loved the guy. There was no relationship, no friendship, nothing but agitation and heartache.

With a flick of an invisible switch, the very deep spiritual storm she had been living with was quieted. What was left was emotional debris, strewn everywhere, that she would have to start cleaning up.

Pest called later that week, and Allie, who had started screening her calls, successfully ignored it. He called back a few times, but when he called again at two in the morning, she decided she had better answer it.

"Things are bad," he said.

And hello to you too. "Pest... how much have you had to drink?"

"Enough. Not a lot for some people, but a lot for me."

It seemed Pest's temperament had deteriorated even more in the past week. This came to a head the other night when he blew up at his rhythm section and fired them. Again.

"How badly did you yell at them? Might they come back?"

"No, they won't come back. I don't want them back. I fired them. Now I don't have a band, I don't have a girlfriend, and my kids are going to be moving to Texas."

Allie did not know what to say to that, so she said, "I don't know what to say to that."

"I know, I know, I shouldn't have called you. It's two in the morning."

"I was up."

"I've been completely self-destructive. Cutting myself, picking fights. The other night at rehearsal, I carved "FUCK YOU" into my chest with a razor blade. Carl tried to stop me, and I told him to back off or I'd to do the same to him."

"Pest, this is way out of my league. And I think it's out of yours as well."

"What do you mean?"

"I think you have too much happening to you right now, all at once. You just had this thing with Tracy, now you've lost your band, your kids are moving, and you have no coping skills to begin with. It's too much. I think you need to talk to somebody, you know, professional. "

"I can't afford a shrink."

She heard him gulp down more beer.

"Maybe this isn't the best time to be talking about this," she said.

"Well, I know I'm kind of paranoid right now, but when I hear you talk about this I think: 'She wants me to go there so they'll convince me to make an honest woman out of her.'"

This guy didn't know her at all. "'Honest woman.' Interesting choice of words."

"No, I know you are suggesting this because you're worried about me."

"Yes, well, when you tell me you've carved 'Fuck You' onto your chest, I think that's cause for worry."

Pest laughed, and it seemed to Allie he was off the ledge for the moment. She had no illusions, however, that he would stay there.

The next day, she received a call.

"I don't need a shrink, okay? I'm fine the way I am."

Allie could hear in his voice that he was anything but fine.

He was slurring his words.

"You just want to control me! And I may have cheated on Tracy, but you're just as guilty. You kept me involved with you. You're evil. Never contact me again —"

Although he was still talking, Allie said "Okay" and hung up the phone.

For a moment she let herself feel hurt, then guilty, then insulted. But with the clarity of thought that came from no longer having her head up her ass, she realized that this was not coming from a clear-headed person. While he wasn't wrong, this outburst had little to do with her.

She uttered a heartfelt and very sad, "Wow."

EPILOGUE

BLUE: *Crystal Blue Persuasion* (Eddie Gray,
Tommy James and Mike Vale)

— recorded by Tommy James and the Shondelles,
released 1968

DECEMBER 31, 1996

"Hey, you like Pest's stuff, you'll love my friend Zoe."

It was true. Buck knew just about everybody.

Hundreds of thousands of people were in Times Square for New Year's Eve, but Buck and Allie, Greg and Rihanna, and Danny and Natia were further downtown at the Rodeo Bar. Tonight's band, Zoe Navarro and the Mustangs, were seated at one of the tables, quickly gulping down their complementary dinner before they started playing.

Zoe, who hailed from San Antonio, was sporting a traditional rockabilly embroidered shirt and skirt. She was petite, with crazy black hair piled high on her head and custom cowboy boots that had guitars painted on them. Her guitar, which she did not play at her knees, was a bold shade of red, and her long, matching fingernails somehow did not get in the way of her furious fingerings. In a battle of guitarists, she could have easily matched Pest.

The band's drink of choice, tequila, was brought to the stage several cups at a time throughout the night. Zoe called various musicians up from the audience to join her as the show went on, and at one point there were so many people on the stage it was hard to see the demitasse Zoe behind the mob.

At a break in the music, Zoe took note of the "No Dancing" sign.

"Is that for real?" she said, and when everyone assured her it was, she said, "We can't have that," and took a napkin from one of the tables and tucked it in over the sign, covering the "No" part.

The clock was about to strike twelve, and, after the official countdown and traditional New-Year's-moment-hug-and-kiss fest, the tables were pushed back, and everyone started doing his or her own version of dancing. By the time the band stopped playing, there were peanut shells, beer bottles, cigarette butts, chips, salsa, and pools of stray margaritas all over the floor. The revelers were sweating so hard it looked like it had rained on them.

Allie's friends said their goodbyes, and Zoe came up to Buck and Allie and said, "We're going out, right?"

Exhausted, Buck and Allie looked at each other with trepidation.

"I've been working all night," Zoe said. "I want to go out. Where can we go?"

Buck thought about it. "Marylu's on 9th Street. They'll be open."

The manager of the Rodeo Bar told the band they could leave their equipment in the upstairs office overnight, so after everything was securely packed away, Zoe, the Mustangs, Buck, and Allie piled into the band's van and headed to West 9th Street.

They drove down a deserted 2nd Avenue, and when they stopped at a light, Allie looked out of the window and gasped.

"Buck! Look!"

There it was, the reconstructed, fresh-out-of-the-box Night Crawlers. A new, blue, neon sign proudly announced the name of the bar in cursive. There were floor-to-ceiling windows where the old metal gates had been, and inside there were couches and lounge chairs and TV monitors playing music videos. Night Crawlers had finally become part of the gentrified East Village, a *Stepford-Wives* version of its former self. It even had a velvet rope.

It was late enough, or rather, early enough in the morning,

that parking spots were easy to find, and Zoe and friends were able to park across from the bar. A private club, Marylu's had a reputation for having an odd mix of patrons: well-known rock musicians, notorious mob guys, bikers, people who looked like rock musicians and mob guys, plus the not-so-occasional famous actor or two who would show up there to do research. After hours, it would open its doors to anyone, and at four a.m. that New Year's Eve, anyone, that being Zoe and her crew, wandered in.

Marylu's turned out to be nothing more spectacular than a bar with a small extra room and piped-in music. The "dance floor" was carpeted and the lighting bright, and except for the small disco ball, they felt like they had all stepped into someone's living room.

"What are we drinking?" Zoe asked Allie.

"Aren't you drinking tequila?"

"I was, but pick something else."

They decided on vodka martinis. An older man in a fancy cowboy shirt and hat approached Zoe and started up a conversation about Texas, no doubt seeing a bonding opportunity in their respective outfits. Three women in black handkerchief dresses latched onto Zoe's rhythm section, and two inebriated men who were leaning on each other for support approached Allie and Buck. One tall, the other short, they both were wearing black dress jackets over t-shirts that were emblazoned with the logo for a show called *Naked Men Singing*.

The shorter man handed Allie a promo card for the show, which she pretended to study. "You should come," he said.

The taller one addressed Buck. "Are you two together?"

Allie and Buck stared at him.

"No?" the man continued, figuring he got his answer when he did not get one. "You two aren't dating? Why not?"

"We're friends," Allie said.

"Are you with other people? Is that why you're not together?" the shorter man asked.

The words, "None of your business," sprang to mind, but Zoe came over and inadvertently ended the interrogation.

"Come with me to the ladies' room," she said. She grabbed Allie's arm. "That gentleman I was talking to is here with his wife, but he started hitting on me, trying to kiss me, asking me for my number. And his wife was there the whole time, hanging on him and laughing."

They pushed against the ladies' room door, but something was pushing back. When the door finally opened, they saw that the room was full of people of both sexes in various stages of undress, snorting coke off each other's bodies. A mirror full of coke was passed to Allie and Zoe, but they passed it on without partaking and backed out.

After their third round of drinks, Zoe and company left Marylu's. In the van, Allie was thinking about inviting herself over to Buck's and seeing how that might go. It wouldn't be fair to Buck, though; she was in no condition to judge whether that was what she really wanted, or if she just didn't want this night to end. She said nothing and let them drop her back at her apartment.

Six a.m. was not an hour Allie often saw voluntarily, certainly not wide-awake and sitting on her stoop. The sky was starting to lighten, and St. Marks Place was all but completely unpeopled. Tinnitus, fatigue, sweat, inebriation, and longing kept her sitting there awhile. Eventually, she made herself go into the building, when it was clear that the sun had made it up over the horizon and was determined to make things very bright very soon.

ACKNOWLEDGEMENTS

First, I have to thank my friend and beta reader Dushka Petkovich, who has read the many iterations of this manuscript about 7,092 times. Thanks to my dad, Dominic, and sister, Sandy. Thanks to friends Victor Mignatti and Janet Rosen for their early feedback.

ABOUT ATMOSPHERE PRESS

Atmosphere Press is an independent, full-service publisher for excellent books in all genres and for all audiences. Learn more about what we do at atmospherepress.com.

We encourage you to check out some of Atmosphere's latest releases, which are available at Amazon.com and via order from your local bookstore:

Twisted Silver Spoons, a novel by Karen M. Wicks

Queen of Crows, a novel by S.L. Wilton

The Summer Festival is Murder, a novel by Jill M. Lyon

The Past We Step Into, stories by Richard Scharine

The Museum of an Extinct Race, a novel by Jonathan Hale Rosen

Swimming with the Angels, a novel by Colin Kersey

Island of Dead Gods, a novel by Verena Mahlow

Cloakers, a novel by Alexandra Lapointe

Twins Daze, a novel by Jerry Petersen

Embargo on Hope, a novel by Justin Doyle

Abaddon Illusion, a novel by Lindsey Bakken

Blackland: A Utopian Novel, by Richard A. Jones

When I Am Ashes, a novel by Amber Rose

Melancholy Vision: A Revolution Series Novel, by L.C. Hamilton

The Recoleta Stories, by Bryon Esmond Butler

ABOUT THE AUTHOR

Connecticut-born Robin D'Amato moved to New York City to attend New York University, fell in love with the City, and never left. In 1984, she was introduced to the Macintosh computer and has worked in the publishing industry as a pre-press specialist ever since. She also spent several decades pursuing dance and choreography. Her first novel, *Somebody's Watching You*, won a 2021 second-quarter Firebird Book Award for fiction. She currently lives in Manhattan's East Village with her 3,000-LP music room and her two cats.